BEYOND THE SUNSET

Molly Rimmer, swept up in the atmosphere of celebration on the evening of Queen Victoria's Jubilee in 1897, accompanies her friend Flo to the centre of Blackpool. During the festivities she meets Joss, a distinguished gentleman who is clearly smitten by her. Her future seems full of promise but her dreams are dashed when tragedy strikes her family and she has to take responsibility for her siblings, leaving her ambitions, and Joss, behind. Life is a struggle but in time she marries Hector Stubbins, believing she has found love and security, but Hector is not the man he first appears to be...

BEYOND THE SUNSET

BEYOND
THE SUNSET

by

Margaret Thornton

Magna Large Print Books
Long Preston, North Yorkshire,
BD23 4ND, England.

British Library Cataloguing in Publication Data.

Thornton, Margaret
    Beyond the sunset.

    A catalogue record of this book is
    available from the British Library

    ISBN   0-7505-1802-2

First published in Great Britain in 2000 by Headline Book Publishing

Published in Large Print 2002 by arrangement with
Headline Book Publishing Ltd.

Magna Large Print is an imprint of Library Magna Books Ltd.

Printed and bound in Great Britain by
T.J. (International) Ltd., Cornwall, PL28 8RW

Chapter 1

'Poor old lady. She didn't last very long, did she?' Molly Rimmer and her friend Flo Palmer leaned against the railings near North Pier, gazing out across the Irish Sea. Not that they had to gaze very far. The awesome sight that was commanding their attention and that of scores of other folk, residents and visitors alike, was the wreck of Nelson's battleship, the *Foudrayant*, now a poor broken-up skeleton of its former self, lying on Blackpool sands near to the Metropole Hotel.

'Yes, it's hard to imagine, isn't it, that we were on it only the other day?' replied Flo. 'Such a grand day it was an' all last Sunday. Not a cloud in the sky. Who'd've thought it could change so quickly? Still, that's Blackpool for you. Seems that even Lord Nelson's ship didn't stand a chance with our famous gales.'

'You're right there, lass,' said the man standing next to her. 'Never seen 'owt like it, have you, Charlie? Twenty foot high, them waves, I'll be bound...'

'Aye, we were here at six o'clock, this morning, weren't we, Nora, watching all t'goings-on?'

'Well, thank God the crew are all safe, that's all I can say...'

Molly and Flo, listening to the comments from the crowd around them, smiled a little sadly at one another. Blackpool was renowned for the free

11

shows it provided, its glorious sunsets being one, the vagaries of the wind and weather another, but seldom had they caused such havoc so near to the town.

At Whitsuntide 1897, Nelson's man-of-war the *Foudrayant* had been moored a mile or so out to sea. She was to be yet another attraction for the rest of the year at least, it was hoped, to entertain the holidaymakers who were flocking to the resort in their thousands. Pleasure steamers were very soon busy ferrying people every hour out to the stately two-decked ship. Molly and Flo, somewhat timorously, neither of them having ventured on to the sea before, had last Sunday afternoon boarded the *Clifton* a paddle steamer painted white and lavishly gilded on its paddle boxes, at the North Pier jetty.

That was nothing, however, compared to the wonders of the *Foudrayant*. The two young women had 'oohed' and 'aahed' along with the rest of the visitors, who were swarming over the decks, marvelling at the leather fire buckets, the cutlasses, flintlock muskets and bayonets, and the motto 'Remember Nelson' inserted in brass letters on the poop deck. The most awe-inspiring spectacle was that of the Admiral's cabin itself, the walls of which were decorated with portraits of Nelson, Lady Hamilton, Sir Ralph Abercromby and former captains of the ship. On the table were facsimiles of letters in Nelson's handwriting, somewhat scrawly because, by that time, Nelson had lost his right arm.

And now not only the great man, but the great ship was no more. At dawn on Wednesday, 16

June, a strong westerly wind had arisen and the *Foudrayant*, her sails still furled, had started to drag her anchors. The news had speedily spread through the town, and hundreds of spectators had watched the destruction of the once-famous battleship. They saw her drifting helplessly towards the beach, battered and tossed about by the waves. The Blackpool lifeboat was launched as soon as it was possible to do so, and the crew of the ship was quickly rescued. Not a moment too soon, because as the ship finally came to ground the main mast and the foremast crashed over the side and the upper parts of the mizzen mast collapsed into the sea. As the tide turned, the wind died down almost as quickly as it had sprung up. Now, in the mid-afternoon, a brilliant sun shone down on the wrecked hull and already a crowd of holidaymakers could be seen descending on the ship, hunting for souvenirs.

'They're like vultures,' said Molly. 'It's making me sad just looking at 'em.' She tucked her hand through her friend's arm. 'Come on, Flo. I've seen enough, haven't you? Let's go and look at the decorations, shall we? It'll happen cheer us up a bit. And we don't want to waste our half-day, do we?'

'I should think not,' replied Flo. 'And the sun's shining, for once.'

The two young women, both aged seventeen, were employed in shops on Jubilee Terrace, Molly at the confectioner's and Flo at the draper's two doors away. There were, in fact, only six shops on this rather exclusive terrace, right opposite the Metropole Hotel, facing the sea. It had been built ten years ago at the time of Queen Victoria's golden jubilee, hence the name. As well as the confectioner's and the draper's there were a chemist's shop, a toyshop, a photographer's studio and a shop which advertised itself as selling high-class boots and shoes.

Now, the Jubilee Terrace shops, along with many other establishments in the town, were setting out their stalls and vying with one another to present the best display of decorations in celebration of the diamond jubilee of the Queen, another grand old lady who, unlike the *Foudrayant*, seemed indestructible.

The actual celebration, to be observed as a public holiday throughout the town, was to be on the following Tuesday, 22 June, but already the town appeared to be in a festive mood. Running south, down the length of the promenade, the lines of flags, pennants and streamers made an attractive and colourful scene. In Talbot Square streamers ran from the central drinking fountain to the poles erected outside the shops on either side of the square. On the Tower buildings national flags decorated the turrets on the balconies and, no doubt, come the great day, flags would be flying from the summit of the Tower as well.

'I dare say your dad's had summat to do with that lot, hasn't he?' remarked Flo as they walked past the Tower. Molly's father, William Rimmer, was employed as a janitor and odd-job man at the Tower, and he was well known for his cheerfulness and eagerness to help out with any job that needed doing.

'Yes, he's had a hand in putting them up,' smiled Molly. 'He's full of it at the moment, I can tell you. They've got some special acts – swimmers and gymnasts and trapeze artists – performing in the Pavilion. And there's an Old English village in the elevator hall – you know, the place where the Tower lifts go from – with all the stalls decked out like the "Good Old Days". Don't quite know when they were. When Queen Victoria came to the throne, I suppose, or even earlier than that, maybe. Dad has been on at me mam for ages to go and see it. I expect he could sneak her in, although you know what a stickler he is for always paying his way. Anyroad, Mam doesn't seem interested. Well, to be fair I don't suppose it's that she's not interested. She gets very tired at the moment.' Molly lowered her voice. 'And she doesn't like folk seeing her now she's such a size. Not that she's said so, but I know me mam.'

'When's the baby due then?' asked Flo, her voice just a whisper. 'It can't be very far off?'

Molly pursed her lips. 'A couple of weeks, I think, that's all. Mam's very cagey about it. She didn't tell me for ages that she was expecting, and she hasn't told our Em at all. Em asked me, though, why Mam was getting so fat, so I had to tell her. I tried to explain, but it's hard to know what to say. I think she understood – at least I hope she did. You know how quiet she is, our Em. Like Mam, really. Never says two words when one'll do.' Emily was Molly's eight-year-old sister, a shy, withdrawn sort of little girl; as Molly said, like her mother. Whereas Molly knew that

15

she herself took after her father, at least in disposition: cheerful, outgoing and – her friends would say – kind, helpful and brimful of optimism.

'Come on,' she said now as they turned off the promenade into Victoria Street. 'Let's go and have a look in Donnelly's windows, shall we? Not that we can afford their prices, but it doesn't cost anything to look.' Thinking of her mother, had, momentarily, dimmed her optimistic outlook. She could not help but worry a little about her, although their good-hearted neighbour, Maggie Winthrop, had assured her that Lily would be fine and that she, Maggie, would be there to see to her when her time came, as she did for most of the folk in the Larkhill neighbourhood. Maggie was usually in attendance not only at the arrivals into the world, but at the departures from it as well. She was an expert at laying out, but Molly knew it was the births, not the deaths, that Maggie delighted in, and it was her proud boast that she had 'never lost a bairn yet'. But as Lily Rimmer had suffered two miscarriages to Molly's certain knowledge in the past few years, as well as possibly others besides, she was bound to be concerned. When they had had a peek at Donnelly's windows Molly knew she would have to be on her way home before Emily arrived back from school.

'Right you are then, Donnelly's it is,' said Flo. 'Let's have a see what the posh folk are wearing this summer.'

Donnelly's Draper's, as it was commonly called, occupied a prominent site on a corner of Bank Hey Street, just behind the Tower and only fifty yards or so from the sea. It was much more than a draper's, although that was how it had started out some thirty years before. Now it was a high-class department store selling not only elegant ladies' wear, but clothing for men and children; corsets, undergarments and hosiery; gloves, handbags and jewellery; and a vast array of materials and all the requirements for the home dressmaker. There was also a restaurant on the top floor serving morning coffee, teas and lunches.

The two girls pressed their noses flat against the plate-glass window behind which was displayed a selection of ladies' dresses, neither of them speaking for several moments. The array of styles and colours was really breathtaking for a couple of young women who were accustomed to making the same blouse and skirt last all summer, with, if they were lucky, a change of garments for 'Sunday best'. Such new clothes as they were able to afford were not really 'new' – only to them – purchased from a second-hand shop or run up on the sewing machine from a remnant, usually the end of a roll, bought at a market stall. Molly's father, William, had bought a second-hand Singer sewing machine from a colleague a couple of years ago, thinking it would be handy for his wife to make clothes for herself and their two daughters. It was Molly, however, who used it, Lily never having mastered the treadle movement operated by the feet; and now she and Flo had become quite skilful at adapting the same paper pattern to make a variety of blouses.

Flo broke the silence. 'Oh, I say, Molly, look at that green dress, the one at the front. I could just see you in that. And the hat the model's got on, an' all. What a good match. Emerald green, they call it.' Flo was an expert on colours, working at a draper's herself. 'It would go lovely with your ginger hair ... sorry, auburn you like to call it, don't you?'

Molly laughed out loud. 'Pigs might fly! Yes, it's very nice, I'm sure, but a bit fancy, don't you think, for serving in the shop or scrubbing the floor?' The green dress had the fashionable leg-o'-mutton sleeves and the sort of high stand-up collar favoured by Alexandra, the Princess of Wales, and was lavishly decorated on both the bodice and skirt with bands of cream lace. The hat, too, the size of a huge dinner plate, was a cornucopia of artificial flowers, lace and ribbons all intertwined. 'Anyroad, I can't go in and buy it today, can I? It's Wednesday – they're closed, like our shops. What a pity, eh? Look, all the dresses in this window are green, different shades, though. I don't know who does their window dressing, but they've got the knack all right. You'll have to tell your boss to come and have a look, Flo. She'd happen pick up a few ideas.'

'Huh! You tell her if you're so keen on the idea,' scoffed Flo. 'She wouldn't take any notice, would she? You know what she's like: way behind the times.' Miss Amelia Perkins, owner of the draper's on Jubilee Terrace, a spinster of indeterminate age, was not noted for her stylish window displays. The other shopkeepers on the terrace, determined to make their row of shops one of the most fashionable in Blackpool, often despaired of her. 'She's put up a few red, white and blue streamers and a banner saying "God Save the Queen". What more can you expect? Yes, this green display's all very well, but not terribly patriotic, is it? Haven't Donnelly's got a special Jubilee window?'

'I expect they will have,' said Molly, moving further along the street. 'Oh yes, look at these children's clothes. That's more like it.'

In the next window there were dresses for little girls, in bright red and royal blue, and one in snowy white with an accordion-pleated skirt and bodice decorated with rows of white lace, finished off with a red bow trailing from the neckline. The suits for the little boys were all an adaptation of the sailor suit which had first come into fashion in the 1850s after Queen Victoria had had a portrait of her son Bertie, the Prince of Wales, painted in one. Some had knickerbockers fastening at the knee instead of long trousers, jackets with shiny buttons and they all sported a lanyard which passed under the square collar which was piped in white braid. In the centre of the window was a model of a little boy in Highland dress. The royal family's obsession for all things Scottish had led to many little boys of the era being dressed as highlanders, although no self-respecting Scotsman would ever had worn the stiff Eton collar and the bow tie which this model sported, or the lavishly decorated sporran which almost obscured the kilted skirt.

And in the next window, the one nearest to the main door of the store, was a huge photograph of

19

the Queen herself. She was dressed all in black with a locket round her neck on a black ribbon, the only touch of lightness in the portrait being a white collar to the dress and a white widow's cap with long streamers. Her face was glum, the mouth down-turned, with deep lines scoring her upper lip and chin. Not a very cheerful picture, but then no one had ever seen a picture of Queen Victoria looking at all happy.

'Looks as though 'er face'd crack that there window,' remarked Flo. 'You'd think she'd try to smile a bit now. Her Albert's been dead for – what? – must be thirty-odd years, but she still looks as miserable as sin.'

'She loved him very much,' replied Molly, smiling wistfully. 'So they say, but what do the likes of us really know about what goes on in their big castles or whatever?' It was common knowledge, however, that the Queen, following the death of her beloved Albert, had shut herself away, first at Osborne House on the Isle of Wight, and then at her castle at Balmoral. Only after an uproar in Parliament had she been forced to return to London, and during the last few years, since her Golden Jubilee, she had become, once more, a very popular figurehead. 'Anyway,' Molly went on, 'she's given us a cause for celebration, hasn't she, the old girl?'

'And a day's holiday, an' all,' remarked Flo.

'You speak for yourself,' countered Molly. 'Mrs Makepeace says we'll have to open next Tuesday, public holiday or not – well, part of the day, at any rate. There'll be hundreds of folk on the prom, all wanting cups of tea and cakes an' whatnot, and Dolly Makepeace isn't one to turn trade away. She's not such a bad boss, though. I dare say she'll let me finish early, then happen we can go out in the evening, eh, you and me?'

''Course we will,' said Flo. 'Where d'you fancy? The Raikes Hall Gardens? Or the Empire, p'raps. They've got some special acts on there in honour of the Queen; Bransby Williams, the actor, and some girl dancing on a rolling globe; that's what it says on the bill outside. "La Belle Rose", she's called. Or I tell you what'd be real exciting, Molly. There's a cinematograph show on at the Theatre Royal, the first time ever outside of London, it says.'

'Cinematograph? You mean moving pictures?'

'Yes, so I've heard. You can see men and women actually walking across a screen, and horses and carts and Niagara Falls – you know, that big waterfall in America – an' all the water coming down.'

'Sounds good,' Molly nodded. 'We'll do something, Flo, but on second thoughts I'd best wait till nearer the day and see how Mam goes on. She'll be near her time then and she might not want me to go and leave her, especially if Dad has to work. It's all right them saying it's a public holiday, but they forget that the entertainment places have to stay open.' Molly, in her eagerness to listen to Flo's description of all the exciting events that were taking place in Blackpool had, just for the moment, forgotten the situation at home. She knew, of course, that her mother must have the first demands on her time until her confinement was over, and afterwards, possibly, she might need help with the new baby. Flo, the youngest of four children and the only one now living at home, knew nothing of the demands that an ailing parent could make. Flo's parents, though they were in their fifties, were both hale and hearty, whereas for as long as she could remember, Molly's mother had suffered from indifferent health and lassitude.

Molly stared bemusedly into the window, realising that soon she must be heading homewards. She had promised she would only stay out for a couple of hours.

'Eye-catching, i'n't it?' Flo's remark brought her out of her reverie. 'You're right, Molly. Miss Amelia really ought to come and have a look-see at this. Them reds and blues – did you ever see such gorgeous materials?'

Donnelly's had certainly gone to town with their Jubilee window, the *pièce de résistance* among all the splendid displays. At each side and above the central portrait, which was mounted on a large easel, there were swathes of the materials that would be on sale in their haberdashery department, skilfully draped and falling in graceful folds. Rich red velvets and satins, royal-blue silks and cottons, and snowy white lace and net. Across the top of the window were strung the flags of the Empire, and the flowers of the realm – the rose, the thistle, the shamrock and the daffodil – decorated the sides of the Queen's picture.

'Yes, I must agree it's a bonny display,' said Molly. 'But all I could afford out of that lot is that blue silky cotton. It'd make a nice skirt for best, but I'm never sure about blue, not with my brown eyes. It'd be all right for you, though, Flo.' Flo had blue eyes and fairish hair, and most colours would suit her, although, like Molly, she was usually dressed in a serviceable black skirt and white blouse.

Flo sniffed. 'Since when could we afford Donnelly's prices? Yes, it's very nice, but we could pick up a remnant in the market for next to nothing, or if Miss Amelia's feeling generous she might let me have the end of a roll. Still, one of these days, you never know... We might meet a millionaire, each of us. Come on, let's be making tracks. I know you're anxious to get back to yer mam.'

Molly knew that Flo's remark about the millionaire was spoken in jest. When did girls such as them get to meet fellows with pots of money – the gentry or well-heeled businessmen and the like – let alone millionaires? What was more, did they really want to do so? They were working class; it had been drummed into them from an early age that it did not do any good to ape your betters or to attempt to hobnob with them. That was the view of William and Lily Rimmer, and of Flo's parents as well.

The Palmers, moreover, had their religious conviction as well to support this view. Sunday by Sunday they sat in the pew at their local Methodist chapel, Flo at their side, listening to the preacher's exhortation, 'Blessed are the meek', or some such sermon. And Flo, since being a tiny girl, had sung the children's hymn which stated most definitely that this was the way

God had decreed that things must be.

> The rich man in his castle,
> The poor man at his gate,
> God made them, high or lowly,
> And order'd their estate.

Molly for her part, unlike her friend, was not much of a church- or chapelgoer. Her parents – most unusually for the good-living, abstemious sort of people they were – did not attend a place of worship and had never encouraged their children to do so. Molly did not know the reason, but then there was a good deal she did not know or understand about her parents, especially her mother. She had been with Flo occasionally to her chapel, to a special Harvest Festival service or when there was a particularly dynamic visiting preacher whom Flo recommended she should hear. On such occasions Molly had felt moved, momentarily, aware that she might be missing something, but the moment had always passed. Flo asked her periodically if she would go with her to her Young Ladies' class on a Sunday afternoon, which she attended in addition to the morning service, but Molly always smilingly declined and her friend did not persist.

But Molly knew there was another side to Flo, a fun-loving side, and that Flo enjoyed a night out at one of the local dance places or a carefree walk along one of the piers as much as she did. They enjoyed one another's company and they did not worry too much about the differences between them.

Molly said goodbye to Flo when they had drunk in their fill of the delights of Donnelly's window. Flo continued along Bank Hey Street to her home in the Hound's Hill area, not far away, whereas Molly turned back towards Talbot Square, walking then away from the sea and promenade along Talbot Road towards the railway station.

Her home was in Larkhill Street, in one of the much less salubrious areas of Blackpool. It was near to the railway sidings and the coal yards; and the trustees of the land, though well-connected and affluent themselves, did not believe in holding back development by insisting on too onerous building conditions. Consequently the building plan was haphazard, and rows of terraced cottages, workshops, warehouses and beerhouses had been erected cheek by jowl, in a higgledy-piggledy maze. The area had become a haven for tramps and itinerant hawkers since a large common lodging house had opened in nearby Seed Street. There were other similar establishments throughout the area, and recently a marine store dealer had moved in.

The Rimmers' home was at the far end of Larkhill Street where it intersected with George Street. This was the rather more respectable end, verging on the area where working-class holiday-makers could find cheap accommodation in the height of the season. There would be no room in the Rimmers' house, however, for any other than the immediate family, consisting as it did of just two rooms upstairs and two down, these being a kitchen-cum-living room and a tiny front room

25

which Lily Rimmer referred to as her parlour.

Lily, though she lived in a somewhat dubious district of the town, had never succumbed to the slovenly and lackadaisical ways of many of her neighbours. Some of them used the downstairs front room as an extra bedroom to accommodate several of their large brood of children. Others used the room for guests, either long-term lodgers or families who were seeking cheap digs for the week, sometimes sleeping three or four or more to a bed. But Lily's parlour was her pride and joy, containing an over-sized horsehair sofa and two chairs, a china cabinet, which held her best tea set and various ornaments she had acquired over the years, and in pride of place in the window stood a shiny-leaved aspidistra on a tall spindle-legged table known as a whatnot. The house stood out from many of its neighbours; the lace curtains were kept freshly laundered and the doorstep, window sills and even the flags outside the front door were washed down at least twice a week. Never would it be said that Lily Rimmer was one to let her standards drop even when she was so near her time that she could scarcely get around.

Truth to tell it was Molly who was keeping things spick and span at the moment, and the couple of hours she had spent this afternoon enjoying the delights of Blackpool's promenade and shops had been a welcome respite from the drudgery of the washtub and the cooking range. She did most of the shopping now as well, slipping out to the nearby market for a few essentials during her midday break, and Mrs Makepeace, her employer, sometimes let her bring home a loaf which had not been sold in the shop or a few left-over cakes or the odd pie.

'Hello there, Mam,' Molly called out as she came through the door, which was always left unlocked. There was no answer. Lily was asleep in the chair by the side of the range. The fire had burned low and Molly knew she would have to mend it, despite the warmth of the summer day. The fire was essential for cooking, which was done in the fireside oven, also for heating the boiler, which was at the other side of the range and provided the only hot-water supply in the house. The boiler had to be filled with water carried in cans from the cold-water tap over the kitchen slopstone. Molly knew her father would have seen to this before he set off for work this morning, but it might need topping up. First things first, however, and her mother would be ready for a cup of tea as soon as she awoke.

Molly filled the kettle and set it on the hob, but she did not wake her mother. She was apt to cry out in alarm when awakened suddenly. Molly had done it once and Lily had screamed, then stared at her daughter as though she had no idea who she was, the fear in her eyes gradually fading as she realised where she was and with whom. Molly looked at her fondly and a trifle anxiously now. Lily's face was flushed from the heat of the fire, but beneath the redness her unhealthy pallor was apparent. Her auburn hair, which curled naturally, as did Molly's, clung to her moist forehead, then hung limply on either side of her sunken-in cheeks. She had put on a good deal of weight during her pregnancy, too much, Molly guessed, for comfort, but it was all centred in one place; the bulge which pushed out her flowered apron and which Molly could see, even now, was moving slightly. The stirrings of the unborn child showed that at least he or she was still all right, and would, God willing, not be stillborn as had happened on two occasions.

God willing. Although Molly echoed those words in her mind, a phrase she had picked up from Flo, they were not the kind used much in this household. God was seldom mentioned. Lily, in fact, purported not to believe in Him at all, hinting that a God of love could not possibly allow such dreadful things to go on in His world, or happen to her, Lily, personally, as she believed had been the case. There was a great deal that was a mystery about her mother, Molly thought again now. She uttered a silent prayer inside her head that all would be well in spite of Lily's disbelief. Molly knew that her mother was not yet forty years of age – just how old she was being something else of which her daughter was not sure – but at that moment she looked much, much older. Her hands and wrists protruding from the sleeves of her dark working dress were skeletal, and no doubt her legs, hidden beneath her long black skirt, were the same. Lily did not like anyone to see her in a state of undress, but there had been occasions when she had been forced to let Molly see her in her night attire. There were times when Lily was forced to take to her bed, a victim of the debility and melancholia which engulfed her now and again and which gave rise to all manner of minor ailments. Molly, seeing her bird-like limbs and slender frame, wondered at her frailty, and was amazed too at how, when she was feeling well, her mother could cope with all the back-breaking domestic chores she forced herself to do. For Lily was renowned in the neighbourhood, when she was in good health, for the whiteness of her sheets and towels strung across the alleyway, for the shine on her windows and furniture, and the huge kitchen range, which was black-leaded every week.

These chores, however, were now being done by Molly. It had been several weeks since Lily had been able to tackle the housework. Molly gently rattled the teacups, thinking it was time her mother awoke. Lily opened her eyes, putting her hand over the straining mound of her stomach. No doubt its movement, as well as the clatter of crockery, had roused her.

'Hello there, Mam,' said Molly again. 'I'm just making us a pot of tea I'm sure you're ready for one aren't you? It'll have done you good to have a sleep.'

'Yes, thank you, love. I'm gasping for a drink. I don't know...' Lily shook her head impatiently, '...sleeping in the middle of the day. Whatever's up with me, eh? Not like me, is it?'

'You're having a baby, Mam, that's what's the matter,' said Molly, smiling. 'Have you forgotten?'

'No ... no, I haven't.' Lily, not endowed with a great sense of humour, did not return her smile. Her mouth was set in a prim line. 'And the least said about that the better. Whatever time is it?'

She glanced anxiously at the large wooden clock on the mantelshelf above the range. 'Good heavens! Nearly quarter past four. I'd no idea I'd slept so long. Our Em'll be home from school in no time and you know how I like to behave as though there's nowt wrong when she's here. Not that there is anything wrong, mind. I'm going to be all right this time, Molly.' The brown eyes, so like Molly's own, were full of apprehension – fear, almost – as she looked at her daughter. 'But I don't want our Em knowing owt about it. She's only a child. Plenty of time for her to find out about ... things when she's as old as you are.'

Molly sighed. 'She's not a baby, Mam. I know she's only eight, but she's too old to go on believing that babies come in the doctor's black bag.'

'I won't need no doctor.' Lily shook her head emphatically. 'Maggie Winthrop'll do for me.'

'No, but you know what I mean. We can't fob our Em off with fairy tales about storks or gooseberry bushes. There aren't any round here anyroad, are there, either storks or gooseberry bushes?' Molly smiled. 'She knows you're having a baby. I told her because she was asking questions.'

'She knows? She's never said owt to me.'

'Well, she wouldn't, would she?' Emily, even more taciturn than her mother, was not one to chatter freely or to divulge her secret thoughts. Molly was the only one who seemed to be able to gain the little girl's confidence. 'You're sure Maggie will do for you, Mam?' Molly asked now. 'We can get Dr Paige if you like. We can afford it, you know.' Molly recalled that Dr Paige had, in fact, been called in at the time of her mother's last miscarriage.

'No, I've told you, I'll be all right this time. Maggie may be a bit rough and ready, but she's got a heart of gold and a real gentle manner underneath all that bluster. And she's very good at ... at that sort of thing. I've promised her, anyroad. I'd not want her to think I don't trust her.'

'All right, Mam. Just as you say.' Molly nodded, but she knew that Dr Paige's home was only a few minutes' walk away, just off Dickson Road, should the need arise. 'Here's your tea. I've put the sugar in for you.'

'Thanks; you're a good lass.' Lily smiled a trifle wearily at her elder daughter, then cocked her head at the sound of the door opening and closing again. 'Here's our Emily. Hush now; no more talk of doctors an' all that.' She raised herself up in the chair. 'Hello, Em. Molly's just made a cup of tea.' Her voice sounded brighter now. 'Come and have one with us, then you can tell us all about school. What have you been doing today, eh?'

'Nothing much.' This was Emily's usual answer to queries about her day at school. 'Reading, spelling, needlework, drill this afternoon.' The child gave a little shrug. 'That's all.' When would her mother realise, thought Molly, that maybe the little girl didn't want to talk about school? She was bright enough as her end-of-term reports always showed, intelligent and hard-working, though Molly guessed her sister was

31

just as quiet and uncommunicative at school as she was at home. Her white frilled pinafore which she, along with all little girls, wore over her dark dress was always as spotless when she came home at teatime as it was when she went out in the morning, and the brown ribbons which fastened her long hair in two bunches were still neatly tied. Em's hair was auburn, like that of her mother and sister, but of a brighter, more reddish, hue. She had the pale complexion and freckles which went with such hair too. She took after her father, though, not her mother, in build, being quite tall and sturdily made.

Molly saw her sister glance somewhat fearfully at the bulge beneath her mother's apron, then just as quickly look away again. 'No, I don't want any tea ... thank you,' she said. 'Sarah's asked me if I'll go round and play. She's got a new whip and top. Can I go, Mam?'

'Yes, of course you can, love. So long as you're back for tea. Mrs Winthrop'll happen ask you to stay, but you must say no. Maggie's already doing enough giving you a bite to eat at dinner time.'

The child seemed relieved to go. Molly reflected that young Sarah Winthrop, one of Maggie's large family and in the same class at school as Emily, would be the one to bring her little sister out of her shell if anybody could. She was pleased the two girls seemed to be getting friendly. It had come about because Maggie had offered to give Emily her dinner during the school's midday break when Lily was feeling too tired to cook – an all-too-regular occurrence these days, but no doubt her mother would get back into her old routine once the baby was born. Molly certainly hoped so.

'What's for tea today?' her mother asked now. 'Did you bring summat home with you, lass?'

'Yes, Mrs Makepeace has given me a couple of meat and potato pies that were left. I'll mash some extra spuds and make some gravy. And there's some of that apple pie from yesterday. I'll have it ready for when Dad gets home.'

'Good lass.' Lily smiled her thanks and Molly smiled back. Her mother was always grateful and Molly didn't mind, but there was no denying that it was hard work coping with the demands of her family as well as her job at the shop.

Chapter 2

Molly was always aware of a lightening in the atmosphere of the household when her father, William, arrived home. There were times when her mother's sombre aspect – not exactly moodiness, but more of a deep-seated sadness – got Molly down, and her little sister too was affected by the same tendency towards the blues. Not so William. His was a happy, carefree disposition. You could not help but feel better when you saw the cheerful grin which spread over his reddish face and the glint of humour in his merry blue eyes. Even Lily responded to him. She was always more relaxed, more at peace with herself it seemed, when her husband was with her. Molly did her best. She loved her mother and she knew she was loved in return, but she often felt she came a poor second when she saw the deep affection that her parents still felt for one another after so many years of marriage.

It must be eighteen years at least, possibly more. Molly sometimes wondered, secretly, why her father had married such a dispirited sort of woman as her mother was; not all the time, but far more than was natural.

'It's not been easy for her,' Molly's father had tried to explain to her a few years ago when Molly had questioned why her mam was often so sad. 'She went through an unhappy time when she was a girl. Her mother died when she was only eight, you know, and that upset her very much. And then she found out–'William stopped abruptly. 'It's no use, Molly lass, I can't tell you about it. I promised yer mam that I'd never talk about it and I never have done. We don't mention all that's gone on in the past. I've tried me hardest all these years to help her to forget, to jolly her along, like ... but I don't always succeed.' He gave a wry smile.

'Don't worry yer head about yer mam. She's all right. Just a bit more serious than you and me, eh? And our Em; she's another quiet 'un. Still, it wouldn't do for us all to be alike. Yer mam's father was a right sobersides, an' all. Albert Grimshaw – you never knew him, of course. He was good to her, mind, after her mother ... died. Thought the world of her, he did, though I always thought he was a bit old to be her dad; more like her granddad really. Anyroad, when the old feller died I thought we were ready for a change of scene, and yer mam fancied living in Blackpool. We'd had a couple of day trips here and she thought it was a grand place. So did I – well, I still do. There's no place like it in my book, 'specially since the Tower went up.'

'But it didn't make Mam any happier?'

'Well, it did and it didn't. She's up and down, you know. And it hasn't been all beer and skittles for us since we moved here. We've had a few setbacks, but we've got one another and we've got our two grand lasses. Aye, we make out. Don't you fret about yer mother. I'll always look after her.'

Molly guessed he was referring to the miscarriages Lily had suffered, also the several job changes he had endured. Not that he had ever been out of work for long. William was an industrious soul, but Molly knew it must have been quite a wrench for him to give up his good job as a tackler in the cotton mill in Preston, which was where they had lived previously, and find employment in another town. A very different sort of town with none of the huge mills where men, and women too, could generally find jobs. William had worked in a factory making sweets, as a coalman, a builder's labourer, then as a pier attendant, before finally getting regular employment at the Tower. He was a jack of all trades there: handyman, caretaker, lift attendant, even zoo keeper when the regular man was absent. There were few jobs, in fact, to which he could not turn his hand; but because he had not been settled in one job for very long, William had not improved his living conditions, as he had hoped he might do. The Rimmers were still in the small rented house in Larkhill Street which they had taken when they first came to Blackpool.

'Off you go now and enjoy yerself,' William said to his elder daughter on the evening of Jubilee Day. 'As luck would have it I'm not working tonight so I'll be able to look after yer mam. I told 'em she was getting near her time, like, and I didn't want to be doing no extra. I wouldn't've minded going up to t'top, though, and having a look-see at all them beacons they're lighting in Lancashire. Fifty-four of 'em, they say, all over

36

t'county, and you'll be able to see 'em grand from t'top o' t'Tower – well, six or seven of 'em, happen. They're running t'lifts till one o'clock, but like I say, it's not my pigeon tonight. So off you go with Flo and have a good time.'

'All right. Thanks, Dad ... if you're sure.' Molly had half promised Flo that she would meet her just outside the North Pier entrance at half-past seven, providing all was well with her mother. The unborn baby had been very active for the last few days, so much so that even Lily, who was normally very sensitive about such personal matters, had commented to her daughter that the bairn was kicking her to death. Now, though, there seemed to be a period of quietude, and Lily herself appeared calmer than she had done for weeks.

'Aye, you go, lass,' she said now. 'Yer dad'll get Maggie if owt happens, but it's not going to happen tonight.' She gave a rare chuckle and what for her was a bold remark: 'I think it must've gone to sleep. I'm getting a bit of peace, anyroad. Our Em'll be back soon from Sarah's. I told her to be home at half-past seven, but she can see to her own supper.'

Em, along with all the other Blackpool children, had had a day off school. Maggie Winthrop had taken her, together with Sarah and a couple more of her brood, to the Raikes Hall Gardens where the children were presented with Jubilee medals and souvenir mugs; and then they had partaken of a Jubilee tea of sandwiches, pork pies and fancy cakes. Emily, unusually for her, had come home pink-cheeked with excitement,

37

thrilled to bits with her enamel mug and begging to spend the rest of the day with her best friend, Sarah.

'You deserve a bit of time to yerself,' Lily went on to Molly. 'It wasn't fair making you work today when the rest o' t'town were on holiday.'

'Not all of them, Mam,' replied Molly. 'A lot of those that are connected with the holiday trade have had to work. Like Dad, for instance – he's only just finished, hasn't he? The Tower never closes, does it, not when there's money to be made?'

'Aye, that's true. Well, our Emily's had her bit of fun today. I've never seen her so excited, so now it's your turn. Don't rush back, love. Yer dad says there'll be all sorts going on on t'prom. Lit-up trams and a torchlight – what did you call it, William? A tata or summat – on the sands.'

'A tattoo, love,' smiled William. 'Soldiers marching and bands an' all that.'

'Aye, that's it,' Lily nodded. 'And where are you thinking of going, you and Flo?'

'Uncle Tom's Cabin, we think,' replied Molly. 'It doesn't get as crowded up there as it does at some of the other places. I should imagine the Winter Gardens and Raikes Hall will be packed out tonight.'

'Uncle Tom's Cabin,' repeated Lily, musingly. A smile lit up her face, which had of late looked so tired and careworn. Only today had the lines of anxiety faded away and now, she looked almost like a young girl again. 'D'you remember, William, how we used to go dancing there when we first came to Blackpool?' She turned to Molly.

'That was afore you came along, love, although we've been a few times since. Not for ages, though. Eeh ... I wish we could go again. Wouldn't it be grand, William?'

'And so we shall, love. No reason at all why we shouldn't go. Once the babby arrives and you're on your feet again our Molly can look after him – hark at me, saying him! – and we'll have a night out, just you and me, eh?'

William was kneeling on the hearthrug at his wife's side, her hands clasped tightly in his. As Molly put on her straw hat, securing it firmly with two long hatpins, her parents were gazing into each other's eyes like a couple of young lovebirds. 'Tara, Mam. Tara, Dad,' she said softly.

'Tara, love...' It was her father who replied, but she felt that neither of them was really aware that she had gone.

The 'going out' clothes of Molly and Flo were almost identical. Both girls had exchanged their workaday black skirt for different ones of dark serviceable colours, Molly's bottle green and Flo's navy blue. They both wore floral-patterned blouses, high-necked and with the fashionable leg-o'-mutton sleeves, though not quite so full as those worn by the more well-to-do. The bright green ribbons on Molly's straw hat picked up the same colour in her blouse, toning well with her deep brown eyes and auburn hair. Flo's straw hat had an artificial flower at the side, just the same blue as her eyes and the cornflowers on her blouse. Both girls carried short black jackets in case the evening should turn cold later on, but it had, by and large, been a glorious Jubilee Day.

The early morning clouds had soon drifted away, leaving a bright blue sky with fleecy clouds. As the day wore on the sun had come out in full warmth and splendour, making the sea dazzle and glitter like a million golden coins and putting everyone in a joyful mood. Flo, whose shop had been closed for the day, had been able to enjoy to the full the relaxed holiday spirit that pervaded the town. Molly, although she had worked for part of the day, had not been immune to the feelings of revelry either. Everyone who entered the shop had worn a bright smile, and the ringing of St John's church bells for an hour in the early morning had set the tone for the day. And as Mrs Makepeace had let her finish after the lunch-time crowds had dispersed she had been well content.

She nodded across at Jubilee Terrace from the other side of the road as they walked northwards along the prom. 'One of these days I'm going to own one of those shops, not just work in one. P'haps not on Jubilee Terrace, but ... somewhere. You just see if I don't.'

Molly enjoyed her work. Not only did she serve in the shop, but she also took her turn at waiting at the few tables which formed the little café at the rear. And in the early morning, before the customers started arriving, she helped Dolly Makepeace take the loaves out of the oven and set the meat pies, sausage rolls and all kinds of delectable cakes on trays for display in the window or under the glass-topped shop counter. But there were times when she longed to be more than just a shop assistant.

Her friend hooted with laughter now at her remark about owning a shop. 'Oh aye? And where d'you think you're going to get the brass to pay for it?'

But Molly just nodded emphatically. 'I mean it, I tell you. Great oaks grow from little acorns. I've heard Mrs Makepeace say that, and it's true. They started off with just a little stall in the market and look at them now. A shop in the poshest part of Blackpool, orders going out all over the town, boarding houses and them big smart houses on Whitegate Lane, and a café an' all. Only a small one, I know, but that shop's a regular little gold mine. For them that owns it, I mean.'

'Yes, but look at the hours they have to work, Molly. You've told me, haven't you, that Mr Makepeace works all night sometimes baking the bread and everything. And Dolly pulls her weight, an' all. She doesn't sit down on the job like some bosses do.'

'No, that's true. I don't begrudge 'em what they earn,' replied Molly, 'and they're certainly not mean with me and Cissie.' Cissie Dean was the other assistant, a married woman many years older than Molly.

Makepeace's was a family-run business. Dick Makepeace worked through the night and the early hours of the morning in the bakehouse at the rear, catching up on his rest during the day. Their son, Fred, a lad of fifteen who had recently left school, was learning the trade, and he took over the baking of the bread and pies when his father finished at six o'clock or thereabouts. It

41

was Dolly who was responsible for the cakes for which Makepeace's was renowned: the sultana and madeira cakes, the swiss rolls, almond tarts, iced fancies, meringues and eclairs. Her sister, Maisie, came in to help in the bakehouse for a few hours each day. Molly, too, under Dolly Makepeace's guidance, was gradually mastering the art of mixing and measuring, icing and piping, and learning how to control the heat of the ovens, most essential if the delicate cakes and pastries were not to be spoiled. She knew that Dolly found her to be an eager and willing assistant, but Molly, of late, had found herself wishing she could be rather more than a mere assistant. Admittedly she was only seventeen, but she had already been working at the shop for four years, ever since she'd left school, time enough for her to have learned quite a lot about the business and to know that she would love, one day, to be the manageress or, better still, the owner of an establishment such as this. Not necessarily one on Jubilee Terrace, as she had hinted to Flo, but just such another shop as the one where she was employed, selling all manner of delicious sweetmeats, breads and savouries. One with a larger café area, however, than Makepeace's had, with a team of waitresses wearing frilly caps and aprons, serving those of the holidaymakers and residents who desired something a little more refined than the standard meal of fish and chips, or meat pie and peas.

Lily's fastidious ways and her insistence on keeping up one's standards had, to a certain extent, rubbed off on her daughter. Though

Molly knew her place in society as did Lily, there was no harm in wanting to improve one's way of living through one's own efforts. If Dolly and Dick Makepeace, who were quite ordinary folk, could do it, then so could she, Molly Rimmer ... one of these days. But for the moment she knew it had to remain just a dream. It was, in fact, the first time she had ever mentioned her ambition to anyone, and she had surprised herself by her unguarded declaration to Flo. It must be the Jubilee spirit that was affecting her, she decided.

'You think I'm daft, don't you?' she said now, grinning and linking her arm through her friend's. 'I don't mean yet, of course. I haven't got the money for a wheelbarrow, ne'er mind a shop, but ... sometime. Like you might have a draper's shop like Miss Perkins', one of these days.'

'No ... I don't think so,' replied Flo, in all seriousness. 'That's not what I want. But d'you know what I'd really like? I'd like to be a dress-maker, a proper one, I mean, with customers coming to me for their posh dresses and costumes. It's working with all them lovely materials, y'see, and when I saw all those in Donnelly's window it started me thinking, just like you did about the shop. That's what I'd like to do: make dresses like that for meself as well as other folk. Ne'er mind, eh?' She turned to smile at her friend. 'At least we've got a bob or two to enjoy ourselves tonight, haven't we, and that's all that matters for now. Have you got yer penny ready for the toll? Oh, I say, we are grand, aren't we? Walking in Claremont Park with all the nobs!'

43

The Claremont Park Estate was the area of the promenade between Cocker Square, near to the North Pier, and Gynn Square, a mile or so to the north. It was a private enclosure with laid-out paths, flowerbeds and shrubberies and had been in existence for about twenty-five years. Tolls were charged, a penny for pedestrians and three-pence for carriages, though it was doubtful that much profit was made. People paid their pennies not only because it was a pleasant area in which to walk, but because it was far preferable, and much safer, than walking on the path along the top of the crumbling cliffs. Starting just opposite Cocker Square and continuing for the best part of a mile along the sea front, work was well under way with the construction of a Lower and a Middle Walk along the promenade and a strong wall as a defence against the rough seas, but further north the sea defences were known to be very inadequate. The cliffs were quite visibly crumbling, wearing away at an alarming rate, it was said.

Molly and Flo's path took them past many of Blackpool's most elegant hotels, the largest and most impressive of which was the Imperial Hydropathic Hotel. The northernmost toll gate was near to the Gynn Inn, a whitewashed building dating from the mid-eighteenth century in what appeared to be quite a rural setting, although it was less than a mile from the centre of the town. A path led inland from the inn towards the hamlet of Warbreck, and just visible on the skyline was the rooftop of The Knowle, an imposing house standing in extensive grounds, which belonged, or so it was said, to a family of the nobility. Just exactly who they were Molly and Flo did not know, neither had they ever seen the house from close quarters. It was very rarely that they ventured that far.

Another path, the one they took, led along the clifftop to Uncle Tom's Cabin. This had long been one of the chief attractions and places of amusement that Blackpool had to offer, but now, since the advent of the Winter Gardens, Raikes Hall Gardens and the Tower, its popularity was somewhat in decline. Also – and this was a fact which could not be ignored – the cliffs on which it stood were gradually being worn away by the sea and now Uncle Tom's Cabin stood some thirty yards nearer to the sea than it had done when it had first opened forty or so years before.

'Ooh-er, look at that,' Flo remarked as the two girls began the climb up the steep path to the promontory a hundred feet above the sea. 'Looks as though it's moved, doesn't it? I'm sure it wasn't so near the edge the last time we came.'

'It's not the building that's moved,' said Molly, smiling. 'It's the cliffs. Never mind; so long as it doesn't topple into the sea while we're here tonight. I must say, though, it doesn't look very busy, does it? I say, Flo, d'you think we've made a mistake coming here? P'raps we should've gone to the Raikes Hall Gardens or the Tower after all, eh?'

'Give it a chance,' replied Flo. 'I'm sure it'll liven up in a while. Anyway, you know neither of us is all that keen on crowds and rowdy behaviour. You get that sometimes at the Tower when some of the fellers've had too much to drink.' Flo was a mite strait-laced and most definitely teetotal, due to her Methodist up-bringing. Molly knew she had 'signed the pledge', as she called it, when she was twelve years old, and sometimes went along to the Band of Hope meetings that were held at her chapel. But Molly did not make fun of this. She, also, was a quite strictly brought-up girl though she might not have the same religious leanings as her friend. Her parents had always kept a watchful eye on the friends she made and they thoroughly approved of Flo. Molly had learned to abhor unruly behaviour, especially drunkenness. There was not much chance of that tonight, she thought, as she glanced at the mere handful of people sitting at the outside tables, nor of much frivolity at all, although the night was young.

'Come on, let's get ourselves a drink anyway, while we're here,' she said. 'I'm fair parched after that climb. Maybe some more folk'll arrive in a little while.'

They purchased their drinks – ginger beer for Molly, dandelion and burdock for Flo – at a counter inside one of the huts, then carried their brimming glasses to a trestle table overlooking the sea. There was a grassy area in front of the wooden cabin on which boards were laid for dancing and the tables were arranged around the perimeter. The sun was still quite high in the sky on this midsummer evening, the clouds just faintly tinged with pink at their edges as the sun began its descent, and the turquoise-blue sea sparkling and shimmering as though diamonds

had been scattered on its surface. The sea at
Blackpool was often grey or muddy brown, with
black lowering clouds above it, but at the end of
this Jubilee Day it seemed as though the
elements were set to behave themselves. It was
the sort of evening on which there would be a
glorious sunset.

'Old Uncle Tom's still up there, anyroad,'
remarked Flo, glancing up at the three wooden
figures perched on the roof of one of the buildings. 'And little Eva and Topsy. That's a good
sign, isn't it? They haven't been blown off in a
gale. I thought they might've come a cropper in
that storm that wrecked the *Foudrayant*.'

'They seem to be all in one piece,' Molly
nodded. 'Have you read that book, Flo? You
sound as though you know all about it.'

'What? *Uncle Tom's Cabin*? Of course I haven't.
A bit too serious for me, I should think. Although
I must admit I like Dickens. I've read a few of
them and—'

'Dickens didn't write *Uncle Tom's Cabin*,'
interrupted Molly. 'It was a lady called Harriet
Beecher Stowe.'

'All right, Clever Clogs!' Flo retorted. 'I know
he didn't. D'you think I'm stupid or summat? I
was just going to say – only you didn't let me
finish – that they have Dickens evenings sometimes at our chapel. You know, people that like
reading out loud – lay preachers an' that –
reading their favourite bits. It's really good.
Happen you'll come along sometime, eh, Molly?'

'Yes, maybe I will.' Molly looked anxiously at
her friend. 'I wasn't trying to be clever, you know,

and I haven't read that book neither. I only know that this place is supposed to be called after it, so some people say.'

'Who's bothered?' Flo grinned at her. ''S all right. I'm not offended. I know you weren't trying to show off. Hey, look – I think things are livening up a bit. That chap's getting his fiddle ready and his mate's sitting down at the pianner. They must've been waiting for a few more folk to come.'

Whilst they had been talking and sipping their drinks, quietly enjoying the ambience of the peaceful surroundings, more people had arrived. Then the small orchestra, comprising a pianist, violinist and cornet player, struck up with a lively tune and the entertainment began. Molly and Flo just watched at first. The crowd of young people, who were the latest arrivals, all seemed to know one another; then a few middle-aged and elderly couples came to join in the dancing. Uncle Tom's Cabin was still a popular venue for folk who remembered it with nostalgia from the days of their youth. Molly recalled her mother and father and how they had been reminiscing when she came out. She could imagine them now, sitting in the firelight, holding hands and being loving together when Emily had gone to bed. They had seemed to be in a very sentimental mood this evening.

Molly and Flo danced together to the strains of 'See Me Dance the Polka', an energetic dance which made the wooden boards reverberate with the clattering and thumping of scores of feet, some of them shod in quite heavy working boots and shoes. There were several more people there now and for the next dance, a veleta, both the girls acquired partners.

Flo's partner was a young man she knew vaguely from a neighbouring chapel. Not her own chapel, which was why she didn't know him all that well, she whispered to Molly in the pause between dances. Molly could tell he had taken quite a shine to her friend and she wasn't surprised when he asked Flo for the next dance. From the look of it it seemed as though Flo had got herself a partner for the evening, and she wasn't averse to this either, judging from her flushed cheeks and the light in her eyes. Molly did not mind. She knew her friend well enough to know she would not leave her to walk home on her own, should this prove to be a budding romance. He seemed a pleasant young man, a year or two older than herself and Flo, she guessed, with a fresh complexion and fair hair which was cut very short.

For her part Molly was content enough, for the moment, to sit and watch the dancers and enjoy the music performed by the very able little band, much of it consisting of melodies from the very prolific Mr Sullivan. Sir Arthur Sullivan, to be more correct, and Molly thought it was a pity that his partner, Mr Gilbert, had not been similarly honoured by the Queen. Their catchy tunes were heard all over the place, played by brass bands in the parks and promenades, whistled by errand boys and men at their work, and performed on the music-hall stage and in amateur productions. Molly knew quite a few of the songs. She had been with Flo to the music hall a couple of times and she had seen *The Pirates of Penzance* performed by a local church group.

'*Poor wandering one*,' she sang quietly to herself, '*though thou hast surely strayed...*', swaying gently from side to side to the rhythm of the music. She hoped she would not have to sit here on her own for very long, though. Her partner for the veleta, a friend of Flo's companion, had had just the one dance with her – out of politeness she supposed, because she was with Flo – and had then disappeared back to his own little crowd.

'Hello there,' said a voice close to her elbow. 'You look rather lonely sitting on your own. Would you do me the honour of dancing with me?'

Chapter 3

Molly looked up into the bluest pair of eyes she had ever seen, bluer even than those of her friend Flo, in which could only be called an extremely handsome face. His dark hair, worn rather long, waved back from a high forehead and, like many young men of the day, he sported a small moustache but no beard. He was not all that young, Molly realised at a glance, not as young as Flo's dancing partner, for instance. He was more likely to be in his mid-twenties, she guessed, and you would most definitely call him a man and not a lad. She knew at once from his well-cut suit, a three-piece in fine grey wool with a faint white stripe, and a gold watch chain dangling from his waistcoat pocket, that this was no ordinary fellow.

Not that there was anything wrong in being ordinary. Most of the lads Molly knew, the ones in her street and at Flo's chapel, and the one her friend was dancing with now, were ordinary and none the worse for that. But this man's voice, as well as his dress, set him apart; cultured and well-modulated, yet not without just a trace of the broad vowel sounds which suggested that he was a northerner. Not a working-class one, however. This man belonged to what Molly had been brought up to think of as the middle class. Which was why she hesitated, just for a moment, before

51

she answered him.

'Why ... yes. I'd like to dance. Thank you very much. That would be ... very nice. Thank you.' Even though he was way out of her social class there could be no harm in having a dance with him, maybe two if he asked her again, and chatting to him for a while. He seemed extremely pleasant, and no one who smiled at her so kindly, and with such a glint of humour in his eyes could be anything but ... nice.

'You don't need to thank me,' he said as they took to the floor. 'I told you – it would be an honour if you consented to dance with me. And I am delighted that you have.'

Molly smiled at him unsurely, not knowing what to say. She had not met anyone before who spoke like that.

'And you dance very well too,' he went on as they circled round to the strains of the waltz music.

Molly knew that this was true. She enjoyed dancing, and though she did not indulge in the pastime all that often she knew she had an instinctive sense of rhythm. Her feet knew exactly what to do, responding surely to the beat of the music and following accurately the lead set by her partner. She had no fear that she might fall over his feet as she had seen less graceful dancers do sometimes.

'Do you often come dancing?' he asked.

'No, not very often,' she replied. 'It's ages since I was here. I've been to the Winter Gardens and Raikes Hall, just once or twice.' She could hardly tell him that she could not afford to go more often, nor that the only other place at which she had danced was Flo's chapel, where they occasionally had social evenings consisting of parlour games and dancing followed by a light supper. Not this man's cup of tea at all, she imagined. Indeed, he looked somewhat out of place in the relaxed, far from sophisticated surroundings of Uncle Tom's Cabin.

'Yes, I've been to the Winter Gardens too,' he said, 'and the Tower. But it's more friendly here, don't you agree?'

She nodded. Her feelings exactly. Maybe he was the sort of person who fitted in well in whatever environment he found himself. 'Do you live here then? In Blackpool, I mean?' she asked.

'No...' her partner replied, a mite hesitantly. 'Not exactly. My family has–' He stopped rather abruptly before continuing, 'No, I don't live here, but I often visit. I live quite near, you see. In Preston, to be precise, so it's quite easy to pop over to Blackpool at the weekend. And tonight, of course, I've come because it's the Jubilee. I believe there will be all manner of celebrations going on in the town centre later tonight. And what about you?'

'What about me?' she frowned slightly. 'What do you mean?'

'I'm sorry.' His glance was warm, slightly amused as he smiled down at her. 'I didn't express myself clearly, did I? What I meant was – do you live here in Blackpool? Or are you a visitor, like me?'

'Oh no, I'm a local lass,' Molly replied, smiling up at him. He was several inches taller than she, five foot ten or so, she guessed. 'I'm what they call a sand grown 'un – born and bred here. As a matter of fact, both my parents were Preston people, but they came to live here before I was born. And we've lived here ever since.'

'I see. I rather guessed you were local, but you looked so lonely sitting there on your own, it made me wonder. You didn't come here alone, did you?'

'Oh no, I came with my friend Flo. But she met a lad she knew and they seem to be getting on quite well, so...'

'So she's left you in the lurch, eh?' He raised a quizzical eyebrow, smiling sympathetically.

'Oh no, nothing like that.' She couldn't have him thinking badly of Flo. She was the best friend any girl could have and Molly knew she would be along soon to invite her to join their little group. Flo would not abandon her to her own devices all evening. 'I can go and sit with them if I like. I just thought I'd give my friend a chance to – well – get to know her partner a bit better. I can tell she likes him.'

'I understand.' The man nodded soberly. 'And you don't want to play gooseberry, eh? Very thoughtful of you, but I'm quite sure you wouldn't have been sitting on your own for very long. Some other young fellow would have come along and asked you to dance if I hadn't been bold enough to do so. I'm not very bold, not really. I wouldn't want you to get the wrong impression, but I would like to buy you a drink, now, if you would allow me to.' The dance had come to an end and the couples were leaving the floor. 'And ... perhaps I could be permitted to come and sit at your table for a while, if you don't mind?'

'Of course I don't mind. But there's no need – to buy me a drink, I mean. Just because I was on my own.'

'But that's what I want to do, very much ... I'm sorry, I don't even know your name.'

'It's Molly.'

'Very well then, Molly. What was that you were drinking?' He nodded towards the empty glass on the table.

'It was ginger beer. It's very nice. Yes, I would like another one, please.'

'Very good. I'll be back before you can say Jack Robinson... Don't go away, will you?' He smiled at her a trifle ruefully and she shook her head.

'No, of course I won't.' She did not yet even know his name, but she could feel a ripple of excitement deep inside her such as she had never felt before. And never had any man smiled at her the way this one did. He really was very nice. She stared bemusedly at his retreating back, in such a brown study that she did not notice her friend at her side.

'So there you are. I saw you'd got a dancing partner.' Flo was looking flushed and happy. 'Come over here and sit with us. I didn't mean to leave you on your own – you know I wouldn't – but I'm getting on quite well with Sam. There's a crowd of them from his chapel, so you'll be very welcome. They're a nice lot. Come on... What's up?'

'I ... well ... I can't. I've met this young man.

55

He's just gone to get me a drink so I can't very well go and sit somewhere else. Besides ... he's really nice, Flo, and he says he wants to sit with me for a while. I can't be rude, can I?'

Flo frowned. 'But you don't know him, do you? You don't know anything about him. What's he called?'

'I ... I don't know – yet.'

'There you are, you see. You don't know the first thing about him. I noticed him, Molly. You couldn't help but notice somebody like him, could you? Posh suit and gold watch chain and polished boots an' everything. He sticks out a mile. But he's not our sort. You know what yer mam and dad always say, and mine an' all – stick to yer own kind. And he's out of the top drawer if anybody is.'

'For heaven's sake, Flo, I'm only going to have a drink of ginger beer with him! Where's the harm in that?' Molly spoke crossly, partly because she knew every word her friend spoke was true. He was, indeed, way out of her class, but she didn't want to admit it. She knew she wanted to spend some time with him however ill advised it might be. 'I'll be here and you'll be over there, so you'll be able to see exactly what we're doing. Anyway, what about you and ... Sam, did you call him?'

'What about us?'

'Well, you've obviously taken a shine to one another.'

'Don't be daft! I only said we were getting on quite well. Besides, I know him, don't I? At least, I know the sort of lad he is. Ordinary, like me.'

'I know what I'm doing Flo, all right? You go and have a good time with your Sam, and let me have a talk with ... this young man. Then we'll go home together, won't we, you and me?'

'Of course we will. What do you take me for?'

'He's coming now.' Molly looked towards the entrance of the hut from which her companion was emerging with two glasses, one full of an amber liquid, obviously ale, and the other of ginger beer. 'If you stop and say hello to him you'll see how nice he is.'

'No, thanks. I'll see you later.' Flo edged away quickly and Molly could not help but feel irritated. Anybody would think this man was the Prince of Wales or something. No, the Prince of Wales was old and fat. This young man was more the age of the Duke of York, but he was much more handsome than any of them.

He sat down on the wooden bench at her side, placing the glass of cloudy foaming ginger beer in front of her. 'There you are, Molly. I may call you Molly, I hope?' She nodded happily. 'It looks good, that ginger beer. I may have one myself when I've finished this. After all, it's what made Uncle Tom's Cabin famous, isn't it, ginger beer and homemade gingerbread?'

'Er ... I don't know. Is it?' she replied. 'I'm sorry, but I don't know your name either.'

'Of course you don't!' He slapped at his knee with impatience at his forgetfulness. 'How very stupid of me. I'm so sorry, Molly. I was so concerned with getting your drink, and making sure you didn't mind me sitting with you that I completely forgot I hadn't introduced myself.

My name is Josiah, but most people call me Joss.'
He held out his hand in a formal gesture and
Molly, somewhat dazedly, took hold of it. 'How
do you do, Molly? I am very happy to make your
acquaintance.'

'So am I,' she answered, not really knowing
what should be the correct reply. 'I'm very
pleased to meet you, Joss. Joss ... what? What is
your other name?'

'Oh, it doesn't matter.' He gave a slight shrug of
his shoulders. 'Just call me Joss. That's all that
matters for the moment. And I'll just call you
Molly. I will have to anyway because I don't
know your surname, do I?'

'No, you don't, and you're not going to
neither,' she answered pertly, grinning at him,
although she was surprised at her own daring. 'If
you won't tell me yours then I'm not going to tell
you mine.'

'Touché,' he replied, nodding and regarding her
keenly. She was not sure what he meant by the
word, one she had not heard before. She half
smiled at him, feeling mesmerised by the deep
blueness of his eyes and the intensity of his gaze.
'And where do you live, Molly?' he asked. 'The
north end of the town, I suppose, seeing that you
have come here tonight. Do you live quite near to
this place?'

'No, not really,' she replied, surprised at his
question. He obviously did not know a great deal
about Blackpool or he would realise that there
were very few houses in this part of the town,
except for the scattering of large mansions on the
cliffs at Bispham and Norbreck which belonged

to the well-to-do. There was a thriving community at Bispham, of course, further inland – maybe he thought she lived there? – but to the inhabitants of Blackpool it was a rural village, not visited very often. 'I live near Talbot Road, not far from the station,' she told him. 'And I work at a shop in Blackpool,' she added, deciding to move quickly away from the subject of where she lived. Not that she was ashamed of living in Larkhill, but it was not the sort of confidence that you blurted out on first acquaintance with someone, especially to a well-set-up fellow such as this.

'Oh ... and what sort of shop is that, Molly?'

'It's a confectioner's. Quite a high-class one.'

'Of course. I'm sure it must be.' His voice sounded a little teasing and she wondered, fleetingly, if he was making fun of her. But the twinkle in his eyes was such a kindly one that she decided just as quickly that he wasn't.

'In fact we're quite famous for our cakes and pastries,' she went on. 'We send out orders to lots of the big houses and hotels. I serve in the shop and sometimes I wait on in the little café. And I'm learning all about baking and confectionery as well. What I'm really doing is ... is learning the trade. I hope to have a business of my own, one day,' she added. She knew that this was a deviation from the truth, but only a slight one, she told herself. Not the part about having her own business; that was true, although it might be but a dim-and-distant dream, but she was quite sure that Dolly Makepeace did not see her as anything but an extra pair of hands to help out at busy times in the bakehouse. She was not, in

59

truth, a trainee confectioner, serving her time to the trade, which was what she was implying. She felt a little ashamed of her white lie. Molly was not given to deception or to exaggeration, but all the same she knew, deep down, that she was guilty of trying to impress this charming and handsome young man, if only a little. There could be no harm in it. She was not likely to see him again after tonight ... was she?

'And I'm sure you will have your own business eventually, Molly,' he replied seriously. 'I can see you are a young lady with lots of spirit and perseverance. And the best way to learn any trade is to start at the bottom and work one's way up. At least – that is what I've always been told – he added, almost to himself.

Molly had the impression he was speaking personally. 'Why, is that what you are doing?' she asked. 'What sort of business are you in ... Joss? What do you do for ... er ... for a living?'

As soon as she had uttered them she wondered if she should have spoken the last few words. Maybe he was the sort of well-heeled young man who did not need to work for a living at all; one of the gentry, as her parents would say. His reply intimated that this could be true.

'Oh ... this and that,' he said evasively. 'Let's say I have not quite decided, yet, which direction my life – my career, if you like – is going to take. There are a few options. The trouble is one cannot always do exactly as one wants to do in life. There are always other people to consider – their wishes, their hopes and ambitions for one's future. One has to try to ... to fit in, but it is not always easy.'

She pondered on his words. She had always thought that the gentry had it made; that they could pretty much please themselves about what they did or did not do. But maybe they too had their problems, even if they did not have the fear of being thrown out of work or worrying about where the next meal was coming from. She frowned a little, wondering about him, eager to know more, but at the same time realising that such knowledge would be futile. She and him, they were poles apart.

'Hey, don't look so worried.' He grinned easily at her and she noticed that his teeth were white and evenly spaced. He either visited his dentist regularly or they were false, but she did not think they were. 'My problems are not yours so let's forget about them. Would you like to dance again? They're playing a waltz and I think we're very good at that, aren't we? Come along – let's show them what we can do, shall we? Is that your friend over there, the young lady you called Flo? She seems to be watching us very intently. Keeping her eye on you, is she?'

'Yes, that's Flo,' replied Molly. 'The one with the blue flower in her hat. We came together, you see, so I expect she's wondering–'

'Whether I'm a suitable companion for you, eh?' His blue eyes twinkled even more. 'Don't worry, Flo,' he called out as they waltzed past her table. 'I will take very good care of your friend.'

Flo's face went pink and she looked away in obvious embarrassment. Joss smiled. 'It's good to have friends,' he said. 'I expect you and Flo are quite close companions, aren't you? I could tell she was rather anxious, but she does not need to be. As I told her, I will look after you ... Molly.' He spoke her name softly, like a caress, holding her a little more closely and gripping her hand more tightly. She was aware of his breath on her forehead and the faint touch, now and again, of his moustache. It was the closest she had ever been to any man, save her father, and she was finding the feeling almost overpowering.

'I'm forever blowing bubbles,
Pretty bubbles in the air...'

All around them carefree voices were singing along to the music of the small orchestra.

'They fly so high, nearly reach the sky,
Then like my dreams they fade and die...'

Molly sang along with them very quietly, almost under her breath. The whole of this evening was taking on the semblance of a dream. She could not bear to think that, come tomorrow, it could so easily fade away and die. She shook herself mentally, coming back to reality.

'Yes, Flo and I are good friends,' she told Joss when the dance had ended and they'd returned to their table. 'She works at the draper's near to where I work. I suppose she's the next best thing to a sister – well, better, perhaps, because sisters don't always get on, do they?'

'I take it you don't have any sisters, then? Brothers, perhaps?'

'No brothers, but I do have a sister, only a little one though. Our Emily's eight so there's a big gap between us – nine years – so I suppose that's why we've not got a lot in common. There's just me and Em, and me mam and dad, of course ... er, my mother and father,' she corrected herself. 'My mother's not had very good health over the years. That's why–' She stopped herself just in time. What on earth was she thinking of? It would be most improper to tell this young man that her mother's ill health had caused her to lose several babies. 'What I was meaning to say was ... I will be having a brother or another sister quite soon. My mother is...' Goodness, how did you say it without sounding indelicate?

'Your mother's near her time, is she? I see. Which is why you are a little agitated tonight, is it, Molly? I can tell you are not completely at ease, but I was hoping it was not because you were not enjoying my company. Now I understand. You are a little worried about her, are you? Your father – is he with her? He is a ... good husband?'

'Oh yes, one of the best. She couldn't have a better husband than me dad. She's always saying so. He adores her. I wouldn't want you to think...' She spoke with vehemence, not wanting him to get the impression that her father was a drunkard or a wastrel or wife-beater as, unfortunately, several of the fellows were in their neighbourhood.

'I don't think anything, Molly,' Joss answered quietly. 'How can I when I hardly know you? But I hope to remedy that before long. Try to enjoy the evening, hmm?' He covered her hand with his where it lay on the table. 'Your mother will be all right, I'm sure.'

'I am enjoying it,' Molly replied, leaving her hand beneath his. It felt safe and comfortable there. 'Honestly I am. And I'm not really worried about Mam. The chances are that it'll be a few days yet before the baby is born.' It had certainly seemed that way when she had left this evening. 'My father insisted that I needn't rush back home. He wanted me to enjoy some of the things that are going on in the town. He knows I'll be all right with Flo. I suppose we'll have to be making a move before long, though, Flo and me...' She cast a slightly anxious glance in the direction of her friend's table. Flo was not there, but then Molly caught sight of her and her new friend, Sam, in the throng of couples on the dance floor. There were several more of them now, jigging around energetically to the music of a military two-step.

Joss had noticed her too. 'There's Flo,' he said, 'in the middle. She looks as though she's having a good time. I don't think she'll be worrying too much about you.' The dance came to an end and they saw Flo and Sam returning to their corner holding hands and talking animatedly as though there was no one else that mattered. She did not even glance in Molly's direction. 'So stop worrying your head about your friend. I'm sure that young man will see her safely home, and that is just what I intend to do with you... Don't look so alarmed. I'm not a big bad wolf, and it's the least I can do after enjoying your company all evening.

If it will make you feel any better I'll go and have a word with her. We could all leave at the same time, if you wish – if you need a chaperone ... but somehow I feel that idea may not go down very well with Flo.'

'No, no, it's all right,' Molly answered hastily. It was becoming obvious now that Flo had other fish to fry. Molly was not at all alarmed at the prospect of being alone with Joss – she knew instinctively that she could trust him – but she was at the idea of him taking her right home and seeing where she lived. That would put an end to any friendship between them, should there be the remotest chance of Joss wanting to see her again. She decided she would have to deal with that problem when it arose. She would think of something; try to get away from him before they got too near to the seedy environs of Larkhill. 'Thank you for offering to see me home. There's no need, but ... thank you.'

'Molly, Molly, why must you keep on thanking me? It will be a very real pleasure.' He smiled disarmingly at her. He really had the most charming manners. 'But we do not need to go just yet. The night is still young. Relax and enjoy it. Forget all your cares, yes?'

As the evening drew on she found herself relaxing more and more, enjoying his company and managing to push to the back of her mind her worries about their difference in status and about what might happen if he discovered where she lived. They danced again, several times, and chatted easily together, though not about their respective families. Molly could not help but notice the omission. Very well then, she thought to herself; if he is going to be tight-lipped about his family and his job – if, indeed, he has one – then I am jolly well going to keep my mouth shut about my relations. She decided she had already told him as much as he needed to know, especially as there was little likelihood of her ever seeing him again after tonight. The thought pained her, though, and she hastily pushed it to one side.

They found they both loved the music of Gilbert and Sullivan, a goodly selection of which was being played this evening, the works of Mr Charles Dickens and the poetry of Keats and Shelley. Molly's mother had volumes of their works she had inherited from her own mother; and Molly, seeing Lily reading them in introspective moments – of which there were many in her life – had come to appreciate them herself although she did not always understand them fully. And they discovered a mutual fondness for Blackpool. Brash and brazen though it might be, they both agreed there was no place like it, and there could be no better town in which to live. It sounded as though Joss had adopted it as his own hometown, and it would seem that he spent as much time here as he did in his native Preston; or at least he would like to do so.

'Are you staying here tonight,' Molly asked, 'or are you going ... home?' She guessed the trains would be running late on this Jubilee evening.

'This is home, Molly,' he replied. 'At any rate, it seems like it, much more so than Preston ever does ... especially now.' The look he gave her was meaningful; the trouble was, what exactly did it mean? she could hardly dare believe that he meant he wanted to go on seeing her. But he was evasive about where he was staying.

'Oh, not very far from here,' he answered. 'It's where we always stay when we're in Blackpool.' One of the big seafront hotels, she guessed, in the prestigious Claremont Park; probably the Imperial Hydro, but he would not like to admit it, not to an ordinary girl such as she was.

She could not have been more surprised when Joss reached into the breast pocket of his jacket and pulled out a small sketch pad, about six inches by four, and a pencil. 'This is one of the things I do, Molly,' he said, 'amongst others. At least I try to. I am an artist, of sorts, and I would very much like to draw you – if you would allow me?'

At first she was covered with confusion. She opened her mouth to protest, but then thought – why not? This was just one more incredible happening in an evening that was becoming more magical with every passing moment. 'Of course I will.' She smiled at him in a friendly manner. 'I feel very flattered. Now – how do you want me to sit?' She began to smooth her skirt and rearrange her hat and hair.

'No, Molly, please. Stay just as you are. Act naturally. Look out to sea, as you were doing a moment ago. That was the expression I wanted to catch. Your eyes on the horizon as though there is something ... just out of reach.'

She looked at him wonderingly, not answering. Could he read her thoughts? 'You can talk if you wish – I would like you to talk – but keep your eyes on the sunset. It won't take me long; I just want a lightning sketch that I can work on later. That is the way I usually work.'

In truth it was Joss who did most of the talking whilst he was sketching, Molly just sitting listening and making the occasional comment. He told her that he painted in watercolours, often taking his paints and easel – all the paraphernalia, he said – into the countryside around Preston: the Ribble Valley, or, nearer to the town, the parklands that reached down to the river. Whilst staying in Blackpool he had painted the fishing boats at Fleetwood, the ancient churches at St Michael's and nearby Bispham and peaceful scenes in the villages and hamlets along the River Wyre. There was, alas, little of scenic beauty in Blackpool, but the glory of its sunsets had to be seen to be believed. Joss had painted them once or twice, but he admitted modestly that he had failed to do them justice. Often, however, he preferred to work from his spur-of-the-moment sketches, capturing in an instant something that had taken his fancy, then refining it later. He sketched people, after asking their permission, just as often as he did scenes and buildings. Never was he without his sketch pad.

'If we had been here earlier in the day we could have had our photographs taken,' he said. Often, at Uncle Tom's Cabin, a photographer was in evidence, setting up his tripod on the green, then disappearing beneath his black canopy. 'But I prefer this way of producing a likeness. Photographs can look so stilted, so ... false, even

68

though they say the camera can never lie.'

'Are you going to let me see it?' Molly asked shyly.

'Maybe ... one day.'

Her heart gave a leap at his words. They could only mean he intended to see her again.

'It is only a rough sketch. There is a lot of work to be done to it to do you justice, Molly. But...' he pursed his lips, putting his head to one side and half closing his eyes, 'there can be no harm in letting you have a peep. See...' He held the pad out to her.

She was astonished at his skill. He had captured in only a few moments the essence of her: her half-smile, the faraway look in her eyes and, more prosaically, the jaunty ribbons fluttering from her hat and the tendrils of hair curling over her forehead and ears.

'It's very good,' she said. 'You must be – I mean, you are – very talented.' She wondered about him again. Could he possibly be an artist, a professional one, doing this sort of thing for a living? Or was it, maybe, an ambition not yet realised?

The sunset Molly had been watching as Joss sketched her was a fitting and spectacular climax to the day of Jubilee sunshine. The sky was a glory of gold and rose as the sun, a fiery ball of such brilliance that it almost hurt her eyes to look at it, began to sink behind the shimmering silvery blue sea.

'The end of a perfect day,' said Joss now, putting away his sketch pad and pencil. He laid his hand upon Molly's. 'Shall we go?' She nodded contentedly. 'And your friend?'

'Oh, I think we could safely leave her to her own devices,' said Molly. 'I'll go and say cheerio, though, if you don't mind?'

'No, of course not. I'll go and find my hat.' Joss disappeared in the direction of one of the smaller wooden buildings.

Flo, in truth, seemed to have forgotten all about her. Molly decided her friend must have come to the conclusion that Joss was, after all, a trustworthy young man and that she could, therefore, concentrate on her own affairs. Her head was very close to Sam's and they were holding hands beneath the table. She appeared startled, as though suddenly brought back to earth when Molly spoke to her.

'Joss is seeing me home. You ... er ... don't mind, do you?' She couldn't resist a roguish grin at the pair.

Sam, who seemed a cheerful and friendly sort of lad, just right for Flo, grinned back at her. 'I should jolly well think not, Molly. I say, you don't mind me calling you Molly, do you? We haven't been properly introduced an' all that, but I'm sure I shall get to know you before long, seeing as how you're such a good friend of Flo's. She's been telling me all about you. and I've told her not to be so mistrustful, like. That feller of yours looks all right to me. A bit la-di-da, happen, but you can't go blaming him for that if he were born with a silver spoon in his mouth. Anyroad, we won't be far behind you – we were just thinking of making tracks, weren't we, Flo? – so we'll be able to see if he gets up to any hanky-panky.'

Another infectious grin told Molly that Sam was only kidding and she decided she liked him very much.

Flo smiled at Molly at she tucked her hand through Sam's arm in a proprietorial manner, her smile seeming to say, Isn't he grand and aren't I lucky? 'Yes, you go and enjoy yourself, Mol,' she said. 'Sam's convinced me that that feller seems very nice. Look – he's waiting for you. See you tomorrer then...'

When Molly rejoined Joss he was wearing a straw boater, a very elegant one with a blue ribbon around it which just matched the colour of his eyes. She would not have been surprised to see him carrying a silver-topped cane, but that was not the case. He held out his arm for her to hold and they set off down the cliff path that led to the Gynn Inn.

From there the tramtrack led along Warbreck Road to Blackpool town centre. It was this road they took now instead of continuing along the cliff path because, in the distance, they could see approaching them an illuminated tramcar. Dusk was falling, and though the sky was not yet fully dark the incandescent lamps which decorated the tramcar created a dazzling spectacle in the gloaming. 'All seasons – all climes', were the words formed by the pink and green light bulbs, and over the windows similarly coloured stars added a further touch of brilliance.

Molly could hardly speak, so overcome was she by the splendour of this scene and the many many more she saw later that evening, even though her father had told her a little of what she might expect.

She felt that the words she uttered were trite banalities, but all around them she could hear similar comments from the folk in the crowd: 'What a sight, eh?' 'Bloomin' marvellous, ain't it?' 'Did you ever see the likes of that?' And Joss at her side held her arm more tightly and smiled fondly at her, seeming to understand perfectly her delight in it all.

The crowd grew denser as they came nearer to the centre of the town. They saw other tramcars along the promenade bearing the inscriptions '1837–1897', 'Empress of India and Australasia' picked out in various glittering colours.

It was not only the tramcars that were illuminated. The periphery of the Big Wheel was outlined on either side with electric lamps, and several of the cars on it were lit up. So was the dome of the Winter Gardens and the Empire Theatre; but the centre of attraction, as was only to be expected, was Blackpool Tower.

Molly and Joss stood by the sea railings almost opposite the Tower from where, along with thousands of others, they had a magnificent view. It must have been at about half-past ten, although Molly had lost all sense of time, that a display of Roman candles was set off from the first platform. The multi-coloured balls of fire, rising and falling in the darkening sky, drew the admiration of the crowd, but this was nothing to what they were to see next. As the last of the fireworks died away the whole ironwork structure of the Tower became illuminated from top to bottom with vivid red electric light. This effect

72

lasted for several minutes, then, as the brightness faded away the electrical decorations on the seaward side of the Tower blazed out in their full brilliance: 'VRI – 1837–1897'. The heading was fashioned in huge letters with coloured lamps, and a decoration consisting of a crown, star, rose, shamrock and thistle with the words 'Victoria, for 60 years our Queen' formed a striking centrepiece. Then a searchlight from the summit of the Tower was directed on to the three piers and the now inky blackness of the sea, whilst rockets were sent up at intervals from the North and Central Pier jetties. Molly felt that the scene on the promenade and the cheers of the crowd echoing in her ears would stay in her memory for evermore; to say nothing of the young man at her side, quietly protective, but seeming equally enthralled by it all.

The crowd was thicker than ever now, and Molly gathered from the comments around her that they were all waiting to see the Torchlight Tattoo which was to take place on the sands. She remembered her father telling her mother about it and the sudden recollection reminded her that she really should go home, that it would be thoughtless of her to stay out any longer, despite her father's words that she must enjoy herself. She could hear in the distance, beyond the murmurings of the crowd, the sound of a brass band approaching.

It was as though Joss could read her thoughts. He put his head close to hers. 'Are you thinking it is time you were going home, Molly?' he asked gently. 'I understand. You are thinking about your mother, are you not?'

'Yes, that is ... if you don't mind. I've had such a lovely evening, but I don't think I should stay and watch the parade. You can, if you like. I don't live very far away.' The thought had also returned to her that now had come the tricky part: getting away from Joss without him finding out where she lived. 'I can easily walk home from here.'

'Don't talk silly.' It was the first time all evening that he had looked sternly at her, though she knew it was only mock severity. 'You know perfectly well I would not allow you to do that. Come along.' He put his arm right round her, guiding her through the throng of people. 'If we don't make our getaway now it will become more difficult later. Did you ever see such crowds?' They were crossing the tramlines now and when they reached the opposite pavement, near to Talbot Square, he stopped in his tracks. He turned to face her, holding her gently by her arms.

'Molly ... Molly, my dear, I have enjoyed being with you tonight far more than I can say. Far more than I have ever enjoyed anything. You will let me see you again, won't you?'

'I would like to, Joss, but—'

'Molly, my love, there could be so many buts, for both of us. Try to put them out of your mind. I know what is in your mind, believe me, I do. But ... will you meet me again?' His eyes were glowing with a light which Molly could not quite interpret. She dare not think it could be the light of love. She was a sensible girl and she knew that Joss could not love her, not yet – he did not know enough about her. It was more the light of affection she could see in his eyes, of tenderness and friendship and a deep liking which, given the time, could grow into love. And she knew that this was just the way she felt about him too.

'Yes, Joss,' she said without any hesitation. 'I would love to see you again.'

'That is wonderful.' His kiss on her cheek was just the slightest brush of his lips against her skin, but the feeling of warmth it evoked spread right through her. 'Now, up Talbot Road, I guess? You said you lived near the station?'

He set off walking more briskly and Molly matched her steps to his. She could have told him that the shop where she worked was just round the corner on Jubilee Terrace, but the moment had passed and Joss was now talking about when and where should be their next meeting. Neither had she told him her father was employed at the Tower although she might so easily have done so.

'What about Sunday, Molly? I will be in Blackpool again this weekend with... That is to say, I will be here. Sunday afternoon – would that be convenient for you?'

'Yes, that would be lovely. I shall look forward to it.'

'Not nearly so much as I will, I can assure you.' His look again was of such tenderness and warmth that Molly could have no doubt that she was doing the right thing. 'Now, where shall we meet? I will understand if you do not wish me to come to your home ... not yet. But later on, of course, I hope to know much more about you, Molly ... and I will tell you more about myself, when we meet on Sunday.'

They agreed upon the North Pier entrance – where Molly and Flo had met that evening – at two o'clock on Sunday afternoon. Near to the junction with Cookson Street a middle-aged man and woman drew alongside them. 'Hello there, Molly,' called out the woman. 'Been to see the sights, have you? Lovely, weren't they?' Molly recognised them as Mr and Mrs Jackson, a friendly couple who lived about halfway along her street. Mrs Jackson did not wait for an answer. 'Sid and me have just been watching t'fireworks. I'm dying to get me feet up and have a cup of tea. G'night, luv. Be seein' yer...'

'Good night, Mrs Jackson.' As the couple hurried past Molly seized her opportunity. 'Joss, you don't need to come all the way home with me, honestly.' She stopped dead, pulling at his arm. 'I'll walk home with Mr and Mrs Jackson. They live down our street and ... it would be silly, wouldn't it, for you to come any further?'

'Very well then.' Joss seemed to understand. Again he kissed her cheek, holding her close to him for just an instant. 'Off you go and catch up with them. Good night, Molly. See you on Sunday, hmm?'

'Yes, of course. See you Sunday. I'll look forward to it. Good night, Joss.' She smiled at him, looking deep into his eyes for a brief moment before she hurried away.

Chapter 4

'Bit of a toff, eh, Molly? Is he a friend of yours? Your young man, happen? No, I don't suppose he is or he'd come right home with you, wouldn't he?'

Molly smiled to herself. Mrs Jackson was well known in the street as something of a gossip, though not in any malicious way. She was a kind woman, always ready to do anybody a good turn, but she did like to know what was going on. Molly didn't know her very well as her mother always preferred to steer clear of neighbours who were nosy. Lily would not discuss her family or her private affairs with anyone and she had tried to instil in Molly the same attitude. This was one of the reasons Molly had been so reticent with Joss.

'Unless your mam and dad don't approve of him, of course...' Mrs Jackson was determined not to give up and Molly felt obliged to answer.

'No, he's not my young man, Mrs Jackson. He's just someone that I know ... quite well.' She felt the white lie was excusable; it would soon be true, anyway. 'I happened to meet him by chance tonight, so we stayed together, that's all.'

'Mmm.' The woman nodded. 'Out o' t'top drawer, though, Molly, eh? I reckon you could do all right for yerself there.'

'He's ... er, yes ... not without a bob or two. But

there's nothing like that between him and me. He's dashing off to catch his train now.'

'Oh, I see. Where does he live then?'

'Preston.' Was Joss catching a train back tonight? Molly was not sure. She could not quite remember what he had said. He had told her that he often came to stay in Blackpool, but she had no idea where; and had he said he was staying there tonight? Her mind was a maze of incoherent thoughts and impressions and memories, but through them all one thought shone clear: she was seeing him again on Sunday. But that brought a host of fresh problems. How was she going to get away from home without telling her parents exactly where she was going ... and with whom?

Immediately she thought of Flo. Flo had asked her so many times if she would accompany her to her Sunday afternoon Bible class. Perhaps she could say she was going there? Her parents would not object to that, even though they seemed to have little interest in religious matters themselves; and Flo would not let on that she had been elsewhere, not if Molly had a cautionary word with her...

No, that would not do at all. She stifled the thought almost as soon as it entered her head. On no account would Flo tell lies for her; she was much too honest and God-fearing to do that. And did Molly really want her to do so? In her heart of hearts she knew that she did not. Molly had been brought up to be truthful. 'Tell the truth and shame the devil' was a favourite saying of her mother's, though whether Lily believed in the devil any more than she believed in the Almighty was questionable. No, Molly knew she must try to tell them the truth: that she was meeting a very nice young man called Joss whom she had met at Uncle Tom's Cabin. One stumbling block was that she did not know his surname. Should she say – although it was not quite truthful – that they had all been together in a crowd and she had not had the chance to find out? Oh goodness, what a quandary she was in.

'...So I says to Sid, "Me ankles are all puffed up like balloons wi' all that standing around." So he says, "We'd best get home, lass, then you can stick 'em in a bowl of hot water and mustard." Nowt like it, Molly, for sore feet.' Molly had been only half listening to Mrs Jackson, who had moved on from the subject of Molly's young man to that of her own aches and pains. She did not require any answers so Molly had become immersed in her own problems. 'We'd like to have seen that there tattoo, wouldn't we, Sid, but ne'er mind, eh? It's been a grand night. The old Queen's done us proud, God bless 'er. We'll say cheerio then, Molly. Be seein' yer, lass.'

They had reached the Jacksons' door and Mrs Jackson began to fumble inside the letter box, no doubt feeling for the key which hung on a string at the back of the door.

'Hey up, Molly. Here's yer dad comin' along. He's moving as though his shirt-tails are on fire.' It was the first time Mr Jackson had said a word since Molly had met them. 'You'd best go and see what's up. Unless he's out looking for you, eh? In hot watter, are you, lass?'

'No, I don't think so, Mr Jackson,' Molly called over her shoulder as she hurried up the street to meet her father. She was suddenly filled with an awful dread. Her mother – something had happened; and one look at her father's stricken face told her she had every reason to be concerned.

'Molly, thank God you're here. I'm just on me way to fetch the doctor. Maggie can't cope any longer. Yer mam, she's badly. Started soon after you went out. Anyroad, I'd best get off.'

'Dad, let me go instead.' She seized hold of his arm. 'Dr Paige, Cocker Street, isn't it? I can run. I'll be there in no time.'

'No, lass – leave go.' He pulled away from her. 'You're hindering me. I've got longer legs than you and I can run faster. Go and see to yer mam.' William rushed off down the street and Molly ran to her front door.

She could hear her mother's moans as soon as she entered the house. She dashed straight up the stairs and flung open the door of the room where her parents slept. Maggie Winthrop's was the first face she saw, turning away from the figure on the bed and staring at Molly in desperation. Maggie's cheeks were always rosy – she was a buxom, healthy woman who boasted she had never had a day's illness in her life – but now her face was bright red with runnels of perspiration running down. Her wiry grey hair too was soaked with sweat and her eyes were fearful.

'I've done all I can, Molly, lass, but I reckon it's too much for me this time. Yer dad's just gone to fetch Dr Paige. Happen he can do summat. I pray to God he can.' And this was Maggie Winthrop, whose proud boast it was that she had never lost a bairn yet.

Molly's first reaction was one of anger. 'For God's sake, Maggie – why on earth didn't you send for the doctor sooner?'

'Because she was all right. She was doing fine. Your dad came to fetch me – about half-past eight, it were – and everything was quite normal. You know I wouldn't take no chances, Molly. And then all of a sudden, this happened. She started bleeding an' I can't stop it nohow.'

Peering round the bulk of Maggie's body Molly looked, for the first time, at the prostrate figure of her mother. She was half sitting, half lying, propped against a pile of crumpled pillows. Her face was deathly pale and she did not even open her eyes at the sound of her daughter's voice. Molly guessed she was far too gone in pain to do so; she was moaning all the while as though in deep anguish. Molly did not want to look, knowing how her mother would hate to feel that her privacy was being invaded, but she could not help but see, in the dim gaslight, that the bulge of her stomach had moved lower, her legs were wide apart and the towel which had been thrust between them was soaked with blood. So was the sheet and a couple more towels on the floor at the side of the bed.

'But this is no place for you, lass.' Maggie was speaking in an authoritative manner now and Molly knew that the woman liked to be left alone when attending a birth. But this was an exceptional case, surely?

'But ... can't I do anything?' pleaded Molly. 'My poor mam, she needs some help, and so do you. I'm so worried.'

'Worrying'll get you nowhere.' Maggie's tone was brusque. 'You'd best start praying.' Her last words were almost a whisper and Molly was not sure if she had heard correctly. 'No, there's nowt you can do. Go and see if the kettle's boiling, there's a good lass, then you can bring me another bowl of hot water, eh?' Her voice was kinder now, more sympathetic. 'And then – well – it'd be best to keep out o' t'road. The doctor'll be here afore long. Dr Paige'll be able to get it moving.' Maggie turned again to Lily, and Molly could tell from the look in her eyes that the midwife was scared to death.

But then she was not a real midwife, thought Molly, as, moving like an automaton, she made her way downstairs. Why on earth had her father not insisted, all along, that her mother should have proper medical care; a qualified nurse, a doctor, a stay in hospital if needs be? But she knew it was largely a question of money. They could not afford very much; besides, this was the way it was always done round here. Maggie did what she could at the birth and it was all conducted with the minimum of fuss and bother. Not really aware of what she was doing, her hands obeying her mind involuntarily, Molly filled an enamel bowl with boiling water. An agonised scream from the room above almost made her drop it, but she managed to reach the bedroom without any of the water spilling.

'For God's sake, Maggie, what's going on?' She

placed the bowl on the floor, hardly daring to look at her mother writhing in agony on the bed.

'She's in labour, lass, that's what. She has to scream – they all do. It's quite normal.' Maggie did not look at Molly as she spoke; she was concentrating solely on her patient. 'Come on, there's a good girl. Pull hard on this, eh? It won't be long now and doctor'll be here soon.'

Molly noticed that, amidst her cries and moans, her mother was pulling desperately, as much as her weakened state would allow, at a knotted towel that was tied to the back of the brass bedstead. She knew that although the screams might be normal the condition of her mother was most definitely not. A sudden thought struck her and she stopped in the doorway. 'Where's our Em?' she asked.

'She's with my lot,' said Maggie hurriedly, not turning round. 'Don't fret yerself. She'll be all right with our Sarah, and my old feller'll see to 'em all. Now, get along with you, Molly. Go downstairs and wait for t'doctor... What's happened to him, for Christ's sake.' Her frenzied mutterings revealed how anxious she was.

The doctor, with her father, arrived a few moments later. The clip-clop of the horses' hoofs on the road outside told Molly they had come in a hansom cab, which would, in normal circumstances, have been a rare treat for her father. Without even stopping to take off his bowler hat and without a word to Molly, Dr Paige dashed upstairs, his black bag in his hand. How simple it would be, she thought, if babies did indeed arrive in the doctor's bag, as children were often told.

No pain, no blood, no anguish, no fear of ... of anything going wrong. She did not let the dreaded word take shape in her mind. Whatever would they do – above all, what would her father do – if anything were to happen to her mother?

'Come on, Molly lass; let's have a cup of tea. There's nowt we can do and Dr Paige is one of the best. She'll be all right now.' Her father was calmer now, as though he had placed his trust completely in the doctor and in so doing had laid the burden of his anxiety upon him. Molly did not voice her own fears although she had never felt so worried in all her life. She was surprised when her father asked, 'Did you enjoy yerself tonight, then? You saw the fireworks, did you, and the tattoo?'

She realised he was trying to focus his mind on something else, to distance himself from what was taking place upstairs, but his words came as a shock. So much had happened in the last half-hour. She had been catapulted out of the enchanted world in which she had been wandering, so joyous and carefree, with her new companion, straight back into stark, grim reality. The events of the evening already seemed like a dream; and she felt a premonition that it had indeed been a magical moment in time, so far removed from real life that it could not be true, and that she would never see Joss again.

'Yes ... er, yes, we saw the fireworks, Dad,' she answered him. He would think that 'we' referred to herself and Flo. What did it matter anyway? What did it matter if Mrs Jackson – Molly suddenly remembered her – started probing about

84

her 'young man'? Nothing mattered now except that her mother should be safely delivered of her child. Not even the child mattered, thought Molly, though despising herself for the thought, so long as her mother survived. 'We didn't stay to watch the tattoo,' she went on. 'And it's a good job I didn't, isn't it?' She glanced towards the ceiling. 'With Mam being bad I'd never have forgiven myself if I'd stayed out any later. As it is I feel dreadful, leaving you alone with her. I never dreamed it would be tonight. It's early...'

'Aye, about a week or so, she reckoned, but you can never tell exactly. Don't blame yourself, Moll. Happen your mam and me needed that little bit of time to ourselves.' Her father's eyes grew misty. 'I love her very much, you know, lass.' She could see a tear glistening in the corner of his eye.

They sat in silence for several moments. It had gone quiet upstairs as well now. Then a different sort of cry invaded the silence; the unmistakable wail of a newborn baby.

William sprang to his feet. 'There you are, you see. It's all right. She's had the baby. She's going to be all right.' He was making towards the door, but Molly restrained him.

'Just a minute, Dad. They'll come and tell you when you can go and see her ... and the baby.'

'What? In my own house, my own wife? I've every right to go. Why shouldn't I?'

'Well ... there are things they've got to do first, aren't there? Washing the baby's face and ... tidying up a bit.' She did not know if her father had seen the state of the bedroom. It had looked more like a slaughterhouse when Molly had seen it and she hoped it had been cleaned up as much as possible by now.

'All right, Molly, if you say so; I'll wait.' William sat down again, legs apart, his hands on his knees, rocking to and fro in agitation. 'I wonder what it is, eh? Another little lass, or a lad? She wanted a boy this time – not that it matters so long as–'

The door opened and Dr Paige stood on the threshold. 'Mr Rimmer, you have a fine healthy son.' The doctor's face, however, was unsmiling and Molly did not like what she could read in his eyes, a look of sympathy tinged with sorrow; nor did he congratulate her father, as was customary. 'You had better come now, right away, and see your wife,' he said. As William stumbled to his feet the doctor put his hand on the man's arm. 'I'm sorry, Mr Rimmer. We have done all we can, but ... but I am afraid–'

'Afraid of what? What the hell are you trying to tell me, man?' William dashed from the room and Molly, filled with fear and foreboding, followed him as he bounded up the stairs two at a time.

Her father dashed into the room, but Molly stood hesitantly in the doorway, not daring, nor feeling that she ought, to go any further. She was relieved to see that the room was cleaner and tidier now. The blood-stained towels and sheets were bundled together in a corner and the sheet on which her mother was lying was a clean one. Her face was as white as the sheet beneath her and her eyes were closed. Molly thought at first that she was dead, but as William rushed over to her, crying out her name, she opened her eyes.

'Lily ... oh, Lily, my love. What have they done to you? What ... what have I done?' He kneeled at the bedside, seizing her pale hand and smothering it with kisses. 'Lily, I'm so sorry. I never meant–'

'It's all right, William.' Molly could tell it was an effort for her mother to speak. She could hardly hear the words and although she had the feeling she was intruding on something very private Molly knew she had to listen. Neither of her parents was aware of her presence, just as it had been when she left them earlier that evening. 'That's what I want you to call him – William. We've got a son, Will, a lovely lad. Take care of him ... won't you? I love you, Will. I always loved you ... so much.' Lily's head fell to one side, her hand, which had been grasping her husband's arm, dropped to the counterpane, and Molly knew her mother was dead.

She felt she would never forget as long as she lived the tormented cry which broke forth from her father. 'Lily, Lily! Don't go. Please don't leave me.' His arms were around his wife, shaking the lifeless body his face contorted with grief and the tears raining down his face. Then he suddenly let go of her, burying his face in the bedclothes and sobbing as though he would never stop. 'What have I done?' Through his sobs Molly could just make out the words. 'Oh, God, what have I done to her? It's all my fault...'

Molly stepped forward, unsure of what she should do. Her poor father. She knew how deeply he had loved her mother, but to see him in a state such as this shocked her. She had never before seen him cry. Men were not supposed to show their feelings in this way. It had not fully sunk into her muddled mind yet that her mother was dead, that she too should be weeping. She put out a tentative hand to touch her father, but the doctor stepped in front of her.

'Come along now, Mr Rimmer.' He took a firm hold of his shoulder. 'You really must try... This is not your fault, you know. It is no one's fault. We did everything that could be done – both Mrs Winthrop and myself – but it was no use. Your wife was losing too much blood, and the child – well, he was a big baby. A fine child. Come along and take a look at him. You have a lovely son, Mr Rimmer.'

At last William staggered to his feet. His face was still ravaged with grief, but he was managing to control his sobs. 'I'm not saying it's your fault, Doctor,' he said gruffly. 'You came when I asked you. But it was her. It's her fault.' He pointed an aggressive finger at Maggie, who had, all this while, been standing on the other side of the bed with the baby, wrapped in a blue blanket, asleep in her arms. 'She should've said as how she couldn't manage. It were too much for her. By the time she got round to admitting she needed some help it were ... too late.'

'Please don't blame Mrs Winthrop,' said the doctor, quite calmly. 'I have the greatest respect for all she does in this neighbourhood. I have worked along with her quite a few times when there has been a difficult labour. Believe me, Maggie knows her job.' He turned to give an appreciative nod and half-smile in her direction. 'I have every confidence that she acted responsibly, but there was nothing that either of us could have done. Mrs Rimmer – your wife – knew of the danger. She had been warned, hadn't she? But she willingly took the risk to have another baby. And you knew the risks too ... didn't you, Mr Rimmer?' he added quietly.

'Aye, aye ... I knew.' William hung his head despairingly. 'But what could I do, eh? I loved her so much ... and she loved me an' all. I'm sorry, Maggie.' He raised his head and looked at her. 'I'd no business to go blaming you. It weren't your fault, but I ... I had to hit out at somebody. If there's anybody to blame then it's me. Like I said afore, it's me. An' I'll never forgive meself.'

Nobody had been taking any notice of Molly as she stood quietly listening to the conversation between her father and the doctor. She had not spoken since she came upstairs; neither, she realised, had Maggie. Molly knew that her father's words, condemning the woman, had been spoken in haste – and who could blame him for that? – but she also knew that he would just as soon repent of them. William Rimmer was a mild and even-tempered, very gentle sort of man. The term 'gentleman' could very well be applied to him. Not because of the social class into which he had been born, nor because of his upbringing was he a gentleman, but he was more deserving of the title than many of the nobly born whose manners and conduct were less than admirable.

Molly went over to Maggie now. 'May I see him?' she asked, carefully pulling the blanket to

89

one side. The baby's face was red and – if it could be said about a newborn child – angry and resentful. His lips were pushed outwards in a pout and there were two tiny scowl lines between his eyes. His hair was dark and inclined to curl, like his father's, and he appeared to have inherited William's sturdy frame as well. As Molly stared down at him, not feeling anything about this baby at the moment – neither joy nor sorrow, just a dreadful emptiness – he suddenly thrust out a clenched fist, catching her on the chin. At the same time he opened his eyes and looked straight at her. He opened his mouth too, from which came a loud wail.

'Is he hungry?' asked Molly fearfully when the wailing persisted. She knew very little about newborn babies, though it was gradually impinging on her consciousness that she would have to find out, and quickly, too. She had been nine when Em was born and had helped her mother with the baby, but that was not the same as having full responsibility.

'No, he can't be, not yet awhile,' replied Maggie. 'He's just letting us know he's here, aren't you, my lamb? That's right, laddie, let it all out. You have a good yell. God knows, there's plenty to yell about.' She turned a tormented face towards Molly. 'I'm sorry, lass – I can't say no more than that, and whatever I say it won't bring her back.' There were tears in Maggie's eyes. She was usually so brusque and matter-of-fact, some would say hard-hearted. She had to be, of course, doing the job she did, but Molly was seeing another side of her tonight.

'Aye, it's a tragedy all right,' Maggie went on, 'for this little chap as well as the rest of us. Not that he'll know owt about it... He'll never know his mam. God bless him,' she added, almost under her breath. She turned to look at William, who was standing like a lost soul at the foot of the bed. 'Will, come and take a look at your son,' she said gently. 'I know it's hard, lad, and I can't begin to tell you how badly I'm feeling...' Her voice cracked with emotion. 'But ... he's a lovely child. I reckon you'll have reason to be proud of him in a few years' time, happen.'

'Aye, mebbe I will, mebbe I won't.' William stared uncomfortably at his feet before taking the few hesitant steps to Maggie's side.

'Here, Molly, you take hold of him.' Maggie placed the blue-blanketed bundle into Molly's arms. 'Happen it'd be better if you took him downstairs. Go and sit by the fire with him. He's dropped off to sleep again now, so p'raps you could put the cot up, eh, Will? See...' Tenderly she stroked the baby's cheek. 'Isn't he a grand 'un?'

William nodded silently. He was staring broodingly at the child, not making the slightest gesture towards him and when, after a few seconds, he lifted his head and looked at Molly, she thought she had never seen such abject despair in anyone's eyes. 'Aye, I'd best see to the cot,' he said in a choked voice. 'He's took us by surprise, this 'un. Lily were asking me...' He swallowed and hastily dashed a tear from his eye. 'She were asking me to put it up, then it all happened so fast...'

The doctor was clearing his throat and Maggie

91

was making a movement towards the bed, at the same time looking imploringly at Molly. The girl realised they were anxious that she and her father should remove themselves from the scene as soon as possible. There were other things to be done, and Molly remembered, with a jolt of horror, that Maggie, as well as acting as a midwife in the neighbourhood, also did the laying-out of the dead.

'Come along, Dad. We'd better let them ... see to things.' Molly, carrying the baby, led the way out of the room and William, reluctantly, followed her.

Her father had assembled the oak cot which had served for Molly as a baby and, later, for Emily, and the child now lay there asleep, for the moment at least. Maggie had prepared a bottle of boiled water and sugar for Molly to give to him when he awoke, urging her to try to get some sleep herself. She sat alone with only the glow from the fire dimly illuminating the room. She had turned off the gaslight, thinking she might snatch an hour or two of sleep, but now, in the early hours of the morning, sleep seemed as far away as ever.

She had persuaded her father to go upstairs to bed; to the bed in the back room which she and Emily usually shared, as her mother, after Maggie's ministrations, still occupied the bed in the front room. Come the morning there would be all sorts of things to see to. The undertaker would have to be summoned and her mother laid in a coffin in the parlour – the room of which she had been so proud – so that the neighbours might come and pay their respects. Em, too, would have to be told the sad news, but Maggie had promised to do that and also to look after the little girl for the next few days.

Molly knew they had a great deal for which to thank Maggie Winthrop, but as far as baby William was concerned, it was becoming more and more apparent to Molly that he was her responsibility and no one else's. Maggie, helpful though she may have been in many ways, had already made that very clear. The baby's mother had died and so, obviously, it was the elder sister who had to step into the breach. Who else? William was the breadwinner and as such could not be expected to have anything to do with the care of a newborn baby.

'Your dad'll come round,' Maggie had whispered, whilst he was out of the room. The doctor had gone and Maggie had finished her necessary work upstairs. 'A lot of fellers don't know how to react to a new babby, and it's only natural he should feel bitter, like, about yer mam. That was why I didn't bother about him having a go at me, poor chap. They were like a couple of bloomin' lovebirds, him and yer mam. They say time heals, though, don't they, and I dare say he'll have his hands full afore long so he'll not have time to brood. He'll be too busy keeping a roof over your heads. 'Cause he'll be the only one working, won't he? You won't be able to go off to that shop of yours, will you, with a new baby in the house? Unless you farm him out, of course. Plenty do.'

'No – definitely not.' Molly's reply had been

unequivocal. She would not put her brother into the hands of a baby farmer. There were one or two in the neighbourhood of whom she had heard varying reports and rumours. If Maggie herself had offered her assistance Molly might have considered it, but looking after infants after they were delivered was not a service that Maggie undertook. 'I'll ... I'll look after him myself,' Molly said. 'And our Em'll help me. It'll take her mind off Mam, won't it, having a new baby to see to? So long as you'll help me, Maggie. You know – advise me, like, about what I should be doing. I don't know anything about babies.'

'Most of it's common sense, lass,' replied Maggie. 'At least, it comes naturally to mothers. I know you're not one, but you'll be the next best thing, eh?' She beamed at Molly, her good humour rapidly returning and, with it, her brusque, somewhat bossy manner. 'This little lad'll come to think of you as his mam, make no mistake about that, and I'm sure you'll do a grand job an' all.'

Molly felt her heart sink at the woman's words. It was not that she didn't want to take responsibility for the child, but she was only seventeen. Some girls were married and already had children at seventeen, she knew that, but she was not one of them. She had her whole life ahead of her: her job she enjoyed so much at the shop, her friends ... including the young man she had met earlier that evening. NO! She immediately squashed that thought before it could properly take shape. It was no use; it had never been any use. Just an impossible dream right from the start. And now it was even more impossible.

'The first thing you'll need, of course, is a wet nurse,' Maggie had told her. 'I dare say I can find one for you. There's a woman in Seed Street just had a baby.'

'A ... wet nurse? You mean ... to feed the baby?'

'Well, of course that's what I mean. How else d'you think you're going to feed him? You can't do it.'

'Oh ... I see.' Molly thought about the woman in Seed Street with her own baby at her breast, then of baby William taking his place. Then she thought of her mother. 'I don't think I fancy the idea of that,' she said. 'Somebody else, instead of ... my mother. Can't he have the same milk as we have?'

'Too rich,' said Maggie abruptly. 'Happen in a while he can, but not yet. I believe there's summat as they're selling now that might do if you're going to turn yer nose up at somebody else's titty.' Molly tried not to let her stab of distaste show. Maggie could be very uncouth at times. 'There's summat called soluble food for babies, made by a German firm, I believe. They say the stuff that's in it is just the same as what's in mother's milk.' She gave a derisory sniff. 'Don't see as how it can be meself, but it's worth a try if you're going to be all la-di-da about it. It's for them rich folk, really, them pampered women who don't want to breast-feed and can't be bothered to find wet nurses neither. But I don't see why we shouldn't have it if it's available.' She had smiled a little more kindly at Molly then. 'I'll have a look in t'chemist's in the morning. Till then he'll not go wrong wi' boiled water and sugar. Eeh, I'm that sorry, lass. I know how you're feeling. Take no notice of me being sharp. It's just me way ... and I was fond of yer mam. She was a good friend to me even though she were ... well, she were different to a lot of 'em round here. Try and get some sleep, Molly.'

But sleep would not come. Molly could not get out of her mind the dreadful grief of her father and the way he had kept saying it was all his fault. This was something she had not considered overmuch. She knew that her father and mother were devoted to one another. It was a talking point amongst the neighbours – Molly had heard them – how Will and Lily Rimmer were still all lovey-dovey after goodness knows how many years of marriage. William did not fit into the conventional mould of many husbands of this community: down at the pub every night, drunk on at least two nights of the week, indifferent to the needs of their family – vicious and brutal in many cases – and treating their wives as nothing more than skivvies, except when they wanted to claim what was known as their conjugal rights. This was not true of all husbands, though, not by any means. Molly guessed there were many who were hard-working, sober and respectful of their wives, but there could be few as caring as William.

Molly was not unaware of the facts of life; not that her mother had ever told her anything, except when she had started with her monthly periods, and then the necessary information – just the bald facts – had been imparted with the greatest reluctance. Molly had known about it anyway. She was not a shy girl and she had talked things over with her friends. She thought she knew about what went on in the marriage bed, and sometimes outside of it, between a man and a woman, some of it, at least.

When it came to her own parents, however, this knowledge was something of a stumbling block. The almost nightly sounds issuing from her parents' bedroom through the inadequately thin wall told her all too clearly what was going on, but it was something to which she had always tried to close her ears and her mind. Until now. Now, with a sick feeling of revulsion and dread that was making her turn against her father, she was beginning to wonder if he, and he alone, had been responsible for her mother's death.

'It's all my fault, it's all my fault,' he had kept saying.

'Your wife knew of the danger and you knew the risks, too, didn't you?' The doctor's words came back to her now as she sat in the dwindling firelight with the child still sleeping in the cot at her side. Her father had known how dangerous it could be for her mother to have another child, and yet he had still gone on making love to her – 'claiming his rights', as some would say round here – although Molly guessed that her mother would not have been unwilling. Such a sad, dispirited little woman she had seemed to be at times, with a timid air and a primness verging on prudity, and yet the way Lily had looked at her husband, and he at her, with such naked passion in their eyes had oftentimes made Molly feel like an outsider.

She felt a sob rising up in her throat, and tears of anger as well as sorrow welling in her eyes. Could they not have controlled their emotions – her father more so than her mother, it would be up to him to take the lead – knowing what might be the outcome? And something else had just occurred to her. 'Happen your mam and me needed that bit of time to ourselves,' her father had said to her as they awaited the birth of the baby. 'I love her very much, you know...' Was he actually meaning that they had made love that evening, when Molly had gone out and Em was still round at her friend's? Another wave of revulsion swept over her as she recalled the swollen mound of her mother's stomach, then, later, her pallid face and screams of agony and the blood-soaked sheets and towels. If they had ... done that ... then that was why the baby had been born early. Her father had not been able to exercise any self-control even when his wife had been within a few days of giving birth. At that moment Molly almost hated her father. He had caused it. It was because of his selfishness, his lack of self-discipline, that his wife had died. And when it came to the crunch he was no better than the rest of the men round about who came home drunk and abused their wives on a Saturday night.

The grief that had, so far, been held in check now broke forth from Molly in a crescendo of sobs that almost seemed to tear her apart, and she felt the tears at last cascading down her cheeks. It was a relief to cry it all out. She had felt numb, unable to believe fully what had happened, but now her senses were returning. After several moments her sobs ceased, but as they did so the baby at her side began to whimper, quietly at first, little snuffling cries, then increasing in volume to a loud repetitive din on a single note – wah, wah, wah ... She picked him up and, instinctively, laid him against her shoulder. The cries stopped for a moment, then started again until she sat down with him in her arms and gave him the bottle of water and sugar which had been keeping warm on the hob.

Her mind was clear now. Her mother was dead and the child she was holding depended on her and her alone for his existence. She knew she would not be able to let him down, not now, nor ever.

Chapter 5

'What a dreadful thing to happen, Molly, love. I could hardly believe it when I heard.' Flo's blue eyes were full of sorrow and as she put her arms round her friend, giving her a hug, Molly could feel the wetness of Flo's tears on her own cheeks. Dear, dear Flo; she was such a good friend and, at this moment, Molly felt more in need of friends than ever.

'Come on in,' she said, speaking in a hushed voice, which was fitting with her mother's body laid out in the parlour and the curtains drawn in the front rooms. 'It's good of you to call, Flo. Folk have been very good, in and out all day. In fact I've scarcely had a minute to myself. Go right through to the back. Mother's in there ... in the parlour. Perhaps you'd like to take a look at her later, would you?'

'I'll look at her now,' said Flo, staunchly, biting on her lips to try to stem the tears. 'I've brought her these, see.' She held out the small bunch of flowers she was carrying; simple flowers – sweet peas, pinks, marigolds and, most appropriately, sweet williams. 'I thought you'd have got her in her little parlour – she loved it, didn't she? – and happen you can put them on the mantelpiece ... or somewhere. She liked flowers, yer mam.'

'They're lovely,' said Molly, smiling sadly at Flo. 'What a nice thought. You're so kind, Flo, and I know Mam would think so too. She was always pleased you were my friend. She liked you, you know.'

'Happen she knows, eh, about the flowers?' said Flo softly. 'You must try to believe she's gone to a better place, Molly, and p'raps they know what's going on down here.'

'Mmm, I'm not so sure about that.' Molly shook her head confusedly. She had not thought about where her mother might have gone. She only knew she was not here and that there was an aching void in the place where she felt her heart should be, a sort of emptiness and sadness that would not go away. 'But thank you, anyway.' She pushed open the door of the parlour. 'Come in, Flo. I'll put them in this little vase.' She picked up a green glass vase from the top of the china cabinet. 'I'll just have to get some water. You'll be all right ... on your own?'

'Of course I will. I'll just remember your mam, and say a little prayer.'

'Here she is then.' Reverently Molly lifted up the small white towel which had been placed over her mother's face. 'Peaceful, isn't she? I'll ... I'll be back in a minute.'

Returning to the parlour she placed the flowers on a little spindle-legged table near the head of the coffin. Their fragrance very soon permeated the room, along with the other faint but sickly smell which was already there.

'Poor, poor lady,' said Flo, gently stroking Lily's marbled forehead. 'What a terrible thing, and after she'd been so well these last few days. You said last night, didn't you, how well she seemed?

You wouldn't have gone out, else. Poor lady,' she repeated. 'And she was a lady, you know, Molly, so polite and, well, ladylike.'

'Yes, I know.' Molly gave a quiet sigh. 'She didn't really seem to belong round here, but Father never earned all that much and somehow they never managed to make a move. The money I earned helped a bit, but now – well, it's too late, isn't it, for it to make any difference? Anyroad, I won't be earning anything now. Come on, let's go through to the kitchen.' Once more she covered up her mother's face for what seemed the hundredth time, certainly the tenth or more. They had had a constant stream of callers since the undertaker had finished his work in the mid-morning.

'There's the baby,' said Molly, nodding towards the cot which stood just inside the door of the living room, commonly known as the kitchen. She would ask her father to carry the cot upstairs tonight so that baby William could sleep next to her. By that time she hoped that Maggie would have managed to procure a second-hand pram, as she had promised she would try to do, in which he could sleep during the day. 'We're calling him William,' she explained, 'because that was what Mam said she wanted just before ... she died. It's a bit confusing, I know, with my dad having the same name, but there's nothing else we can do, is there?'

'No, I suppose not.' Flo shook her head sadly. 'No, of course there isn't. You've got to carry out your mam's last wishes. You could happen call him Bill, or Billy.' She leaned towards the baby, tickling him beneath his chin. 'Oh, isn't he a beautiful boy? He's a real bonny lad, aren't you ... Billy? Yes, I think Billy might suit him, eh, Molly?'

'Perhaps,' said Molly, although she had already begun to think of him as William. What was more, to her amazement, she was beginning to think of him as her own child. This feeling was not sufficient yet to fill the emptiness inside her completely, but it would help, and she was confident it would grow. When she held the child in her arms, she knew, even now, that her affection for him was helping to assuage her grief and the pain in her heart.

As she leaned over the cot he opened his eyes and gave a little whimper, and she bent down and picked him up. She had heard Maggie say that you shouldn't pick babies up whenever they cried, you should let them be, but Maggie was not here and Molly decided she was going to do as she wished with her own child. She held him against her shoulder, gently patting his back in a way that was so soon becoming familiar to her.

'Sit down there,' she said to Flo, gesturing towards the armchair at the side of the fire, 'and you can hold him for a bit, if you like. Don't worry, he's been fed and changed.'

Somewhat apprehensively Flo took the baby on her lap. She looked relieved when he closed his eyes again. Molly could see her friend's eyes wandering round the room, no doubt noting that already it was showing signs that there was a new occupant in the house, one, in fact, whose presence was overriding that of the other members of the family. Nappies were airing on a clothes-horse in front of the range; several more, together with tiny nightdresses, vests and cot sheets hung on a rack which was suspended from the ceiling; a half-empty feeding bottle of milk stood on the table and one of boiled water was keeping warm on the hob; and outside the window another line of little white garments was flapping in the breeze. A job that Molly still had to tackle was the boiling of the sheets and towels that had been on her mother's bed. Maggie had left them soaking in a dolly tub of cold water, but, so far, seeing to baby William's needs had taken all her time.

'He's making his presence felt,' said Flo, looking now at the bottle of milk. 'You say he's been fed? What are you giving him? He can't have proper milk, can he, like we have?'

'No, this is something Maggie got from the chemist's,' replied Molly. 'She was there as soon as it opened this morning. I don't know what I'd have done without Maggie – you know, Mrs Winthrop, the ... er ... midwife – she's been very good. This is made by Nestlé's, the firm that make the chocolate. You just add water and it's supposed to be like ... like mother's milk.' Her voice faltered a little. 'I thought it was best. I don't think Mam would've wanted anybody else feeding her baby – you know, one of those wet nurses. She was very particular, everything had to be clean and tidy and ... just so.'

'Here, you'd best put him down, hadn't you?' said Flo. Molly could tell her friend was relieved to hand the baby back. So might she have felt herself a couple of days ago, but so much could happen in such a short space of time. One's whole way of life, of thinking, could be completely turned around.

'What was that you were saying about not being able to earn anything any more?' Flo was asking as Molly laid William down in his cot again. 'I didn't quite understand what you meant. You'll be going back to work at the shop, won't you?'

'How can I?' Molly sat down in the armchair opposite her friend and leaned forward, looking earnestly at her. 'How on earth can I go on working? Who would look after William?' The name came naturally to her. She knew she would never call him anything else.

'I don't know.' Flo was frowning a little. 'I just thought you might ... well, I mean, he's not really your responsibility, is he? You're just his sister.'

'You thought I might what? Farm him out, leave him with somebody else? I can't, Flo. Yes, I know I'm only his sister, but there's only me to see to him, isn't there?' She noted the perplexed look on her friend's face and gave a wry smile. 'I would've thought just like you're thinking a few days ago, believe me; that it was somebody else's responsibility, not mine. But, well,' she gave a slight shrug. 'I've come to accept it and ... and I don't really mind.'

'What does your dad say about it? Where is he, anyway?' asked Flo.

'Oh, he's off out somewhere.' If Molly sounded a little indifferent then that was how she was feeling. She felt sorry for her father. He was like a broken man, but she couldn't rid herself of the niggling thought that it was he who had caused her mother's death through his own blind selfishness. And that was something she could not share with Flo. 'He has all sorts of things to see to. He's not going into work today, of course. I don't know when they're expecting him back: tomorrow more than likely. I can see to things here. He hasn't said anything about the baby, hardly looked at him, in fact.'

'Poor man, it's understandable,' said Flo. 'He must be grieving dreadfully about your mam.'

'Yes, so he is.' Molly knew she sounded a little curt, but Flo didn't seem to notice. 'He can't think of anything else at the moment but that Mam has died, I know that. I think he's taking it for granted that I'll look after the baby, but I don't really know what he thinks 'cause he's not said. I'm just ... carrying on.'

'And what about your Em? Where is she?'

'At school at the moment. Maggie and I thought it was best she should go. She had a good cry about Mam, but Sarah's looking after her – that's one of Maggie's kids. She's only the same age as Em, but she likes to mother her. And she's staying at Maggie's until after the funeral. That's on Friday.'

They both fell silent for a few moments. Then, 'How have you managed to come here this afternoon?' asked Molly. 'Shouldn't you be working?'

'It's Wednesday,' replied Flo. 'Half-day closing. Had you forgotten? Well, I suppose you must've done with all that's been happening.'

'Yes, I'd forgotten,' said Molly. 'Wednesday – of course. And how did you find out ... about Mam?

106

I suppose Mrs Makepeace told you, did she? I sent a message with Maggie's lad, Tom, this morning, that I wouldn't be coming in.'

'Yes, bad news travels fast,' said Flo. 'Everybody on the terrace is ever so sorry about it. Miss Perkins said I had to be sure to give you her condolences. They'll all miss you, Molly, if you don't come back.' Flo looked wistfully at her friend. 'And I shall miss you more than any of 'em. We'll still be able to see each other, won't we?'

'Of course we will. Why not?' Molly tried to smile encouragingly, but it was dawning on her that their little jaunts to a dance hall or variety show, or even a walk on the prom, would now be sadly curtailed.

The same thought had occurred to Flo. 'And to think that only last night we were so happy, having such a lovely time,' she said. 'And today ... well, it must seem as though it was ages ago, almost as though it never happened.'

'That's exactly how it seems,' replied Molly. 'As though it were years and years ago, or unreal, just like a wonderful dream.' She looked keenly at her friend, trying to steer her own thoughts away from her sadness. 'Your Sam was real enough, though, wasn't he? Are you seeing him again? He was nice, Flo; just right for you.'

'Yes, I'm seeing him again. Tonight, as a matter of fact,' said Flo hurriedly. 'But I don't want to go on about it now.' Molly knew that Flo was trying to consider her, Molly's, feelings which was no doubt why she had not mentioned Joss. It was Molly who brought his name into the conversation. She couldn't help it; besides, she knew Flo would be wondering about him. 'And that young man I met – Joss – he was real enough too; although I can hardly remember what he looked like now, it all seems so far away.'

'Did he ask to see you again?' asked Flo hesitantly.

'No,' replied Molly. 'No ... he didn't.' The lie was against her nature, but she felt it was for the best. She knew it was impossible now for her to meet him on Sunday. The funeral would be over, but she would be in mourning and she could hardly go gadding off to meet some young man her father had never heard of at a time like this. Besides, there was baby William to consider. She couldn't arrive at the entrance to North Pier on Sunday afternoon pushing a perambulator. Whatever would Joss think?

'He ... he saw me home,' she went on, continuing with her half-true story. 'At least he walked most of the way with me, then I met some neighbours going my way so I left him. I think he was hurrying to catch his train – he lives in Preston. He was a very proper sort of young man – very gentlemanly. You could tell that, couldn't you, just by looking at him? So I suppose he knew it would only be right to see me home. But I won't ... I won't be seeing him again.'

'What a shame,' said Flo. 'He seemed very nice. I thought he might've asked you–'

'You've changed your tune,' Molly interrupted. 'Weren't you telling me that he wasn't our sort, an' all that? That he was too posh for the likes of us?'

108

'Happen I changed my mind,' said Flo. 'Sam told me not to be so disapproving. He said that – what did you call him, Joss? – looked a very genuine, caring sort of chap; and he certainly seemed to be looking after you all right, Molly. Oh dear, I'm so sorry, love – about your mam – and about Joss as well. I could tell you liked him. It would've cheered you up if you could've seen him again, wouldn't it?'

'It's no use, Flo.' Molly shook her head decidedly. 'I couldn't have met him anyway, not with William to see to.' She had been almost tempted to tell Flo the truth, but then her kind-hearted friend would have tried to think of a way of getting round the problem; meeting the young man herself, maybe, and explaining about Molly's predicament, or even offering to look after the baby. It would all get too complicated. Besides, it would all come to nothing in the end. It was no use pursuing what could never be. Her mam was dead; she had a newborn baby to rear; her life had changed completely since yesterday; it was pointless now to wish for romance – pointless and selfish too.

'I think he must have decided that it wouldn't be suitable,' said Molly, 'him and me. After all, that's what you thought, isn't it Flo? It was lovely to spend the evening with him, but that's all. You can always get along with what you can't have. Mam used to say that,' she added musingly.

'Mmm ... what you want and what you get are two different things. That's what my mother used to say when I was a little girl,' replied Flo.

'It seems as though you might have got what

you want now though, eh, Flo?' asked Molly, a little teasingly.

'Oh, we'll have to wait and see.' Flo gave a coy smile, but it was quickly replaced by a look of genuine concern. Her blue eyes were misting over with tears again. 'I'm really sorry, love, about it all. I feel – oh, I don't know – as though I haven't any right to be happy when all this has happened to you.'

'You must be happy, Flo.' Molly tried to smile back at her. 'You deserve to be happy.' Be happy while you can, she thought to herself, because you never know how soon it might all be snatched away. She knew that the ache in her heart and the feeling of emptiness inside her were not due entirely to the loss of her mother. Joss... For a brief few hours she thought she might be falling in love. Now she knew she had to put the idea right behind her.

Joss Cunliffe waited for half an hour outside the entrance to North Pier on Sunday afternoon before deciding that it was no use. Molly must have changed her mind about coming. Or maybe she had never intended to come at all? He found that hard to accept. She had seemed so eager to meet him again after her initial hesitation. 'I would love to see you again...' That was what she had said, and, seeing the look of wonder and excitement and barely suppressed longing in her lovely brown eyes, he had wanted so much to believe her. To believe that she, too, had fallen in love – or was rapidly on the way to doing so, just as he had done.

Love at first sight. Romantic and idealistic though he was, he would have scoffed at the idea at one time; or maybe that was because he had never before met anyone who had attracted and charmed him the way that Molly had done. And though he tried hard not to let them influence him or his way of thinking too greatly, Joss knew, nevertheless, that his family tradition and background had, until now, played a major part in his life and development.

His father, Henry Cunliffe, owner of Cunliffe Mill in Preston, was typical of many cotton mill owners: shrewd, level-headed, ambitious, and always with his eye on the main chance, which was, of course, to make money. There were dozens of mills in Preston, both large and small, the largest and best known being that of Horrockses. It covered acres of land in the Stanley Street area, near to Preston prison, and was so large that it was almost a town within a town. Horrockses had their own shops, pubs and houses, with virtually the whole community being dependent on the benevolence – or otherwise – of the mill owners. Horrockses, to give them their due, were considered to be pretty fair to their employees. Henry Cunliffe reckoned that he was a satisfactory boss too, although his mill was nothing like the size of Horrockses.

Henry's mill, set up in the mid-eighteenth century by his forebears, was at the other end of the town, near to North Road. It was a weaving mill, as were most of those in Preston. At one time Cunliffe's mill, along with others, had done all the processes right through from carding and

111

spinning the cotton to weaving, bleaching, dyeing and printing. Now, in the late nineteenth century, the spinning mills were, by and large, situated in south-east Lancashire and the weaving mills in the central and north-east. Cunliffe's was a prosperous mill, though comparatively small, with a couple of hundred employees. Henry owned just two of the streets of two-up, two-down houses in the vicinity of the mill, and his workforce, with almost as many women as men, all lived in the immediate area.

Cunliffe's concentrated on plain cotton fabrics for household use – for making into sheets, pillowcases, working shirts, frocks and overalls – as well as checks and ginghams of two and three colours. There was also a smaller department where hand printing and, of late, cylinder printing with more complex patterns took place.

Lord Shaftesbury and his ilk, with their parliamentary endeavours, had put paid to employing very young children in Henry's father's day. Nowadays the youngest working at Cunliffe's were thirteen years of age; too young to be of any real help on the looms, but quite capable of sweeping the floors, lighting the gas burners in the weaving sheds and collecting the workers' breakfast cans and filling them with boiling water for the eight o'clock brew; and all the while learning the trade.

Joss knew that his father considered himself to be philanthropic in the extreme to his workforce, although he closed his eyes to the impoverished, often insanitary, conditions in which many of them lived. And it was possible that Henry was, indeed, benevolent when compared with his father or grandfather. Tales of the arduous conditions in the olden days – losing nothing in the telling, no doubt, but based on indisputable facts – had been passed down through the generations. Joss was thankful that things had improved more than a little, but that did not stop him feeling guilty oftentimes about his own affluence and the comfort of his life.

It would help, of course, if he could throw himself wholeheartedly into his work at the mill; but Joss had found on leaving school and starting work there that he was unable to do so. Five years later – he was now twenty-three – he found that he still had not developed a consuming passion for the mill, as had his two elder brothers, or, indeed, much interest in the business at all.

His father had insisted that Joss should start at the bottom and work his way up. He had had no objection to doing this; he had never found it difficult to get along with people in any walk of life. Because Cunliffe's was now solely a weaving and finishing mill he had been sent, first of all, to his uncle's spinning mill in Oldham where he'd learned about the early processes, unpacking the bales of raw cotton which then had to go through the processes of scutching (loosening the tightly packed cotton), carding and combing before it could be spun. Joss had stayed there only three months, then had returned to Preston, relieved that his father's was a weaving and not a spinning mill. Surely, he thought, he would be able to work up more enthusiasm for the finished product – rolls of cotton material – than he had been able to do for cotton thread.

But he had discovered, as he had feared would be the case all along, that he could find no keenness in himself, no motivation for working in the cotton mill. Mindful that he must try to placate his father and not disappoint his mother, whom he loved dearly, he had tried to adapt. His two brothers – the elder, Percy, in charge of the office work and finances, and Edgar, responsible for the warehouse and the dispatching of orders – had enthusiasm enough for a dozen men. And his father, born in the early years of Victoria's reign, but still as youthful and vigorous as ever, was the undisputed head of it all; a whirlwind of a man with little time for slackers or malingerers or, indeed, for anyone who did not live, breathe and exist solely for the manufacture of cotton cloth, as did he and his elder two sons.

Joss, gentler, quieter and far less forceful than the rest of the menfolk in his family, at times felt overshadowed by such eagerness and vitality; but never completely so because he knew he had the sympathy of his mother, Charlotte. He believed that he, the youngest of her three children, was her favourite, although she had, of course, never said so. It was at Charlotte's suggestion that Joss had been given charge of the dyeing and printing shed. She knew it was the only process of them all at the mill which would provide him with any scope for his artistic talent; a talent which he had inherited from her. Henry had agreed, but in his view this was only a sideline to the proper business of the mill. However, if it would keep the lad happy... Heavens above, he had shown very little aptitude for anything else. Joss knew only too well that, compared with his brothers, his father considered him to be a poor sort of fellow; but the work in the printing shed had proved fulfilling, if only to a degree. Some of his own designs and patterns had been adapted for printing on the materials, but cotton was not, alas, in his lifeblood.

He got away when he could to the countryside, or to Blackpool where the family owned a second home on the cliffs at Norbreck; not so often, though, for his father to accuse him of slacking. Henry, and Percy and Edgar, however, showed at times that they could play just as hard as they could work; and sometimes the whole family spent the weekend, after the mill closed at midday on Saturday, at their Norbreck home, Cunliffe House.

That was where Joss was heading now, after turning away dejectedly from the North Pier entrance. Molly was not coming. However could he have been such a fool as to ever think she would? And yet surely he could not have mistaken the look in her eyes, the warmth and promise of affection in her voice? No, he was quite sure he had not imagined any of it, but he also recalled her automatic response when he had first spoken to her, the way she had reacted, as though he were a gentleman – which he was, of course – but more than that, as though she regarded him, somehow, as better than she was, in a different class. Joss felt his jaw tightening and his fists clenching into balls at the thought of this as he walked northwards along the promenade.

As if it mattered, any of it. And yet Molly must have thought that it did.

He was in a different class, he supposed, from the lovely girl he had met five days ago. He had known straight away, at his first glimpse of her, that she was from a poorer sort of home: working class, but most definitely respectable. She had obviously taken pains with her appearance. Her white cotton blouse, sprigged with a green floral motif, had shown signs of frequent washing, but it was scrupulously clean, as were her face and hair and fingernails, something which Joss always noticed. He remembered how the green ribbons on her straw hat had fluttered in the gentle breeze up on the clifftop, and how the colour had toned so perfectly with her lovely deep brown eyes and her rich auburn hair. She was a beautiful girl – there was no doubt about that – and it was her serenity that had attracted him first of all as she sat there quietly on her own while her friend was on the dance floor.

And then, later, he had found in her a warmth and gaiety and a sense of fun; common sense, too, and optimism, all the qualities he most admired in a young woman, but which, so far, he had never found in such abundance. Clearly, though, her optimism had not been sufficient to overcome the difference in their class and up-bringing. On second thoughts she must have decided that it would be no use and that they could have no future together.

Joss had the sense to know that if he had con-tinued his friendship with Molly it would have been comparable to walking out with one of his father's mill hands. He came across them from time to time in his daily work – lovely lasses, some of them, but none of them had appealed to him particularly. He would have shown no hesitation about being friendly with one of the mill girls, in spite of what his father's and his brothers' reaction would have been. But it had not happened. Besides, Joss was involved in an ongoing, casual relationship with Priscilla Cartwright, the daughter of one of his father's friends, another mill owner. It was only a friendship, nothing more, but both Joss and Priscilla felt that Henry Cunliffe would like the relationship to progress beyond that. At the moment Priscilla seemed no keener than Joss for it to do so. And Charlotte, Joss's mother, appeared actively to oppose the idea of a marriage, although Joss had never discovered why. At least his mother would not have raised any objection to his friendship with Molly, Joss mused, as he made his way back through Claremont Park. Charlotte Cunliffe treated everyone – her peers, her family, her servants and her husband's employees – with the same friendliness, courtesy and quiet charm.

It was because he had guessed how Molly might react that Joss had declined to tell her his surname or to divulge much about himself. Cunliffe House, a large sturdily built mansion on the cliffs, was less than a hundred yards from Uncle Tom's Cabin, though further back, away from the encroaching tide and crumbling cliffs. It was more than likely that Molly would recognise the name; it was written on the stone pillars beside the iron gates for all to see. Many wealthy industrialists from the Lancashire inland towns, some from as far away as Manchester or Liverpool, had built themselves houses along the Fylde coast, and Cunliffe House had been built in Joss's grandfather's day. The Cunliffe family, all or some of them, spent most weekends there, especially during the summer season, and they had made a special visit there at the time of Queen Victoria's jubilee when the mill had been closed in honour of the event.

How Molly had enjoyed herself that evening, thought Joss. How thrilled she had been at all the sights: the illuminated trams and buildings, the fireworks, the fun and laughter and the feeling of being part of a momentous occasion. He could hardly bear the thought that he might never see her again. He was already cursing himself for not having told her, at least, his name and his profession – after all, she would have had to find out eventually if he continued seeing her – and for failing to find out more about Molly herself. Tit for tat, he supposed. She had laughingly refused to tell him her last name and he could not blame her for that. He had understood too her reticence about the area in which she lived. Joss did not know Blackpool as well as he knew Preston, but he did know that the district known as Larkhill was one of the poorer parts of Blackpool, and it was there, evidently, that she lived.

But why should he not try to find her again? It occurred to Joss that Molly had been worried about her mother, who was in the late stages of her pregnancy. It was quite possible that the baby had been born earlier than was expected and that

Molly was tied up with all sorts of commitments at home. He had realised she was a thoughtful and dutiful daughter and she must have found it impossible to get away today, or to let him know. He felt almost cheered at the thought.

He reached into his breast pocket and drew out the sketch, somewhat crumpled by now, that he had done of Molly. He had made a copy of it at home and had already started work on a portrait of the lovely girl he had met and known for such a short time. But he would find her again. he would not rest until he had done so. He realised he had not much to help him: a sketch which bore a likeness to the girl, and the knowledge that she was called Molly and lived, more than likely, in the Larkhill area. And – yes, of course – she was employed at a confectioner's shop some-where in Blackpool. Little enough information, but Joss was determined.

Today was Sunday. The shops were closed and he was due back at work tomorrow or else he would incur the wrath of his father. It would not be possible for him to begin his search until next weekend, on Saturday afternoon, after the mill had closed. He would catch the first available train to Blackpool, then he would ask in all the confectioners' shops he could find if they had in their employ a young woman called Molly.

Chapter 6

William was not an easy baby. The belligerent expression that Molly had seen on his tiny face only a few moments after he was born became more pronounced as the days went by; and his sister feared that his strident yells could be heard the whole length of the street. She supposed that he cried only when he wanted something, but his wants seemed to be many and often. She knew it was, of course, the baby's only way of drawing attention to himself, and he always stopped when she picked him up.

'A bairn only cries if he's uncomfortable or hungry or unhappy,' Maggie told her. 'It's his way of telling us that there's summat wrong. And in young Will's case it can only mean that he's wet or hungry 'cause he can't be unhappy. What has a little mite like that to be unhappy about, eh? Nowt at all, especially with you always picking him up and cuddling him the way you do. You should let him yell sometimes, Molly. It won't do him any harm. Never mind the neighbours. They've all had kids of their own. You're making a rod for your own back, I'm telling you. You're spoiling him.'

But Molly did not take too much notice of what Maggie said, not in that respect. If she wanted to pick up her baby brother and cuddle him then she would do so. Besides, she was concerned about the neighbours, and about her father, who tended to get irritable when the baby cried.

William, some three weeks after his wife's death, was showing very little interest in his son or, indeed, in anything else. He had retreated inside himself and was a shadow of the man he had once been – cheerful, friendly and thoughtful towards others. Now he was morose, withdrawn, appearing to think only of himself and his own needs. He went to work and came home again, ate his meals, then read his newspaper, performing all these actions in a mechanical fashion as though he were scarcely aware of what he was doing, and speaking only when it was necessary to do so.

Molly's initial bitterness towards him, blaming him, as she had done, for the death of her mother, had now lessened. When she saw the anguish on his face and the look of desperation in his eyes she could not help but feel sorry for him. Her sympathy, though, was tinged a little with exasperation. She felt that he should try to pull himself together and take more notice of his son. After all, she had had to do so, and quickly too; and young Emily, also, after her early distress at losing her mother, was becoming very competent at doing little jobs around the house and in helping to care for her baby brother.

But Molly could not find it in herself to rebuke her father nor, on the other hand, to commiserate with him and tell him she understood. All she could do was watch him anxiously and hope that, in time, his sorrow would decrease and he would find some pleasure and consolation for the loss of his beloved wife in his new son. As she, Molly, had done.

Little William was not difficult and fractious all the time, though Molly could see that as he grew up he might well have an aggressive streak. He could be a child who would want his own way and move heaven and earth until he got it, but there was another side to him as well. When she picked him up his cries would cease immediately and he would make little gurgling noises in his throat almost as though he were laughing at her. Maggie said that babies as young as William could not smile at you because their eyes could not focus properly yet, but Molly did not believe that. Little William did smile at her, she was sure, and he was already beginning to show signs that he knew who she was; the person who loved and cared for him. The sound of her voice and the feel of her arms around him was enough to calm him, and when he had his napkin changed or had taken several gulps of his bottle of milk there could not be a pleasanter or happier baby anywhere.

He was thriving on the patent baby food which Maggie had suggested she should try and which Molly now bought at the chemist's shop on Talbot Road. You could almost see him gaining weight by the hour, his cheeks becoming chubbier, his limbs sturdier and the bracelets of plumpness on his tiny wrists and ankles more pronounced. His eyes, like his hair, were the same colour as William's – deep blue, although Molly had heard that all babies' eyes were blue at first and that they might change as they got older.

'Eeh, this 'un's the spitting image of his dad', was a frequent comment from the neighbours when Molly wheeled him out in his perambulator. This was a large, somewhat shabby, black vehicle that Maggie had found for her, which was proving very useful for carrying home the shopping as well as keeping the baby comfortable.

'Aye, old Will'll never be dead so long as this one's alive,' was another comment she heard. Not a very tactful one, considering the recent death in the family, but then people did not always stop to consider what they were saying.

If only her father would come to his senses and realise that the child would need the paternal love that only he could give him, as well as Molly's affection. She loved this little baby who had, so peremptorily, been given into her charge. Her initial apathy, the feeling of emptiness she had experienced when she had first looked at him, had passed away very quickly, and Molly knew now that she loved him as much as any mother could love her child. Her feeling for him, not forgetting the hard work involved in looking after him, had helped her to recover from her grief at losing her mother. And as for that other sadness, that other ache in her heart over the young man she had met and known so briefly – well, there was scarcely a moment to dwell on that.

Molly was determined that young William should want for nothing. His baby food was quite expensive, but it was essential; and if the rest of the family had to go without certain things because of it then this was unavoidable. She learned to economise by buying cheaper cuts of meat – cheaper, even, than the very reasonable cuts that her mother had bought – on many days buying no meat at all. She used more potatoes instead, or made broths and stews with root vegetables or cabbage. If you went to the market late in the day you could pick up leftover vegetables and bruised fruit for much less than the normal cost. She and Em made do with bread and dripping, or a scrape of margarine and jam for their tea, instead of the occasional egg or sardines; and as for her father, he never appeared to notice what he was eating or made any comment. He had taken it for granted that Molly would see to their needs, just as she was seeing to baby William.

She missed the items of food she had been able to bring home from Makepeace's when she was working there: the day-old loaves of bread and the cakes, meat pies and sausage rolls. Such luxuries were too expensive to buy and Molly, so far, had not found time to bake anything that was not absolutely essential. A baby took up so much of one's time; she could not have believed how much. Also – the most important fact – there was now only one wage coming into the house – her father's – and there was little likelihood at the moment of Molly being able to resume her work in the shop, or, indeed, to take any job. Besides, Flo had told her that her position at Makepeace's had already been filled. She resigned herself to the fact that the rest of the family must learn to tighten their belts, but on no account must little

William be made to suffer.

It was almost exactly a month after his wife's death that William, at last, began to take notice of his son. Molly might have thought he had never been aware at all that there was a baby in the house, except for his frown of annoyance when the child cried. It was one morning before he departed for work, breakfast having been eaten in the usual near silence, that he stopped by the pram which took up a goodly space in the living room. He leaned over and pulled back the blanket that covered his son, who was sleeping peacefully after his early morning feed. Then he turned round and spoke to his daughter, a little shamefacedly, she thought.

'He's coming on a treat, Molly. He's ... he's the making of a grand little lad, hasn't he?'

'We think so, don't we, Em?' replied Molly, smiling confidingly at her sister. Emily was looking at her father in amazement, clearly as surprised at the turn of events as Molly was, but it would not be Emily's way to comment. Molly had not discussed their father's lack of interest in the baby with her young sister, but the little girl could not have failed to notice.

'Yes,' said Em now, very quietly. '*We* think he's lovely.'

Their father stared down at his feet, looking uncomfortable for a moment or two, before he spoke again. 'You ... mustn't think I don't appreciate all you're doing, Molly. You're ... well, you're doing a grand job. Thanks, lass.' Hurriedly he reached for his jacket and cap, which hung on a hook on the back door. 'I'll be off now. See you tonight.' It seemed as though he couldn't get out of the house fast enough.

'Well, well, well; wonders never cease,' said Molly, more to herself than to Emily. She was astounded at their father's change of heart, but her own heart felt lighter as she grinned at her sister. 'Come on then, Em. Standing around chatting won't buy the baby a new bonnet, as they say. Help me to wash these pots before you go to school, there's a good girl. I'll wash, you dry; all right?'

The little girl nodded and smiled. She, too, looked more at ease than she had at any time since their mother died.

It was the next night, Thursday, 22 July, soon after eleven o'clock, that Maggie came knocking at the door. 'Sorry to disturb you so late,' she said, 'but I could see there was a light on, so I knew you'd not gone to bed.' She sounded out of breath and quite excitable. 'Will you tell yer dad ... tell him the Tower's on fire.'

'What!' exclaimed Molly, although she had heard perfectly well what the woman had said. 'What do you mean? How do you know?'

'I mean that t'Tower's on fire, up at the top, like I said,' Maggie almost shouted. 'Bill's just come home from town – he's been down for a pint – and he's seen it with his own eyes. There's quite a crowd of folk there already, so he says, standing around gawping – you know how they do. So just tell yer dad, Molly. I know he'll be concerned, like, with him working there.'

'Oh dear!' Molly had suddenly turned quite

cold and she felt a spasm of fear run through her. 'He's there! At the Tower. He had to work late tonight.'

'Oh ... oh, I see.' Maggie Winthrop looked worried for a moment, then, just as quickly, she removed the frown from her face. 'Still, not to worry, Molly. Yer dad'll be all right. He's not likely to be up at t' top is he? And the fire brigade'll have come along by now, I should think, to put it out.'

'But how can they do that, if the fire's up at the top?'

'I don't know, lass, but you can be sure they'll try. It's their job.' She reached out and patted Molly's arm. 'You go back inside and wait for yer dad. He'll happen be a bit late with all the excitement, but he'll not be in any danger, don't you fret.'

'No, no ... I must go. I've got to go and see what's happening. My dad – yes, of course I'm sure he'll be all right – but I want to see for myself.' Molly was not at all sure that her father would be all right. She knew about his willingness, his propensity to get involved in things that were really none of his business sometimes, if he thought he could help. At least, that was what he had been like before her mother died, and it would seem now that traces of the old William were showing again. At all events, she knew she could not stay at home doing nothing.

'But you won't be able to do owt...' Maggie began, then she stopped at the look of desperation on the girl's face. 'All right then, lass. You run along and see what's happening, although

I'm pretty sure it'll all be over by now. I'll look after your Em and little Will. Get yer jacket, luv; it's a chilly night,' for Molly had been about to start off without her coat.

Moving more quickly than she had ever done in her life Molly ran down Talbot Road, then Abingdon Street pausing at the corner to snatch her breath, which was coming in noisy gulps, and to ease the stitch in her side. The Tower was visible from here, and the fire at the top. She ran on, finally stopping at the corner of Church Street and Market Street, where quite a crowd had gathered. She stared upwards, craning her neck, gazing at the unbelievable sight of flames shooting out in all directions from the top of Blackpool Tower, and – she began to tremble when she saw them – the figures of several men, black silhouettes against the red of the fire and the grey of the night sky, endeavouring to beat down the flames. Molly almost cried out in her fear, although her common sense was trying to tell her that it was ludicrous to imagine her father might be one of those men. Why should he be? They would be trained firemen, wouldn't they? Or at least men who were experienced at that sort of thing. But the murmurings of the crowd told her that the fire brigade had not yet arrived.

'Where's the blessed fire brigade? That's what I'd like to know. It's their job to get the fire out.'

'But they couldn't do owt if they came, could they? Talk sense, Harold. Their hoses 'ud never reach all the way up there. Anyroad, I dare say the Tower've got their own equipment. They'll be here if they're needed, you can be sure of that. If

128

the roof catches fire.'

And it seemed very likely that this would happen because the sparks were showering in all directions, fanned by the strong westerly breeze, and then large pieces of wood began to drop away from the burning mass, flying through the air like rockets.

'Like a ruddy firework display, i'n't it? Pity it couldn't've happened on Jubilee night, eh?' said one voice in the crowd, only to be silenced by his indignant wife.

'Give over, Bert! What a thing to say! Just think of them poor chaps up there. I couldn't see you risking yer life like that, that's for sure! If you can't say owt sensible, then shut up!'

'All right, all right, I were only saying... Hey, just look at that ironwork; red hot it is. Hey up; they're moving away now, them chaps. Must've realised they can't do any more.'

'Well, thank the Lord for that. It'd be awful if somebody was to get badly burned, or killed.' A thought which Molly echoed to herself as the tiny figures up on the platform disappeared from sight, seemingly still all in one piece after their efforts. She breathed a sigh of relief. Even if her father had been one of them he was away from the danger now.

Suddenly, over the whispered comments of the crowd – strangely, no one was shouting – there came a loud whirring sound, then an almighty crash as something was seen to drop down through the ironwork of the Tower and crash through the roof of the buildings below. Several people, men as well as women, screamed, and those who were nearer to the scene turned and fled for their lives.

'Heaven help us, it's the lift,' cried a frightened voice.

'No, it'll not be the lift. It's the balance weight that controls it,' replied someone more knowledgeable. 'There's two of 'em, them balance weights, what balance the lifts. There'll be another crash afore long, just you see.'

And so there was, a few minutes later; another deafening crash as the second balance weight dropped through the roof, together with more pieces of ironwork, glowing red with the heat. Between the four legs of the Tower, right at the bottom of the building, the circus was situated, as most people were aware.

'Good heavens above! Whatever'll happen to all those poor animals if the girders start to fall in?' cried a woman in the crowd. 'Saints preserve us! We're going to have lions and tigers wandering loose in the streets.'

'Don't talk daft, Ada. The Tower itself won't fall down. How can it? It's made of iron. It's only the buildings that'll cop it. And it looks as though the fire up at t'top is burning itself out now, thank God.'

'All the same, I'm worried about them animals, Fred...'

Indeed, many people were now turning away and leaving the scene as if they too were frightened of wild animals being let loose in the streets.

Then, at long last, the fire brigade arrived. No one was sure why they had been so tardy; at least it seemed to the crowd that they had been so, but once they arrived on the scene they set to work at once, playing their hosepipes on to the roof of the Tower buildings which, miraculously, had not caught fire, and on the roofs of nearby shops which were also in danger.

'So that's that,' said the man standing next to Molly, the one who had seemed to know all about the mechanics of the lift. 'It's all under control now. We can all go home. I hope there's not been too much damage done, that's all. Still, the Tower company can stand it, I dare say.' He turned to Molly, in the way complete strangers were apt to do when they found themselves sharing a crisis or a disaster. 'What do you say, luv?'

'Yes, I hope everything's all right,' replied Molly. 'Well, as all right as it can be. I certainly do. You see ... my father works there, at the Tower. In fact, he's still in there, somewhere.'

'Oh dear, that's too bad,' said the man. 'Sorry, luv; I didn't realise. Still, he'll be all right. I've just heard somebody say that there's no one been hurt, thank God.'

'Yes, thank God,' breathed Molly. She very rarely prayed, but she had been doing so, silently, as she stood there in the crowd. 'I'd best get off home now. I'll go and wait there for my father. Ta-ra then...'

Inside the Tower building, just after eleven o'clock, it was pandemonium. Scores of folk were dashing hither and thither, all trying to help, but frustrated by their own helplessness for they

131

knew there was little they could do. They could only keep a watchful eye on what was going on, and hope and pray that things would not get any worse. At the moment the fire seemed to be contained at the top of the Tower. A few brave souls with fire extinguishers strapped to their backs had already mounted the circular iron staircase that led up through the girders of the Tower, to battle with the flames.

'It should be me up there, fighting that fire,' remarked Jim Walmsley, the night watchman, the one who had first noticed the fire when he was on his last round before the Tower closed down for the night. 'The trouble is I reckon I'd be more hindrance than help, the state I'm in at the minute. Oh dear, oh dear! I can't help feeling it's all my fault. I'm the one that's supposed to notice things like that.'

'And so you did, Jim,' William Rimmer consoled him. 'You were the first one up there, weren't you? That's how you got this lot.' For Jim's hands had been quite badly burned, and William and another colleague, Joe, one of the barmen, were in the process of covering them with ointment and bandaging them. Jim refused to go home or, for the moment, to call a doctor, insisting there were more important jobs to be done. Indeed, he was as restless as the proverbial cat on hot bricks, and William and Joe were having a hard time trying to make him keep still.

'Hold still a minute, lad,' said William. 'We've nearly done. I dare say it'll hurt for a while. You must see a doctor as soon as you can. And let's have no more nonsense about it being your fault.

132

Nowt o' t'sort. I reckon you deserve a medal going up there at all, knowing as how it were on fire.'

'Aye, well, that's as may be,' shrugged Jim. 'I'll never forget it, I can tell you, lads, not so long as I live.' Once again he started to tell the tale that he had recounted to them a couple of times already. 'Aye, we only got as far as the arrival platform.' That was the level of the Tower to which the lifts ascended. 'And we could see then as it were no use; we couldn't get up any further. The whole lot were ablaze, right up to the crow's nest at t'top. It's all wood up there, you know. All that wooden casing and the fancy goods stalls filled with all them bits and bobs; real tempting food for the flames, you might say.'

'What d'you think started it, Jim?' asked William, tying a final knot in the bandaging and still endeavouring to keep his colleague from dashing about.

'Dunno really. Faulty wiring, happen, or wires that were exposed. I dare say the wind and rain got to 'em and made 'em spark, and it wouldn't take much for all that woodwork to take hold. We've had a long spell of dry weather, haven't we, until recently, and it'd burn like straw? Can't help thinking I should have noticed 'em before, though, them wires.'

'Not your job, Jim,' replied William. 'If it comes to that I could say I'm even more to blame. I'm supposed to be the handyman around here, aren't I? Not an electrician, though, I must admit. It were just an accident, Jim; just one of those things, as they say. So stop yer mithering. Anyroad, it's happened before, hasn't it? It caught fire not so long ago.'

'Aye, just a few weeks ago. Same time – round about eleven – and same place an' all. But it were soon under control, not like this lot. It's them balance weights as I'm worried about. Goodness knows how many tons they weigh and if they crash down, well ... God knows what'll happen.'

'If it's going to happen, then it'll happen,' said William resignedly. 'Nowt we can do about it. And judging from what you've told us about the fiery furnace up yonder I should think it's more than likely. You said yourself as how the cables were white-hot.'

'Aye, so they were.'

'The fire brigade's on its way, Jim.' Fred White-side, the head waiter, one of the men who, with Jim, had made the first perilous ascent, had just reappeared on the scene. 'We're frightened of the roof catching fire, you see, with all them sparks flying about, and there's been a few pieces of red-hot timber fallen down already. But the heroes up at t'top have called it a day, you'll be pleased to hear. They're on their way down now.'

Even as they spoke the small group of men came through the door which led to the circular staircase. Their faces were blackened and their eyes red, and none of them, for the moment, seemed to want to speak; which was under-standable, thought William. One of the men was the chief swimmer from the circus. The show always ended with a spectacular display of swim-ming when the circus ring was filled from the bottom with water. He's a brave fellow, thought

134

William, as he glanced at his dejected face and general air of weariness, especially as he was more used to water than fire. Another of the group was the elephant trainer, a man quite used to danger, no doubt, but brave none the less. William wished he could have been up there too. He would have liked to do his bit and helped in a practical sort of way, but by the time he had arrived there after doing a minor carpentry job down near the ballroom the fire fighting had already begun.

He wouldn't have cared about putting his life in danger. After all, what did his life mean to him now that his beloved Lily had gone? Not very much at all. He had his two daughters, of course, and he loved them, just as, he supposed, they loved him; although none of them had ever been very good at expressing their feelings. Maybe he should have told Molly and young Em more often how much they meant to him, but the truth was that the lion's share of his love had always been showered on Lily. He had never had any difficulty in telling Lily how much he loved her, or in showing her. But now Lily had gone and, for a time, William had not wanted to go on living either. Until yesterday when, on a sudden whim, he had looked – he had to admit it was the first time he had *really* looked – at the face of his little son. And he had realised that there might after all be something to go on living for. It would be hard, and he knew he would never stop wanting Lily or cease to mourn her, but maybe, just maybe, the future did hold a ray of hope.

He looked round at the Old English village

which was situated in the elevator hall, the scene now of all the frenzied activity. It was a quaint place, designed for the holidaymakers, of course, with its mock-Tudor shops and stalls selling all kind of fripperies, but it had a certain vulgar charm, as had many of the amusement places in the Tower and throughout the town of Blackpool. William had wanted Lily to come and see it, but she had never done so. And now it was too late.

His thoughts were interrupted by a low ominous rumbling sound and everyone instinctively, began to run away from the centre of the hall where the Tower lifts ascended, to the sides and a place of safety.

'My God, oh, my God! It's the balance weights!' cried Jim. And the next moment there came a deafening crash a noise which struck terror into William's heart even though he had been expecting it, and which he could feel reverberating right through his body, making his heart beat faster. William had started to run, along with the others. Now he found he was rooted to the spot as, a few moments later, there came a second, if possible, even louder crash as the second weight fell.

'That's it, lads,' came Jim's voice from somewhere in the distance. 'It's what we've been waiting for. We'd best go and see what damage has been done.'

But they all seemed too stunned for the moment to make a move. Suddenly, out of the blue and totally unexpected, there came another loud report. All eyes looked upwards, from where the noise came, to see a piece of the iron flagstaff, which surmounted the Tower, glowing red with the heat, crashing down through the roof of the Old English village. They all stared in amazement and horror, wondering why on earth he did not move out of the way, as it came tumbling down on to the head of William Rimmer, felling him to the floor.

Jim, Joe and Fred were at his side at once. Joe, indeed, had started to run a few seconds earlier in an endeavour to pull his colleague out of the way. But it was too late. William lay unconscious on the floor, his eyes closed, his head bruised and scorched and bleeding from the weight of the piece of iron flagstaff.

'Get a doctor. Somebody call a doctor,' cried Joe. 'I think he's badly hurt. He can see to you at the same time, Jim; those hands of yours.'

Fred, the waiter, came to kneel on the floor. He took hold of William's wrist, feeling for a pulse, then, frantically, put his head to the man's chest, listening intently. After a few moments he looked up, his face grim. 'It's too late,' he said. 'Too late for the doctor. I'm afraid he's gone.'

It was necessary to call a doctor anyway, who pronounced that the man was, as they had feared, beyond any help.

'Oh dear, oh dear, that's a bad do. It is that,' cried Jim Walmsley, once again distracted from the pain of his hands. 'I reckon somebody had better go and tell his wife.'

'Not his wife, Jim,' remarked Fred, who knew the dead man slightly better than Jim. 'Don't you remember? He's a widower – was, I should say, God rest his soul. His wife died only a month back. The night of the Jubilee it was. There's a daughter, though, who looks after them.'

'Aye, our Molly, he calls her,' added Joe. 'An' there's a new baby an' all. That's how his missis died, in childbirth. Aye, it's a bad do, whichever way you look at it.'

'I'll go and tell the next of kin,' said Sergeant Beaumont, the policeman who had been on the scene since the start of the fire. 'After all, that's one of our jobs, one of the least pleasant ones, I might say. If you'll just let me have the address...'

It was almost one o'clock in the morning when Molly, waiting up, and growing increasingly anxious, despite the news she'd heard earlier that no one had been hurt, heard the knock at the door. She opened it to see, to her horror a policeman standing there. She knew from his face that the news was bad; besides, a policeman on the threshold usually indicated something drastic.

'Miss Molly Rimmer?' he asked.

'Yes. What is it? Is it my father? You've come to tell me there's been ... an accident?'

'I'm afraid so, luv. If I could just come in for a minute...'

Silently she led him through to the living room where Maggie was still sitting. She had stayed to keep her company till William arrived home. Maggie sprang to her feet. 'What is it?' she also cried.

Although they had both guessed. The sergeant made sure that Molly was sitting down before he broke the news. And when she heard that her father was dead she started to scream and scream. Maggie feared she would never stop.

Chapter 7

At first, on that dreadful night, Maggie Winthrop had felt worried about the poor girl's sanity. On hearing the news about her father she had screamed and carried on alarmingly for a full five minutes, with Maggie's arms around her and the police sergeant standing there shuffling his feet and looking most uncomfortable.

'You're a relation, are you?' he asked quietly, when Molly's sobs and cries had subsided just a little. 'I know she hasn't got a mother, poor lass.'

'No, just a neighbour,' replied Maggie. 'Well, more than just a neighbour; a very good friend.'

'That's all right then,' said the sergeant. ''Cause that's what she's going to need. We hate having to break news like this, Mrs...?'

'Mrs Winthrop,' said Maggie.

'...Mrs Winthrop, but it's part of the job, worse luck, and I'd been there on the scene since the fire started.' He cast an anxious look at Molly who was now staring unseeingly into space, her chest still shaking every few seconds with violent, though now silent, sobs and her hands clinging tightly to Maggie's as though she was frightened to let go of her. 'I can leave her in your capable hands then, can I?' He lowered his voice. 'They're seeing to ... everything down there, the fellows at the Tower. The – er – undertaker an' all that. I should imagine they'll bring him home – Mr

Rimmer, that is – sometime tomorrow.'

Molly did not appear to be registering what he was saying. Maggie, kneeling on the floor at her side, freed one of her hands that the girl was grasping so tightly and put an arm around her shoulders. 'Aye, I'll be here to see to things, don't you worry. I'll take good care of Molly here. She'll be all right,' she added in a whisper, 'when she's got over the shock, like; I'm sure she will. She's a strong lass – strong in spirit, if you know what I mean. It's a terrible thing, though, losing 'em both within a month. I can scarcely take it in myself. Now, can you see yourself out? Unless you'd like a cup of tea before you go, Sergeant?'

'No ... no thanks, Mrs Winthrop. I'd best get along now. Make one for the young lady, though. I reckon she could do with one; strong and plenty of sugar. Well, I'm sure you know, don't you? You'll have dealt with this sort of crisis before.'

The sergeant turned to Molly, his rugged and homely face full of compassion. 'Good night then, Miss Rimmer. I'm ... I'm so very sorry, my dear. They asked me to tell you – all the chaps at the Tower – how sorry they are and that they're thinking about you.'

Molly showed no sign that she had heard, and Maggie realised that the girl had not spoken at all, apart from one anguished cry of 'Oh no!' since hearing the dreadful news. She appeared to understand when Maggie told her now that she was going to brew the tea, and then, obediently, she drank the beverage, but her eyes were glazed over and her face was expressionless. Maggie knew she would not dare to leave her on her own

140

that night – alone, that was, apart from the young children – but she had to let her husband know that she would not be coming home.

'I'll not be a minute, luv,' she told Molly. 'I'm just popping along to see Bill.' But when she returned a few moments later it looked as though the girl had not moved a muscle. She sat motionless by the fireside, her cup and saucer in her hands, her mouth partly open and her eyes still with that vacant, almost inane, look in them that was frightening Maggie to death. It seemed as though the lass might be losing her senses.

She did not speak at all that night, and Maggie began to fear that she might have been struck dumb. She had heard that a severe shock could have that effect. Like a submissive and brow-beaten child she obeyed Maggie's suggestion that she should go upstairs and get into bed. She rose to her feet and made for the door, but there she stopped and, still not speaking, cast a frightened look in Maggie's direction. 'I'll be here,' said Maggie. 'Don't worry, luv; I'll not leave you. I'll sleep down here by the fire. Up you go now and try to get some rest.'

Maggie thought she might go and stretch out on William's bed for a while when Molly had gone to sleep, if the poor lass ever did. It would be more comfortable than the sagging armchair, although she doubted that she, Maggie, would be able to sleep with all the traumas of the night.

To her surprise Molly appeared to be sleeping when she crept into the room to take a peep some fifteen minutes later. At least, Maggie could see by the faint light filtering through the thin curtains that her eyes were closed and one arm lay protectively across her young sister, Emily. It was a mercy, and a miracle too, that the little girl had not woken, nor baby William. He had had a late night feed only half an hour or so before the policeman came, and Molly had told her that he usually managed to sleep through the night now, not waking until six o'clock or thereabouts.

It was as Maggie had feared. Sleep would not come to her. It was a relief to rest her weary body, although the day had been no more nor less busy than normal; her days were always filled to capacity with the demands of her family and the jobs she did in the neighbourhood. But her mind was too full, too burdened with anxious thoughts for her to sleep. What a tragedy, to be sure, for that poor lass, and for little Emily too. Baby William was too young to know what was going on. He didn't know his father, and from what Maggie had gathered, William had been making no effort to get to know his son until yesterday – or so Molly had been telling her just before the awful news came. And now it was too late. All three of them were orphans.

Aye, William Rimmer had a lot to answer for, he had that... Maggie immediately rebuked herself for the uncharitable thought that had come into her mind. You should never speak ill of the dead. That was what folks said, and she wouldn't say one word against the fellow, not to anyone. But you couldn't always help your thoughts, could you? He couldn't have wanted to get himself killed, of course – that was just a tragic accident – but happen he could have been more careful. He would have been here, there and everywhere, she had no doubt, seeing what he could do to help – that was William all over – but not giving a thought to his three children at home.

But as far as his wife, his poor Lily, was concerned, then Maggie did blame him and him entirely. Dr Paige had warned him – and Maggie herself had warned not William, but Lily – that it would be downright dangerous for them to have any more children. And what did he do but take no notice. He went right ahead and got his wife pregnant. Oh yes, it took two, Maggie was well aware of that, but Lily wouldn't have wanted to refuse him. She thought the sun shone out of him as he did of her. Proper embarrassing it had been sometimes to see the pair of them together, billing and cooing. Maggie did not doubt that they had loved their two girls, but their daughters had taken second place as far as Lily and William were concerned, second place to their adoration of one another.

Such an unlikely couple, too, to have known such passion. Lily had always seemed so prim and proper and William such an ordinary sort of bloke. She could be a real misery at times as well, could Lily, when one of her black moods came upon her. William had once confided in Maggie that Lily had had a tragic life. Her mother, Alice, had committed suicide when Lily was only eight years old, the age that Em was now, and that was the reason for her despondency and fits of malaise. There was something else too, another tragedy further back in the family which William had hinted at but never divulged. Tragedy seemed to strike at the women of the family, he had said, and that was the reason he had never wanted to tell Molly how her grandmother had died, or even hint to her about that other distant catastrophe. It would not be right, William had said, for Molly to go through life anticipating trouble when there was none.

But now there was trouble indeed. The hand of fate had struck again, with another dose of tragedy, a double one this time. All the time that Lily had been pregnant Maggie had gone on affirming, of course, that she had never lost a baby yet. What else could she have done? But she had had her fears all along, though she had kept them to herself. Though in that last week or so, Lily had seemed so much better that even Maggie had started to believe all might be well. She had blamed herself afterwards, when poor Lily had died, for not insisting that the woman should go into hospital for the birth, or at least have a doctor in attendance all the time. But Lily's faith in Maggie had been touching, and besides, hospitals cost money; so did doctors. In the end it had all happened too quickly, but Maggie was relieved that Dr Paige had been there to share the responsibility with her ... and the blame.

William was the one who was mostly to blame for his lack of restraint, but Maggie, in her more reflective moments, could not help but feel guilty about what had happened. Especially now, when those poor children had lost both their parents. She made up her mind there and then, as the faint light of dawn crept through the curtains and she still had not slept, that she would make it up to Molly. The girl, most certainly, would have to go back to work; if not to her original job at the confectioner's, then to some other such employment. They had been relying solely on William's wage for the last month and now there would be no money at all coming into the house. Maggie doubted that they had any savings. Any money the Rimmers had had to spare had seemed to be spent on knick-knacks and bits of – what Maggie considered to be – totally unnecessary furniture for that blessed parlour of Lily's. What did a working-class couple want with a china tea service, for goodness' sake, or a whatnot or an aspidistra? And William, silly besotted fool, had had no more sense than to indulge Lily in her high-falutin whims. It was the one thing about Lily that had annoyed Maggie, her delusions of grandeur, although she had always gone on insisting, nevertheless, that she and William knew their place in the world, and so did the girls.

A tremendous sigh shook Maggie's body. It all made no difference now – she felt a tear pricking at the corner of her eye – for Lily was six feet under; and she would soon be joined by her husband. And poor Molly was left with the burden of providing a home for herself and her little sister and brother. Should she fall behind with the rent the landlord would show no mercy. Molly would be out on the streets and those two little mites would be packed off to the orphanage...

Maggie tugged back her rambling thoughts.

Whatever was she thinking of, letting her mind run off in that ridiculous way? Such a thing was impossible; Molly would never allow it to happen. She thought the world of her brother and sister. Besides, she, Maggie, was going to look after them for her. Young Em was no trouble; such a quiet little mouse of a child she was, and she already spent a lot of time with Sarah. And as for baby William, well, one more would make no difference in an already crowded household. Bill might grumble a bit. He had made up his mind there would be no more babies when the twins, Betty and Billy Junior, were born four years ago. But Bill was out all day delivering coal – he worked for Henry Hall, the well-known coal, lime and slate merchant – and most likely the baby would have been returned to his sister by the time Bill came home. Anyway, Maggie knew that she had very little choice in the matter. The girl needed help and Maggie would see that she got it.

And she would need help now in facing the day that lay ahead. Maggie heaved her heavy body out of the strange bed and quickly straightened the clothes. It would not do for Molly to find her here, in her father's bed, when she had said she would sleep downstairs. Always supposing that Molly was in a fit state even to think about it; she had been lost in a world of her own last night, poor lass. Maggie crept downstairs and went down the yard to the closet, then she swilled her hands and face at the kitchen slopstone before setting to work to mend the fire and make a pot of tea. It was while she was setting out the crockery on the table – she must insist that the two girls had a bite to eat – that Molly appeared in the doorway. She was already fully dressed, and was holding baby William in her arms, although Maggie had not heard her moving about. Molly's face was grave and her eyes full of sadness, but Maggie was relieved to see they no longer had the vacant and abstracted look that had so alarmed her the night before.

'My father is dead, isn't he?' she said, her voice a monotone. 'That is what he came to tell us, didn't he, that policeman? I wondered if I might have dreamed it, but I know it's true. He's dead.'

'Yes, I'm afraid so, luv. That's why I stayed, you remember? I didn't like to leave you.'

'I'll be all right, Maggie. I will have to be all right. William needs feeding, and then I must wake Emily and tell her ... tell her that Father is dead.' Even though the light of understanding had returned to her eyes her voice was still impassive. 'You must go home, Maggie, to your family. They will need you. I can manage. I'll have to manage without them now, my mother and father, they are both dead.'

Her words struck a chill into Maggie's heart. It was as though in repeating the words – he is dead; they are both dead – Molly was trying to convince herself of the dreadful fact. Last night the girl's frenzied screaming, though understand-able, had been uncharacteristic, so had her subsequent silence and her air of inanity. But now her awareness had returned, she seemed too calm.

'I can stay a little while,' said Maggie. 'It's not

147

six o'clock yet. Sit down and have a cup of tea and I'll see to young Will's bottle for you.'

'I'll see to it, Maggie. I always get William's bottle ready. He's used to me.' She laid the baby in his pram, whereupon he started grizzling, though not actually crying. 'He's called William, not Will,' she said impassively. 'That was what my mother said – to call him William, after my father. And now my father's dead.'

Mechanically the girl moved around the kitchen, collecting the bottle, the tin of baby food, the boiling water from the hob, while Maggie watched her, at a loss for words.

'You must let me do summat, lass,' she cried out eventually, made uneasy by the silence. 'How would it be if I ... if I went and broke the news to your Em? Not that I want to take your place – don't think that, Molly; I don't want to push myself – but the little lass has got used to me with spending so much time with Sarah.' Maggie was worried that Molly, in her present state of mind, would not impart the awful tidings in a sympathetic manner.

To her relief Molly nodded. 'All right; it might be better for you to tell her. Tell her that Father is dead. Er ... thank you, Maggie.' The last words sounded like an afterthought, but Maggie was not offended. The girl was not herself at all and the Lord only knew when she was likely to be.

Maggie went back upstairs to the room which the sisters shared. Em was sitting up in bed, a puzzled, almost frightened look on her face. It was as though the child already knew that there was something sadly amiss in the household.

148

'What's up?' she cried. 'Where's our Molly? I woke up and she wasn't here. What are you doing here, Auntie Maggie?'

Maggie went to sit on the edge of the bed and took hold of the little girl's hand. The springs in the iron-framed bedstead beneath the lumpy flock mattress creaked as she put her weight on them. All the furniture in this room was old and rather shabby, but the sheets and pillowcases were dazzlingly white; the floral curtains at the window and the bedspread, though faded with frequent washing were also spotlessly clean. Molly was obviously taking a leaf out of her mother's book with her scrupulous care of her home. Aye, the lass could teach me a thing or two, young as she is, Maggie observed to herself wrily. Maggie was not renowned for her tidiness or her fastidious housekeeping. She was clean enough in her person, however, and no one ever had cause to complain about her observance of the necessary hygiene in her confinements or layings-out; as hygienic as it was possible to be, that was, in some of the mucky holes she visited.

'Molly's looking after baby William, isn't she?' she said now. 'Where else would she be, love? She's giving him his bottle.' Oh God, please help me, she prayed silently now as the child continued to regard her questioningly, a worried frown on her face.

'Why are you here, Auntie Maggie?' she asked again.

'Because ... because I have something to tell you, love; something very sad. I'm afraid you will have to try to be a very brave girl. There was an accident last night at the Tower – a fire up at the top – and your dad was trying to help. You know how he always tried to help people, didn't he, Em? Well, I'm afraid he got hurt, very badly hurt, and that means ... he didn't come home. He won't be coming home any more, Emily love, because he's gone to be with your mam. He loved her very much, just like he loved you and Molly, but now ... now your mam and dad are together again. Do you understand, Em? Do you know what I'm trying to tell you?'

The child looked even more puzzled and she shook her head in bewilderment; not in denial, Maggie understood, but because it all must be so very hard to take in. First her mother, now her father, however must she be feeling?

'You mean he's dead – like Mam's dead?' she asked after a few seconds.

'Yes – I'm sorry, love – that was what I was trying to tell you. It's very, very sad for all of you – you and Molly and baby William – but your mam and dad, well, they're both with God now, aren't they? In heaven. And that must make them very happy, to be together again.'

Maggie was well aware that the name of the Almighty was scarcely ever mentioned in this house. She had never really understood why; she just knew that both of them, William and Lily, had professed not to believe in any God, and neither of the lasses had ever been encouraged to go to Sunday School, which Maggie thought was a crying shame. For her part, she was not a great church- or chapelgoer – when was there ever time to go to church, for goodness' sake? – but

150

she had been brought up in a God-fearing family and all her own children had been sent to Sunday School. And Maggie honestly believed that William and Lily were now reunited in heaven, despite the fact that they had denied Him most of the time. After all, it said in the good book, didn't it, that He loved us all, so she couldn't see that He would shut them out. Anyroad, if it would be any comfort to poor little Em then that was what she had to say.

The child cried then, a more normal crying than her sister's hysterical outburst of the night before, while Maggie held her in her arms and stroked her hair, then mopped her face with a large handkerchief, a fairly clean one, which she withdrew from her apron pocket. After a few moments Emily stopped sobbing and looked soberly at Maggie. She was such a solemn little girl; she had inherited much of her mother's taciturnity, Maggie feared.

'You said there was a fire?' she asked. 'My dad – was he burned then? Is that why he died?'

'No, no, he didn't get burned, love. And we have to be thankful for that. Something fell on him, something heavy and it – well – it killed him straight away, Emily. So he didn't suffer; he didn't have any pain. It happened so suddenly that he wouldn't have known anything about it.'

'Until he found he was with Mam again,' said Em, in quite a matter-of-fact way. Maggie was glad she seemed to have accepted without question the somewhat facile explanation she had given. Maybe in a little while, and provided Molly was in agreement, it might be a good idea to send the little girl to Sunday School along with Sarah and Billy and Betty. For the moment, though, Emily must be reassured that she would be well looked after.

'Yes, I expect that was how it was, love,' said Maggie, sighing deeply. 'And now your Molly is going to look after you, isn't she? She's very sad at the moment, though, Em. You must try not to worry if she doesn't talk to you very much. She's very upset, of course – we all are – and she has a lot to do as well, looking after the baby.'

'I help her,' said Em, even smiling a little at the mention of baby William. Maggie had noticed how the little girl doted on him. 'Molly says I'm a tremendous help to her. She says she doesn't know how she'd manage without me. I nurse the baby, Auntie Maggie, and sometimes Molly lets me give him his bottle. You have to tip it up very gently, you see, so that he doesn't get too much at a time. And he has to keep having a little rest so that he doesn't get wind. Perhaps ... perhaps I could stay away from school today, could I, so that I can help our Molly?'

Maggie smiled sadly. 'Yes, that might be a good idea. I don't think you need to go to school today, Em.' On the other hand, Molly might not want the little girl in the house. She would have her hands full, poor lass, dealing with folks coming to express their sympathy and the undertaker arriving with the coffin. It might be as well to remove Emily away from the scene. 'I tell you what,' Maggie went on, 'how would it be if you and baby William both come to stay with me today? We'll look after him together, shall we?

Then p'raps we could take him for a nice long walk along the prom.'

The little girl nodded seriously, but after her burst of chatter she had gone silent again.

'Now, I'm going to bring you up a nice cup of tea,' said Maggie, 'before I go back home to see to my lot. A little treat for you, eh?' The child loved her cups of tea as much as any grown-up, old-fashioned little thing that she was. 'Then you can get yourself washed and dressed and see if Molly wants any help. You're a very brave girl, Em. I'm proud of you.'

It had all gone far more smoothly than Maggie had dared to hope. The younger girl had accepted the tragic news much more calmly than her sister had done the night before. Molly was nursing the baby when Maggie re-entered the kitchen. The empty bottle was on the table, but she was making no move to put William back into his pram. From her rapt expression as she looked down at the baby Maggie doubted that the girl would agree to part with him today, but to her surprise Molly raised no objection when Maggie informed her of her plan.

'So I'll come back when I've got Bill off to work and the kids to school,' she said. 'Em's going to help me and it'll leave you free to do ... whatever there is to do. Now, you'll be all right, won't you, lass, while I just slip home?'

'I'll be all right, Maggie. I've still got our Em and little William. We've just got to carry on, haven't we? What else can we do, now that Mother and Father are dead? We've just got to go on.'

It was her impassivity now that was worrying Maggie. It was almost as though last night's tragedy and her bereavement of only a month ago were not touching her.

Molly was surprised by her own calmness. It was not that she was unmoved by her father's death. She remembered how she had carried on when she first heard the news, crying and screaming, but afterwards the enormity of what had happened had seemed to recede to a distant part of her mind. It was as though she were witnessing all that was going on through someone else's eyes, or as a series of pictures, like that cinematograph show that she remembered Flo telling her about. She was aware that Maggie had stayed the night with her and that the woman was being very, very kind, but she couldn't talk to her about how she was feeling. Because, in truth, Molly didn't know how she was feeling. She only knew that the numbness such as she had experienced shortly after her mother's death had overpowered her now to a much greater degree. She found that she could not even express her thanks to Maggie as she knew she should, nor could she talk to Em about what had happened.

Had she tried to do so the immensity of her grief and the burden of care she was bearing would have become insurmountable. Molly did not fully understand this, but those closest to her – Maggie and Flo – in those dreadful few days following her father's death could see it more clearly.

One misfortune was that there were no relatives

on whom Molly could call for help. She had never known any of her grandparents. Her mother's family story was veiled in mystery. All Molly had learned, from the little her father had told her, was that her mother, Lily, had had an unhappy time as a girl. Lily's mother had died when she was eight and her father, though good to her, had been old enough to be her grand-father. If there were any other relations Molly had never heard of them. And her father's family was just as much of a puzzle. They were a Preston family, she knew that much, but the only remaining relative was an elderly man whom her father had referred to as Uncle Silas. But this uncle, apparently, had wanted nothing more to do with William after the young man had married Lily and gone to live in Blackpool. Molly had never asked why, and her mother and father had never seemed unduly concerned about their lack of relations. They had been a close-knit little family, relying on one another for love and com-panionship. Neither Lily nor William had sought friends outside the family circle, except for Maggie and one of William's colleagues at the Tower, Joe Turner.

It was Joe who called round to see Molly the afternoon following William's death. Molly had met him before on her occasional visits to the Tower, but he had never been to their home; her parents had had few visitors. He was a good-natured, usually cheerful man, about the same age as her father, and it was easy to see the two of them might have been friends or, at least, close colleagues.

'We can't begin to tell you how sorry we are, lass,' he began, holding on tightly to the tin box in his hands. 'It's been a terrible shock to all of us at the Tower. He were well liked, yer dad. We've had a bit of a collection, see. It'll happen help – we know as how you've got yer little sister and brother to look after.' He handed the box to Molly and she noticed, on the periphery of her mind, that it had a picture of Queen Victoria on the lid. 'Aye, it's a bad do, Molly lass, especially after yer mam, an' all. If there's owt else we can do...'

'Thank you, Mr Turner,' said Molly. She tried to smile at him, but her mouth felt frozen and her eyes too would not respond. 'It's very kind of you. No ... I don't think there's anything ... anyone can do.' She felt suddenly light-headed and she momentarily closed her eyes, opening them again to see Joe Turner looking at her in some concern. He took hold of her arm.

'Are you sure there's nothing we can do for you, Molly? You're only a young lass to be coping with ... all this lot. And I've heard Will say as how you've no relations in Blackpool. My missus 'ud be only too glad to come round and give you a hand – with the kids or anything ... or just to keep you company.'

'No ... thank you. I'm all right; really I am. I've got Maggie – she's a neighbour. She's looking after the children for me now. And my friend Flo. I expect she'll come round ... as soon as she can.' Molly's words, to her own ears, sounded far away and as though they were being uttered without her volition. 'Would you like to look at Father, before you go?'

'Aye, I'll do that, lass.' Joe hung his head, then followed Molly into the parlour. 'And of course we'll be at the funeral, some of us, if you can let us know when it is. And they said as I'd to tell you that the Tower Company'll look after all the expenses, for t'funeral, like...'

Molly noticed a tear in his eye, this big cheerful robust-looking man, as he looked down at the body of his workmate. This was the part that seemed most unreal to Molly; her father lying exactly where her mother had lain a month ago. The lines – mainly they had been laughter lines and not lines of care – had gone from his face and the bruise on his head was concealed by the skilful draping of the shroud.

'It'll be next week sometime,' she replied automatically. 'I'll let you know, Mr Turner.'

She opened the box when he had gone. It contained what she thought would amount to two or three pounds, although she did not bother to count it straight away, in threepenny bits, sixpences, shillings and the odd florin and half-crown. She had given little thought as to how she would manage without her father's wage. Molly, at the moment, could not see any further than the next few hours.

It was Flo who tried to make her look more clearly at the hard facts of her situation. She called that evening when the children had gone to bed and Molly was on her own. Maggie had been reluctant to leave her, but Molly had insisted, once again, that she would be all right. At the sight of her good friend Flo, Molly felt

157

something akin to warmth and emotion stirring inside her, but still the sense of unreality was pervasive.

'You poor thing,' said Flo. 'I couldn't believe it when I heard. "It can't be true," I said to Miss Amelia when she told me. "Not Molly's father, so soon after her mother." There's no justice, is there? It makes you wonder sometimes about God's ways, what He means by it all. I suppose we've got to go on trusting, that's what they teach us at Chapel, but it's hard at times.' She stopped abruptly, eyeing Molly a little warily. 'I'm sorry, love. I shouldn't be saying all this, should I? I wasn't thinking. I was forgetting for the minute that you don't ... well, you don't go to–'

'Go to church? Don't believe in ... everything, like you do?' said Molly, but not unkindly. She smiled sadly and shook her head in a bewildered way. 'Blessed if I know what I believe, Flo. But if I did – well, it would make me wonder, like you say.' She gave a deep sigh. 'At the moment I don't believe anything. I can't take it in at all, that all this has happened. It all seems so ... far away, so distant, as though it's happening to somebody else.' But though she had been talking to Flo for only a moment the mere presence of her friend was beginning to bring her back to reality.

'That's nature's way of helping you to cope, I dare say,' said Flo. 'Your father, is he ... in there?' She motioned towards the parlour door.

'Yes,' said Molly briefly. 'Like ... Mam was.'

'Then I'd best pay my respects, hadn't I?' said Flo. 'Although I didn't really know him as well as I knew your mother.'

'How will you manage,' asked Flo a little while later, when they were settled in the kitchen with a cup of tea, 'if you don't mind me asking?'

'Manage? What do you mean?' Molly stared at her. 'Same as I've done since Mam died, I suppose. I had to give my job up then to look after Em and little William, because Dad ... well, I'm not going to say anything wrong about him, especially not now, but he wasn't bothering much about them. No, it's up to me to look after them, nobody else, and I shall just go on doing it.'

Flo gave a little tut of annoyance. 'But haven't you realised? There won't be any money coming in, will there? Not now your dad's gone.'

Molly looked at her blankly, then she began to feel a tiny flicker of fear at the edge of her consciousness. It was the first time the thought had occurred to her, although it should have been obvious; there would be no money. 'There is some money,' she replied, still unable to grasp the seriousness of the situation. 'Mr Turner, one of Dad's workmates, he came round earlier. They'd had a collection.'

'And how much was there?' asked Flo, matter-of-factedly.

'Oh, I don't know. A couple of pounds, maybe. It's in that tin box on the sideboard. Have a look if you like.'

'We'd best count it,' said Flo. She tipped the contents on to the plush cloth that covered the kitchen table when it was not in use for dining or cooking. Deftly she fingered the coins, putting them into piles. 'Three pounds, two shillings and threepence ha'penny,' she announced. 'Not bad,

I suppose, but not a fortune, not when it's to look after three of you. Isn't there anything else, Molly? No savings? Your dad had a regular wage, didn't he? And he wasn't a drinker.'

'I think they spent it, most of it,' said Molly. 'Mam liked nice things, you see.' She saw Flo cast her eyes towards the ceiling, but without comment. 'And there was a bit of insurance money when Mam died. Dad paid a few pence a week on a policy, but that 'ud be to pay for the funeral. If there is anything it'll be in the tin box in the sideboard. I haven't looked,' she added.

'Then don't you think you'd better do so?' said Flo. 'I don't want to poke my nose into what's none of my business, Molly, but you've got to sort yerself out.'

The black tin box contained five sovereigns and a few half-crowns and florins, also an insurance book which showed there would be a few pounds to collect on William's death. He, like her mother, had been insured for a few pence a week. 'And the undertaker, and Joe Turner, who worked with Dad, said that the Tower company were taking care of the funeral expenses,' said Molly, 'so you don't need to worry, Flo. There's enough to keep us going for ages.'

'Not for ever,' replied Flo. 'Not for all that long if you think about it properly. What about the rent money? And the coal and the gas meter and the food and milk? And your William's special baby food?'

'We'll manage,' said Molly. 'That's the most important thing; William's food. I've got to take care of William, and Em. I don't need much to eat myself. I haven't been very hungry lately, anyway.'

'And it shows an' all!' replied Flo. 'You're nearly skin and bone, Moll. I had a shock when I saw you, I can tell you. You mustn't let yourself go to pieces, love.' She reached out and clasped her friend's hands in her own. 'I know it's been a shock to you, all this, and you've been wonderfully brave, really you have. And I know I couldn't have coped anything like as well with a new baby and a little sister. But when – when it's all over, happen you could think about going back to work, eh?' Molly opened her mouth to protest, but Flo hurried on. 'That new girl they've got at Makepeace's, well, I've heard as how she's not all that popular with the customers and Dolly 'ud like to get rid of her. I know she'd have you back like a shot, and baby William's more settled now, isn't he, with his feeds and everything?'

'No, Flo. It's out of the question. I won't leave him.' Molly shook her head vehemently. She knew she was being somewhat stubborn and Flo was only trying to help, but she would never leave the baby, come what may. 'I told you before, when Mam died, that I wouldn't farm him out.'

'Seems to me as though you'll have no choice,' said Flo, a little less patiently now. 'You can't live off fresh air. And there must be somebody you know who'd look after him without having to go to one of them baby farmers.'

'Yes, there is,' said Molly. 'Maggie Winthrop. She was on about it this teatime. She offered to look after William; she's never wanted to do it before, she says, for anybody else, but Billy and Betty are older now and she thinks I'm a special case.'

'Well, there you are then.'

'But I told her no, just like I'm telling you. I shall never leave William with anybody. Poor little mite; he's lost his mam, and now his dad. He's not going to lose me as well.'

She even found herself smiling at her friend's look of pity, tinged with more than a little exasperation. Flo, in spite of her plain-speaking, had helped to cheer her up. Molly knew too there was a lot of truth in what her friend said. The money would run out. And then what would she do? Molly didn't know, but she would think of something.

'Don't worry ... I'll manage,' she said again.

Chapter 8

Maggie could not understand the girl at all. She would not leave baby William, not even for a couple of hours while she attended her father's funeral. The child was with her at the graveside, wrapped in a white woollen shawl which made a sharp contrast with the stark black of Molly's clothing. Little Em too was dressed all in black, her coat, dress and wide-brimmed hat having been bought – second-hand – at the time of their mother's death. Molly had not wanted her sister to attend Lily's funeral so she had been looked after on that occasion by Mrs Jackson. But this time Molly had insisted they should all be there – herself, Emily and baby William, as a sign of respect, not only to the father they had lost, but in remembrance of their mother, too.

The three of them made a poignant picture: Molly, so pale and fragile-looking of late, her auburn hair, curling beneath the brim of her hat, the only splash of colour about her person; young Emily, even more solemn than usual and perplexed by all that was going on, clinging tightly to her sister's skirt, her ginger hair, of a brighter hue than Molly's, making her freckled face look even whiter; and baby William, not visible beneath the folds of the shawl, but making his presence known by his snuffling cries. He had been quiet in the chapel, but when the clergyman threw the earth on to the coffin and indicated that Molly should do the same, the child gave a piercing shriek, just as though he understood what was going on, poor lamb, thought Maggie.

William Rimmer was being given a Christian burial in the cemetery at Layton, he who had always vowed he was an unbeliever. But even William had paid heed to the proprieties when his wife died and had agreed that a clergyman should be present to conduct her funeral. It was what people would expect and he hadn't seemed to care what happened that day, so overcome by grief as he had been. Now, a brief month later, he was joining Lily in the deep pit which had been dug in the heavy clay soil. It was all so un-believably sad, and Maggie felt the tears welling up in her eyes again. She had shed more tears just lately over this family and its troubles than she had over her own for many a long day.

There were more people attending this funeral of William's than had been at his wife's, mainly because of the goodly number of his workmates from the Tower who had turned up to say their farewells, and the neighbours from the Larkhill area. William had been generally better liked than his wife. Maggie knew that several of their more rough and ready neighbours had thought she was a snooty piece who, in truth, had nothing to be stuck-up about. Yes, William had had lots of acquaintances, folk who had liked him and said he was a good sort, but surprisingly few close friends. He and Lily had been too wrapped up in one another, that was the problem; whereas Molly, with her cheerful disposition and her ability to get along with folk, would make friends wherever she went. Maggie was sure she would, although the lass had little to be cheerful about at the moment. Maggie was the first to admit that the girl had problems, but she couldn't help being a little exasperated with her because it seemed as though she would just not help herself. And, if she were honest, Maggie was rather offended that Molly had turned down her offer to look after the baby.

Only a handful of people attended the funeral meal provided at Mrs O'Hanlan's confectioner's in Talbot Square. It was just a stone's throw away from Molly's previous workplace, but Mrs Makepeace did not have the same facilities as Mrs O'Hanlan – who boasted an elegantly equipped private tearoom – being able to provide only a few tables at the rear of the shop. Anyway, it was the undertaker who had made the arrangements and Molly had fallen in with his plans, especially as the ham and salad tea and the cream cakes were being provided by the generosity of the Tower company. Joe Turner and his wife were there, plus two of the Tower officials, Maggie and Bill Winthrop, Flo and, of course, Molly and her sister and baby brother. Maggie could not help but feel that the little gathering was conspicuous by its lack of any relatives at all.

They had been transported to and from Layton Cemetery, a good mile up Talbot Road, then New Road, by horse-drawn landaus, but they were to make their own way home when the funeral feast was over.

'Let me carry him for you, Molly,' said Maggie,

as they came out of the café. 'You must be tired out, struggling with him all afternoon. I can see he's getting restless – wanting his feed, no doubt. He's getting to be a real big bonny lad, aren't you, William?' Maggie tickled his chin and was rewarded by a gummy grin. Young as he was he seemed a volatile child, quickly changing from crochety cries and whimpers to smiles and gurgles of delight. 'That food you're giving him is certainly bringing him on a treat.'

Molly nodded silently as she handed him over. Maggie was relieved, if a little surprised, that she had agreed to do so. The girl had held William on her lap all through the meal, trying to eat her tea with one hand while restraining the active child with the other. 'Yes, he's a handful,' she said now, with a trace of a smile. 'Getting heavy, I mean, but he's no trouble. Well, very little, but we don't mind, do we Em?'

Em shook her head solemnly. 'He cries and wakes me up sometimes,' she said, 'but I don't mind. It's only 'cause he's hungry, isn't it, Molly?'

'Have you thought any more about what I said?' asked Maggie, falling into step beside the young woman. 'You know, about looking after young William?' She always remembered now, after Molly's correction, to call the child by his full name and not refer to him as Will. It was quite fitting anyway, now that the older William had gone. 'I'd love to have him, and Bill doesn't mind, do you, Bill? I've talked it over with him.'

'No, it's all right with me, lass,' agreed Bill. 'It's up to you, of course, Molly. Mind you, I don't think Maggie'd do it for anybody else, only for you.'

'It's very good of you to offer,' said Molly, at the same time shaking her head, 'but, no, thanks all the same. I can manage. No, I can't leave him. We'll be all right – for a while.'

'For a while, yes, but after that? What then?' asked Maggie, a little more sharply than she intended.

'It's no use, Mrs Winthrop,' said Flo, from the other side of Molly. 'I keep trying to make her see sense, but she won't listen. He'd be all right with Mrs Winthrop, really he would, Molly. And I've been talking to Mrs Makepeace. She says you can have your old job back.'

'No! Leave me alone, can't you, all of you? I'm staying at home with William until ... until he's old enough to go to school. And if we're hard up, well then, that's my business, isn't it? I'll do something. I'll take in washing. I'll – I'll go out cleaning – and take him with me. I don't care what I do, but I'll never leave him. So you can just shut up, the lot of you!' And to the astonishment of Maggie and Bill, Flo and Emily and more than a few passers-by, the girl burst into tears.

'Now look what you've done,' said Bill in a harsh whisper. 'The lass is right. You shouldn't keep on at her.' He put his arm around Molly, pulling her aside into a nearby shop doorway away from inquisitive eyes. 'Go on, lass, have a good cry. Never mind what folks are saying. You'll feel better for it.'

She seemed calmer again after a few moments,

when Bill had wiped her eyes and she had blown her nose. 'Sorry,' she mumbled. 'I didn't mean to do that, but just leave me alone, please.'

Maggie, holding on to baby William, felt guilty and more than a little concerned at the uproar she had caused. She hadn't meant to upset the girl. Still, it might do her the world of good to have a cry and Maggie was sure the floodgates would open again once Molly reached home. She had been far too detached since that dreadful night when the policeman called.

Molly started to weep again as soon as she arrived home, regardless of Flo who had come in with her and who immediately began to busy herself making a pot of tea at the other side of the kitchen. Em had asked if she could go and play with Sarah, who would, by now, be home from school, and Molly had readily agreed. Anything to help the little girl to put the sadness of the day to the back of her mind.

'That is, if you don't mind, Maggie,' she had asked a little timorously, feeling ashamed of her outbreak of emotion.

'No, it's all right with me, lass. I'll send her back in an hour or so.' Maggie's answer had been rather curt and Molly could not blame her. The woman had only been trying to help and she really did have a heart of gold. But Molly was getting so tired of people trying to run her life for her.

'Let it all out, luv,' said Flo after a few moments. 'It'll do you good. Don't mind me. But give me the baby, for goodness' sake. You're giving him a right shower bath and no mistake.'

Molly gave a weak smile as Flo took William off her lap. 'He's ready for his bottle, and he'll need changing.'

'Then I'd best see what I can do, hadn't I?' said Flo brightly. 'It'll be good practice for me for one of these days. Just tell me what to do and I'll do it. You sit there and drink your tea.'

'No ... no, I'm all right now,' said Molly. She wiped her face with her handkerchief, then stood up and took off her coat and hat, hanging them on a peg behind the door. 'Sorry about that, but I feel better now; much better than I felt earlier, at any rate.'

There had been a tight knot of tension at the heart of her, but the scalding tears that had broken forth again once she was in her own home had been cleansing and healing. Her tension had gone and with it much of her pain and sorrow and anxiety. 'I'll make William's bottle while you nurse him a bit. Or have a go at changing him, if you feel like it.' She smiled again at her friend, feeling her lips respond in a way they hadn't done for ages and she felt that the smile might even have reached her eyes. 'There's a clean napkin on the clotheshorse, and you can put the wet one in the bucket under the sink. I don't think he'll be anything worse than wet.'

'Flo, thanks for putting up with me,' said Molly a little later, when William was cleaned and fed and lying in his pram. She leaned forward in her chair, looking intently at her friend. 'I've been a pain, haven't I, just lately? Not wanting to face up to anything. And I feel dreadful about going on at

Maggie like that. I don't know what came over me. Whatever must she think of me?'

'She won't think anything,' replied Flo, 'and neither do I. You've been under a lot of strain lately, Moll. Good grief, it's unbelievable what you've just gone through.'

'And it's only just beginning,' said Molly, speaking more rationally than she had at any time since her father died. 'I know it'll be a struggle, Flo, looking after the pair of them. But they're my responsibility – Em and William – until they're ... well, until they're grown-up, I suppose; nobody else's. That's why I can't hand them over to Maggie. Yes, I know Em's round there now. I don't mind that – it's for the child's sake rather than mine, to take her mind off things. But I couldn't bear to see William growing up thinking that Maggie is his mother and not me.'

'But you're not his mother.'

'No, but you know what I mean. He's mine, mine and Em's. We've got to do the best we can for him.'

And Molly knew it would not be the best thing for William to grow up in the slapdash environment of Maggie's home. Molly felt that her housekeeping left a lot to be desired, probably because the girl was comparing it with her own mother's fastidious ways. Young Billy and Betty were quite often seen playing out in the street with a slice of jam and bread in their hands, instead of sitting respectably at the table in the way Molly and Em had always been made to do. Molly was surprised her mother had allowed Em to go round there so often, although she had been so tired towards the end of her pregnancy that she supposed she had had no choice. And Maggie would have insisted; she was a most forthright and forceful person. There were so many of them too; Billy and Betty, Sarah, Arthur, aged eleven and Tom, who had recently started work as a butcher's assistant in town. To say nothing of Maggie's married daughter, Alice, who often came round with her two young babies. A haphazard household, where pots and lace curtains and jammy faces were often left unwashed, newspapers were piled high in corners and dust accumulated on cupboard tops so thick you could write your name in it. A happy household, none the less, where love abounded, but not the surroundings in which Molly wanted her baby brother, given so unexpectedly into her charge, to be reared. Her loyalty to Maggie, however, stopped Molly from revealing her exact reasons for her refusal of the woman's offer.

'Maggie has quite enough to do anyway,' she said now, in way of explanation, 'and, as well as that, I have to admit she's rather bossy. Well, you've heard her, haven't you? I've got to live my own life, Flo, in the way I want to. Well, no ... that's not strictly true, is it? It's not the way I would have chosen, but life has taken an unexpected turn, hasn't it, and I've got to go along with it? But, I can't be told what I must do. I've got to sort things out for myself.'

'You didn't mean it, did you,' asked Flo, 'when you said you would take in washing, or go out cleaning?'

'No, not really,' admitted Molly with a wry

grin. 'Not that there's anything wrong with that. Lots of women have to do it.'

'But your mother never resorted to it, did she?' said Flo. 'Nor has mine. Your mam wouldn't've liked it, not for herself nor for you.'

'No, that's true enough.'

'Then what will you do? I don't want to nag you, but you really must try to think about it. You'll have to earn some money somehow.'

'And it doesn't grow on trees,' Molly added, smiling sadly. 'That's what Mam used to say. I expect it's something all mothers say. And I have been thinking about it, Flo, in spite of what I said. At least, I've got an idea. What I thought I might do is open a shop.'

Flo gaped at her. 'A shop? But where? You'll hardly be able to afford the rent on the house, never mind a shop.'

'Here, in Mam's parlour,' said Molly. 'A house shop, that's what I mean. Selling all sorts of odds and ends that people run out of. Sarah came round to borrow a cup of sugar for her mam – it was just before Dad died – and I thought then that that was what we needed in this area; a house shop. That's another thing about Maggie: she's always running out of something or other. She doesn't mean to, I suppose, but she's so busy and then she forgets. She was always borrowing stuff off Mam. Mind you, we always got it back.'

Flo nodded. 'Yes, some women are like that, a bit feckless. My mam isn't, and I know yours wasn't. But d'you think you'd be able to make enough with this house shop to make ends meet?'

'I can but try. I've only just had the idea. I've

been mulling it over in my mind for the last day or so and I think it's something that might go well round here. I've seen them in other places, but there isn't one near here. The nearest shops are on Talbot Road – quite a way to go if you suddenly run out of something.'

'Only down the street and round the corner.'

'Quite a long way all the same if you want to do some baking and you find you've no baking powder, for instance, or you're short of an egg.'

'And will you stock all these things?' asked Flo. 'My mam gets our eggs at the market.'

'So do I, but I thought I could get a few extra and have them in stock, as I was saying, for the sort of folk who run out of things. They'd have to pay a bit extra, mind you; a ha'penny or so, but they'd be paying for the convenience of it, you see.'

'Mmm... You're sounding like a real business-woman, Molly.'

'Not at all, not yet. But ideas keep coming to me. I thought I'd have some sweets as well, for the kiddies to spend their Saturday pennies on.'

'And where are you going to get all this stuff – all your stock? I say, that sounds real posh, doesn't it? Stock – like a proper shop.' Flo gave a little laugh, but Molly was not laughing.

'I'm not a little girl playing at shops, you know,' she answered, a shade indignantly. 'I've got to make some money, as you keep reminding me. There's a big warehouse down Central Drive way, I believe. I thought I'd have a trip down there and see what I can find. I can load lots of things in the pram. There's a big empty space underneath where the baby lies, and I always put my shopping there.'

'You'd be able to load a lot more if the pram was empty,' said Flo. 'I tell you what: if you don't want to say anything to Maggie just yet – and I don't think you do, do you?' – Molly shook her head – 'then why not let me look after William when it's my half-day? That's tomorrow, isn't it? I could come here and see to him and to your Em when she comes home from school. It would give you a free afternoon to get your stock sorted out. I wasn't laughing at you, Moll, really I wasn't. I think you're ever so brave, and adventurous an' all. It sounds like a real good idea to me.'

'Thanks, Flo,' said Molly. 'I think I will take you up on your offer. I'm sorry as well – I didn't mean to snap at you. I'm still a bit on edge. I dare say I will be for a while yet. And thanks for coming today. I do appreciate it. How did you manage to get the time off? I thought Miss Perkins might've been funny about it.'

'Oh no, she can be quite understanding, can Miss Amelia, 'specially when it's something like this. And she always liked you, Molly, when you were working on the terrace. She's real upset about ... what's happened. She's been a lot easier to get on with lately because – I nearly forgot to tell you – she's selling up.'

'She's giving up the shop?'

'Yes, she's sold the business. She's getting on for sixty – at least I think she is – so I suppose she thinks it's time she finished. And the new people – two sisters, she says – are taking over next month.'

'Goodness, that's a surprise,' said Molly. 'What about you, Flo? Will you still have your job?'

'Oh, yes; Miss Amelia says they're quite willing to take on the existing staff – that's me and Minnie – if we want to stay. That's all I know at the moment, but Miss Amelia says we're both good workers so there shouldn't be any problem. Anyway, that's enough about me. I'll come round tomorrow then, shall I, as soon as I've finished work? I'll have a sandwich before I leave instead of going home for dinner. I think you're ever so brave,' Flo said again. 'It'll be a step in the dark, as they say, won't it? But I hope it'll work out for you.'

'I hope so too,' replied Molly. 'I've got to give it a try, whatever happens.'

The warehouse was crammed from floor to ceiling with the largest assortment of goods Molly had ever seen in her life, all displayed in open-top boxes. A bald-headed man in a brown overall appeared almost as soon as she entered, having left the perambulator at the entrance.

'Hello, young lady. And what can I do for you? I don't think I've seen you here before, have I? I'm Albert Ogden.' He held out his hand. 'How can I help you?'

'How do you do, Mr Ogden?' Molly shook his hand. 'No, I haven't been here before. I'm Molly Rimmer – Miss Rimmer – and I'm starting a little shop in my home. I want – well, a bit of everything, I suppose.'

'Then you'll find it here, that's for sure. We're short of nothing we've got, as the saying goes.'

The man beamed at her. 'I'll leave you to browse around and if you want any help just give me a shout. Here you are.' He handed her a big cardboard box. 'Put it all in there. It'll hold plenty and you can have another one if you need it.'

Molly was mesmerised by the hundreds of articles on display and so spoiled for choice she did not know where to begin. It all looked so tempting. Her eyes were immediately drawn to the sweets. She had always had a sweet tooth, although her mother had never allowed her to overindulge, but she decided she would leave the luxury items till later and concentrate on the essentials. She started with household goods: reels of cotton, packets of pins and needles, cards of shirt buttons, elastic, small balls of darning wool, matches, bootlaces, candles, tapers... Then on to kitchen items: salt, soap, baking powder, tins of Colman's mustard, jars of Bovril, packets of Bird's blancmange and jelly crystals. Rather a luxury, these last items, but housewives who came in to buy a box of matches, for instance, might be tempted. She put in a couple of packets of each, then hesitated by the tea and sugar. These were in huge barrels, to be sold loose, not ready packaged as were most of the goods.

Mr Ogden appeared at her side. 'Now, how are you doing? You'd like some tea and sugar, would you?'

'Yes, I think so,' said Molly unsurely. 'But the trouble is, I don't want very much. I thought I could sell it in small amounts. You know – in a little paper bag, or even a cup, if they bring their own – for people who find they've run out of tea or sugar.'

'A splendid idea, Miss Rimmer. I can see you've got your head screwed on the right way. I'll let you have – what shall we say? – five pounds of tea to be going on with: Brooke Bond's blended – I think that'll be the best for you. And the same amount of sugar. Is that all right?'

'Yes, thank you, that'll be grand.' Molly was making quick calculations in her head, working out if she could afford it; she had set aside a good portion of the insurance money for this venture. She was pleasantly surprised at how helpful Mr Ogden was being. He was no doubt hoping she would come again and he dealt only with cash on the nail. A large notice on the wall stated this and Molly decided she would adopt the same policy in her shop; no credit, or 'putting it on the slate' as it was often called.

'Now, if I may make a suggestion,' said Mr Ogden, 'what about a few medicinal remedies? For when they can't get to the chemist's shop. You'll find they'll sell like hot cakes.'

Molly, on Mr Ogden's advice, invested in headache powders, senna pods, Epsom salts, Beecham's pills, Carter's liver pills and a few packets of Fisherman's Friends, the well-known throat lozenges which were manufactured up the coast at Fleetwood. And, lastly, a variety of sweets for the younger customers she hoped would come, and for their mothers, too, who might indulge themselves with a penny chocolate bar along with the more necessary items. She chose lollipops, toffee bars, liquorice sticks, aniseed balls, pear-drops, acid-drops, dolly mixtures and Cadbury's chocolate bars.

It was amazing how quickly the time had flown and at the end of an hour Molly's pram was full to overflowing – it was a good job she had agreed to leave William at home with Flo – but her purse was, alas, empty.

'Thank you for your custom, Miss Rimmer,' said Mr Ogden, after he had helped her to load her purchases. 'And the best of luck with your new venture. I hope I will see you again.'

'Thank you; I'm sure you will,' replied Molly, smiling at him.

She felt more hopeful than she had been for ages. Not since Queen Victoria's Jubilee night had she felt so optimistic. But that was a time she would not let herself think about. Whenever thoughts strayed into her mind of the personable young man she had known so briefly she immediately banished them. She pushed away the intrusive thoughts of him now as she wheeled her heavy perambulator back along Central Drive towards her home, forcing herself instead to think about the little shop she was going to open. A new beginning, hopefully, for them all.

Chapter 9

Joss had begun his search, the week after Molly had failed to turn up at their proposed meeting place outside North Pier, just opposite there, at the hub of the Blackpool scene, Talbot Square.

His first call had been at the premises of Mrs O'Hanlan, a prestigious-looking confectionery business with an elegant tearoom at the rear which he could not help but admire. He had been tempted to stop for a cup of tea, but after his enquiry about the young woman named Molly had drawn a blank – as he had guessed it might; he could hardly hope to strike lucky the first time – he had decided to continue his quest.

Talbot Road, Clifton Street, Abingdon Street, Lytham Street, Church Street ... confectioners' shops abounded, both large and small, in the quarter square mile or so of streets to the rear of Talbot Square, but no one, it seemed, had heard of Molly or recognised the sketch of her that Joss proffered. Some of the people he asked, harassed shop assistants and waitresses, or snooty cashiers behind their oak desks had looked at him as though he were somewhat lacking in the top storey, as he was beginning to think he might well be.

He looked further south the following week – Bank Hey Street, Victoria Street, Coronation Street – but with no more success. He had thought the proprietors and staff of these establishments might know one another, be on friendly terms, even, seeing as they were in the same line of business. But that did not seem to be the case. Occasionally he came across a shop with the same name as one he had visited previously; successful businessmen – or women – these, with more than one branch in the town. For instance, Mr Ramsden of Talbot Road and Church Street also had a shop in Fishergate, Preston, which Joss had visited occasionally. By and large, though, the shops operated independently, jealously guarding their own success and their own clients. They were not interested in where an unknown young woman might work if she was not employed by them.

Central Drive, the area he decided to try next, was much further out, and by the third week of his search Joss was beginning to feel more than a little disillusioned. Was he, after all, pursuing an impossible dream? It could be that Molly had forgotten all about him, that she had changed her mind as soon as she left him on that Jubilee night and had never had any intention of seeing him again. But, deep down, he could not believe that; or was it, he asked himself, that he did not want to believe it?

All his family, his mother and father and his two brothers, were staying at Cunliffe House this weekend. Up until now, Percy and Edgar in particular had been very curious as to Joss's whereabouts and his reasons for dashing off to Blackpool every Saturday. He had told them that he wanted to paint. The white lie had sufficed as they'd never showed any interest in the fruits of his labours. But this weekend his two elder brothers were all set to have a good time, a well-earned break, they declared, from the hard work they had been putting in at the mill. There had been a backlog of orders which had resulted in longer working hours, both for the mill hands and the office and warehouse staff. Joss, in the printing and design shed, had not been affected by this, but he realised that if he did not wish to incur his brothers' displeasure any further – already there had been hints about Joss's job being 'money for jam' – then he must humour them and go along with at least some of their plans for their weekend's entertainment. He did not want to be seen as a spoilsport or a wet blanket. He was neither of those things; he could enjoy himself as much as the next man when he felt inclined. But as soon as he'd met Molly the pursuit of pleasure for his own personal gratification had begun to seem meaningless. He had felt by the end of that evening that he wanted to share the rest of his life with her.

He had known for some time the sort of girl he wanted; a girl who was not only charming, good-humoured and spirited, but natural and gentle as well, a girl who could relate to anything or anyone, not just to his own rather snobbish and insular background. In short, someone very much like his own mother, Charlotte. A tall order, he would have thought; then, on Jubilee night, he believed he might have found her. He had had a few minor flings with rich highly suitable young women, some of them conceited and condescending, some of them just plain boring. Priscilla Cartwright, however, was not like that. She was a nice, pleasant girl and he was fond of her, but he knew, alas, that she was not the girl for him. At last he had found the girl of his dreams. Now he wondered if he had been deluding himself.

At all events, he had agreed to meet Percy and Edgar at the entrance to the Tower towards the end of the afternoon. That gave him time for a search in the Central Drive area of the town. He knew instinctively, however, as soon as he began his quest, that this was not where Molly had been employed. It was too far from her home, for one thing and also it did not feel right. He had got the impression she had worked in a more salubrious area than this. But where? She had given him no clue at all.

Dispiritedly he trudged back, past Central Station, the Palatine and the Royal hotels, remembering to put more of a spring in his step and a smile on his face before he reached the Tower or his brothers would accuse him of being a killjoy.

'We've only just arrived,' said Percy, slapping him on the back. Joss was glad about that or he might have had to suffer an inquisition about what had taken him so long. 'Come on, little brother. Let's go and sample the delights o' t'Tower, eh lad?' His Lancashire accent was assumed and Joss gave a polite little laugh in acknowledgement. Percy considered himself no end of a wag.

It was not the first time by any means that Joss

had been inside the Tower building, although he had not been as frequent a visitor as his two brothers. Opened in 1894, three years previously, the Tower boasted an aquarium, a menagerie, a circus ring with a sinking floor and water tanks beneath it, for a stupendous final scene to the show, a ballroom, and various bars and refreshment rooms; not to mention the lifts installed by the well-known Otis Elevator Company to transport people the 500 feet to the top of the Tower. It was, in reality, 518 feet to the crow's nest and flagpole at the top, but the lifts did not ascend quite so far.

The chairman of the Blackpool Tower Company and the prime mover behind its conception was Sir John Bickerstaffe, a member of one of Blackpool's most prominent fishing families. Sir John was determined that the sixpence entrance fee to the Tower should provide the customers with a glimpse into an exciting and glamorous world, far removed from their ordinary workaday lives. Each Saturday special excursion trains ran from towns in east Lancashire, including Preston, to Blackpool Central Station – a mere stone's throw away from the Tower – the admission price to the Tower being included in the half-crown fare. Mill workers in plenty filled the trains, returning on the home-bound train at around one thirty in the morning. Joss and his brothers, however, having their own house in Blackpool – albeit at the other end of the town – would not be returning to Preston until the following afternoon.

The sixpence entrance fee meant little to the

three Cunliffe brothers, whereas to their father's employees it would be quite a sizeable amount; reasonable enough, though, when you considered all you got for it. Percy and Edgar, however, were determined to get true value for their money. Joss accompanied them, first of all, through the simulated limestone caverns of the aquarium, where fish of all shapes, sizes and hues swam silently through the green waters. It was cool and peaceful down there, unlike the menagerie, which they visited next. The cages were heavily barred and the animals, apart from the bears and a bored-looking lion, not terribly fearsome. Joss felt sorry for the poor creatures although Jacko, the baboon, seemed to be happy enough displaying his repertoire of tricks to a crowd of screaming, delighted children. Joss was glad to escape to the roof gardens where real palm trees, vines and floral plants flourished in abundance, and an orchestra played for the entertainment of the more discerning ladies and gentlemen who reclined on the comfortable seats.

On the same floor as the roof gardens was the Old English village, a medley of mock-Tudor black-and-white houses, leaning towards one another at crazy angles – a church too, and shops where visitors could buy souvenirs and presents to take home for a penny or twopence. Some considered it vulgar and phoney, but who was to say what an old English village really looked like anyway? And it did attract thousands of holidaymakers – residents too, in small numbers – during the height of the season. From this floor, also, you could take the lift to the top of the Tower for an extra 'nimble sixpence', a phrase coined by Sir John Bickerstaffe himself.

'I don't think we'll bother today, eh, lads?' said Percy, in reply to an overeager attendant anxious to lure them into the lift. 'We'll go and get "us teas", shall us, before we see what's on offer in the ballroom?'

Above the village a staircase led to a balcony with an outdoor tearoom, providing a pleasant view over the sea and promenade and, on the other side, a view of the bear pit. 'There you are, a grand sea view and you can watch the antics of Bruin and his missus, an' all,' said Percy, leading his brothers to a vacant table. 'What more could you want, eh?'

'And it's plenty high enough for me,' said Joss. 'It's a splendid view from here without going right to the top.' Little did he know that in a few days' time a disastrous fire would prevent anyone from venturing up there.

They could see practically the whole length of the promenade, stretching away on either side of them, and a vast expanse of golden sand dotted with bathing huts, ice cream carts, a Punch and Judy show, deck-chairs, rock sellers and hundreds and hundreds of people. To the south were South Pier and Victoria Pier jutting out over the sea; and, to the north, the new promenade under construction, the gradually crumbling cliffs with Uncle Tom's Cabin perched near the edge, and further back, just visible, their own Cunliffe House.

Joss averted his eyes away from North Pier and

Uncle Tom's Cabin, concentrating instead on the menu offered by a young waitress in a black dress and stiffly starched white apron and cap. 'A selection of sandwiches, I think, please, miss. Is that all right for you, Percy, Eddie? Salmon, ham and potted meat. And some cream cakes, please.'

'And lashings of tea – hot, strong and sweet, just the way I like my women,' added Percy with a saucy wink at the waitress who, Joss was pleased to notice, did not bat an eyelid.

'Very well, gentlemen. Will that be all? I'll bring a selection of cream cakes, then you can choose.' Her remarks were addressed to Joss, to whom she had handed the menu, and she gave him a quiet smile; but she paid no attention to Percy.

'Snooty piece, that one,' he observed. Percy hated to be ignored. 'I'd like to show her a thing or two; bring her down a few pegs. Damn it all, she's only a flippin' waitress; she doesn't own the place.'

'How do you know?' laughed Edgar. 'For all we know she might be the chairman's daughter. I thought she looked very nice.' Edgar was always more inclined than Percy to see the best in people.

'Don't waste your time on such as her, Eddie lad,' replied Percy. 'There'll be much better bits of fluff on offer in the ballroom later on. I can't wait...'

Oh dear, thought Joss, listening to the interchange between his brothers, with Percy, as usual, doing most of the talking. He had almost forgotten what an evening in their company entailed: loud laughter, lewd comments and a fair bit of drinking, although, when it came to chasing after the girls his brothers were 'all mouth and trousers'.

Percy, in reality, was engaged to a young lady at home in Preston, Hannah Watson, the daughter of a mill owner in the Stanley Street area. The mill owners, by and large, stuck together, endeavouring to strengthen their positions and widen their contacts by negotiating marriages between their offspring. Percy and Hannah had been engaged for over a year now and plans were underway for them to marry this coming autumn. Percy seemed quite content to go along with it, as did Hannah, and they appeared fond enough of one another on the rare occasions they were seen together; but Joss knew it was not a love match, such as he would desire – would insist on – for himself. His own friendship with Priscilla Cartwright was no love match either, but Joss could see that coming to an end before long, by mutual agreement.

Edgar, at the moment, was 'footloose and fancy-free' as the saying went. Their father had not done any marriage bargaining as yet with his middle son; neither had Edgar shown much inclination for finding a partner for himself.

The Tower ballroom was considered by many to be the *pièce de résistance* of the whole building. The Tower company had spared no expense with its frescoed ceilings and crystal chandeliers, gilded balconies, marble pillars and, most magnificent of all, the parquet floor consisting of small blocks of mahogany, oak and walnut, forming an intricate tessellated pattern. Every

187

night throughout the year it would reverberate to the rhythm of Oliver Gaggs and his orchestra, and the pounding of thousands of feet, daintily clad in dancing pumps or, not so delicately, in working boots and heavy shoes; the floor of the Tower ballroom could withstand them all.

Joss's heart was not really in the evening; neither in the music nor the elegant surroundings nor the company. He had danced a few times, choosing pleasant, not too showy, young ladies for his partners, and he had taken part in the progressive barn dance. He felt bound to show at least some semblance of enjoying himself. The less his brothers knew of his true state of mind, the better. Although, with regard to the elusive Molly, Joss was beginning, reluctantly, to think that he might be pursuing a dream. What did that song say about pretty bubbles in the air? 'Then like my dreams they fade and die...' He and Molly had danced to the tune at Uncle Tom's Cabin, and the orchestra had played it this evening. Joss was deliberating with himself that he would search for just one more Saturday – that would make four in all – then, regrettably, he would have to admit defeat. Deep in the heart of him he knew he would have to be sensible. There was no point in chasing a shadow, a memory. Maybe that was how he would have to try to think of Molly, as a lovely memory. He was aware that his obsession with finding her was affecting everything: his work, his leisure time, his family relationships. He knew he would have to pull himself together; but he would allow himself one more weekend.

'Hey, little brother, come back to earth. You're miles away.' He started as Percy nudged his elbow, almost making him spill his beer. 'Just look over there, in that corner by the pillar. Our brother and ... doesn't that young woman he's with look familiar to you?'

Edgar had been missing from the trio for quite a while and Joss had noticed him dancing a few times with the same girl. A small dark-haired girl who, as he glanced at her now, sitting in the corner of the Long Bar, her head inclined towards Eddie's, certainly did look familiar. Joss had seen only her back view when the two of them were dancing, but now he knew exactly who she was. She looked rather different; her hair, usually scraped back in a tight bun to keep it clear of the machinery, was hanging loose, almost to her shoulders, but she was recognisable as Betsy Pringle, one of the workers at Cunliffe Mill.

'Yes,' agreed Joss. 'I know who she is.' He spoke matter-of-factedly, not wanting to make too much of an issue of it. It was Eddie's business, after all, not his brothers', whom he spent the evening with. 'She works at our mill.'

Percy frowned, then, 'Good God, so she does!' he cried, slapping his hand resoundingly on the table top. 'She's one of our weavers. I knew she looked familiar, but I thought perhaps I knew her from ... somewhere else. She looks different; not a bad-looking lass really, out of her overall. All the same...'

'She's called Betsy Pringle,' said Joss. 'A good worker, from what I've heard. She's in charge of quite a few looms. A nice girl; our Eddie could do much worse,' he added with a sly grin, as much to get his brother going as anything. 'It's about time he found himself a young lady.'

'What the hell are you on about? I should hope our Eddie's got more sense than that. She looks as though she might be all right for the night, but as for anything else...' Percy shook his head. 'How d'you know her name, anyway? Blessed if I know any of 'em.'

'I've met her a few times,' Joss smiled. 'She's been on errands to the printing shed. I tell you, she's a nice lass. I thought she was friendly with Saul Rigby, one of the lads who works for me. But it looks as though I was wrong, doesn't it, or she may well have transferred her affections?' He nodded towards the couple who were now making their way back to the ballroom floor, Edgar's arm tucked companionably around the young woman's waist. Edgar did not so much as glance in his brothers' direction; it was doubtful that he even noticed them there, or else he did not care what they might think.

'He'll send her off with a flea in her ear after tonight, you'll see,' said Percy, dismissively. But that was where he was proved wrong.

Joss and Percy left at half-past eleven to walk home along the promenade. When Joss went to tell Edgar they were leaving, his brother announced, with his arm still protectively around the young woman, that he was staying to see Betsy safely to her train.

'Good evening, Mr Joss,' the girl said shyly.

'Good evening, Miss Pringle,' Joss replied. But

Percy, striding ahead, had refused to say good night to either of them.

'Read all about it, read all about it...' called the newspaper seller outside Central Station the following Saturday afternoon. Joss stopped to read the headlines on the billboard. 'TOWER ABLAZE. GREAT DAMAGE DONE. MIDNIGHT SCENES IN THE STREETS.' He bought a copy of the *Blackpool Gazette* and walked across the promenade to find an empty bench where he could sit and read it.

He read about the incalculable damage that had been done to the Tower, estimated by some at £20,000, considering the loss that the company would sustain during what was the height of the holiday season. It would be impossible to get the lifts working again before the end of September, and the top platforms of the structure would need overhauling and strengthening. 'It is the most serious conflagration we have had in Blackpool or the Fylde in the whole course of its history,' this section of the report concluded.

Joss turned round to gaze up at the tall structure of the Tower. It looked pretty much the same as before, although if you looked carefully, you could see evidence of burning around the woodwork of the veranda, the level to which the lifts had ascended. But there would be no one up there now, except workmen, to take advantage of the view. And to think that he had been in there only last Saturday, amidst all the hustle and bustle and gaiety, mused Joss.

'Bad do, that, isn't it?' A middle-aged man who

had sat down on the seat next to Joss nodded at the headlines in the paper, then pointed behind him to the Tower.

'Yes, very unfortunate,' agreed Joss.

'Thousands of pounds worth of damage,' continued the man, who sounded a real Job's comforter if ever there was one, thought Joss. 'I've heard as how the worst damage was done by the lift crashing down – well, the weights that balance it, at any rate. Would you believe, one of 'em crashed right through the glass roof and ended up in one of the circus boxes. The director's box, no less, but he weren't in it at the time, of course. Anyroad, they're leaving it there, so I've heard. It'd cost too much, y'see, to move it. They'll need a whole new safety system for them lifts; they can't risk it happening again, see. Just imagine, if the lift had been full of folk. It doesn't bear thinking about.'

'No, that's quite true,' replied Joss. 'I haven't heard about anyone being killed, though, so I suppose that's something to be thankful for.'

'Oh no, that's where you're wrong,' said the man. 'One poor fellow copped it. It mentions it in there, on t'next page.' The *Gazette* report was really a series of accounts by various eyewitnesses who had been at the scene, giving a variety of facts and differing points of view. 'I reckon they're playing it down, 'cause it wasn't really the fire that caused it. No, he was struck down by summat falling on his head; in the wrong place at the wrong time, y'might say. He worked there, at the Tower, a sort of odd-job man, I believe. I know somebody as knew him. Will Rimmer was his name. Nice chap, they say, he'd do anybody a good turn. Well, he's done the last of his good deeds, poor feller.'

'Yes, indeed,' replied Joss. 'That's very sad – most tragic.'

'And he'd only recently lost his wife ... in childbirth,' the man added, lowering his voice and nodding sagely. 'And now his daughter's left with a young baby to bring up and she's only a bit of a lass herself, eighteen or so. Eeh, I don't know; there's always trouble for somebody, isn't there?'

Joss agreed again that there was indeed. But he decided he had heard enough about Will Rimmer, whoever he was. People were dying every day, often as the result of tragic accidents. Families were bereaved and left to cope as best they could. You couldn't take upon yourself the problems of the whole world. He had his own problems – insignificant, maybe, compared with those of ... this Will Rimmer's daughter, for instance, but serious enough to Joss. He stood up, nodding a farewell to his lugubrious acquaintance. 'Good afternoon. It's been pleasant talking to you.'

Joss strode away along the promenade, depositing the rolled-up newspaper in the first litter bin he came to. He did not want to read any more about Thursday night's catastrophe. Today he would continue his search for Molly in Dickson Road and the area around Talbot Road Station. After all, he was pretty sure that she lived in this vicinity; it was quite likely her place of work was here too. But after a couple of hours he knew that his mission, once again, had been fruitless. He was not going to find her; it was doubtful that he would ever find her.

He made his way back to the station, frustrated, sick at heart and deeply disappointed, but realising, all the same, that he could not go on frittering away his time and energy in this futile quest. He had intended staying in Blackpool overnight. Now, on an impulse, he decided to cut his losses and return home. And as for Molly ... he smiled reminiscently at the thought of her. She would always be there, at the back of his mind, as a lovely memory. He fingered the sketch of her, now somewhat crumpled, in his jacket pocket. There was one thing, however, that he could, and would, do. He would finish the portrait of her he had started and he would make sure it was the best painting he had ever done.

Chapter 10

Molly pursed her lips and frowned as she looked round the crowded little parlour. The three-piece suite would have to go. That was a pity; her mam had been very proud of the brown plush armchairs and sofa stuffed with horsehair, although they had always been far too cumbersome for the small room. One of the chairs, perhaps, could go in the living room – both of them, maybe, at a pinch – instead of the sagging armchairs that were there at the moment. But all the surplus furniture would have to go to the saleroom to make room for the trestle table Molly had ordered from the same place and which was being delivered later that day.

On a sudden whim she decided to keep her mother's china cabinet and the tea service and ornaments it contained. She had been tempted to sell the lot. She might well still have to do so if the proposed house shop did not prove to be the success she hoped it would be. But for the time being the cabinet could stay where it was. Molly knew that her mother would 'turn in her grave', as folks in their neighbourhood were always saying, at the plans her daughter had in mind for her beloved parlour.

The items that Molly had bought from Albert Ogden's warehouse were stacked in boxes in the living room-cum-kitchen. Several times Molly had seen Em curiously lifting the lid of a box and taking a peek at the contents, or just standing there staring at all their newly acquired 'stock', the evidence that the Rimmer family, very soon, would be real shopkeepers.

'Just like Donnelly's,' the little girl had said excitedly, when Molly had told her of the plans she had.

Molly was glad that the idea of the shop, whether it proved to be successful or not, was helping to take Em's mind away from the double bereavement she had suffered. Although, in truth, Emily seemed to be coping much better with her loss than was Molly. She was much younger, of course, and she still had the warmth and security of her big sister's love surrounding her, and, with the touch of self-centredness that all children possessed, she was thus able to take her mind away from unpleasant thoughts, fixing them instead on this exciting new venture. Whereas Molly still grieved. She could not even now entirely grasp the enormity of what had happened to her family, and at night, alone in the quiet darkness, she was unable to stem the floods of tears that soaked the pillow. This new enterprise was helping, however, during the daytime hours to focus her mind in another direction; and what with coping with baby William and Emily and all the household chores – washing, ironing, cooking, cleaning, shopping – every minute of her day was filled.

She hastened to tell Em that their shop would, in reality, be nothing like the department store Donnelly's, That it would, in fact, not be recognised as a shop at all, except by the folk who used it.

'We'll put a notice in the window to tell people we're selling things,' Molly explained, 'and we'll have to take down the lace curtains so that they can see inside. And we can put the table near the window, with a display of some of the ... er, merchandise on it. That's a big word, isn't it, Em? It just means the things we are selling – a posh way of saying it. What I'm trying to say, love, is that we can't have a proper shop window. It'll be just what they call a house shop.'

Molly knew that if she started to make any drastic alterations – always supposing she could afford it, which she couldn't – she would need to have plans drawn up and get permission from the landlord. Who would more than likely refuse anyway. No, she would have to start in a very small way and see what happened.

'Like a market stall, you mean?' asked her sister.

'Yes, just like a market stall,' said Molly. 'Except that we'll be selling a bit of all sorts of things. Rather like those bring-and-buy stalls they have at church dos.' They had both, on occasions, been to such events.

'And can I help?' Emily asked, her brown eyes so alight with enthusiasm that Molly felt a pang of unease. How quickly, it seemed, children could be distracted from their troubles when something new captured their interest. It seemed disrespectful, somehow, although she was glad of her sister's interest.

'I don't see why not,' Molly answered guardedly.

'When you come home from school you could help for a little while – when I'm busy with William, perhaps.'

'And Saturdays and Sundays?' asked the little girl, still very eagerly.

'Saturdays, yes,' said Molly. 'I'm not too sure about Sundays.'

Molly was undecided as to whether she should open the shop on what was considered by many to be the Sabbath Day; the one special day in the week when no work was supposed to be done. Except by harassed housewives, she thought – those who could afford it, at any rate – who cooked a roast dinner: meat and two veg and gravy and all the trimmings, plus pudding and custard to follow. Her own mother had always cooked an extra special meal on a Sunday, and Molly, since Lily's death, had tried to do the same although that had not been easy in their straitened circumstances. To Lily, of course, there had not been anything particularly holy about Sunday, and Molly, also, did not regard the day as anything special. A time for a rest, maybe, if you were lucky enough to get it, but she knew she would not be so fortunate. And she did not see why she should not sell goods on a Sunday if she wanted to do so. It might be the time, surely, when housewives found they had run out of something or other; custard powder or gravy browning, for instance.

'You won't want to be helping me all the time, though, Em,' she told her sister. She knew it was all new and exciting to the child at the moment, but when faced with the reality of it the novelty might soon wear off. 'You'll want some time to play with your friends, won't you, especially Sarah? But I dare say I'll be glad of a bit of assistance now and again. You're already a great help with William, aren't you? Have you noticed how he smiles now when he sees you?'

The little girl beamed proudly at this. Baby William was taking more notice of his surroundings now, smiling and gurgling a lot of the time, but also grizzling more as well. He was definitely not an easy child and Molly knew her hands would soon be full to overflowing with the extra work that the shop would bring. But it was something she could do in her own home and she was determined to make a go of it.

As far as Sunday opening was concerned, Molly knew there was someone who would disapprove most strongly: Maggie Winthrop. Maggie did not go to church herself, but she believed it should be a day set apart, except for the ritual Sunday dinner and, of course, the event of anyone wanting to enter the world or depart from it. Maggie, in fact, seemed to disapprove of the whole idea of the shop.

'You want your head seeing to, lass,' had been her first remark a few days ago, on hearing of the venture. 'A new baby to bring up, and your little sister, to say nothing of all that housework you seem so keen on doing. How the heck d'you think you're going to have time to run a shop an' all?'

Molly understood, however, that Maggie's remarks were underlined with more than a touch of resentment. The woman was still peeved because

Molly had not taken up her offer to look after baby William. She could well have reminded her friend that, had she decided to go back to work, she would still have had to see to the house, and the children, when they were not with Maggie. But she had replied instead, 'I'm young and strong, and I'll manage somehow. Anyway, I know it's what I've got to do. And our Em's going to help me. She's really looking forward to it. And anything that helps to take the child's mind off ... things, then that's all to the good, isn't it, Maggie?'

'Huh!' Maggie had given an audible sniff. 'Em's only a kid. A fat lot of help she'll be. Aye, I know you're young, Molly, but I don't know so much about strong. You look as though you'd get blown over in a puff of wind these days, girl. Still, on your own head be it, if that's what you want to do.' She'd paused for a moment, then had continued more gently, 'The offer's still there if you want to take me up on it.' But Molly's silence had been answer enough.

'No? All right then; I've offered and I can do no more.' The older woman had smiled then, resignedly, and Molly had seen the concern on her face beneath all the annoyance at her desire to help being spurned. Maggie never remained in a huff for very long and her warm-heartedness was never far below the surface. 'Do try and look after yerself though, lass,' she'd continued. 'Try to think about yerself as well as other folks. You've gone through a lot lately, more than most folks have to put up with in a lifetime. I only thought ... if you went back to work it'd help to

200

take your mind off all that's happened. Not to forget, I don't mean that – you'll never forget – but give you summat else to think about, like you were saying about your Em.' Molly's silence again had been eloquent.

'No, I've said enough, haven't I?' Maggie had grinned. 'That's the trouble with me. Like a dog with a bone, I am, when I get summat on me mind. I never let go. Anyroad, lass, I wish you well. I can't say fairer than that now, can I? Even though I do think you're taking far too much on... But, for heaven's sake, try and get a bit more food inside you. Get a bit of flesh on yer bones. And when are you thinking of opening, like?'

Molly had told her she hoped it would be in a few days' time. She had only just got the stock and there was all the furniture to see to; getting rid of her mam's stuff and preparing the parlour for its new role. She had not told Maggie that she intended it to be an 'Open all hours' kind of shop and that no one would be turned away whatever time of day – or evening – they came round, even on a Sunday.

Since that conversation the shop had not been mentioned again. Molly was busy with her own concerns as Maggie was with hers. They saw one another in the street or when, for instance, Molly went to fetch Em home from her playtime with Sarah. But Maggie did not pop in as much as she had formerly done, especially as she had done during those dreadful days after Lily's, then William's deaths. Molly knew she could not have managed without Maggie's help and bolstering support at that time. That was what Maggie was like, in effect, in looks as well as in temperament. She was like a big cushion, a bolster that you put on the bed. She had cared for Molly and shielded her, as much as she was able, during those agonising times ... and Molly did so want to feel that the older woman was still there for her, should she need her support. She had never wanted to antagonise her. After Molly had lost her mother she had, almost unwittingly, begun to look upon Maggie Winthrop as a substitute mother. If she should lose her friendship and help, Molly knew she would, indeed, be alone.

The trestle table was in position, stretching the full width of the little room. There was hardly room to squeeze past it at one end. The other end was pushed right against the wall. The horsehair sofa had been taken away on the removal cart, together with the dilapidated armchairs from the back living room, or kitchen, as they usually called it. The brown plush armchairs were now in position on either side of the kitchen range, giving the whole room a decidedly less shabby appearance. Molly had always secretly questioned the idea of keeping the 'front room' and all the furniture in it for best, hardly ever used except on high days and holidays. Well, her mother's posh chairs would be put to good use now, sure enough, thought Molly, should she ever have time to sit on them. So would the parlour.

Molly found, to her surprise, that she was unable to suppress a sudden surge of excitement as she began to lay out some of her stock on the trestle table, having first covered it with two of her mother's largest white damask cloths. These, like the furniture in the one-time parlour, had formerly been used only on special occasions. She opened the boxes and took out just a couple of the items from each one, arranging them methodically on the table, larger items at the back and smaller ones at the front. When she had finished it still looked somewhat sparse. Not much like a real shop, she concluded, but as time went on she might be able to be a little more adventurous and invest in a few more lines. The jars of sweets for the children – the red and yellow pear-drops, the aniseed balls and the multicoloured dolly mixtures – helped to add a splash of colour, and the bright yellow tins of Colman's mustard and the attractively packaged blancmange and jelly crystals looked tempting. The rest of the stuff was largely mundane, but all commodities that the average housewife could not do without.

Molly stood back and surveyed it critically. What else did she need? Oh yes; her mother's kitchen scales and the weights, although she would need only the smallest ones – one ounce, two ounces, possibly four ounces. She had bought only five pounds of sugar and tea to be going on with, which she would sell in quarter- or two-ounce bags. Mr Ogden had reminded her at the last minute that she would need paper bags, so she had purchased these from him as well: stiff blue ones for the sugar and tea and a variety of flimsier ones, some square and some cone-shaped, for the sweets and smaller items.

She carried the scales into the front room, placing them at the end of the table. She did not have a till for the money, of course – that was something she would, most probably, never be able to afford – but she would need a good strong tin box with a securely fitting lid. She decided the one Mr Turner had brought, containing the donations of the Tower people at the time of her father's death, would do nicely. It was colourful, too, with a bright transfer on the lid dating from Queen Victoria's earlier Golden Jubilee. She placed that next to the scales. It was all looking much more businesslike now, except that the tea and sugar were still in their paper bags. They would soon split with constant use. She tipped the contents out into her mother's huge earthen-ware jars, labelled tea and sugar respectively, receptacles which had always been far too large for a small family's consumption of those items. She and Em could manage with a couple of basins for their own use. She went back into the kitchen to fetch a scoop for measuring out the tea and sugar, tiptoeing past baby William, asleep in his pram, and while she was there she heard the front door open and close with a bang. Em was home from school.

When she re-entered the front room the child was standing there staring in wonder at the changed appearance of the parlour. 'Gosh, isn't it lovely?' she said. 'You've made it look real grand, our Molly. I don't care what you say – I think it looks like a proper shop. When can we open? Are you going to open it today, right now?'

Molly smiled. 'I think we'll wait till tomorrow

morning. There are one or two things I've still to do. I'll have to make some notices, for one thing.'

The little girl pouted slightly. 'That's not fair. I'll be at school. And you did say I could help.'

'So you can,' agreed Molly. 'You can help me with the notices tonight. If I draw some big letters you can colour them in with your crayons, nice and bright – I think red would be best, don't you? – to show people we're open.' The sound of the baby crying broke into Molly's words. 'Oh-ho, no peace for the wicked, as they say.' She gave a wry smile. 'I thought we were doing too well. You can come and help me now, Em – give William his bottle while I see about getting our tea ready. We'll leave the shop just for now, then we'll add the finishing touches later, when William's gone to sleep.' She did not rebuke her sister for banging the door, which she had told her countless times not to do. No doubt that was what had wakened the baby, but she did not want to burst her little sister's bubble of happiness.

'SHOP – NOW OPEN', read the notice that Molly had hung in the window, suspended from a drawing pin pushed into the woodwork. The large letters were coloured in red and blue – Em's handiwork – and below, in smaller letters, the notice went on to say, 'Molly and Emily Rimmer will be pleased to serve you with a variety of household requirements.'

The little girl was delighted that her name was included, but Molly assured her that that was only fair because she had already come up with a very good idea. It was Em who had suggested they should make up their own lucky bags with a selection of the sweets. She had made a dozen of these – just for a start – painstakingly counting out the required number of dolly mixtures, plus a couple of aniseed balls and pear-drops, and finishing off with either a liquorice stick or a small chocolate bar. 'Some of 'em have little toys in as well, in the proper shops – I mean, in the other shops,' she said to Molly, 'but I think these'll do, don't you?'

Molly assured her that they would be 'just grand' and also promised that they might think about including tiny toys later on. The surprise toy, Molly remembered from her own childhood, was the essential item in the lucky bag and she didn't want her young customers to be disappointed. Whether the toy was what you would have chosen yourself was immaterial. It was the element of luck involved that brought the excitement. Maybe Mr Ogden would be able to tell her where to purchase, at cost price, some sheets of coloured transfers and marbles and things like tin whistles and rings – the sort of gewgaws you found in Christmas crackers – if he did not stock them himself. She could buy them, she supposed, at a market stall, but that would mean paying the full price and every ha'penny counted at the moment.

At any rate, Emily went to bed happy, without the worried expression her sister had seen cross her face from time to time, especially when she said good night to her. It was no end of a job to get her off to school the next morning, but she finally departed, after Molly had reminded her that it would soon be the summer holiday and she would be at home for quite a long time, and had assured her, also, that she could help today when she came home from school; at dinner time, even, should they have any customers then.

Molly stood back for a moment, studying the notice she had written out in pen and ink last night and which she had now propped up prominently on the table, or shop counter, as it now was. 'Please do not ask for credit as a refusal may cause offence.' That was what she had seen written large in Mr Ogden's warehouse, and what was good enough for him was good enough for her, Molly Rimmer. Folk would know exactly where they stood and it would show them that she meant business. She wasn't doing it for fun, but to make a living. She knew of shops, public houses, too, that allowed customers to put their purchases 'on the slate', to be paid for at some future time, but that was out of the question. If you started that sort of carry-on goodness knows where it might end. One of the things her parents had taught her, by example, was to pay for everything 'on the nail'. Never had William Rimmer been even a day late with the rent money, and the coalman and the milkman and all the other occasional door-to-door tradesmen had never had to wait for payment from Lily. Last night too, Molly had written out price labels to place in front of the goods, calculating the mark-up carefully. She needed to make money – she must never lost sight of that – but customers wouldn't return if they found her shop expensive.

Next, Molly propped open the front door with a couple of bricks she had found in the backyard.

It looked more inviting like that, otherwise customers might be unsure whether to knock or to walk straight in. It was still the height of summer, but Molly knew that when the weather was inclement, or as winter approached, the door would have to remain closed. Perhaps she could make another notice, 'Please enter – you do not need to knock', or words to that effect. But she did not have to worry about that today. It was a glorious sunny morning with not a cloud in the sky for her first day in the business. The sort of day that made you glad to be alive, she thought, with a sudden pull at her heart strings, remembering the ones who were not here to see it, and the reason she was doing all this in the first place.

She had been up since six o'clock making sure that all was ready. William had had his bottle and gone down without a murmur, bless him, in his pram at the back of the shop room. Molly had decided she must keep him in there with her and just hope that the clatter of the anticipated customers would not disturb him too much. It would be too risky to leave him in the kitchen, out of sight, especially with the front door propped open. Finally she donned a crisp white apron in place of her flowered overall. Then she stood behind the counter and waited.

She did not have to wait long. The first customer was Mrs Jackson from down the street, the woman with whom she had walked home the night her mother died. Every time Molly saw her she was reminded of that night and of how the ever inquisitive woman had questioned her about the young man she had seen her with – futile thoughts which were immediately suppressed. It was obvious now that Mrs Jackson had come more for a 'nosy' than to buy anything, although, to give her her due, she did make a few purchases.

'Well, I never did!' she exclaimed, her bright beady eyes darting all around and taking in everything at a glance. 'A little bird told me about all this, so I had to come and see for myself. You're short of nothing you've got, I can see that, Molly.' She picked up a few items, one at a time – a reel of white cotton, a pair of black bootlaces and a box of matches – examining each of them carefully as though she had never seen the like before, then putting them down again. Molly stood and waited patiently.

'Yes, Mrs Jackson, I've tried to cater for everyone's needs. Er ... would there be anything you want this morning?' she asked in what she hoped was a businesslike, but not too pleading, voice. Molly was quite used to serving people. She had enjoyed that part of her work when she was employed by Mrs Makepeace, but the difference, of course, was that it had not been her own shop. It had not been so vitally important, as it was now, that the customer should make a purchase.

'Aye, why not?' Mrs Jackson beamed at her. 'I'll have a card of them shirt buttons. Sid's forever bursting 'em off wi' his big belly. And some of them Carter's Little Liver Pills – I'm a martyr to indigestion, you know, Molly.' Her eyes scanned the counter. 'And happen I'll mek us a blancmange for us dinner. It'll be a nice treat for

209

Sid. Now, how much is that I owe you?'

Molly worked it out in her head. She had always been quite good at arithmetic when she was at school and her job at the confectioner's had increased her ability, then she handed Mrs Jackson the change from the florin the woman had given her. The float in the tin box consisted of pennies, ha'pennies and farthings Molly had been collecting. 'Thank you so much, Mrs Jackson. I do hope you will come again.' She smiled at the woman, then, on impulse, she handed her a small bar of Cadbury's chocolate. 'And there's a little gift from me. That's because you're my first customer. It won't ... er ... give you indigestion, I hope?'

'Not on your life! It'll go down a treat. Ta ever so much, Molly.' Mrs Jackson was obviously tickled pink. She glanced all round the room again. 'Aye, you've got the makings of a nice little business here. And I'll tell all my neighbours and friends about it, you can be sure of that.' She lowered her voice. 'I'll just have a peep at his lordship here, then I'll be off.' She tiptoed in an exaggerated fashion to the pram, poking her head beneath the raised hood. Molly held her breath for fear the child would waken. 'Aye, he's coming on a treat, bless him, he is that. Fast asleep, though, so I'd best not disturb him. He's a credit to you, Molly, and I wish you all the best, lass.' With a satisfied nod and another searching glance, a rather longer one this time, at the china displayed in the cabinet, Mrs Jackson was on her way.

Molly felt a glow of warmth at the heart of her

and a slight moistness in her eyes. Mrs Jackson might be a nosy old so-and-so, but she was good-hearted. Most of her neighbours, Molly had found since her parents' death, were kind people. Not that Molly wanted customers to come to her shop solely out of the kindness of their hearts, but it did help when they were sympathetic.

She had the impression as the morning drew on that the majority of folk were coming, as Mrs Jackson had done, as much out of curiosity as any desire to make purchases. But purchase they did – they could not, for shame, do anything else – and Molly was gratified to see the amount of silver coins in the box, in addition to the copper ones, slowly increasing. William woke up and was changed and fed, and in between dealing with him and serving a steady trickle of customers Molly had to get the dinner ready for herself and Em. It was a stew she had prepared the night before which was cooking slowly in the fireside oven, but she needed to keep her eye on it, also on the fire, also on William, now wide awake and, unless she was very much mistaken, getting ready for a good old yell. He seemed to know that he had not got her whole-hearted attention this morning.

By the time Em arrived home at a quarter-past twelve, in a flurry of excitement, her big sister was extremely hot and bothered. 'Goodness, is it that time already?' she cried as the little girl appeared. 'Here you are, wanting your dinner, and the table's not even set. And baby's crying fit to wake the dead. I mean–' She stopped suddenly, aware of what she had said – what a stupid, tactless thing to say in front of Em – but the child didn't seem to have noticed. 'He's making a heck of a din, isn't he, Em?' she amended her words. 'Perhaps you could hold him for a few minutes, eh, while I set the table?'

''Course I will,' agreed Em, sitting down in an armchair ready to receive William on to her lap. 'How've you gone on, Molly? Have you had lots of customers? Come on, tell me. I'm dying to hear all about it.'

Indeed, the little girl did not seem worried about anything, neither the unlaid table nor the lateness of the midday meal, nor the fact that, at the end of the meal, there was no pudding for her today, only about how the shop had fared. Molly had been determined that Emily would not suffer because of the extra duties the shop imposed, but she was already finding that that was easier said than done.

'I'm ever so sorry,' she apologised. 'I meant to do some stewed apples and custard – no excuse, have I, with packets of Bird's custard on sale in the shop? – but I haven't had time to get round to it. I don't know where the time has gone to, Em. Honestly, it's just flown. You'll have to make do with an apple just as it is today. There's one left in the fruit bowl. Yes, I've had ever so many customers. Nosing, I think, most of 'em, but they did buy quite a lot of stuff. Mrs Jackson was the first, you might know...'

Towards the end of their meal they heard a knock at the door, then a voice in the passageway. 'Hello there – shop – anyone at home?'

'Can I go? Can I go, please, Molly?' Em leaped

to her feet and, without waiting for her sister's answer, darted through the kitchen door, Molly close behind her.

It was Mrs Harding, a neighbour from the other side of the street, wanting to buy a couple of ounces of tea. 'Would you believe, when I looked in t'tea caddy it were empty? I can do no good wi' my lot if they don't have their cup o' tea after their dinner. Aye, this shop of yours'll be a godsend, Molly, I can see that already. And you've got an assistant, an' all.'

'I can do it, Molly. Honest, I can.' Emily whispered, and Molly stood back, trying not to watch too critically as her sister weighed out the required amount of tea, tipped it into a small blue bag, then gave Mrs Harding the correct change from her sixpence. Em was quite pink with pleasure at the end of the proceedings.

'It's not a game, though, Em,' her sister reminded her. 'We've got to make it work, make a living from it, you see, if we can.'

''Course we will,' replied Em, with the easy confidence of the young.

But Molly was not so sure. She had got off to a good start with the customers, but it was early days yet. What was worrying her most was how she was going to organise her time. If she got into a fluster about preparing a bit of dinner, as she had done this morning, how on earth was she going to cope when it was wash day, the weekly ritual that had to be faced every Monday? and all the ironing and house-cleaning and baking, to say nothing of the shopping, because their own shop would not supply all their needs; it was only an emergency sort of place.

But manage she did – she knew that she had to – by getting up earlier in the morning and going to bed later at night. When it came to Saturday night the shop had been open for five days and Molly had never been so exhausted in all her life. She looked back to the time when she had been working at Makepeace's and how, when her mother was nearing the end of her pregnancy, she, Molly, had had to make the tea and do a good share of the housework in addition to her job. She had thought she was tired then, but it was nothing to the exhaustion she was feeling now. Still, she told herself, she would get used to the routine and it could only get better.

Emily had now broken up from school, so she would be on hand to help with the washing on Monday. This was possibly the biggest task of all and one that Molly had not yet attempted along with her shopkeeping. She was conscious, however, that she must not make a drudge of the little girl as so many mothers tended to do, especially at holiday times. Molly had always helped her mother in the house, but Lily had made sure she had her playtimes as well, and Molly was determined that Em, also, must have her leisure time.

At all events, tomorrow was Sunday and Molly had already changed her mind about keeping the shop open. Enough was enough. If folks ran out of tea or sugar or whatever then is was just too bad. She was entitled to one day of – comparative – rest and the door would remain shut. That was one reason, but Molly knew, deep down, that there was another reason. Maggie Winthrop had been conspicuous by her absence all week. Molly had seen her once or twice in passing, but her friend had not been near the shop; the shop, in fact, had not even been mentioned between them. And Molly had no wish to antagonise her still further by not observing the strictures of the Sabbath Day.

No, she would cook an especially tasty dinner for herself and Em. They had existed on stews and makeshift meals all week. She had a nice half-shoulder of lamb she had managed to procure, by the skin of her teeth, from the nearest butcher's shop, just as he was closing. And she had bought her vegetables from the greengrocer's cart which paid a twice-weekly visit to the neighbourhood, instead of going to the market. It had cost her a penny or two more, but these door-to-door sellers were a great boon. She might even manage to make an apple pie.

But Sunday or no she would have to catch up on the cleaning she had neglected during the week, then sort out the washing and leave it to soak overnight, ready for tackling the next day. This was definitely one day when the shop must remain closed. There was no doubt, however, that they could do with the money. She had not made quite as much as she had hoped for during the first week, but there was a point beyond which she could not push herself.

It was about half-past eleven on Sunday morning when Molly heard a loud knocking at the door. She was busy shredding a cabbage and Em was peeling the potatoes.

'Oh lor, who the heck's that?' Molly put down her knife and wiped her hands on her apron. 'I'd best go and see, I suppose.' The door, even when closed, usually remained unbolted so that neighbours could walk in, as was usual in the area, but today Molly had made sure the bolt was in place. She did not want any customers. 'I know we're closed, but it might be somebody else, not a customer.'

'But if it is – a customer, I mean – they'll want serving, won't they?' said Em.

'Yes, of course they will,' agreed Molly. 'I tell you what, you go and have a peep through the front-room window, Em, and have a see who it is. Then I can decide. Oh dear, I don't want to offend anybody.' The loud knocking came again as Em disappeared into the shop room. She was back in a few seconds.

'It's Auntie Maggie, Molly. Shall we let her in?'

'Maggie? Yes, of course we must let her in. Oh dear, whatever will she think of me, bolting the door?' Molly hurried to the front door and drew back the bolt.

'And about time too,' said Maggie Winthrop, looking very red and flustered. 'What on earth are you thinking of, Molly, bolting the door? I wondered whatever was up. You've never done that before.'

'No ... well, I don't want any customers,' Molly started to explain. 'The shop, you see. It's Sunday, and we're closed on a Sunday. But I didn't mean to shut my friends out – you know that, Maggie. Anyroad, come on in. I'm ever so pleased to see you.'

Maggie followed her into the kitchen. 'So the shop's shut, is it?'

'Well, yes, of course.'

'What do you mean, "of course"?'

'Well, it's Sunday, isn't it?'

'And how long have you been bothered about Sunday, Molly Rimmer? Folks have to cook their dinners, you know, Sunday or not.' Molly stared at her friend in puzzlement.

'But I thought... You've always told me that Sunday ... was special...' The penny suddenly dropped and Molly grinned. 'D'you mean to tell me that there's something you want, Maggie? You've run short of something?'

'Aye, as usual, lass.' Maggie burst out laughing. 'A bit of custard powder. And happen a cup of sugar. But I suppose it'll be in a bag now as you've gone all lah-di-da. I'll pay – I don't want it for nowt.' She reached into the pocket of her voluminous apron and drew out her purse.

'But we're closed,' said Molly, trying to keep a straight face. 'We decided, didn't we, Em, that we wouldn't open today?' She winked at her little sister, but Emily, like her mother, was not gifted with a great sense of humour and she was looking very worried.

'But it's Auntie Maggie,' she said in a loud whisper.

'And I think for Auntie Maggie we might make an exception,' said Molly. 'Come into the shop, Maggie, and Em will serve you. We wouldn't do it for anyone else, mind.'

'Aye, well, we've all got to eat humble pie once in a while,' said Maggie. 'But it's me apple pie as

I'm worried about. It's no good without custard.'
She looked admiringly round the transformed
parlour. 'Aye, you've worked wonders here, lass.
I'll admit I thought you were making a big
mistake, but I reckon I'll have to eat my words.
All t'neighbours've been telling me what a grand
job you're doing, and now I can see for meself.
How's it going then?'

'Not bad,' replied Molly. She shrugged. 'Could
be better, could be worse. I've made a bit, but not
enough to live on, not yet. If it wasn't for the
insurance money ... well, I don't know. And I'm
tired, Maggie.' She had intended putting on a
brave face, but seeing the concern in Maggie's
eyes she knew she had to unburden herself to her
old friend. She lowered her voice, so that Em
would not hear. 'The truth is ... well, I'm not sure
that I've done the right thing. I can't help wondering and worrying about how it'll work out.'

'You're sure to be tired,' Maggie told her, 'but
it'll get easier, you'll see. And word'll spread
about what a grand little business it is. Cheer up,
lass – it can only get better.'

Molly was pleased she had regained the
support of her friend. Maggie's cheery confidence was just what she needed. But she wished
she felt as optimistic about the future as Maggie
seemed to be.

Chapter 11

Molly found that she was less harassed as the days went on. She was able to organise her time more satisfactorily, fitting in her household chores and caring for William in between serving in the shop. she had to admit, however, that the main reason she was coping so much better now was because Em was at home for the long summer holiday. When the baby cried or needed feeding or changing, Em was there to lend a hand, minding the shop while Molly dealt with him, or sometimes wheeling him up and down the street in his perambulator to lull him off to sleep again. The little girl pushing the big black pram was becoming a common sight in the neighbourhood, and Em didn't seem to resent that this was how she spent her time instead of playing hopscotch or tig or skipping with her friends in the street. Molly feared the child might be getting old before her time. 'Eight going on eighty,' was how Maggie described her, but it was not just recent circumstances that had made her so. Em had always been an old-fashioned, serious little girl.

'I don't mind, honest, Molly,' she frequently told her sister when she had pangs of guilt about the way Em seemed to be missing out on the pleasures of childhood. 'I'd rather be with you, anyway, and our William.'

She was not exactly a clinging child – Molly had been surprised at the self-sufficiency she had shown in dealing with the customers in the shop – but she had no desire to roam the streets or play out till all hours as some children in the neighbourhood did. That was, in part, due to Lily's rearing of her. The slightly snobbish attitude that Lily had always held with regard to her neighbours might well have rubbed off on the little girl if it had not been for her friend, Sarah Winthrop. Her 'Auntie Maggie' and Sarah were the only ones, apart from the family, that Emily had ever allowed into her close-knit little world.

There could not be two children more dis-similar, Molly often thought when she saw the two of them, Em and Sarah, together. Em was quite tall for her age and sturdily built, with ginger hair and the pale freckled complexion that often came with such colouring. Sarah was much smaller and dark-haired and, in spite of her lack of height and her scrawniness, she was a tough little thing, the undisputed leader, not only of the two of them, but of all the neighbourhood children. Very much like her mother, in fact, in temperament if not in build. Em seemed to think the sun shone out of her.

Sarah appeared on their doorstep one Sunday morning towards the end of August. Molly had decided to give up on the idea of closing the shop entirely on a Sunday, so she was working a compromise. The door did not stand wide open on Sunday as it did throughout the week, but neighbours and folk 'in the know' would be served if necessary. The idea was working quite well; besides, Molly needed every penny she could get. She smiled when she saw Sarah.

'Hello, love,' she greeted her. 'What has your mam run out of this time? Let me guess. Gravy browning – it's just about time for making the gravy, isn't it? Or is it sugar again?'

'No, no, it isn't owt like that. She's not short of owt today.' The child sounded quite indignant. She stood on one leg, then the other, hopping up and down. Sarah could never keep still. 'Me mam's sent me to say – would Em like to come to Sunday school this afternoon with me and our Billy and Betty? She's kept meaning to ask you, she says. Can she come? Can I go and ask her?' She skipped past Molly without waiting for an answer, along the passage and into the kitchen where Em was nursing baby William.

'Here's your friend,' said Molly, a tiny bit peeved at the child's boldness, and at Maggie's persistence too. Maggie knew perfectly well that they did not want pestering about religious matters. They had always been quite all right the way they were without any of that. 'She's come to ask you...' She hesitated, then turned to Sarah. 'I'm not sure, Sarah. It's kind of you to ask, but I don't really think that Em–'

'I know what she said,' Em interrupted. 'I heard her. Can I go, Molly?'

'Well, yes, I suppose so. If you really want to. But we've never bothered with anything like that. You might not like it, Em. You'll be starting school again soon, and I've always thought that day school was quite enough, without Sunday school as well.'

221

'It ain't like proper school,' said Sarah. She knelt on the hearthrug next to Em and took hold of William's hands, juggling him up and down. 'It's real good. We sing and listen to stories and colour pictures. There's no sums or spelling or owt boring like that. Anyway, me mam says it's time Em went and heard about Jesus and stopped being such a little heathen.'

Molly bristled. 'I'm sure your mother said no such thing.'

'She did, an' all,' retorted Sarah. 'But she was laughing when she said it. You know me mam – she didn't mean to be nasty.'

'Yes ... I know your mother,' said Molly, smiling in spite of herself. 'Well, it's up to Em. If she wants to go then I suppose she can.' Molly knew it would be churlish of her to refuse to let the child go; she asked so very few favours. 'Do you go on your own, though? There are one or two big roads to cross, aren't there ... Sarah, please don't pull at baby William like that, there's a good girl. He's only just had his bottle and we don't want him to be sick, do we?'

'Sorry.' Sarah let go of him suddenly and he fell back against Emily's chest. 'There's only Talbot Road to cross, then Dickson Road, an' it's just down the next street. We'll be all right, honest. I'll look after her, Molly. I always take our Billy and Betty an' it's not busy on a Sunday. No horses and carts to watch out for, only landaus and posh folk in them hansom cabs.'

'Look out for them then, won't you,' said Molly, somewhat anxious at the thought of letting her little sister loose with the irrepressible

222

Sarah and a couple of four-year-olds. Admittedly Emily walked to school and home again twice a day through the busiest part of Blackpool, but there was always a crowd of children all together and there was safety in numbers. She had never sent Emily on errands to the town centre shops, as Maggie sent Sarah, only to the ones that were near. She knew, though, that she must not keep Em tied to her apron strings, and she was aware also that it was the thought of Maggie pressurising her that was getting her goat.

''Course I'll look out,' said Sarah, pulling a face at Em as she spoke, as if to say, What a fusspot your sister is! 'I always do.'

'Can I go then, Molly?' asked Em again. 'You're sure...?'

'Yes, I'm sure.' Molly smiled at her. 'Go today and see how you like it, then we'll see.'

'Goody!' Sarah leaped up and down from her crouching position on the rug. 'I'll call for you this afternoon at two o'clock. It starts at half-past. I'd best go. Me mam said not to be long. Ta-ra, Em. Ta-ra, Molly...'

The house was quiet when Em had gone out and William was sleeping again, abnormally quiet it seemed, and it was at times like this, when she was all alone, that Molly started to brood. She knew she was managing much more ably than she had done in that first frantic week when everything had been getting on top of her, at least as far as organising her work was concerned. Even Maggie had praised her achievements, saying that the whole thing was running like clockwork, and so it seemed; but the truth was that the shop was not paying its way, not making enough, that was, for Molly and her little family to live on. There was very little money left in the kitty, just a few silver coins remaining from her father's insurance money, and after that was spent Molly did not know how she would manage.

She knew that if she were to go out to work again she would be able to earn considerably more, but she was determined not to admit defeat, which was how she saw it now. Besides, Maggie had not mentioned for ages her initial offer to look after the baby. It was almost as though she had thought better of it, and it was not what Molly wanted anyway. She still intended to care for William herself. It was what her mother, and her father, would have wished.

She was gradually coming round to the idea, abhorrent though it was to her, that she would have to pay a visit to the pawnshop. That was something she knew both her parents would have disapproved of most strongly. Never had Lily had to resort to such measures in all her married life, but then she was fortunate in that she had never needed to do so. There had always been enough money to pay the rent, to keep the roof above their heads. This week Molly had been hard pressed to find the rent money and had managed to do so only by cutting down on their food; not for William and Em, of course, but for herself. Their Sunday dinner today, instead of the usual roast, had been scrag end of mutton, stewed for hours to make it tender, that the butcher had been selling cheap at the end of the day.

She went to the sideboard and took out the tin box which contained everything of value that the family owned: the small amount of money that remained, plus her mother's wedding ring – a thick gold band which had always seemed too large for Lily's slender finger; a silver heart on a chain which had also belonged to Lily – a present from William; a pinchbeck brooch; and her father's pocket watch; his pride and joy which he had always worn, when dressed in his best suit, suspended from a chain attached to his waistcoat button. There were also her parents' clothes, still lying in the wardrobe and chest of drawers upstairs. She would be able to sell them to a second-hand shop for a reasonable amount as there was a good trade done in second-hand, even third-hand, clothes. That would be a help, if she could only make herself do it. Both Maggie and Flo had told her it was something she must do; it was no use hanging on to them and the longer she did so the worse it would get. But the truth was that the wounds left by her parents' deaths were still too raw. She had not felt able to dispose of their most intimate possessions to a second-hand dealer. Now she knew that she would have to.

She could, of course, sell the china cabinet and its contents out of the one-time parlour as she had thought of doing right at the start, but something inside her was protesting against this measure. Maybe it was because of what the neighbours might think. They would be sure to notice its absence from the shop room and surmise that Molly was finding it hard to make ends meet. She was her mother's daughter, in some ways at least, and outward appearances counted with her to a certain extent, though not so much as they had with Lily. And the china cabinet was a reminder of Lily and her pretensions, rather silly though they might have been, that Molly was loath to part with.

Em was back from her visit to Sarah's Sunday school almost before Molly could turn round, it seemed, although she knew she had spent a fair amount of the time in contemplation of her lot. Hastily she shoved the tin box back in the sideboard as she heard the front door open and close.

'Hello there, love. Have you enjoyed yourself?' she asked, putting on a cheerful face as she always tried to do when she was with Em. 'Tell me all about it.'

'Yes, it was real good,' Em replied. 'We sang "Tell me the Stories of Jesus" – I know that one from school – then we sang another one, "Hear the Pennies Dropping", and we all dropped our pennies into this big wooden plate thing. Then those that had birthdays went out to the front and the teacher lit candles and we sang to 'em again.'

'Sounds like an awful lot of singing,' observed Molly.

'Yes, it was. I like singing,' said Em, happily. 'Then we had a story about Jesus, about how he was at a wedding and they had no wine and he made some out of water. Then we drew a picture of it and coloured it, and then we said some prayers, then we sang again, then we came home.

Can I go again, Molly?'

'Yes, I don't see why you shouldn't,' replied Molly, a trifle guardedly. But it could do no harm and it was giving the little girl another interest outside of the narrow confines of her home. Molly was not sure how much of this religious stuff she, personally, could believe. Very little, she admitted to herself. The Almighty – if, indeed, He existed – always seemed to be absent when you needed Him most. Where had He been recently, in all Molly's tribulations? Her mother had always avowed that God had done nothing for them, only let a load of trouble come to successive generations of the family, although Molly had never discovered just what those troubles were. And she knew her mother had tended to take a pessimistic view of life.

Em broke into her thoughts. 'Molly, d'you know what our teacher said? She said if you want something then you have to ask Jesus and He always listens and He always answers our prayers. That's what she said.'

'Did she now?' replied Molly. 'Well, well, well – you learn something every day.' Would that it were so simple, was what she thought.

On Monday morning she was at the pawnshop dead on nine o'clock, just as the door was opened. She had been forced to leave her own shop closed and Em playing out in the street with Sarah while she wheeled William in his pram to the shop on Market Street. It was too much of a responsibility for the little girl to leave her in sole charge, even for half an hour or so.

Her father's watch realised seven shillings and

227

sixpence, her mother's wedding ring four shillings, and with the other bits and pieces the pawnbroker, quite a sympathetic man, made the sum up to fifteen shillings. Riches indeed to Molly. She would now be able to pay another visit to the wholesale warehouse on Wednesday. But she felt that she had betrayed the memory of both her parents.

'You know, you and I have both been very lucky,' Flo remarked to her when she came on Wednesday afternoon. Flo had volunteered to look after the shop and baby William while Molly went to the warehouse, as she had done before. 'Well, I know you've had more than your share of bad luck recently, but before that, I mean, when we were children. We were always well-clothed and well-fed, and we had parents who cared about us and always watched out for what we were doing. Not like some of the scruffy kids I've passed on my way here, Molly. Snotty noses, backsides hanging out of their trousers; some of 'em look as though they haven't had a wash in weeks, nor a decent meal.'

'Not all of them, though,' replied Molly. 'Some of the parents round here take very good care of their kids, just like ours did.'

'No, I don't mean all of 'em, of course not. Not your Em, nor her bosom pal. I saw them sitting on Sarah's doorstep, chatting away like a couple of old women. And some of the others look clean and tidy enough. 'Tisn't fair to lump 'em all together. But you know what I mean; I dare say some of their dads spend all the money on booze and their mams have to make do on what they can scrape together. We've never had to suffer that, you and me. So I shouldn't worry too much about visiting the pawnshop. I expect some of these women are regular customers, aren't they? Just be thankful your own mam was never one of them.'

'That's what makes me feel so dreadful now,' said Molly. 'Whatever would she think? We always had our standards. I had it too easy, I suppose, compared with some kids. I was scared to death, I can tell you, in case I saw somebody I knew, but I didn't, not this time. Anyway, I hadn't much choice. We've run out of quite a few lines in the shop, and Mr Ogden wants cash on the nail, same as I do. I'd best get off, anyroad. William's fed and changed and Em's quite happy where she is. It's ever so good of you, Flo. We'll have a chat when I get back.'

A couple of hours later, after Molly had returned from Central Drive with a laden pram, they resumed their chatter.

'I don't know what I'd do without you, Flo,' Molly remarked. 'You're a friend in a million. Coming here when it's your half-day as well. I'm really grateful to you.'

'I know you are,' said Flo, 'so let's say no more about it. It's no trouble to me looking after the shop; quite good fun, in fact. I've had a nice chat with your neighbours, and I think young William is getting to know his Auntie Flo. Anyway, what else would I be doing on my half-day? I'm not meeting Sam till later tonight.'

Flo's satisfied little smile and the sparkle in her eyes told Molly that all must be going well between her friend and Sam Leadbetter, the young man she had met at Uncle Tom's Cabin the night of the Jubilee.

'Oh, so that's still going strong, is it?' asked Molly. 'You still like him as much?'

'Oh yes, more and more,' enthused Flo. 'Mam and Dad like him too, so I'm pleased about that. He's working hard and saving up because ... well, I'll be eighteen soon and we might ... it's a secret at the moment, Moll, but we might be getting engaged.'

'Really? That's good news,' said Molly, feeling pleased for her friend. Sam Leadbetter worked for a printing firm in Euston Street and, from what Molly knew of him from Flo, he appeared to be a most pleasant and industrious, though somewhat serious, young man.

'Of course we won't be able to get married for ages and ages,' Flo continued. 'So you won't tell anybody just yet, will you? You're the first one I've told.'

'No, of course I won't,' said Molly. 'I thought you liked him right from the start.' She felt a shadow fall across her mind as she recalled that night; her own meeting with Joss, William's birth, her mother's death...

Flo must have noticed the change of expression on her friend's face and guessed the reason for it because she immediately changed the subject. 'Anyway, that's enough about Sam. Let me tell you about the shop. The new owners have taken over from Miss Perkins now. They moved in this week and there's a decorator there already painting the outside of the shop bright blue and putting a posh new sign over the door. "Marianne Modes" – that's what it's going to be called. Bit of a change from Amelia Perkins' Draper's, isn't it?'

'Is that what the boss is called then – Marion?'

'No, there are two of them, I told you. Two sisters; one's called Mary and the other's called Annie. Mari – anne, y'see. And "modes" is French – it means fashions. We're not just going to sell materials like we did before; they're starting up their own dressmaking business. They had one before, in Wigan, they were telling us, then their mother died and left them quite a lot of money, so that's why they've come here. They're quite old – thirty-odd, both of 'em, real old spinsters – but they're very nice and easy to get on with.'

Molly had rarely seen her friend so excited, especially as, under the Misses Fothergill, Minnie was to serve in the shop and Flo, who had always had a flair for sewing, was to be trained as a high-class dressmaker.

'So you're on your way to realising your ambition,' said Molly. Flo had always said that she wanted to learn the trade properly and sew for rich folk as well as for herself and her mother; to own her own business, maybe, one day. 'Good for you, Flo.'

'Seems like it,' said Flo. 'It's a start, anyway. And you've made a start, an' all, haven't you, opening your own shop. D'you remember saying you wanted to have your own shop? Well, now you've got it.'

'I didn't mean one like this, though,' said Molly

ruefully. 'I meant a proper one, with a counter and a till and a big plate-glass window.' She had really dreamed of owning one on Jubilee Terrace, but she didn't mention that. 'I'm only doing this because I've got to make some money and this seems to be all I can do.' She sighed. 'The other was just a dream, wasn't it?'

'This'll do to be going on with,' said Flo. 'You've got to walk before you can run. And it'll get bigger and better, knowing you, Molly. The folk round here've been telling me they don't know how they managed before you opened up.'

Molly was gratified by her friend's words, though she guessed they might be a little exaggerated. But she had felt a resurge of optimism on visiting the warehouse and had invested in half a dozen new lines as well as replenishing her old stock. Time would tell.

'Now, let's go and have a look at your mam and dad's clothes,' said Flo, 'while your Em's out of the way.' The little girl had been home to ask if she could stay for tea at Sarah's. 'You've kept saying you'd see to 'em, and there's no time like the present. It won't take us long if there are two of us...'

Flo chatted away as they worked together in the bedroom, emptying the large mahogany wardrobe and chest of drawers, and piling the clothes on the bed. 'You must come and have a look at us all on the terrace, Molly. You'll find some changes, I can tell you. You should see the window display that Miss Mary and Miss Annie are setting up. Just one costume on a model – a travelling costume, it is, in lightweight wool, one they've made themselves, of course – standing on its own in the middle of the window. Not bits of this and bits of that like Miss Amelia used to have. Real elegant, it is. Miss Mary says that's the important thing – elegance.'

'So there's nothing else in the window, just one costume?' asked Molly.

'There are some of our materials draped at the back of the window, like curtains, showing all the different colours and textures,' Flo explained. 'It's still a draper's, but a much more high-class one now. And there are some suitcases and travel bags scattered around, and I think they're going to put up some railway posters. It's to show what the well-dressed lady wears when she's travelling, y'see.'

'I see,' said Molly. She had to agree it sounded very different from Miss Perkins' motley display of ginghams and cottons, ribbons and lace and knitting wools and buttons. 'Yes, I'd certainly like to come and have a look at it all. Perhaps I'll wheel William down in his pram sometime, though goodness knows when it'll be.'

Planning an outing, even only to go window shopping, was easier said than done. Molly hardly ever ventured further than the end of the street these days, she was so very busy. She had never been back to Jubilee Terrace since she had stopped working there. The fact that she had no time was only one reason, possibly an excuse. Molly knew, deep down, that it would conjure up many memories were she to go back. She had been so happy working for Dolly Makepeace and it had seemed that those carefree days would go on forever. Admittedly she had had her dreams – what girl didn't? – but she had been contented. She knew, however, that she must try to put the past behind her. It would please Flo if she were to go and take a look at the new style shop, and maybe she could pop in and see Mrs Makepeace at the same time. Dolly would no doubt be pleased to see her.

'The chemist's shop's up for sale as well,' Flo told her. 'You remember old Mr Drew, don't you? Well, he's retiring. About time, an' all. That's another shop that could do with bringing up to date.'

'Mmm, it certainly sounds as though there are some changes afoot,' observed Molly. 'Who's buying the chemist's, do you know?'

'Not really. We've heard that someone's been to look at it – a Mr Stubbins, apparently. He's already got two chemist's shops, one on Church Street and one in South Shore, but I don't know any more than that. And the toyshop's started selling books as well as toys. Children's books at the moment, but Mr Merryweather says he's going to stock adult books as well if he can manage it. That should please you. You like reading, don't you, Molly?'

'When I have time,' Molly agreed. 'I used to, but I hardly have time to read a newspaper these days.' And how would she ever be able to afford to buy books? she thought. The shops on Jubilee Terrace had always catered for the more well-to-do, and now, more than ever, such luxuries were beyond her means.

'By the way, I nearly forgot to tell you,' said

Molly, changing the subject. 'Em went to Sunday school last Sunday with Sarah Winthrop. She seemed to enjoy it, so I don't see as it would do any harm for her to go again. I thought you'd like to know.' She grinned at her friend. Molly's own lack of religious conviction had long been, not exactly a bone of contention, but the cause of some good-hearted banter between them. Flo, to give her her due, was not overpersistent about drawing Molly into 'the flock', but she did keep on trying from time to time.

'Yes, that's good news,' said Flo. 'And what about you, eh? The invitation's still open, you know. You're very welcome to come with me to my Young Ladies' class. You could come while your Em's at Sunday school. Different chapel, of course, but it's at the same time.'

'And what would I do with William?'

'You could bring him with you,' said Flo. 'One of the other girls brings her baby when her husband can't have him. He's no trouble. He sleeps all through it.'

'William wouldn't,' replied Molly. 'He seems to know when I want him to go to sleep, the little monkey, and that's when he stays awake. Anyway, I'll think about it, Flo ... when I've got more time. When William's older, maybe.'

'This year, next year, sometime, never,' said Flo, frowning at her in mock reproach. 'But you can't say as I never ask. And you really should try and have a bit more time to yourself, Molly.'

'Huh, chance'd be a fine thing,' said Molly. 'Now, what do you think about this lot?'

There was, in truth, very little of any real value.

Although she had been trying to put on a brave face in front of Flo it upset Molly very much to see her mother's skirts and blouses and her best black coat piled on the bed with her father's shirts and working trousers and his one good suit. Only three months ago the two of them had been so happy together – in this very bed – and now they were lying in the graveyard while their earthly possessions, which only amounted to a jumble of old clothes, were being sorted out to bring a few paltry shillings. Her father's black three-piece suit would fetch the most; possibly five shillings or even seven and sixpence, as it was hardly worn. But Molly did not expect to get much for the rest, although none of it was shabby. The second-hand dealers had to make their profit. She was relieved when Flo offered to take the lot for her to the nearest shop on Topping Street which, fortunately, stayed open on a Wednesday afternoon. It would have felt like the ultimate betrayal to go herself and barter with her parents' intimate possessions, even worse than visiting the pawnshop or turning her mother's beloved parlour into a trading estab-lishment.

In September Em went back to school and it was then that Molly realised what a good help the little girl had been in the shop or as an extra pair of hands to look after William. Now she had to manage all on her own, except at the weekends and the couple of hours around teatime, which was always a busy period in the shop. William was sleeping much less and demanding more and more of her attention. Fortunately he still spent most of the time in his pram or cot. Molly wondered however she would cope when he started crawling, then walking, but she would have to meet that problem when it arose. He was fractious now with cutting his first teeth. They were very early, Maggie informed her; to have two teeth at the age of four months was quite unusual, but Molly guessed that William might be a child who would do all things early; sitting up, walking or talking. Already he was trying to lift his head from the pillow and stare around. His eyes, which had been an indeterminate grey at first, had now changed to a deep brown like those of Molly and Em, and their late mother. Bright and alert they were, seeming to take in everything when he lay in Molly's arms, craning his neck to see all round the room, and lighting up with joy when he caught sight of Molly or Emily. He appeared to recognise Maggie and Sarah too, and Flo, and he did not mind who nursed him or picked him up. Molly loved him unreservedly. She had not realised it could be possible to love a tiny child so much, but he brought problems as well as pleasure and she guessed he always would. He was all sweetness and light when she was giving him her full attention; at other times, when he felt he was being ignored, his screams of anger and frustration could be heard at the other end of the street.

This was how it was one afternoon towards the end of October. Em had been home for her dinner and had gone back to school, and now

William just refused to settle down. Every time Molly laid him in his pram he screamed and, what with one thing and another, she was at the end of her tether. At that moment she could cheerfully have handed him over to Maggie, turned her back on him – and Em and the shop and everything – and gone back to work. She knew she couldn't do this, not immediately – but there was something she could and would do. She made a snap decision. She could get away from the shop for an hour or two. Be hanged to the shop, she thought, as she put on her hat and coat, hung a notice in the window saying 'Closed', then trundled the pram containing the still screaming William along the passage and out of the front door, locking it firmly behind her. She hurried along the street, anxious to get away before any prospective customers might delay her. It was the first time ever that she had closed the shop in the afternoon, but she knew she would have gone mad had she stayed there a moment longer with a crying baby and all her other anxieties weighing heavily upon her.

Already, as she turned into Talbot Road, William had stopped crying and seemed to be asleep, lulled by the motion of the pram. Molly, too, was feeling a little calmer. She tried to think through her situation rationally. The shop was not paying its way, there was no doubt about that. True enough, she had been able to pay the rent each week, and the tradesmen, and there was always enough food on the table, especially for the children, but that was only because of the money she had received from the sale of her parents' clothing and her visits to the pawnshop. She had redeemed the oddments of jewellery the following week, but then had been forced to part with them again. She did not see, now, how she would ever be able to get them back. All the spare money she had was gone and there was scarcely enough in her purse to see them through to the end of the week. Maybe it was foolish, then, to have turned her back on the shop, she pondered, but she had known she had to get away.

She would give it till Monday, she decided, then, short of a miracle, she would have to throw herself upon the mercy of Maggie and put up with all the remarks like 'I told you so', or 'I knew all along it was what you should do'. But would Maggie still be willing to look after William? She had not mentioned it for ages; never, in fact, since the shop opened. What was more, would her old job be available at Makepeace's?

Molly tried to convince herself that that was not the reason she was heading for Jubilee Terrace now. She was going to look at the new 'Marianne Modes' that she had heard so much about from Flo. She had kept promising her friend she would go, but two months had gone by and she still had not found time. The autumn sunshine had cheered her, causing her worries to recede a little. As she turned on to the promenade, walking northwards towards the terrace, she felt a sudden upsurge of her spirits. She had always loved the terrace and the people there. It had been wrong of her to cut herself off so completely and it would be grand to see them all again.

She looked in the window of the draper's shop first. At least, that was what it had been when Molly had worked in the area, but you certainly could not call it by such an ordinary name now, she thought, as she gazed at the striking display in the window of 'Marianne Modes'. The travel display that Flo had described to her had been replaced, she had been so long in paying her promised visit. Now it was an autumn panorama that faced her. Autumn leaves, cut from coloured paper, were scattered on the floor. Swathes of material hung at the back of the window – golden satin, pale orange silk, russet velvet and a rich brown tweed in the finest wool – and in the front there were two models. One was wearing a brown costume made from the tweed which hung at the back, suitable for wearing out of doors, and the other model was arrayed in a fashionable afternoon dress made from the russet velvet, with huge leg-o'-mutton sleeves and a lace fichu at the neck. Hmm, very elegant indeed, thought Molly, echoing in her mind one of Flo's now favourite words. Lah-di-da was the expression that sprung more readily to Molly's mind, and pricey, too.

She peeped through the glass door, not really expecting to see her friend. Flo had told her she was usually busy in the sewing room upstairs, only serving in the shop from time to time. But, as luck would have it, Flo was there and she beckoned to Molly to come inside. Molly left the pram outside as William was asleep and entered the shop. The interior, too, was much changed since Miss Perkins' time. A lot of the stock was the same, but the place now appeared much less cluttered and untidy. Business did not seem to be very brisk at the moment. There were no customers in the shop, nor upstairs in the fitting room, Flo informed her, but it was 'just a lull', she explained. 'We were rushed off our feet earlier, weren't we, Minnie?'

Molly already knew Minnie, the fifteen-year-old girl who was employed there. Now she was introduced to Miss Mary, the elder of the two Fothergill sisters, soberly dressed in black with a tape measure around her neck and a pair of small steel-rimmed spectacles perched on her nose. She looked rather forbidding, but that was only at a first glance. She smiled charmingly at Molly when she was introduced as Flo's very best friend and said she had heard a lot about her. She did not seem to mind her assistant entertaining a friend, although it was obvious that Molly had not come in to buy anything. Molly, however, was anxious not to intrude and she hastily made an exit when two ladies entered the shop.

'I'm on my way to see Mrs Makepeace,' she said in a hurried whisper as Flo smiled welcomingly at the customers. 'I'll see you soon. Goodbye, Miss Fothergill. It's been nice meeting you. 'Bye, Minnie...'

She released the brake on the pram and slowly made her way along the row of shops, pausing for a moment or two at each one. 'High Class Boots and Shoes' looked as though it had not changed at all since Molly last saw it. Mr Finch dealt mainly in bespoke boots and shoes, and there was a small selection of his handiwork in the window. It had never interested Molly overmuch

241

since she could not afford to have her shoes specially made for her. Neither could most people she knew. They went to a multiple shop or bought them second-hand.

She passed on to Mr Merryweather's toyshop next door, which had always fascinated her. It appealed to the child at the heart of her, she supposed, gazing at a longed-for toy which you hoped against hope would appear on Christmas morning. The display of outdoor toys – whips and tops, buckets and spades, hoops, skipping ropes and balls of all sizes – that had filled the window earlier in the year had now been replaced by exquisitely dressed dolls, building bricks, clockwork trains and wind-up animated animals. At the rear was a rocking horse and a large doll's house, and in the centre of the window was a Noah's ark with Mr and Mrs Noah and all the brightly painted wooden animals going in two by two. It would be William's first Christmas in a couple of months, Molly pondered. She hoped she might be able to afford a small toy for him; one of those floppy sailor dolls, maybe, and Em would be intrigued by the kaleidoscope... She moved away. It was no use even thinking about such things at the moment, no use at all.

She passed by the photographer's studio – another luxury well beyond their means – pausing at the corner shop, the chemist's. H. Stubbins and Son, read the sign over the door. Flo had told her the new owner had now taken over, although she did not know, as yet, very much about him. In the window as before there were still the large glass bottles of coloured liquids, and below a wide variety of goods, not only patent medicines and surgical appliances, but soaps, combs and brushes, sponges and bottles of perfume. As with the draper's it now appeared to be better cared for and more modern in approach.

Molly did not linger, however. She turned the pram round and retraced her steps to the confectioner's shop at the other corner. Once again she left the pram outside and opened the door, hearing with a pang of nostalgia the familiar jangling of the bell. It was such a friendly welcoming sound and she felt sure of a welcome here. She was not disappointed.

'Molly! How lovely to see you, and after all this time. Whyever have you left it so long, you naughty girl?' Dolly Makepeace bustled forward from behind the counter, enveloping Molly in a bear hug. Molly kissed the cheek of the bright-eyed, apple-cheeked woman – the first time she had ever done so – feeling quite overwhelmed by the warmth of her greeting. She could smell the aroma of freshly baked bread and cakes still lingering on the air, though it was now the middle of the afternoon, and the scent of tea and coffee brewing from the café at the rear. Yes, it was good to be back.

'We were so sorry to hear about ... everything.' Dolly's smile faded momentarily and Molly could see the genuine concern and sympathy in the woman's eyes. 'What a dreadful time you've had, to be sure. But Flo tells us how brave you've been, picking up the pieces and looking after the baby and your little sister. And you've got your little shop an' all. So things aren't too bad, eh, love?'

'No ... not too bad,' agreed Molly. What else could she say? 'I've left William outside, but I don't really think I should. Would you mind if I brought him inside?'

'Mind? Of course we wouldn't mind.' William was pushed into the shop and, now wide awake and staring around bemusedly, was admired by Dolly and Cissie Dean, the older assistant who had worked with Molly. Dolly's husband and son also emerged from the bakehouse at the rear to say hello to her. Another young woman, too, stepped forward somewhat hesitantly from behind the counter where she had been standing.

'May I have a peep at him? I love babies,' she said, smiling shyly at Molly before turning to speak to Dolly. 'That is if you don't mind, Mrs Makepeace. Seeing as we're not too busy at the moment.'

'Of course you may, Nora,' said Dolly. 'How thoughtless of me. I haven't introduced you, have I? Molly, this is Nora. She's our new assistant. She's going to take over your old job on a permanent basis, we hope, don't we, dear?' She smiled encouragingly at the girl, who appeared to be about sixteen years of age, small and dark and neatly dressed in a black frock and the same kind of long white apron and cap that Molly had used to wear. The two young women shook hands.

'How d'you do?' said Nora, almost bobbing deferentially at Molly. 'I've heard such a lot about you ... Molly. Mrs Makepeace is always singing your praises.'

'How d'you do?' replied Molly. 'I'm very pleased to meet you.' She was smiling brightly, trying to hide the feeling of bitter disappointment which, already, was like a lead weight at the pit of her stomach.

'Credit where it's due,' beamed Dolly Makepeace. 'Molly was a grand little worker, but you're shaping up very nicely as well, Nora.' She turned to Molly. 'The last girl we had was no use at all. Such a surly manner she had with the customers and they didn't like her one bit. I dare say Flo told you, didn't she? So it was by mutual agreement that she left, you might say. We're very pleased to have Nora especially now we know there's no chance of you coming back.'

'No ... no, I can't leave William. And ... there's my own little shop, of course,' faltered Molly.

'He's a lovely baby. Look how he's smiling.' Nora was tickling William under his chin and he was gurgling with pleasure.

'He can take any amount of fussing,' said Molly. 'He's not always like that, I can assure you. You should have heard him earlier this afternoon, screaming his head off. That's why I came out.'

'You won't put me off. I'd like to have lots of babies. When I get married, I mean.' Nora grinned a little embarrassedly and her cheeks flushed pink. 'Oh, excuse me; we've got a customer.' She hurried back behind the counter as a lady entered the shop.

'Come through to the back and have a cup of tea,' said Dolly. 'What about this little lad? Are you going to lift him out for a while? He's wide awake, see. Is it all right if I pick him up?' Molly nodded her assent as Dolly reached into the pram and lifted William out. He stared round the shop, crowing with delight.

'Come on through.' Dolly led the way to the small café area where two tables, which could each seat four, were laid with crisp white cloths and rose-patterned china. Two ladies were sitting at one table and a lone gentleman at the other. He looked up enquiringly as they entered.

'Molly, this is Mr Stubbins, the new owner of the chemist's shop. I don't think you've met, have you?' said Dolly as the gentleman rose to his feet. 'Mr Stubbins, this is Molly. Miss Rimmer, I should say. She used to work here before ... well, before you moved in.'

He held out his hand, regarding her gravely, and Molly was at once aware of the perceptive gleam in his eyes, cool grey eyes that looked as though they could see right to the heart and soul of her. 'How do you do, Miss Rimmer?' he said. 'Are you going to join me?' He gestured to the bentwood chair opposite him.

'How do you do, Mr Stubbins?' Molly replied. 'Yes – that is if you don't mind.' She tried to smile at him, disconcerted by his piercing glance, and she was relieved to see his small, rather prim mouth relax slightly into a smile.

'Why should I mind?' He raised his eyebrows, still continuing to look right into her eyes as she sat down.

'Of course he doesn't mind,' said Dolly, placing William on Molly's lap. 'He quite often comes in about this time for a cup of tea, don't you, Mr

246

Stubbins? Now, just make yourself at home, Molly, and I'll fetch you a pot of tea and a scone. Or how about a nice cream horn? I know you used to like those, didn't you?'

'Yes, thank you. A cream horn would be lovely,' said Molly, beginning to feel somewhat ill at ease beneath the cool regard of her new acquaintance.

'So you used to work here, Miss Rimmer?' he said. 'I have not heard Mrs Makepeace mention you before, but then there is no reason why she should. And I have been here only two weeks myself. Did I hear correctly? She did say you were ... Miss Rimmer?'

Molly was aware that his glance had now transferred to William and she guessed, also, that he was trying to take a peek at her left hand, which was hidden beneath the folds of the baby's shawl. She lifted her hand out now, placing it on the table.

'Yes, I am Miss Rimmer,' she replied, looking at him evenly. 'And this is my little brother, William. My mother died giving birth to him and then ... well, my father died not long after, so that's why I had to leave the shop. To look after William.'

The cool, almost unfriendly, look in his eyes changed to one of concern. 'Oh dear, I am so very sorry to hear that, Miss Rimmer. And also for thinking... Naturally, I assumed ... but that was very wrong of me, I can see that now. Please, do forgive me.'

'You assumed that the baby was mine?' she replied easily. 'Yes, I suppose you would, but he's my brother, not my son. I think of him as mine, though,' she added, a little defiantly, 'and I

247

expect that's how he'll think of me as he gets older, as his mother.'

She knew she could not blame this gentleman for looking askance at her before he became aware of the true facts. To have an illegitimate child, especially to flaunt it in public, would be enough to evoke the censure of any respectable folk. And Mr Stubbins was eminently respectable; a very well set-up young man, smartly dressed in a dark business suit and a high starched collar. His hair was dark, though he appeared to be prematurely balding, and his high-domed forehead gleamed like marble. He sported a moustache, as did many men. But surely he was too young to be the owner of – what had Flo said? – three chemist's shops. He looked much more approachable now he was smiling, and his eyes appeared warmer, almost kindly, although Molly did wish he would not stare at her so. She ventured a question.

'You own the shop on the corner then, Mr Stubbins? And didn't I hear you had two more shops in Blackpool?'

'That's not strictly true, Miss Rimmer,' he replied. 'It is my father who owns the shops, not myself. Although it is a family business and I will inherit them one day, I suppose. I am the only son. My father is Herbert and I am Hector, the son referred to in H. Stubbins and Son, of course.'

Molly learned a little more about him as she drank her tea and ate her cream horn, trying to prevent an active William from grabbing at her cup and saucer. Mr Stubbins' eyes, she noticed, kept straying thoughtfully towards the baby.

'He's a grand little lad,' he observed, though not overenthusiastically, she thought. 'How old is he? Six months, seven months? Not that I know anything about babies.'

Molly told him that William was only four months old, but quite big for his age, and forward too, she guessed. She learned that Hector Stubbins was a bachelor. He did not state his age, but she assumed he was in his early to mid-thirties. He was the manager of the shop on the corner, living alone over the premises, and he had a young lady assistant as well as a young man training as a pharmacist.

Molly said goodbye to him, scarcely giving him another thought as she made her way home. Her plans, thought tentative, for going back to work had been well and truly foiled and she could not see her way ahead, not anyhow. Where and how could she find another job, always supposing that Maggie would have William? But at the heart of her she knew she would never want to leave him. What on earth was she to do?

Hector Stubbins returned to his shop with a decided gleam in his eye and a jaunty spring in his step. Molly Rimmer; what a delightful, most lovely and desirable young woman she was. The moment she had answered him, so calmly and collectedly, that the child was not hers, but only her baby brother, he had made up his mind that he would have her. By hook or by crook, she would be his. Those limpid lustrous brown eyes, with just a shade of defiance in them; that rich auburn hair curling prettily beneath the brim of her hat; that neat little figure in the close-fitting black coat ... all of it added up to the most alluring girl he had ever set eyes on. To look at her was to desire her and Hector would not rest until he had made her his own. He knew he would have to marry her, of course. Anything else was unthinkable for a man in his position. The child was something of a drawback, admittedly. It had come as a relief to know the baby was not her own, but she did seem to be rather possessive regarding him. No matter; it was only a small problem, and he did seem to be quite an amiable child. Hector's eyes glowed with ardour as he began to look forward to wooing and winning Miss Molly Rimmer.

Chapter 12

Today was Thursday. She would give it till Monday, Molly decided, then she would have to do some serious thinking about their future; hers and Em's and baby William's. Maybe she could leave him for just part of the day, if she could get a part-time job, then she could open the shop during the remaining hours. But what about Em? She did like to be there when the little girl arrived home from school, as Lily had always used to be. She had had to rush this afternoon, all the way up Talbot Road, and she had been quite out of breath by the time she reached her door, only a few moments before Em arrived.

'What's up, Molly?' the child had asked as Molly was preparing their tea. 'You've gone all quiet. You've not asked me if I've enjoyed me day or anything. There's nothing wrong, is there?'

'No, nothing,' replied Molly, smiling at her. She knew she was preoccupied, but she must not let it affect Emily. The child had already had far too many upsets. 'Nothing at all. I'm just a bit tired. I've been out, you see, this afternoon and I had to rush to get back. I went to see how they were all getting on in Jubilee Terrace.'

'What? You shut the shop?' Em stared at her in astonishment.

'For a little while, yes. I do need a break from time to time, Em, and it can't make much difference closing the shop for just a couple of hours. If folk want anything they can always come back, can't they?' She spoke unconcernedly, but the truth was that customers would be quite likely to go elsewhere if the shop was shut; also, even two hours could make a difference in the takings, the difference between having enough money or not for the gas meter, for instance... But those couple of hours away had been necessary for her state of mind. Or so she had thought, but now, on returning, she knew she was just as troubled as ever.

'It was lovely to see Mrs Makepeace again,' she went on, 'and Cissie, and Dick and Fred. They made ever such a fuss of our William. They've got a new assistant as well, a girl called Nora who's taking over my job.' She sounded quite matter-of-fact about it, as though she didn't much care, but she was panicking deep inside with fear for what lay ahead. 'And look what Mrs Makepeace has given us for our tea, Em. Isn't it kind of her?' At least their next meal was assured, she thought to herself as she opened the paper bags and took out two meat pies, two sausage rolls and two rather squashed cream cakes that Dolly would have been unable to sell in the shop. Riches, indeed; if it hadn't been for Dolly's kindness they would have been making do, as they did so often, with bread and a smear of butter and jam.

'I've already eaten a cream horn this afternoon, Em. Goodness me, this'll be quite a feast, won't it? Come on, love, you lay the table, there's a good girl, and I'll see if there's a few pickled onions left in the jar. They'll go down a treat with

252

these nice meat pies.'

Em tucked into her meal with relish. It did Molly good just to watch her sister enjoying the unexpected bounty. Although their tea was usually a makeshift meal, Molly tried to make something more substantial at dinner time, even if it was only a meatless stew of vegetables and potatoes. She supposed they were lucky to have one good meal a day, which was more than some poor folk had. Molly now stocked a few what she thought of as luxury items in the shop – such as canned beef, sardines and bloaters, and tins of Heinz baked beans – but she made it a rule that they were not to help themselves to the shop goods. Those were solely for the customers.

Em licked her fingers, which were sticky with jam and cream, then licked her lips in a satisfied manner and patted her stomach. 'Gosh, I'm so full I feel I could burst, don't you, Molly? It's ages since we had cream cakes, not since you worked at the shop. And sausage rolls, an' all. We've not had them neither. Our mam used to make them sometimes; d'you remember? Why don't you make 'em, Molly?'

Molly had never felt more like shaking the child. Why didn't she make sausage rolls, for heaven's sake? Because there were not enough hours in the day, because she was already worn out with shopkeeping and housework, and looking after children. She very nearly said all this, but she managed to curb her tongue.

'I don't have very much time, do I, Em?' was all she said. Her voice was not as controlled as usual and, to her annoyance, she could feel a lump in her throat and incipient tears welling in her eyes. She blinked rapidly and swallowed, but Em did not appear to notice her discomfiture. With the innocence of childhood she blundered on.

'No, I know you don't, but I just thought it might be a good idea. You could perhaps sell 'em in the shop. Like Mrs Makepeace does. She makes all that stuff what she sells, doesn't she?'

'Yes,' replied Molly, curtly. 'Well, Dolly and her husband and son between them. There are more of them, aren't there? And Dolly can afford to pay somebody to do her cleaning, not like...' She sighed. It was not the child's fault if she, Molly, were tired and overwrought and worried sick. 'Come on, let's wash up, love. Then when William's settled down we can happen have a game of ludo. We haven't played for ages, have we?'

The days were much shorter now and it was too dark for the children to play out after tea as they had during the summer and early autumn. There were fewer customers, too, when dusk fell earlier and folk were disinclined to leave their homes. Molly did sell a few small items, however, that early evening, which gave her a few more pennies to feed the gas meter. At least they would not be playing their game of ludo by candlelight or getting up in the dark.

Why don't I make sausage rolls, indeed! thought Molly, a trifle bitterly, the next morning as she put William's soiled napkin and damp nightdress and cot sheet to soak in a bucket, made the beds, riddled out the ash, then got together the materials for blackleading the grate.

This was the job her mother had always used to do on a Friday and Molly had tried to do the same. She had not had time last week and Lily would have hated to see it looking so grimy and lacklustre. There was nothing like the artlessness of children, she thought, smiling wryly at Em's remark. She still wanted to shield the little girl, though, as best she could. Em was already having to grow up far too quickly, and the child really did think she had hit on a good idea. Sausage rolls, indeed...

Somehow Em's words lingered in her mind all morning. There was a fair number of customers, quite a steady flow, in fact, between eleven and twelve o'clock when, to her relief, the black leading was finished and the brass fire irons and brass fender had been polished till they shone like gold. She sold several of the new 'luxury' goods. The novelty of seeing them there on her counter was enough, seemingly, to persuade neighbours to part with their money. A jar of Bovril, a bottle of Lea and Perrin's sauce and a tin of Fry's cocoa – these had all been bought on impulse by customers attracted by the brightly coloured labels.

The last customer – or would-be customer, as it turned out – at twelve o'clock, just before Em was due home for her dinner, was a lad of fifteen or so.

'Got any meat and tatie pies, missus?' he asked brightly. He was a cheerful-looking lad but his face dropped when Molly told him she was sorry, but she did not sell them.

'Oh dear, that's a bad do,' he said, scratching

his forehead beneath his oversized cloth cap. 'Me mam didn't get round to putting up me stay-bit this morning, so me mate told me there were a shop up here where I could happen get summat. Oh dear, I'll have to go back and see if I can cadge a butty off him, won't I, if he hasn't already scoffed the lot.' He grinned at Molly and she could not help smiling back.

'Sorry I can't help,' she repeated. 'I've only got stuff in tins and that's not much use to you, is it? Where do you work?'

'At t'abattoir up the road,' he replied. 'I reckon you'd do a fair trade if you sold meat and tatie pies, missus. You think about it. Ta-ra now...'

Meat and potato pies; whatever next, thought Molly, shaking her head bemusedly. Meat and potato pies, sausage rolls... Somehow she couldn't get the thought of them out of her head. She did not say anything to Em, not that dinner time, but the child, in her ingenuousness, bless her, had given her the germ of an idea. Em and then that lad with his request for a 'meat and tatie pie'.

Molly called to see Maggie that very evening. The idea that had taken root in her mind was now developing. Maybe Em's remark had not been so outrageous after all. It had, at all events, started Molly thinking that there might be a way out of her straitened circumstances. But she would not be able to do it without help, and although it went against the grain after her, Molly's, show of independence, to ask Maggie, she knew she had no choice. And there was no time like the present.

'Hello there, stranger,' Maggie greeted her. 'And what have we done to deserve this honour, eh?' It was somewhat unusual for Molly to call at Maggie's home. It was generally Maggie who did the neighbouring, the popping in and out, although, since the shop opened, the two women had seen rather less of one another. It was usually Sarah who came along to buy the odd items that her mother had run out of. Molly felt that, deep down, her refusal of Maggie's help still rankled with the older woman. Well, very soon all that would be changed ... maybe. Molly metaphorically crossed her fingers and took a deep breath.

'I've come to ask a favour. Can I come in a minute, Maggie?'

'Of course you can.' Maggie peered out of the door, looking for the pram. 'I was just wondering where the little 'un was. It's not like you to leave him on his own.'

'He's not on his own, is he?' said Molly. 'He's with our Em. He went to sleep early tonight, thank goodness. They'll take no harm for a few minutes, though I mustn't be long.'

She followed Maggie into the kitchen at the rear. The whole family was there and, as usual, the room looked overcrowded and dreadfully untidy. The sideboard was strewn with all the paraphernalia of daily living: bills, letters, toys, gloves, scarves, newspapers. The clotheshorse was laden with articles gently steaming from the heat of the banked-up fire, and a pile of clothes, waiting to be ironed, lay on a chair. Billy and Betty, the twins, were playing snakes and ladders on the rag rug by the fire, and Sarah, also seated on the rug, was reading a comic book. Bill, and Tom, the eldest lad, each had his head buried in a page of the local *Gazette*, although Bill looked up welcomingly when Molly entered; and eleven-year-old Arthur was blowing a penny whistle. And Maggie, clad as usual in her flowered pinny, looked as though she might be about to tackle the sinkful of unwashed pots. Molly wondered anew at the idea of catapulting her precious baby brother into this haphazard household. But the room was warm, not just with the heat of the fire, but with the feeling of love and contentment that emanated from it, and she decided that maybe William would not fare too badly here. But, first of all, she had to ask.

'And what can we do for you?' asked Maggie. 'Shut up, our Arthur, blowing that bloomin' thing! We can't hear ourselves think... I reckon it must be summat important, like, for you to be coming here cap in hand, so to speak. Nay, lass, you don't need to look so sheepish. We're all friends here. Come on – what is it?'

'Well, I was wondering, Maggie,' Molly began, 'if you could look after William for me – only a couple of hours a day, mind. You see–'

'Oh aye, you're getting yerself a little job, are you? Or p'raps you've already got one, eh?' Maggie grinned, not exactly gloating, but in a way that was just a little self-satisfied. 'Of course I always knew it would come to this, but you wouldn't have it, would you? But what about the shop now, eh? Folks round here have come to depend on it, even though I thought from the start it were a barmy–'

'Hold on a minute, Maggie,' Molly interrupted. 'I'm not thinking of giving the shop up, far from it. As a matter of fact, I'm thinking of expanding it.'

Aware of Maggie's open-mouthed astonishment she went on to explain her idea, about how Em had mentioned the sausage rolls, then the lad had come asking for a 'meat and tatie pie'. 'So I wondered if, perhaps, I could do just that. Make meat and potato pies, and sausage rolls, maybe, and sell them in the shop. That lad seemed to think they'd be popular with the workmen.'

It was Bill Winthrop who spoke first. 'D'you know what, lass, I think you've hit on a grand idea. Why not? Just think of all t'work places there are round here. That lad came from the abattoir, you said? Aye, then there's the railway station, that's only just up the road, and the marine stores and the brewery. I reckon you could make a fair bit o' brass wi' that lot. You could make it into one of them dinner shops.'

'Hang on, Bill,' Maggie sounded a little irritated. 'Don't get carried away. How d'you know they'd come? Anyroad, I haven't said I'll have the bairn yet, have I?'

'Come on, Maggie – fair dos,' said her husband, tersely. 'You promised the lass. It was you what suggested it in t'first place.'

'All right, all right,' said Maggie. 'An' I'm not likely to refuse now, am I? Of course I'll have the babby.' She smiled a trifle grudgingly at Molly. 'I'll be pleased to help if I can. I said I would, didn't I? But this idea of yours – I'm not saying it isn't a good idea, mind – and Bill seems to be coming up with all sorts of fantastic schemes.' Molly knew that Maggie liked to think she was the one with all the ideas. 'But, well, it's going to be bloomin' hard work for you, isn't it, Molly? If you remember, that was why I was against the shop in the first place. I thought it was too much for you to handle on your own, and this'll make it even harder.'

'That's why I'm asking you to help me now, Maggie,' said Molly simply.

Maggie was silent for a moment before replying. Then she said, 'And you shall have my help, and willingly. What are friends for, eh? But ... meat and potato pies? Very fiddling, I should think, if you make each one separate, like. And you won't have room for 'em all in that fireside oven. I tell you what you could do, and it might be a better idea. You could make it in a whacking big dish – I sometimes use a washing up bowl for my lot, they're that greedy – then stick a crust on the top, and bob's yer uncle. Home-made hotpot, all ready to serve out to yer customers.'

'But what would I put it in?' asked Molly. 'I can't put it in a paper bag, not if it hasn't got a bottom crust, or even in greaseproof paper.'

'No, happen not.' Maggie was thoughtful. 'Tell you what,' she said, after a few seconds' pause. 'You could tell 'em to bring their own basins. You could put a notice up – "Delicious hotpot served daily. Bring your own basin", or summat like that. Yes, I reckon that's the best idea.'

Molly knew that, strictly speaking, this was not hotpot, although meat and potato pie was often referred to, in this part of the country, by that name. Traditionally, Lancashire hotpot was made with mutton chops, or sometimes with scraps left over from the Sunday roast, peas and carrots added, if desired, then covered with thinly sliced potatoes, browned on the top. Molly's 'hotpot' would consist of stewing beef and potatoes, with a dash of onion, cooked slowly for a couple of hours, then topped with a golden brown crust. That should be simple enough to prepare, especially if William was out of the way.

'Yes, that's a very good idea about bringing their own basin, Maggie,' she said now. She turned to Bill. 'What did you mean, Bill, one of them dinner shops? What's that, exactly?'

'Well, they used to have 'em where I lived in Burnley,' said Bill, 'near to t'cotton mill. I haven't seen 'em so much round here, although I dare say there are some, up and down. Mill workers couldn't get home at dinner time, y'see, so they could order their dinner in advance on their way to t'mill, at one of these dinner shops. I've known of many a housewife who opened up her front room for selling dinners, like you're doing, Molly, with your little shop. Happen you could combine the two, eh?'

'It would be the same meal every day, though, wouldn't it?' said Molly. 'Meat and potato pie – or hotpot, whatever you want to call it.'

'Beggars can't be choosers,' said Bill. 'There's nowt wrong wi' havin' the same dinner every day, especially summat as nourishing as hotpot. I'll tell you what else we used to have in Burnley, though – we had any amount of pay oiles.'

'What?' said Molly laughing. 'What on earth are they?'

'Hot pea saloons, to be more correct,' Bill laughed. 'Pay oiles, they always called 'em – pea halls, I suppose. They sold all sorts of peas; green peas, brown peas – parched peas, they call 'em – mushy peas. A ha'penny for a basinful – just a little basin, mind – wi' salt and vinegar provided. And you ate the peas with a spoon and drank the liquid. Mmm ... lovely it were.' Bill licked his lips at the memory. 'Sausages in gravy, they sold, an' all. Or you could have a teacake wi' a sausage inside it, or one with ham inside. It's worth thinking about, Molly, as well as yer hotpot. Mushy peas and sausage teacakes.'

'Give over, Bill. You'll have the lass dizzy with all yer barmy ideas,' said Maggie. 'Take no notice of him, Molly. He gets carried away, I've told you.'

'Perhaps not so barmy,' replied Molly. 'It's given me something to think about.' She smiled. 'Food for thought, you might say. I'll start in a small way, though, with the hotpot. I'll get a notice up right away, then perhaps word'll get round. I could start on Monday, Maggie, if that's all right with you? Anyway, I'd best be getting back. Em'll be wondering where I am.'

'Yes, I'll have the little 'un on Monday,' agreed Maggie. 'You'll have to go to the butcher's bright and early, won't you, to get your stewing beef or whatever. And get that notice up. You'll have to advertise, and I'm sure folks'll soon catch on... Wait a bit, though. Don't go dashing off. Your Em and William'll take no harm for another minute or two.' Maggie whispered a few hurried words to Bill, who listened thoughtfully, then nodded.

'Aye, you're right, Maggie,' he said. 'I couldn't agree more. And don't let her say no.'

Maggie went to the sideboard and took out a tin box, similar to the one in which Molly kept her spare cash, when she had any, and anything else of value. She took something out, closed the box again and put it away, then came across to Molly. 'Here y'are,' she said in a gruff whisper, pushing something into her hand, 'and, like Bill says, we won't take no for an answer. This is to help you get on your feet.' Molly saw that it was a gold sovereign.

'Oh no,' she cried instinctively. 'I couldn't possibly...' She felt tears springing to her eyes. Maggie, despite her brusqueness, really did have a heart of gold, like the sovereign she was trying to make her accept. But both Molly's mother and father had believed in paying their own way and never taking anything that smacked of charity. Molly had always vowed she would stick to the principles they had instilled in her, but she knew that Maggie would be very hurt if she refused to take the gift. 'I can't...' she faltered, but rather less vehemently. 'It's so good of you, Maggie, and you, Bill, but really, I don't think–'

'I've told you, we insist,' said Maggie. 'You can't refuse, and if you do, well then, I shan't help you.' She spoke decisively, but Molly could see the glint of humour in her friend's eyes.

'All right then.' She smiled back at her, weakly though, still feeling more like crying; Maggie and Bill were so kind. 'Thank you, both of you, thank you very much. It's no use pretending it won't be needed. As a matter of fact, I've wondered however I was going to manage, this last week or two, until I had this new idea. And now I can buy all the things I need to get started. But it's only a loan, mind you, Maggie. I'll pay you back when I get on my feet again, really I will.'

'Very well then,' replied Maggie. 'Call it a loan if you must, if it'll make you feel better. Pay me back ... sometime, although there's no need. Now, off you go before your Em starts worrying.'

Molly made the notice, with Em's assistance, the very next morning. It was a rainy Saturday, far too cold and wet to play out in the street, and the little girl was delighted to fill in the letters that Molly had drawn, with her coloured crayons.

'Home-made meat and potato pie served here daily,' read the notice. 'Please bring your own basin.' Molly had decided to call the dish by its correct name so there would be no misunderstanding. Maybe, as time went on and she grew more proficient, she could serve other dishes as well, including the real Lancashire hotpot and the peas and sausages that Bill had spoken of. But she knew she must begin in a small way, as she had done with the shop, and see how things worked out.

Em had been thrilled at the new plan. 'It was my idea, wasn't it?' she said eagerly. 'With me saying about the sausage rolls. It was me that made you think of it, wasn't it, Molly?'

Molly had replied that it was, indeed, Em who had planted the idea in her mind, Em and the unknown lad from the abattoir; but that the sausage rolls would have to wait a little while. 'We have to walk before we can run, Em,' she said, 'but I must admit I'm looking forward to Monday, and you can help me to serve it out when you come home from school.' Provided we get any customers, she added to herself.

But before that, on Sunday afternoon whilst Em was at Sunday school, Molly had a surprise visitor.

She was more than surprised, she was astonished, on opening the door at the forceful knock, to see Hector Stubbins standing there. For a second or two she failed to recognise him, having given him not a single thought since she had met him three days ago in the café. 'Good afternoon, Miss Rimmer,' he greeted her effusively. When she did realise, on hearing him speak, who he was, she was a little discomfited. What on earth was she to do? Might it not be considered improper for her to invite him into the house while she was alone – except for William, of course? On the other hand her good manners prevented her from leaving him standing on the doorstep. But what on earth did he want?

'Oh, Mr Stubbins,' she said. 'How very nice to see you again. What a surprise. Won't you ... won't you come in?' What else could she do? He had taken off his bowler hat in a sweeping gesture and now stood with it against his chest, his head poking slightly forward, his all-knowing grey eyes looking at her intently.

'Yes, thank you, Miss Rimmer. I would be

delighted to step inside for a few moments, if it is not inconveniencing you?'

'No, no, not at all. I have just finished washing up.' Automatically she wiped her hands on her apron, wishing she had taken it off when she heard the knock at the door, but she had assumed it would be one of the neighbours, not someone ... well, someone as important as Mr Stubbins. He stepped over the threshold and she closed the door behind him. 'There's only me here, and the baby, of course. My little sister, Emily, has gone to Sunday school. She'll be back in a little while.' Oh, do shut up, she chided herself. Stop prattling, for heaven's sake. Find out why he's here. A sudden thought struck her in that split second that maybe he had come to offer her a job in his shop. She could not think of any other reason for him being here. If so, it was too late.

He had followed her into the back room. Now he stopped dead in his tracks and stared at her 'Oh, I did not realise you had a sister as well. I was assuming there was just yourself and your baby brother. A sister ... I see.' He nodded, his eyes regarding her keenly. 'How old is she?'

'She's just turned nine,' Molly answered, rather curtly. What business was it of his, anyway? Come to think of it, how did he know where she lived? She answered her own question in her mind straight away. It would be Mrs Makepeace, of course, who had told him. But why had he wanted to know?

'Won't you sit down, Mr Stubbins?' she said politely. Her mother had always told her she must be polite to guests, whoever they were, not that the Rimmer family had ever had many visitors. 'Let me take your hat.' Not his coat, though, his smart Burberry-style overcoat; that would look as though she were wanting him to prolong his stay. She was unsure what to do with the hat, however, when he handed it to her. They did not have a hallstand, so she placed it on the sideboard which, fortunately, was much less cluttered than the one in Maggie's house. The whole room, in fact, was reasonably tidy, warm and welcoming, too, with the fire irons and fender gleaming brightly and the armchairs and cushions she had rescued from Lily's one-time parlour adding a touch of, if not exactly elegance, of respectability.

'I'll make you a cup of tea, if you would like one?' she said, watching as Mr Stubbins took off his overcoat, without being invited to do so, and laid it over the back of a chair.

'If you don't mind, Miss Rimmer,' he said, 'it is very warm in here.' He sat down in one of the armchairs. 'I won't have any tea at the moment, thank you. Later, maybe. Sit down, won't you, Miss Rimmer? I want to talk to you. You must be wondering why I have come.'

'Yes, I am, rather,' said Molly, sitting down in the chair opposite him, not relaxing, though, as he appeared to be doing. She perched on the edge of the seat. 'I expect it was Mrs Makepeace, wasn't it, who told you where I live?'

'Yes, indeed it was that lady,' replied her guest, fixing his eyes upon her again in a way she found more than a little disconcerting. 'When I met you on Thursday I knew that I would like to get to know you better. To be your friend, if you would allow me to be, Miss Rimmer?'

Molly stared at him, completely taken aback.

'I realise how difficult it is for you,' he continued. 'You are on your own, apart from your brother ... and sister, of course. Mrs Makepeace has told me a little more about the tragic loss of your parents. I am so very sorry. It must have been dreadful for you, and to be left with a young family to care for as well.' She could see the sympathy in his eyes and she felt his concern was real.

'Thank you,' she said with a sad smile. 'Yes, it has been hard for us, but we are managing. We have the shop, you know.'

'Yes, Mrs Makepeace told me a little about the shop. And I knew about the baby, of course, but she did not mention your sister.'

'Yes, our Em,' Molly smiled fondly. 'She's a very good little girl, no trouble at all, and she's a great help to me with the baby, and with the shop.'

'I am sure she is,' replied Mr Stubbins politely, and a trifle indifferently, she thought. 'I saw your notice in the window,' he added. 'A new innovation, I take it, selling meat and potato pie?' He raised his eyebrows quizzically.

'Yes, very new. We start tomorrow,' said Molly, aware that she sounded a shade defiant. 'Things have not been easy, Mr Stubbins, I can't pretend they have. I have to earn a living.'

'And I admire you for it, Miss Rimmer, I do indeed. I am full of admiration for all you are doing, but I hope it may be ... only a temporary measure?'

Molly opened her mouth to reply, but no words came. She was not sure, in truth, what it was she wished to say, but it did not matter because Hector Stubbins did not wait for an answer.

'As I was saying, I appreciate what a difficult position you are in, a young woman alone in the world. If you had a father I would, of course, be asking his permission to ... to see you, but as you are on your own, then it is you I must ask.' His eyes bored into hers.

'Miss Rimmer, let me tell you a little more about myself. You already know I am a bachelor and I manage one of my father's shops. Apart from that I am ... a Methodist local preacher,' he said this with some pride and she could almost see his chest swelling, '...at the Ebenezer Chapel just round the corner from Jubilee Terrace. It is very convenient now I am living, as you might say, on the doorstep. However, to come to the point. I would like to invite you to come with me to our chapel anniversary weekend, next Saturday and Sunday. We are having what we call a Faith Tea on the Saturday, followed by a concert; then on Sunday we have a special guest preacher. I do hope you will say yes.' He paused for just a few seconds before adding, 'And I hope it may be the first of many similar outings for us.'

Molly was flabbergasted. Her initial reaction was to refuse, quite definitely. So Mr Hector Stubbins was a religious man, was he? She had not known that, and she wanted nothing to do with religion. But she could not say that to this earnest young man, not so bluntly. That would be extremely rude. Besides, the chapel he had mentioned was, coincidentally, the one that Emily was attending at this very moment. And so, when she replied, she found herself prevaricating a little.

'That is very interesting, Mr Stubbins. Quite a coincidence. That is where my sister has gone this afternoon, to your chapel. I told you, didn't I, that she had gone to Sunday school?'

'Really?' His eyes gleamed even more intently. 'Well, that is remarkable. I assumed that she had gone to the Church of England school. I happen to know, you see, that you, yourself, are not what you might call a regular worshipper...'

Not a worshipper at all, thought Molly, let alone a regular one. What else did the fellow know about her, for goodness' sake?

'...and when people do not go anywhere they usually say they are Church of England, or they send their children there. But perhaps I could persuade you to come with me, especially as your sister is acquainted with the place? Please say you will, Miss Rimmer. You would make me very happy if you were to say yes.'

Molly was not unmoved by the fervent expression in his eyes. She started thinking about how much Em enjoyed her weekly visit to this chapel and how she always came home in a joyful mood, ready to tell her sister about all that had gone on there, much more readily than she talked about the happenings at day school. Maybe, just maybe, there was something that she, Molly, was missing.

'Yes,' she found herself replying, much to her surprise. 'Yes, I think I might like that. Thank you, Mr Stubbins. I will come with you. That is, if I can bring Emily with me. I expect my neighbour will look after William, but I don't like to leave Em as well.'

'Of course, why not?' he answered jovially, clasping his hands together. 'There should be quite a few of the Sunday school children there, those whose parents attend, so she will not be on her own. Excellent, Miss Rimmer. I am delighted you have said yes. If I may, I will call for you ... both of you, at four o'clock next Saturday afternoon?'

'Yes, that will be lovely,' replied Molly, feeling bemused at the way she had changed her mind. But it was ages since she had had an outing of any kind, apart from her visits to the warehouse, not since Jubilee night. Em would enjoy a treat too, and she was sure that Maggie would agree to have William. 'Now, you must let me make you a cup of tea, Mr Stubbins.'

'My name is Hector,' he replied, regarding her gravely. 'I would be honoured if you would call me by my name, and perhaps I might be permitted to call you Molly? Seeing that we are about to become friends?'

Molly nodded as she rose to fill the teapot from the already steaming kettle. 'Yes, most people call me Molly, so I see no reason why you should not do so...' Her voice petered out. She was overwhelmed at the speed in which things were happening. What on earth was she doing? Only half an hour ago Hector Stubbins had been the furthest thought in her mind, and now she had agreed to ... what? To start walking out with him? Was that what he had in mind? It certainly sounded like it, but Molly knew that she could not, must not, commit herself so far. Not that she had anything against him. From the little she already knew of him he seemed to be a very steady and worthy young man. Well bred, too. Certainly not someone for whom she could use the everyday earthenware crockery that she and Em used. Shades of Lily, she thought wryly as she excused herself to her guest and went to fetch the flowered china cups and saucers from the cabinet in the front room.

'I will be pleased to come with you on Saturday,' she said, trying to keep both her hand and her voice steady as she passed him the cup of tea, 'but it is just for the once ... Mr Stubbins.' She knew she could not yet call him Hector. 'Beyond that, well, I can't promise anything.'

'I understand, Molly.' He nodded gravely. 'Just as you say. One step at a time, that's your motto, eh?'

'Something like that,' she muttered. She was relieved, at that moment, to hear the front door open and close. Here was Em, home from Sunday school. That, at least, should stop Hector Stubbins from hurrying things along too fast.

The little girl was dumbstruck at the sight of the guest. She just nodded silently when Molly explained that this was Mr Stubbins, the chemist from Jubilee Terrace, and he had come to invite them to a tea and concert next Saturday, 'At the chapel you go to with Sarah. That will be nice, won't it, Em?' Molly said brightly.

But Emily did not seem at all pleased at the idea. Rather reluctantly she took hold of the hand the gentleman held out to her, murmuring 'How d'you do?' as she had been taught she should. Then, to Molly's consternation, she put her head down and did not speak another word to either of them. She took her colouring book and crayons out of the sideboard drawer and sat down at the table, colouring away furiously.

'She's rather shy,' Molly explained, feeling that she could shake the child, although, on the other hand, she thought she could understand why Em was acting like this. She had never been at ease with strangers. Hector Stubbins said that he understood and seemed relieved, as soon as he had gulped down his tea, to take his leave of them; especially as William was now stirring in his pram, making the aggressive noises which showed he wanted attention.

'That wasn't very polite to a visitor, was it Emily?' Molly chided her gently when he had gone, 'refusing to talk like that.'

Em shrugged. 'Who is he, anyway?'

'I've told you. He has the chemist's shop on Jubilee Terrace and I met him the other day. He thought it might me nice for us to go to the concert on Saturday,' said Molly. 'I think it was very kind of him,' she added crisply.

'Well, I don't like him,' said Em. 'So there!'

Molly sighed inwardly. This was not going to be easy. Hector Stubbins did not appear to be at ease with children any more than Em was at ease with him. A sudden memory came to her of a pair of twinkling blue eyes and a winning smile, and she was transported back in thought to that joyous Jubilee evening. 'Just like my dreams they fade and die...' The words of the song echoed in her mind. Almost angrily she pushed the thought away and reached into the pram for the now screaming William.

Chapter 13

Joss Cunliffe, at the same time, was thinking of Molly.

Here, at the Oldham home of his Uncle Walter, his father's elder brother, and his Aunt Miriam, he had been made to feel most welcome. His large bedroom faced north across a bleak stretch of moorland. It might prove rather chilly, he guessed, as winter approached, although his aunt had assured him he could ask for a fire to be lit any time he wished. However, the clear northern light streaming through the window was ideal for his painting. It was the portrait of Molly to which he was putting the finishing touches at the moment.

Molly ... whose other name he had never discovered, gazing out across the Irish Sea, her deep brown eyes fixed on the horizon, the green ribbons on her straw hat lifting slightly in the gentle breeze, her auburn hair curling softly across her forehead. He doubted that he would ever be able to capture her true beauty in paint, but he had done his best. He felt, though, that he had done justice to the sunset, the pinkish-orange flow of the sky and the shimmer of gold on the turquoise sea. He had tried to face up to the fact that he was unlikely ever to see this lovely girl again. The memory of her and that wonderful evening had become almost like a dream to him, but she would live forever in his mind and in this portrait of her.

During the mellow early autumn days of September and October Joss had sometimes hired a pony and trap to take him out on to the moors around Oldham. The hillsides were harsh and bleak, lightened only here and there with the odd patch of heather or the flame of a gorse bush, but the dark shadows which drifted across the moorland and the grey lowering sky gave the landscape a beauty all of its own, providing Joss with ample scope for his artistry. Or he would take a train out to Hebden Bridge, just over the border with Yorkshire, and with his haversack on his back and stout boots on his feet he would tramp along the pathways of the beautiful Calder Valley, or up into the lower stretches of the Pennine hills. There he would set up his small easel and try to capture on paper some of the colourful glories of the scene around him; the rich brown of the bracken clothing the moors, the russet and gold of the trees in their autumn foliage, or the silver-grey shimmer of a small waterfall cascading between the rocks. Sometimes he sketched, rather than painted; an odd-shaped tree growing out of a rock or a trio of inquisitive sheep who had wandered close to him, perfecting his rough drafts later in the solitude of his room.

Uncle Walter and Aunt Miriam were restful people, his uncle the very antithesis of Joss's blustering dictatorial father. It was partly his desire to be free for a while from Henry Cunliffe's domination that had made Joss apply for the course in textile design at the Manchester college. He had been surprised when his father had not opposed his request but, rather, had actively encouraged him. Henry, as a rule, took the opposite view in anything his youngest son suggested, but not so this time. He could easily find someone else to take his place in the design shed, his father had told him, which was not very flattering, but suited Joss admirably. He came to the conclusion his father was just as glad to see the back of him as he, Joss, was to depart. It was Henry who had arranged that he should stay with Walter and Miriam in Oldham, travelling into nearby Manchester each day on the train. His mother had been regretful, even tearful, but she could see it was for the best and, Joss consoled her, it would only be for a year. And he would be able to come home now and again for the weekend.

So far, he had been home only once since he started the course in September, for the wedding of his eldest brother, Percy, to Hannah Watson. It had been a lavish affair, the ceremony taking place at St John's Church and the celebration afterwards at the nearby Booth's restaurant. Joss, wishing the happy couple 'all the best', wondered, in truth, how happy they would be. He liked Hannah. She was an uncomplicated, rosy-cheeked, rather horsy-faced lass, very pleasant and amiable, and he thought she deserved better than his brother Percy, who was turning out to be a carbon copy of his father. At the moment he seemed fond of her, in a casual sort of way, as she did of him, but the attraction for Percy – and for his father – had undoubtedly been the dowry she brought with her. Hannah's father too was a mill owner, of a somewhat larger mill than Cunliffe's, and she was the only child. It did not take much working out to see that Henry and his eldest son had their eyes on the main chance.

Henry had been in the best of spirits that day, which was a blessed relief to all the members of his family, as he had been in a foul mood since the summer – ever since he had found out about his middle son, Edgar's, friendship with a mill girl, one of his own weavers, whom he had met, of all places, in the Tower ballroom at Blackpool.

'Has tha no sense, lad?' Henry had cried when Edgar, quite boldly and unashamedly, had admitted it was true. He was seeing the said young lady, Betsy Pringle – he had stressed the word 'lady' – he was, in fact, walking out with her. 'Lasses like her are all right for a bit of that there, but not for owt else.' Henry had never tried to disguise his Lancashire accent and the broadness of his vowels, but they became even more pronounced when he was angry. 'You'd best watch out, lad, or she'll get her claws into you good and proper, then you'll be up the creek wi'out a paddle. Ah'm tellin' yer. Even you couldn't be such a fool as to think of marrying her, surely?'

It had not happened overnight, but by September it had been quite obvious that that was exactly what Edgar did have in mind. He was quite brazen about it, too, and Joss could not but admire him for his stand. He knew it was exactly how he would have reacted if he had been in a similar situation. If he had had the good fortune to track down the elusive Molly he would not have let anyone stand in his way. But Blackpool was a big place, he had not known where to look next, and always, at the back of his mind, there had lingered the niggling doubt – she had not turned up to meet him when she had promised to do so. Maybe the unpalatable truth was that she had simply changed her mind. He had not been back to Blackpool since July, not since the night that Eddie had met Betsy Pringle.

Acrimonious words had been bandied back and forth all through the summer. Joss had been surprised that his father had not shown Edgar the door and told him to find work elsewhere – God knows, he had been angry enough. But the truth was that Edgar was a good worker, invaluable in the warehouse and with the dispatching of orders. Not impossible to replace – no one was indispensable – but Henry would have to look a long way to find someone of Edgar's capability and shrewdness. Besides, Joss guessed that, beneath his rage and bluster, Henry was too fond of his middle son to become estranged from him. It was possible that Henry might, in time, even come to relent over the friendship with Betsy Pringle. As Edgar had reminded his father very forcefully, Henry's wife – the mother of his three sons – had been a weaver, just like Betsy.

This remark, though true, had almost caused Henry to have an apoplectic fit. 'How dare you, you cheeky young devil?' he had raged, going red in the face, the veins standing out alarmingly on his forehead and neck. 'How dare you speak about your mother like that? Get out of my sight

279

this minute, before I kick you out. Get up to your room. Go on, before I give you a damn good hiding!'

This angry exchange had taken place at the dinner table about a week before Joss had been due to go to Oldham. Edgar, obediently, had departed – he had finished his meal, anyway – but not before he had delivered a parting shot. 'But it's true, Father, so why get into such a state about it? Mother was a weaver, wasn't she, just like Betsy? Though we all know you'd like her to forget all about it.' He'd been through the door before the table mat, which Henry hurled, hit the wall behind him.

'There's no need for all that, Henry,' Charlotte had interposed calmly, as was her way. 'After all, you can't deny the lad's speaking the truth. That's what I was, when all's said and done, a weaver, just like the lass there's all the fuss about.'

'Don't you start sticking up for him, woman.' Henry had turned on her angrily. 'It's all water under the bridge, anyroad, all a long while ago, and we've come on a long way since then. I want summat better for the lad than a jumped-up mill girl.' Which Joss had considered was a very tactless remark to make to his wife who had risen from the self-same occupation. The fact had always been known to the three boys – Charlotte had made no secret of it – but never talked about it in any detail. Joss and Percy had exchanged uneasy glances then, but had made no comment. Percy, though sometimes loud-mouthed, could keep silent when he felt it was expedient.

'You were a weaver at Father's mill – Cunliffe Mill – weren't you, Mother?' Joss had asked Charlotte one evening when they were alone together. He could not understand all the secrecy and had often wanted to find out more about it, but had not liked to do so. Then, on the eve of his departure to his uncle's home and his new course in Manchester, he had felt it might be opportune to enquire.

'No, not exactly,' his mother had answered, sounding a little hesitant. 'That is to say – I was a weaver, as you already know, but not at your father's mill. No, I worked at Seth Cartwright's mill.' She had lowered her eyes, fixing them on the floral pattern on the carpet at her feet, and her voice had been so quiet Joss had almost had to strain to hear her words. 'Well, it was Seth's father's mill in those days, of course, just as Cunliffe Mill belonged, then, to your grandfather. The two young men – Seth and your father, I mean – were good friends. Still are... It was through Seth that I first met Henry. But as he so rightly says, it's all a long time ago. A lot of water has flowed under the bridge since then. Your father wants me to forget those days – my humble origins.' She'd given a slight shrug of her shoulders. 'And I've tried to do so.'

She'd looked up at him, smiling a little uncertainly. Joss had sensed her discomfiture, although he hadn't been sure of the reason for it. He had always been aware of a certain restraint between his mother and Seth Cartwright – Priscilla's father – whenever the families met together. This was not very often, although the two men still appeared to be on friendly terms. His mother, however, had never seemed keen on Joss's friendship with Priscilla; neither had Seth, he realised now when he thought about it. It was his father who had tried to matchmake, as he had done with Percy and Hannah. But although he, Joss, liked Priscilla well enough as a friend, there was no vital spark between them or the sort of affection that could lead to marriage. They had made a mutual agreement recently, as he was going to Manchester, that they would go their separate ways. Joss had wondered now if there had been something, way back – a feeling that was more than friendship – between his mother and Seth Cartwright. He'd decided not to ask, however. She would tell him if she wished him to know, and he'd been aware that she seemed ill at ease, thinking about the past.

'I had always assumed you worked for Father – well, for Grandfather,' Joss had said, trying to sound casual. 'I suppose that's because Father had never really explained.'

'Henry's been good to me,' Charlotte had replied, looking at her son almost defiantly. 'We've been happy. He's brusque, I know, but beneath it all he's ... well, he's very good at heart. I have a lot to thank him for. All this...' She'd moved her hand in a gesture that took in the whole room.

This was, strictly speaking, the morning room, the small room that was Charlotte's private sanctum where she gave instructions each day to the housekeeper and dealt with servant problems when they arose. Always trivial ones in this household, as all the servants agreed that Madam was the most kind and agreeable person to work for. It was a cosy place to spend an evening hour as well. The deep salmon pink of the velvet curtains, drawn now against the dark, matched exactly the shade of the plush boudoir chairs, and the floral pattern on the carpet picked up the same rich colour. There was an elegant rosewood writing desk where Charlotte dealt with her correspondence and the minor household bills, and a display cabinet, also in rosewood, which contained a collection of Royal Crown Derby, Minton and Coalport china, and the Dresden figurines which Henry loved to buy for his wife.

'Yes, it took a while for me to get used to all this,' Charlotte had continued. 'After what I'd been used to ... or hadn't been used to, you might say.' Joss knew little of his mother's early life, save that she had been brought up by an elderly aunt, who had died a long time ago, in a small terraced house near to Cunliffe Mill. Near to Cartwright Mill as well, for the two mills were near neighbours. 'But your father was a good tutor, and I reckon I haven't done too badly for him. Anyroad ... anyway,' she had corrected herself, 'I have done my best, though I have to admit I don't always agree with him.'

Only occasionally did Charlotte's broad vowel sounds and her use of the vernacular show in her speech. In truth, she spoke much more refinedly than did her husband. 'I think you've done splendidly, Mother,' Joss had assured her. 'Father couldn't have a better wife nor a more loyal one. It gets my goat the way he puts you in your place sometimes. But it's no use telling you to stand up to him, is it?'

'Not really, dear,' Charlotte had smiled. 'It's just his way. All bluff and bluster. He doesn't like to lose face, that's his trouble, but he usually comes round to things in the end. Like he did with you and this course in Manchester.'

'He didn't oppose it at all, Mother, if you remember,' Joss had said. 'In fact he seems only too keen to have me out of the way.'

'Oh no, I'm sure that isn't so,' Charlotte had replied, not altogether convincingly. 'You're mistaken, Joss. He wants what is best for you, as I do, and he knows that design is your speciality, isn't it?'

'Not his, though. Father couldn't care less about new designs. He's only interested in the ordinary stuff that makes more money for us. I'm not as much use to him as Percy and Edgar.' His mother had declined to answer and Joss had decided to change the subject. Her loyalty to her husband was unquestionable. 'Do you really think he'll come round, then, with regard to Eddie's ... er, lady friend. He seems very set against it at the moment.'

'I think he will eventually,' Charlotte had replied. 'What else can he do? He won't want to lose Eddie, and the lad's of an age to do as he likes.'

He wouldn't be so concerned at the thought of losing me, though, Joss had mused.

'She seems a very nice girl, this Betsy,' his mother had continued. 'I've only seen her a few times, at the mill, of course – he hasn't been able

284

to bring her to the house – but I hope he will be able to do so fairly soon. Perhaps after Percy is married your father may see reason. What's the difference, anyroad, between her and me? Not a scrap of difference.'

His mother had fallen silent again and Joss had sensed that she was more troubled than she was admitting. She had been quiet all day, though, and Joss had known it was the thought of his departure that was making her sad. The two of them had always had a close relationship.

'So that would be two of you settled,' she'd said after a few moments, speaking quite cheerfully. 'Percy and Hannah, Eddie and Betsy, happen. And what about you, eh, Joss? You've not met anyone yet who's taken your fancy?' She'd smiled at him and he'd recognised that the clear blue of her eyes was just the same colour as his own. She had a lovely smile, just like the girl who was still constantly, though hopelessly, in his thoughts.

'I did ... a little while ago,' he'd begun, 'but it seems as though I've lost her again.'

A small frown had creased his mother's brow. 'Do you mean ... Priscilla?'

'Oh no, not Priscilla. That's not who I meant. I thought you realised. Priscilla and I both know that it's no use. We're good friends, but nothing more.'

Charlotte's face had relaxed again and she'd given a decisive little nod. 'Of course. I know that was what you said. Quite right, she is not the girl for you,' she'd added dismissively. 'So ... who?'

'A girl I met in Blackpool on Jubilee night.' Joss had taken out the sketch which he always kept in his inside pocket and showed it to his mother. 'I did this drawing of her. It's very tattered now, but you can see how lovely she is ... was.' He'd shrugged. 'I seem to have lost her.'

'You mean she didn't want to see you again?'

'I'm not sure. Maybe not ... or maybe something went wrong for her. I don't know. I've tried to find her again, but I can't. So I know I've just got to think of her as a lovely memory.'

'She's certainly a very lovely girl.' Charlotte had handed the sketch back to him. 'But there will be other girls, I'm sure. Maybe in Manchester... You will write, Joss, won't you, when you have time? And you'll try to get home now and again? I know it's only a year, but I'm going to miss you very much.'

His mother was the only member of the family that Joss really missed. But, having left home, he was not at all sure now that he would want to return there after the year's course was finished, despite his assurances to his mother that he would do so. There was not much scope for his talent at his father's mill, nor at his uncle's mill here in Oldham. That, like many others in the town and in neighbouring Rochdale, was a spinning mill, not concerned with the weaving of the product and the setting up of new designs. Maybe he could find employment as a textile designer at another of the Preston mills. Disloyal to his father though it may seem, he did not think that Henry would care overmuch. Or he could try further afield, maybe, in Blackburn or Burnley. Weaving mills abounded throughout the whole of east Lancashire.

But that was in the future. There was still more than two-thirds of his course to run. Joss was enjoying the lectures, the new ideas and the challenge of it all, and the companionship of the other students – male students, in the main, although there were a few women: rather intense, blue-stocking sort of girls, one of whom, as the only child, was in line to inherit her father's mill. But there was no one of the opposite sex who could stir a spark of interest in Joss. He entered into the camaraderie at the college by day, but the evenings and weekends were spent quietly with his aunt and uncle and, occasionally, his cousins and their families. The children of Walter and Miriam, two boys and a girl, had long been married and left home. The sons, Clem and Jonas, carrying on the family traditions, held positions of authority in their father's spinning mill. Their visits to their parents' home were confined to weekends, and not every weekend at that. Walter and Miriam, living alone, had been glad of 'a bit of young blood', as Walter put it, to enliven their solitude.

As for Joss, he was contented enough at the moment with his own company or that of his aunt and uncle with whom he had always enjoyed an easy relationship. He walked on the moors, dutifully attended church on a Sunday morning, read from his favourite Trollope or Dickens, and worked on his portrait of Molly.

By the end of the first week of her new enterprise Molly had reason to believe that it had been a good idea. There were just a few customers on the Monday and Tuesday for the meat and potato pie, and Molly and Em, eating the leftovers for tea as well as dinner – there was a limit to the number of times you could warm it up again, certainly not to serve to customers – felt that they could soon become sick of the sight and taste of it. By Wednesday, however, the word had spread, and on Thursday and Friday Molly had sold out of the dish by one o'clock and had to turn people away. And, more importantly, there was a steadily growing amount of silver in the tin box in the sideboard.

Molly decided it could be time to branch out. Maybe next week she would make some sausage rolls as Em had suggested. It would mean rising at the crack of dawn, or even before, to put them in the oven, so that they would be cooked before it was time for the meat and potato pie to go in. There was a limit to the amount that the fireside oven would hold. Or, alternatively, she could make them the night before. At all events the sausagemeat would have to be fresh and she would not have time to keep running to the butcher's shop. Maybe she could have a daily order of sausagemeat and the stewing steak she needed each morning delivered by the butcher's boy. So far, she had been sending Em to buy the meat when she came home from school, having decided that the little girl was now old enough, and assuredly sensible enough, to run errands; but there was a limit to what she could ask the child to do. Yes, a standing order might be best; like a real businesswoman, Molly thought to herself with a certain pride as she considered it.

But before that there was the outing to the Ebenezer Chapel on Saturday with Hector Stubbins. Molly had been so busy all week that she had scarcely given the young man a thought, but now, as the day approached, she began to wonder if she had done the right thing in accepting his invitation. Em had not mentioned him at all since her outburst the previous Sunday when she had declared that she did not like him, but she too had had other things on her mind all week. Em seemed happier, much more settled in her mind, Molly thought. The little girl knew that their new business venture was proving successful, and if her sister was less worried then it was bound to affect her favourably. Molly decided, on the Friday night, that it might be a good time to broach the subject of the next day's outing.

'You haven't forgotten we're going out tomorrow, have you, Em?' she ventured. 'To that tea and concert with Mr Stubbins? Auntie Maggie is going to look after William for us, so it'll be a nice change, won't it, after we've been working so hard all week? I'm looking forward to it,' she added, her forceful words aiming to convince herself as well as Em.

'I've not forgotten,' replied Em. 'I told Sarah about it, 'cause it's at the same place as we go to on a Sunday, and she says she'd like to come with us. Children can go if they're with a grown-up, Sarah says – they've had 'em before, these concerts. And Auntie Maggie can't go 'cause she's looking after William. Anyway, she never goes to church or anything, does she? So can

Sarah come with us? Auntie Maggie says it's all right.'

'It's the first I've heard of it,' replied Molly. 'Maggie hasn't said anything to me about Sarah going.'

'No, 'cause Sarah's only just asked her, so I said I'd tell you. Can she come with us then?' Em's brown eyes were fixed intently on Molly's and there was just a shade of belligerence in her voice. 'I shan't go unless Sarah can go.'

'It's not really up to me,' said Molly. 'I don't know what Mr Stubbins...' She noticed the narrowing of Emily's eyes and the slight pouting of her lower lip. 'Oh, all right then. I don't suppose he will mind. Yes, Sarah can come. After all, she does go to the Sunday school.' The two girls would be company for one another, she thought to herself. And there would be nothing worse than dragging along a recalcitrant little girl who was being forced to go somewhere against her will.

'No, of course I don't mind. The more the merrier,' declared Hector Stubbins, when Molly asked if Sarah might accompany them. 'So you're Emily's little friend, are you, my dear?' He beamed somewhat fatuously at Sarah and Molly suspected, as she had before, that he had had little to do with children.

'Yes, tha's right,' replied Sarah. She grinned at him, not at all shy at meeting a strange adult. 'Em and me's best friends, ain't we, Em?'

Em nodded and Molly was relieved to see that she was, so far, not showing any antagonism towards the man. Neither was she going out of her way to be friendly, but at least they had got off to a fairly good start, and Sarah would help to relieve the tension.

'Good, very good,' said Hector Stubbins heartily. 'I think Emily was rather shy of me the other day, eh, Emily? But we'll soon bring her round, won't we, Sarah?' His broad smile encompassed all three of them, and Em actually smiled back at him, though she still appeared a little ill at ease.

'Righty-ho then, let's be off, shall we?' He held out his arm to Molly and, after a moment's hesitation, she placed her hand near his elbow, very lightly. It felt uncomfortable there, but to refuse to take his arm would have seemed ill-mannered. She was very self-conscious as they walked along the street then down Talbot Road, aware of the curious glances of a few of her neighbours. The two little girls, who knew the way, were skipping ahead quite unconcerned.

'I've got some money to pay for meself,' said Sarah when they arrived at the chapel. 'Me mam gave it to me.' She offered the coin to Hector, but he refused to take it.

'Oh no, most certainly not. My treat today, Sarah.' He beamed expansively at them all again, and at the middle-aged lady who was seated at the door, dropping the sixpences and shillings into a glass sugar basin.

'Ta very much, mister,' said Sarah cheerily. She dragged at Em's arm. 'Come on. Let's go and see if there's any of the others here.'

'Wait a minute, dear,' said the lady on the door.

'You need a ticket for your tea, both of you. That's to show you've paid.' She handed them each a small pink card. 'We've got a special table for children at the far end of the room. We thought they would like to be on their own for a while, away from their ... mothers and fathers.' She glanced curiously at Hector, then at Molly. 'Your ... nieces, perhaps, Mr Stubbins? I did not realise–'

'Oh no, just friends,' replied Hector. 'This is my friend Miss Molly Rimmer and her little sister, Emily, and Sarah.' But the two little girls had disappeared. 'Molly, my dear, this is Mrs Wotherspoon, one of the stalwarts of our chapel. We don't know how we would manage without her at these chapel teas, do we, Mrs Wotherspoon?'

'Oh, how very kind of you to say so, Mr Stubbins,' twittered Mrs Wotherspoon, the cherries on her black straw hat bobbing up and down at each movement of her head. 'We do our best. Not just me, of course, oh no, not at all. I'm just a small cog in a very big wheel. We have a loyal band of helpers. We're always willing to do what we can in the service of our Lord, like you're always reminding us we should do, aren't you, Mr Stubbins?' The woman was clearly in awe of him, and Molly was somewhat embarrassed when Mrs Wotherspoon turned to her and went on, 'And it's so lovely to see you here today, my dear. Just wait till I tell them all that I was the first one to meet you. We kept saying it was time he had a nice young lady friend. We hope you'll come again and again, don't we, Mr Stubbins?'

'Er ... thank you,' muttered Molly, longing to

put the woman right, to tell her that she was not his young lady friend, but at the same time feeling completely at a loss.

'Indeed we do, Mrs Wotherspoon,' said Hector. 'I hope this will be the first of very many visits for Molly. Come along, my dear.' He tucked his hand beneath her elbow in a proprietorial manner and led her into the hall.

Molly felt, as she had when he called on Sunday, as though she were being propelled along partly against her will, but there was no doubt at all of the warmth of Mrs Wotherspoon's greeting, nor of the welcome she received at the tea table. Hector fussed around her, taking her coat and hanging it on a peg at the side of the room with a row of other coats, then drawing out her chair and making sure she was comfortably seated. Em and Sarah were already sitting down at the end table, both appearing quite at home in their surroundings – understandably, as they came here every Sunday – and chattering away to another couple of girls of a similar age. It was the first time Molly had been in this building, which consisted of the Sunday school hall and a few smaller rooms adjoining the main chapel. The chapel that Flo attended, and which Molly had visited occasionally, was at the other end of the town. But, newcomer though she was, Molly was made to feel at her ease immediately, not only by Hector, but by all the other people at the table.

As soon as they were all seated they had to stand again to sing the grace. At a chord from the piano they all began to sing loudly and, on the whole, melodiously,

'Praise God from whom all blessings flow,
Praise Him all creatures here below...'

Molly was glad that she knew the words and the tune from somewhere way back – her schooldays, maybe? At any rate, she was able to join in. Then they all sat down again before going, a few at a time, to a long table at the side which held the food.

Each table, apart from the long one for the children, seated ten, and Molly felt by the end of the meal that she had known some of these people all her life, such was the friendliness and sincerity of these warm-hearted Methodist folk. Maybe she had been lucky, she mused, in her choice – or, rather, Hector's choice – of table companions. Surely all the members of this congregation could not be so free and easy and genuinely welcoming of a stranger in their midst. But it was certainly true of this cross section of them and the feeling began to grow in Molly that maybe there was something in her life that had been missing till now: companionship, fellowship with a wider group of people than that of just the family circle. She had had a few friends when she was at work – she had never found it difficult to make friends – and now she was at home there was still Flo and, of course, Maggie. But you could not help but be aware in this church hall that they were all members of one big family – a happy family too, by and large – which engendered in Molly a glow of warmth and contentment. In spite of the misgivings she had felt about accompanying Hector to this place – doubts she was still harbouring, if she were honest – she was beginning to feel already that she belonged, that she could be happy here.

The folk on their table appeared somewhat older than Molly; three married couples, and two middle-aged ladies – there seemed to be a preponderance of such – as well as herself and Hector. The couple opposite Molly and Hector were particularly amiable, introducing themselves as Ralph and Violet Prosser and going out of their way to make sure Molly was amply provided with food and drink and friendly conversation. She had puzzled over the term 'Faith Tea'. She now learned it was a meal to which each person brought a contribution – some sandwiches, half a dozen buns, tarts or a fruit loaf; whatever they wished – and the offerings were then shared out between everyone. You had to have faith, Molly thought amusedly, that there would be enough to go round. Which there undoubtedly was. The table at the side from which everyone could help themselves was practically groaning beneath the weight of homemade cakes, buns and jam tarts; fruit loaves and currant teacakes; sausage rolls and meat pies; large dishes of fruit salad and trifle; and a huge variety of sandwiches – potted meat, salmon paste, and boiled ham as well as the more mundane cheese or egg and cress.

'Why didn't you tell me?' Molly whispered to Hector when she discovered what a Faith Tea actually was. 'I feel dreadful now – I haven't brought anything.'

'But I have,' he assured her. 'I called in earlier with my contribution. Sausage rolls and a large meat pie – Mrs Makepeace's best. I've told you, today is my treat, so just enjoy yourself.'

'Yes, you tuck in, luv,' said Violet Prosser, the woman who had been particularly welcoming to Molly. Molly guessed she was in her mid-thirties, short and plump with a round rosy-cheeked face and round blue eyes smiling from behind a pair of round steel-rimmed spectacles. Her whole aspect was one of cheerful roundness. 'There's always far too much, anyroad, at these dos. Like the feeding of the five thousand, it is. That's what some folk think happened, you know, when Jesus fed the multitudes. Everybody took out their own little picnic, like, that they'd brought with them, and shared it.'

'Well, fancy that,' said Molly, rather nonplussed at hearing the name of the Lord used so openly in ordinary conversation. That was certainly something she was not used to. However, she was aware of Hector at the side of her bristling a little.

'I have to say that I do not agree with you, Mrs Prosser,' he declared. Molly was learning that every sentence that Hector spoke was more of a declaration than a casual remark. 'The feeding of the multitudes was a miracle, pure and simple, and to suggest anything different is to minimise the power of our Lord.'

'What does it matter?' said Ralph Prosser, with an amused glance at his wife. 'She didn't mean any disrespect, did you, luv? Aye, they're a good idea, Miss Rimmer, these Faith Teas. We quite often have 'em here. Some folk like to call 'em a

Jacob's Join. Same dog washed, as they say. What's in a name, eh? Now, more tea, Miss Rimmer? Over here, Mrs Wotherspoon, please.' He beckoned to the lady with the nodding cherries on her hat, who was now, with another lady, making her way between the tables, bearing enormous enamel teapots. 'This young lady will have a drop more. Anyone else?'

The tea was hot and strong, more dark brown in colour than any she had seen before. 'Please call me Molly,' she reminded Mr Prosser. 'I'm not used to being called Miss Rimmer.' She remembered, at the same time, that she had yet to call Hector Stubbins by his Christian name. She knew she would have to make an effort to do so. She was glad now that he had invited her here and she was enjoying herself far more than she had thought she would.

Molly noticed, however, that he was 'Mr Stubbins' to most of the people gathered round the table, only one of the men occasionally referring to him as Hector, and they seemed to regard him with some awe, as she had noted Mrs Wotherspoon had done. It was an awe, though, she felt, that held more apprehension than admiration or respect. She learned during the course of the meal that Hector, as well as being a lay preacher, was also one of the chapel stewards – a group of people, six in number, who dealt with the running of the church – and a class leader too. This was a new concept to Molly. She had thought it was only the children who were taught in little groups on a Sunday afternoon but it appeared that the adults, also, in the Methodist chapels, were divided into classes, under the guidance of the prominent members of the congregation who were known as the class leaders. She remembered that Flo was a member of such a group – her Young Ladies Class – which met on a Sunday afternoon. The classes at Ebenezer met on various nights of the week, some in members' homes and others here, on the chapel premises. Hector's class met in one of the Sunday school rooms every Wednesday evening, and it was this class to which Violet Prosser, Molly's informant, belonged.

'You'll be coming along, I dare say, won't you?' she said to Molly, 'seeing that you and Mr Stubbins are … er … friendly.'

'I don't know,' replied Molly, evasively. 'He hasn't asked me about it yet. As a matter of fact, I haven't known him very long. I wouldn't want you to think that we are … well, what I mean is, we're not walking out together or anything.' Hector had by now risen from his chair and was talking earnestly to a man at the next table so Molly felt she could talk more freely. Even so, she lowered her voice because she did not want the rest of the people on the table to hear her conversation. She felt, however, that she could confide in Violet Prosser. She had taken to the woman immediately. 'As I was saying, I only met him just a week ago. I was flabbergasted when he asked me to come here today. He hardly knows me.'

'He seems smitten, though,' said Violet with a smile, 'and it takes a lot, let me tell you, to get our Hector to unbend. Proper stiff and starchy he can be at times, you wouldn't believe... Oh dear, pardon me.' She put her hand to her mouth. 'I shouldn't be saying anything against him, should I? I'm sorry, luv. It was very naughty of me, but we were that surprised when the news got round that he had invited a young lady along.'

'Why?' asked Molly. 'Hasn't he ... hasn't there been anyone else, before?'

'Not that we know of,' replied Violet. 'No, he's always seemed wedded to his work – the shop, I mean – and to his preaching, of course.'

'And is he a good preacher?' asked Molly, who had heard so few sermons in her life that she knew she would not be competent enough to judge. 'Do you like listening to him?'

'I'm blessed if we can understand what he's on about half the time,' said Violet, laughing, and with a candour that Molly found refreshing. 'There again, I shouldn't be criticising, should I? Yes, he's reckoned to be pretty good, I must admit. Very theological, you know' – Molly did not know, so she just nodded – 'very deep and learned. Anyway, you'd best come along and hear him for yourself. You'll be coming to the service tomorrow, won't you? Not that Hector'll be preaching tomorrow. We're having a guest preacher.'

'Er ... yes, I expect I'll be coming,' said Molly, surprising herself by her reply. She did not know yet what she would do about William, but she felt it would be ungracious of her to refuse to come to the service after enjoying the tea and concert. The Chapel Anniversary, she gathered, was quite an occasion in the life of the folk here at Ebenezer.

'Yes, we've got a chap from Rochdale coming to preach tomorrow,' Violet went on, 'a friend of our own minister, I believe, one that'll make us sit up in our seats and take notice. You know what I mean.' Molly again nodded politely. She didn't really know. 'Mind you, our own fellow is well worth listening to. That's our minister over there – the Reverend Richard Allbright.' She nodded towards a middle-aged man with a clerical collar sitting at the other side of the room. He was quite short and stocky, with a shock of wiry grey hair and a ruddy complexion. He looked to Molly more like a manual worker than a minister of the church. He was not unlike her father, she mused, especially when she saw him turn and smile at the woman next to him. His face seemed to radiate an inner joy, similar to the happiness she had so often seen illumine her father's face when he had smiled at her mother. Molly felt sad for a moment, and lonely too, wishing she had someone who cared about her in that special way.

'And that's his wife, next to him,' Violet went on. Mrs Allbright was similar in age, and in looks, to her husband: fiftyish, homely and friendly looking. 'They're a grand couple. They've really worked wonders at this place since they came just over two years ago. There's nothing they won't do in the service of our Lord.' There it was again, that free and easy reference to the Lord that made Molly feel a shade embarrassed, though she could not have explained why.

Hector returned to his seat with an enquiring smile at Molly. 'I'm sure you've been all right in Mrs Prosser's capable hands, haven't you, my dear? I just had a few details to sort out about the service tomorrow,' he added importantly. 'Mrs Prosser has made you feel at home, has she?'

'Oh yes, thank you. Mrs Prosser and I have had a lovely chat,' said Molly, smiling at the woman she was beginning to think of as a new friend. 'I've been hearing all about the classes and about your minister...'

The Reverend Richard Allbright stood up at that moment and clapped his hands, at which the hubbub of noise gradually decreased, then stopped altogether. He certainly seemed able to command their attention. He thanked all the lady helpers for organising the tea and all the people who had brought the food. Now, he said, it was the men's turn to do some work; they were to move the tables and put the chairs into rows for the concert 'to which we are all looking forward immensely. We know it will be a grand event in the true Ebenezer tradition.'

An army of aproned ladies, for the most part still wearing their hats, descended on the tables and quickly piled the crockery on to large trays which were then carried into the adjoining kitchens for what Molly guessed must be the mammoth task of washing up.

'Can I help?' she asked, feeling bemused and a little guilty too at all the flurry of activity going on around her. But Violet told her most definitely that she was a guest today and, what was more, she, Violet, had been given the job of looking after her. 'They'll soon get through it,' she said cheerfully. 'There's enough of 'em to help and plenty of hot water. That's the important thing;

301

we had a new geyser put in last year and it's been a godsend. I'd best make the most of it, hadn't I? I've only been let off today because you're here. Mind you, we'll get you working the next time you come. We all have to do our bit.'

Molly assured her she would be only too pleased to help ... the next time. She already felt that this would not be her one and only visit to Ebenezer. She felt, too, that the reason for this would not rest entirely with Mr Hector Stubbins. Em and Sarah came running towards her and she was pleased to see Em's happy smile and bright eyes. Obviously the child's earlier reluctance had been overcome by Sarah's presence and that of her other Sunday school chums, as well as the carefree ambience of the place. The two little girls were quite clearly at home there.

'This is my sister, Emily, and her friend Sarah,' Molly told Violet. Em, as well as Sarah, smiled at Mrs Prosser in a friendly way, but it was Sarah, of course, who said to the woman, 'We know you, don't we? You teach in our Sunday school.'

Violet Prosser agreed that she did, but she was in charge of the 'babies' class', not the grown-up girls like Sarah and Emily. And her fifteen-year-old daughter, Daisy, had also just started to teach there. 'So we're all one big happy family here, aren't we?' she said cheerily to the girls. 'And we're hoping your sister will come along and join us as well. That would be grand, wouldn't it?'

'Yes, we're all going to the special service in the morning,' said Em, with an eagerness that Molly found unusual. 'You'll come an' all, won't you, Molly? You can bring William. Our Sunday

School teacher says you can.'

'Perhaps,' said Molly, a trifle guardedly, feeling, once again, that events were taking over and sweeping her along out of her control. 'I'll have to see.'

'That means yes,' said Sarah. 'When me mam says "I'll see" she always does it in the end.'

Violet grinned knowingly at Molly as the two little girls followed their friends into another of the wooden partitioned rooms; they were to play quiet games with one of the teachers until it was time for the concert to start.

'I hope you'll come,' Violet said quietly. 'You are really most welcome here, you know. I take it you don't belong ... anywhere else?' To another church or chapel, Molly assumed she meant. 'We wouldn't want to poach, you see, on another congregation.'

Molly assured her new friend that she did not 'belong' anywhere else and, with a sense of fatality, added that she would most probably be there at the morning service. They all stood around in small groups, chatting, while the menfolk pushed the chairs into rows facing the stage. Then Hector joined the small gathering of women of which Molly and Violet were a part. She noticed that the conversation waned a little at his presence, but he did not seem to be aware that he was causing any discomfiture amongst the ladies.

'Come along, my dear.' He took hold of Molly's arm again in the possessive way she had noticed before, and was not sure she was ready for – at least, not yet – and led her to a row of chairs near

303

the front. 'The concert will be starting soon and I want you to have a good view.' She was relieved to see that Violet and her husband, Ralph, joined them, Violet seating herself on the other side of Molly. Sarah and Em were already sitting down on the front row, no doubt at the instigation of Sarah, who appeared to be as much of a leader here as she was with the children in the neighbourhood of Larkhill.

Molly found the whole concert most entertaining, although she had been to few such gatherings and had nothing with which to make a comparison. It was such a pleasant change from the routine – often, she had to confess, drudgery – of her day-to-day existence. For a couple of hours she was able to forget, or at least to put to one side, her problems with a fractious baby, the housework, the shop, the continual cooking of meat and potato pie – which, though profitable, was also exhausting – and lose herself in the music and poetry.

It was not a particularly light-hearted programme. These Methodists were not given to a great deal of levity such as cracking of jokes, and frivolous song and dance, but the entertainers seemed to be enjoying themselves, as was the audience, and certainly they put their hearts and souls into making the evening a success. What the tenor singing 'Love Could I Only Tell Thee' lacked in the sureness of his top notes he made up for in volume and enthusiasm. A little girl, about the same age as Emily, touched all hearts with her singing of 'Won't You Buy My Pretty Flowers?', and the same hearts were stirred, but in a different way, by the gentleman who recited 'Ye Mariners of England' followed by 'O Captain, My Captain'. The lightest touch of the evening was provided by the young lady who sang a selection of songs by Gilbert and Sullivan. Molly had heard only snatches of them before, whistled by errand boys and performed by the little orchestra at Uncle Tom's Cabin. Now she listened in delight to the words and music of 'Little Buttercup', 'The Sun, Whose Rays', and the lovely song from *The Gondoliers* about the Merry Maiden who was about to be married.

But the words that stayed with her after the concert ended and she walked home through the dark streets with Hector were those from the poem 'Remember' by Christina Rossetti. It had been recited by a dark intense-looking girl who, Violet had whispered, was one of her fellow Sunday school teachers.

'Better by far you should forget and smile
Than that you should remember and be sad.'

Molly found the words most poignant, and relevant, too, to her own circumstances. Maybe it was time to try to put the past behind her; all her sadness and grief for her mother and father, and the yearning, too – for, if she were honest with herself, she had never stopped hoping and longing – for a young man who could never be hers, and to look towards the future.

Hector at her side was holding forth – with Hector it could never be called chattering – about the various people they had met that evening, whilst Em and Sarah, as before, skipped on ahead of them. He did not require an answer, only an occasional 'Yes' or 'Mmm...' of agreement or a nod of the head. They stopped at her door and Molly's dilemma as to whether or not she should invite him in, whether it would, indeed, be proper to do so, was settled by Hector's words.

'I will not come in tonight, Molly, my dear. I know you will be anxious to collect your baby brother and to see to this young lady here. Long past your bedtime, eh, Emily?' Em's slight frown showed her disapproval of being treated like a baby, but she took hold of the hand that Hector politely held out to her, then to Sarah, muttering, 'Good night, Mr Stubbins. And thank you for taking me.'

'Me an' all,' added Sarah, and Hector actually laughed. Molly was glad her sister had remembered her manners, and without being prompted. Maybe, after all, Em might turn out to be not so much of a problem as she had feared – if, that was, she should continue to see Hector Stubbins.

'Perhaps, on another evening, Molly, I could avail myself of your hospitality?' She took the hand he offered to her, unsure of what to say. He was taking it for granted there would be a next time and she could not find it in her to object.

'Er ... yes, of course,' she murmured. 'And thank you for a lovely evening ... Hector.'

His eyes glowed at her first use of his Christian name. He bent his head gravely, stooping to kiss her hand. 'I will call for you in the morning to escort you to the service.'

Molly had already agreed to go, but it was useless for her to protest that she could easily get there on her own. Hector was most insistent and, as she was already learning, he was not a man who could be easily dissuaded.

Chapter 14

Molly and Hector were married in May 1899, some eighteen months after their first meeting. It was not a long courtship compared with many, and Flo, who had been walking out with Sam Leadbetter for several months longer than Molly and Hector had been courting, with still no wedding date in sight, seemed a trifle envious, a trait certainly not usual with Flo.

'It's all right for some,' she had said when she first heard the news, at the beginning of January, that the marriage was to take place in the late spring of that year. 'Of course, you can afford to get married, can't you? At least he can; with him having his own business and that. D'you remember saying, Molly, that you would have one of those shops on Jubilee Terrace one day? Well, your wish is coming true, isn't it?'

Molly had pointed out to her friend that it was not the same thing at all. What she had meant was that she would like to be the owner of one of the shops, not just be married to a man who owned one. Besides, Hector did not really own the shop. It belonged to his father and Hector was the manager.

'As good as, though,' Flo had countered, 'and it'll be his one day, won't it? Not that I begrudge you any of it, really I don't,' she'd added, sounding a little as though she were trying to convince herself of the fact as well as Molly. 'I'm so pleased that things are going well for you at last. You deserve all the happiness you can get after what you've been through. You are happy, aren't you, Molly? About getting married and ... everything?'

Molly had assured her friend she was happy about her forthcoming marriage, although contentment, rather than happiness, would have been a more accurate way of assessing her state of mind. More like resignation, she thought to herself in her more reflective moments, but this was a pessimistic way of looking at things when she knew she was really very fortunate. Molly was convinced she was doing the right thing in marrying Hector, although she was aware that there was little of the ecstatic joy in their relationship, such as she had seen in the love her parents had had for one another, and that she saw in Flo and Sam's friendship too. You could see in the eyes of that couple when they looked at one another how much in love they were. Theirs was a true romance, but the word 'romance' was not one that Molly would choose in describing her relationship with Hector.

Admittedly, she had perceived a gleam of ardour in his pale grey eyes at times – he had such a habit of staring at her – and she had looked away, feeling uncomfortable and, if she were honest, a little fearful. But Hector was always most circumspect in his manner towards her. They had been going about together for several months before he had asked her, formally, if she would do him the honour of becoming his wife...

It was a balmy evening in late May and they were walking home together, arm in arm, from the weekly class meeting which Hector took every Wednesday. Molly did not always attend, but Hector had particularly wanted her to be there that evening. She had left William in the care of Emily. The little girl was growing up and loved to have full charge of her baby brother, now almost one year old, although it was only on rare occasions that Molly would allow her to do so.

'I have prepared an interesting discourse on Moses and the Ten Commandments,' Hector had told her. 'I would like you to hear it, my dear. I am sure you would find it enlightening.'

It was invariably some Old Testament figure that he chose to talk about, many of whom Molly had never even heard of, but Moses, at least, was familiar. She had to admit she found the subject matter slightly less tedious than the lectures she had heard previously, and Hector seemed to be in a jovial, almost light-hearted mood. She found herself warming to him as they made their way home. It was almost a year now since the death of her parents and she realised that meeting Hector and having his companionship had been quite a solace to her. She knew that the worst of her grieving was over and that this was, in part, due to Hector.

Emily had taken herself off to bed, having left the living room tidy, the pots all put away and the fireguard placed around the banked-up fire.

'Em is such a good girl,' Molly remarked, smiling fondly as she took off her coat and hat. 'Of course she has had to grow up quickly with all that has happened, but she really is a very great help to me.'

'Quite so.' Hector smiled politely and, she thought, a trifle dismissively. He took off his coat, laying it carefully over the back of a chair, at the same time taking a small box from the pocket of his coat. Then, precisely – he was precise in all his movements – he laid his bowler hat on the seat of the chair and turned to Molly.

'Sit down, my dear. There is something I want to say to you.' Obediently she sat in the armchair. She had seen the small box in his hand and it came as no surprise to her. She had been expecting this moment for some time now, though not with joyful anticipation; more with a sense of ... inevitability. She was somewhat taken aback, though, when he kneeled on the hearthrug at her side and took her hand in his.

'Molly, my dear, I think you realise how much I care for you. Since I first met you, six months ago, my feelings for you have grown deeper and deeper, and now I want to ask you if you will do me the great honour of ... becoming my wife. Molly, my dear, will you marry me?'

She agreed after only a second's hesitation. 'Yes, Hector ... I will marry you.'

The myriad thoughts that rushed through her mind in the few moments while he proposed to her were a mixture of those that had been with her constantly over the past few months. Hector was a good man, upright and worthy, and although he was not universally liked at the chapel, his preaching and his good works there spoke for themselves. How could a man of God be anything but honourable and deserving of all the affection she could give him? She knew she did not love him, but she had convinced herself that the attachment she was already feeling towards him would grow. She often thought of her parents, a devoted and loving couple if ever there was one, and she was well aware that the same vital spark did not exist between herself and Hector ... but it might develop, given time.

Molly knew, also, that in marrying him she would be gaining some vital security, not only for herself, but for Em and William as well. Admittedly, Hector did not take very much notice of them, but neither did he totally ignore them; and this, too, was something which would grow, given time ... wouldn't it? She knew he had never had very much to do with children. He was the only son of somewhat elderly parents and so he had no nephews or nieces. In fact she knew very little about his background or about what he had done in the years before he took over the shop in Jubilee Terrace.

Hector had told her he had worked as a chemist in Yorkshire and had come back to Blackpool only a few years ago at his father's request. Mr Stubbins, Senior, had wished to open a third shop and had wanted a reliable and experienced manager. His parents lived in Marton, at the south end of the town and were members of a Methodist chapel in that vicinity. Hector had taken Molly to meet them just once, and she had been made very welcome in their home; a modest home, not at all showy or grand, although Molly gathered that the Stubbinses were not short of 'a good bit of brass'. But neither did they set much store by this or let it affect their simple, God-fearing way of life. Molly decided that she liked them very much and she had wondered why Hector had not taken her to see them again. She had sensed a certain restraint between the three of them, something she could not quite put her finger on; nothing as definite as antagonism or bitterness, but she realised they were not so free and easy in their dealings with one another as her own family had been, or as Maggie's, for instance, always were. But she had dismissed her doubts, telling herself that not all families could live up to her ideal.

And so she agreed to marry Hector and he slipped the sapphire and diamond ring on to her finger. It really was a beautiful ring, just the one she might have chosen for herself, but it was Hector who had chosen it. Then he kissed her for the very first time, gently and – so it seemed – without a great deal of passion or feeling. She did not know whether to be glad or sorry about his restraint.

Their courtship progressed and his kisses, at least at the start, were always chaste and very seemly. Inevitably, they were often alone together, in Molly's home or in Hector's rooms above the shop on Jubilee Terrace, but never did he take advantage of the situation and let his feelings get out of hand. His embraces became a little more ardent, his kisses longer and a mite more passionate as the wedding day approached, but she felt that Hector was keeping a tight rein on himself.

313

Her feelings about the wedding night and what would take place were ambivalent. She did not know everything about such matters. She realised that there were few girls who did know all the facts, although she and Flo had talked quite openly about it. All that Molly knew was that Flo and Sam would approach their wedding night with joyful anticipation, happy in their love for one another, whereas she, Molly, was apprehensive to say the least. She was doing the right thing, though; she was sure of that. Hector had told her that he loved her, and she believed him. He had made it obvious from the start that he wanted her for his wife, in spite of the fact that she had her younger sister and baby brother to care for.

Hector had been unable to disguise entirely his lack of rapport with the children; any children, not just Molly's siblings. He still largely ignored William, now nearly two years old, and treated Emily with the same forced bonhomie that he had shown when he first met her. Molly continued to tell herself that it was only because he had never been used to children; the vast majority of men, anyway, took little notice of their off-spring, leaving their upbringing solely to their wives. So it would be in their marriage – no different from thousands of others – and she would have the added advantage of help with the housework and the children. She had to admit, when she had got used to the idea, that that, indeed, would be a luxury.

Molly had argued against the idea of hiring a nanny to look after William, which was what

Hector had at first suggested. What would be the point when she would, after her marriage, have more time to spend with her little brother than she had ever had before? Her dinner shop, successful though it was, would, of course, come to an end when she married Hector. But she had agreed, though reluctantly, to his appointment of a maid of all work who would live in and assist with the cooking, cleaning and – on the occasions when Molly would allow it – caring for William. The girl Hector had chosen for this position was sixteen years old and a regular attender at the Ebenezer chapel. She was called Rosie Hewitt, one of a large family who found it hard to make ends meet, or so Hector had told Molly. Molly was sure the two of them, she and Rosie, would have a lot in common. She knew the girl by sight from her own visits to the chapel and liked what she saw. Rosie Hewitt was a girl such as she, Molly, had been when she was struggling to make a success of the house shop after the death of her parents; poor, clean and tidy, though somewhat shabbily dressed, but always managing to raise a cheerful smile. Molly was not at all happy about the idea of employing a servant of any kind, but she knew that, in marrying Hector, she was taking a step up in the world and so she must conform to his idea of what was right and proper. If Hector said they should engage a maid then that was what they must do.

Immediately after their marriage and the honeymoon in the Lake District that Hector had arranged, they were to move into a house of their own in Warbreck Road, some five minutes' walk from the shop. The rooms that Hector occupied at the moment could be used as storerooms or, at a later date, rented to a suitable occupant. Molly was grateful, too, for his thoughtful provision of a home for them all. It was a terraced house with four bedrooms; one for Hector and Molly, one for the two children, who would share a room as they were quite used to doing, a small one for Rosie, the maid, and a spare bedroom. It sounded like a veritable mansion to Molly, and to Flo as well. Another reason, Molly feared, for her friend's slight envy, and who could blame her?

'Sam and me, we'll be lucky if we can even afford to rent a place,' said Flo. 'We want a place of our own, y'see. We don't want to move in with my parents or Sam's, like a lot of couples have to do, but we'll need money for furniture an' all. We're saving up like mad, but Sam doesn't get very much at the printing firm he works for, and Miss Mary and Miss Annie don't pay me much neither. I'm getting my training, of course, and that counts for a lot. I'd still like my own business, one of these days. If Sam and me get a little house of our own I could p'raps use the front room as a fitting and sewing room – you know, like you use your front room for the dinner shop...' Flo stopped, wrinkling her forehead thoughtfully before giving a laugh. 'Hark at me! We've not even fixed a date yet. It must be making your wedding dress that's getting me all jealous. No, I'm not really jealous – you know what I mean, Molly. Just that I wish it was me; me and Sam, of course, not me and Hector.' She burst out laughing as though such an idea was preposterous. 'Although you seem quite suited with him, I must admit. Come on now. Slip this over your head and let's have a see if I've got the fit all right this time.'

It was Flo who had come up with the suggestion that she should make Molly's wedding dress, and Molly had jumped at the idea. It would be good practice for her friend, who was doing it in her own time, in her own home, and it would cost much less than having it made by 'Marianne Modes' – where it would be Flo doing most of the sewing and fitting anyway – or by the dressmaking department at Donnelly's. Molly was still very conscious of the cost of everything, though the dinner shop was doing well and she knew that quite soon, when she was married to Hector, she would no longer need to count the pennies. Now, six weeks before the wedding, the ivory satin dress needed only the finishing touches adding to it, as did the bridesmaids' dresses, which Flo was also making, for herself and Emily.

'Yes, Hector's quite a nice fellow when you get to know him, isn't he?' mumbled Flo, crouching on the floor, her mouth full of pins, as she adjusted the hem of Molly's dress. 'Not such an old sobersides as he seems at first. He preached at our chapel once and we couldn't make head nor tail of him, at least I couldn't. But he's quite jolly and friendly when he's with you, isn't he? I was surprised ... I'm real glad, Molly, that he's got you coming to chapel. You've never regretted it, have you?'

'No, no, I haven't,' answered Molly with

complete sincerity. She recalled a conversation she had had with Maggie Winthrop a few days before, a similar conversation, in fact, to the several she had had with Maggie from time to time over the last few months, ever since the announcement of her engagement to Hector Stubbins.

'Now you are sure, aren't you, lass? You're not just marrying him to get a roof over your head and a bit more brass? 'Cause there's no need, is there? Your little shop's doing well, far better than I ever thought it would, to be honest. It seems a shame to give it all up... And marriage is for a lifetime. You've got to be sure.'

'You don't like him, Maggie, do you?'

'Oh, I wouldn't go so far as to say that. He's charming enough, I've got to admit, and he thinks the world of you – I can see that. I just wish he'd take more notice of little William... But your Em doesn't like him, does she?'

'She hasn't said so,' Molly had replied. 'Not since that first time. She's said very little about him since then.'

'She doesn't need to say owt. I can tell by the look on her face,' Maggie had said, with the all-knowing expression in her voice and in her eyes that tended to annoy Molly. 'Still, if you're happy with the fellow...'

'I am,' Molly had insisted that last time, as she had many times before. 'Not all my friends think like you do, Maggie. Flo seems quite taken with Hector. He's been ever so friendly towards her and Sam.'

'Oh aye, well, he would be, wouldn't he? He's

318

one o' them, isn't he? That's why they can't see owt wrong wi' him. You're marrying that lot as well as Hector Stubbins, aren't you, lass? Come on now, admit it. They've got a real hold of you, that Methodist lot, haven't they?'

'I enjoy going there, yes,' Molly had agreed. 'They've all been very kind to me. But that's not the reason I'm marrying Hector. Of course it isn't.'

'All right then, if you say so...'

But Molly knew, deep down, that what Maggie said was true. In marrying Hector she was, in a sense, marrying into the whole of the chapel community as well. She agreed readily with Flo now that not once had she regretted going along with Hector, first of all to the Faith Tea and concert – that had been the start of it all – then to the morning service and to many other services and class meetings. She had met with such warmth and friendliness there as she had never experienced before. And Molly, still grieving over the untimely death of both her parents, still perplexed at the strange turn her life had taken, had gladly accepted their welcome into the bosom of their church family. She had little family of her own to speak of. Now, suddenly, she found herself a member of a much larger family group who truly seemed to care for one another with a complete lack of self-interest.

She had gone along to that first morning service, the day after the tea and concert, in some trepidation. What was she letting herself in for? she had wondered. She had sat with Em and Sarah, with baby William on her lap, about halfway back in the congregation. The baby, for once, had behaved remarkably well. There were other small children there too, so the occasional whimper and yell were to be expected and, Molly noticed with relief, were not frowned upon. William appeared mesmerised, as Molly herself was by the strangeness of her surroundings. It was the first time she had been in the Ebenezer chapel and she was struck, first and foremost, by the homeliness and simplicity of it all.

There was a large pulpit in the centre of the building, not to one side, as she knew, from her very occasional visits to the Church of England, was usual in their places of worship. Here, as in all Methodist chapels, preaching of 'The Word' was of primary importance, hence the central position of the pulpit. It was a square wooden box, raised high above the heads of the congregation, furnished from the same warm brown highly polished oak as the pews. Molly was impressed by the way everything gleamed, and Hector told her later that the cleaning of the chapel – the polishing and scrubbing, as well as the more decorative jobs, such as flower arranging – was undertaken by faithful members of the congregation. There was a rota of such women who assisted the chief caretaker in his work. There was a simple wooden cross on the communion table – Molly soon learned that this was the name given to that piece of furniture in Methodist chapels; never must it be referred to as an altar, as in the Catholic churches and in some Church of England ones – and on either side of the cross a vase containing large chrysanthemum flowers of purple, white and a deep golden yellow. The stained-glass windows, interspersed between the ones of frosted glass, were pleasing to the eye, although Molly was unsure which Bible stories they depicted. The Bible, until then, had been a closed book to her, but that was very soon to change. Molly was not fully aware, that first morning, of the change taking place within herself. All she was aware of was a feeling of peace and serenity and the conviction that it was right for her to be here, in this place. This feeling, however, had little to do with Hector Stubbins, although it was because of him that she was there.

Hector was not sitting with Molly and the children because he was taking part in the service. He read one of the lessons – from an obscure Old Testament book she had never heard of and the content of which she did not understand at all – in a deep sonorous voice. It was his normal speaking voice, for he always spoke in resounding tones, but his voice was louder now and echoed round the chapel. He was soberly dressed in a black suit and stiff-collared white shirt, as was the minister who preached the sermon. Molly had expected the preacher to be dressed differently, in some sort of regalia like a long fancy robe, maybe, but she was to learn that dressing up by the clergy was most definitely frowned upon by the Methodists. She could not remember the content of the sermon that first time. Violet Prosser had told her that this man would make them all sit up and take notice, and they all, certainly, seemed very attentive. But Molly was wool-gathering for part of the time. It still seemed very strange to her that she was there at all; strange ... but right. All she could recall later from the preacher's words was that the God they worshipped was a God of love.

She had known she would go again, and so she did, to many other services and to Hector's class meetings as well, when Maggie or Emily was willing to mind the baby for her. She was forced to agree with Violet, though. You could not always understand what Hector was on about. He talked a lot about sin and repentance, obedience and duty and judgement. A harsh God He seemed to be, this God that Hector worshipped, one who expected total obedience as well as worship and adoration. She realised in the discussions that took place after his talks that Hector's class members did not always agree with him, and that some of them were not afraid of telling him so. But always he endeavoured to have the last word. Molly kept very quiet during these discourses, not because she felt embarrassed, as she might have felt at one time to be talking about God so openly, but because she was still very ignorant about such matters as religion and faith. How could she express an opinion amongst these folk who had been chapelgoers all their lives, she who had been brought up, if not to denounce, then largely to ignore the Almighty? But gradually the feeling was growing in her that her parents had been wrong to leave God out of their lives so entirely, whatever had been their reasons.

One thing Molly had noticed was that Hector

rarely mentioned the name of Jesus in his sermons. But Mr Allbright, the minister at Ebenezer, did so frequently. She heard much about conversion and rebirth, about turning away from sin and letting Jesus into your life. It was all very perplexing, so difficult for her to understand: she had not thought that she, Molly Rimmer, was such a sinner, so much in need of repentance and forgiveness.

Strangely enough, she did not ask Hector about matters that puzzled her. When they were alone together, she and Hector, he never brought up the subject of religion at all. He was eager enough for her to go to chapel with him, and he seemed to take a pride in the fact that she was there at his side, or on his arm, or sitting in the congregation whilst he preached. But never had he asked her what she thought about this or that – although Molly was learning that, to Hector, the opinions of women mattered very little – nor had he questioned the state of her immortal soul. A high-flown phrase 'immortal soul' was one she did not entirely understand, but one which she had heard Hector use frequently. At all events, she thought, it might have been of some concern to Hector how her soul stood in relation to God, but it appeared that this was not so. She was to learn that it was not Molly Rimmer's soul that was of primary concern to Hector.

It was Violet Prosser who answered her questions and helped Molly along the road to what Methodists liked to call Salvation. Her conversion, if it could be called that, came very gradually and not in a blinding flash of light such as she had heard others say they had experienced. It was at the end of November 1898, on the Sunday she now knew was called the First Sunday in Advent, that Molly knew, beyond all doubt, that there was now a new dimension to her life and that she need never feel alone any more.

'O come to my heart, Lord Jesus,
  There is room in my heart for Thee.'

She sang the words of the Advent hymn along with the rest of the congregation. And how they could sing, these Methodist folk. Sometimes it seemed as though the roof would lift off with the volume of their joyous upraised voices. Some people were so stirred that they left their seats and went to kneel at the communion rail, so as to affirm their belief in the baby of Bethlehem, their Lord and Saviour, that they were singing about. But Molly did not join them. She just knew there was room for Him in her heart, also. She quietly rejoiced in the assurance that had come to her that she now belonged, not only to this family here at Ebenezer, but to a much wider family. There had been times following the death of her parents when she had felt so alone. Even in the company of her sister or Flo or Maggie she had felt desolate and lost. Now she knew that loneliness, and grieving too, were things of the past.

She had, in fact, been a full member of the Ebenezer chapel for some time now. Following their engagement, several months ago, Hector had made sure of that. And so Molly was now able to take part in the service of Holy Communion – or the Lord's Supper, as they liked to call it – drinking raspberry cordial from tiny thimble-sized glasses which fitted into holes along the communion rail.

Hector exasperated her at times, but at other times it was this same quality in him – his pomposity – which amused her, as she knew it amused other members of the chapel. There were those who sometimes had a quiet laugh at him behind his back, of which he remained blissfully unaware. Not that he was a figure of fun. He was far too staid and serious to be that, but his self-importance and his pedantic manner and way of speaking just lent themselves to ridicule amongst those who were not his most ardent admirers. Some of the older ladies, though, seemed to adore him, lapping up his words of praise and falling over themselves to do his bidding.

But all the folk at Ebenezer, his critics as well as his admirers, would have been in agreement about one thing. His engagement to that lovely lass Molly Rimmer had made their lay preacher more human – not much, mind you; only slightly so – and there was not a man amongst them who, secretly, did not envy him a little. What on earth did she see in him? they might well have asked. Why, in heaven's name, was the lass marrying him?

Molly would have found it hard to answer. Mainly for security, she supposed. Marriage to Hector would mean that she and the children would never again need to wonder where their next meal was coming from. And gratitude as well. She was grateful to Hector for his companionship at a time when she was very low and lonely, and for introducing her to a whole new group of friends and way of life. There was the house, too, into which they would be moving after their honeymoon; and Rosie Hewitt to assist with the housework. Yes, Molly knew she was a very fortunate girl and there were many who would envy her.

Maggie, who was sitting, at Molly's invitation, in the front pew at the Ebenezer chapel, reflected that she had never seen the young woman look so beautiful. This was a seat usually reserved for the bride's mother, but no one was more entitled to it than Maggie, Molly had said, the woman who had been a surrogate mother to her ever since Lily had died. Maggie felt a huge lump come into her throat as she watched Molly walk down the aisle on Bill's arm. It had been Molly's wish that Bill Winthrop should give her away, in the absence of her own father. And when Maggie saw Hector turn to smile at Molly as she reached his side, a smile, or so it seemed, of such warmth and tenderness, she even began to think that she might have been mistaken; that maybe, after all, the lass was not making such a disastrous mistake as she, Maggie, had feared.

To give the girl her due, she would not say a wrong word about the fellow, and that was the way it ought to be. He certainly appeared loving and attentive enough today, but so he should be, on his wedding day. Hector was the height of elegance in his morning coat and pin-striped trousers, a sartorial touch which Maggie guessed that Molly, left to her own devices, would have preferred to do without. But the Stubbins family, chemists of some renown in the town, did have certain standards to maintain. Herbert Stubbins, Hector's father, was similarly attired, as was Hector's cousin, Martin, who was acting as his best man; he was the son of Herbert's younger brother. Maggie knew that Molly, working-class girl though she might be, would not give the Stubbins family any reason to be ashamed of her. And, to be fair to them, from what the girl had said they seemed to have welcomed her into their family quite readily. Hector, though, had not seen all that much of his parents since leaving the family home in Marton to take over the managership and the living accommodation of the shop on Jubilee Terrace.

Yes, Molly really looked a picture in her ivory satin wedding dress, made so professionally by that clever young woman Flo Palmer. The leg-o'-mutton sleeves, still quite fashionable, were not overexaggerated, and the high neckline and the close-fitting bodice and skirt, ending in a slight train, emphasised Molly's slender figure; although the girl had, of late, filled out a little, Maggie was pleased to see, losing the hollow-cheeked fragility she had shown soon after her parents' death. Her short veil was held in position with a headdress of wax orange blossoms, and she carried a bouquet of white and yellow roses.

The bridesmaids' dresses, Flo and Em's, were

of forget-me-not blue, which suited the colouring of both girls; Flo's fair-haired prettiness and Em's vivid ginger hair and pale complexion. They wore large straw hats trimmed with flowers of a matching blue and they too carried small posies of white and yellow roses. Em appeared quite self-possessed today – she had matured a lot of late – although she glanced round from time to time, as if for reassurance, grinning at Maggie and her best friend, Sarah, at Maggie's side.

Maggie watched the child thoughtfully as she, in turn, watched her sister go through the wedding ceremony with Hector Stubbins. What did the little girl really think about it all? She had said very little, other than that they were all going to live in a big house and that Rosie, a girl from their chapel, was going to live there and help look after them. She had seemed pleased at that and excited at the idea of the big house – what child wouldn't be? – and at being a bridesmaid for her sister. But how would she feel about sharing her sister, who had been virtually a mother to her since Lily's death, with a man like Hector? Maggie knew, instinctively, that he would be a possessive husband. The way he was looking at Molly now intimated this. Looks of love they may well be, but Maggie sensed acquisitiveness there too; the desire to own this young woman completely. She guessed that Hector Stubbins, once married to Molly, might be jealous of anything and everyone that threatened to come between them. She felt a stab of fear for the little girl in the pretty blue dress and for the boy sitting on her, Maggie's, lap.

William, soon to celebrate his second birthday, was also dressed in blue, a hand-smocked dress that had also been made by Flo. He was not yet old enough to be 'breeched', but he was a sturdy little fellow, running around and getting into everything if he wasn't watched, and already starting to talk. He could say 'Moll' and 'Em', and Maggie was convinced he tried to say 'Mag'. As well he might, because Maggie had looked after him for quite a lot of the time whilst Molly was getting to grips with the dinner shop. Maggie was to be left in charge of both children, William and Emily, whilst Molly and Hector went on their honeymoon. How could she have refused to have them? The lass was entitled to a honeymoon. Besides, it was only for a few days, then they would all be back in their new home in Warbreck Road; and goodness knew when Maggie would see them then. Certainly not as often as she had done of late.

William kicked and struggled as she picked him up whilst they were singing the second hymn, 'O Perfect Love', so she put him down again to scrabble around on the floor with a pile of hymn books. He was not really a naughty child, just wilful at times, wanting his own way, and Molly, understandably, had spoiled him more than a little. Would he understand the new regime, she wondered, having a man living permanently in the house when he had never been used to one? Would he settle down in his strange surroundings? Of course he would, she chided herself. Molly would be there and she would see that everything carried on the same as before ...

or nearly the same.

Maggie could feel herself getting agitated again, as she had many times over the last few months. For the life of her she couldn't understand why the lass wanted to get married at all, not to Hector Stubbins, at any rate. It wasn't as if she were in dire straits any longer. The dinner shop had proved more successful than Maggie – or Molly – had ever dared to hope. She had, long ago, repaid Maggie's loan to her, despite Maggie's insistence that the gold sovereign had been a gift. As well as meat and potato pie Molly now sold sausage rolls, sausages in rich gravy, parched peas and mushy peas (such as they sold in the famous 'pay oiles' in the inland towns that Bill had told her about) and barmcakes filled with boiled ham. She had been unable to cook all that in the small fireside oven and so she had had one of those new-fangled gas cookers installed. Queues formed every dinner time and she often had to disappoint customers when the food ran out. Why had she decided to give it all up ... for such as him?

Maggie knew, however, that she was prejudiced – maybe quite wrongly – and she was not being fair to the girl. It was Molly's decision, as it had to be, and she was a sensible lass, not one to dash into something without due consideration. She also knew that she, Maggie, was more than a little upset at losing not only her close friend and neighbour, but the two children who had come to mean so much to her over the last two years. She sighed to herself, then resolutely she picked up little William so he could wave to Molly, coming down the aisle on the arm of her new husband. Then she followed the crowds of folk out into the sunshine.

After they had all stood outside and chatted for a few moments the guests then adjourned to the adjacent Sunday school hall where the reception was to be held. The chapel had been more than half-full for the service; there were almost as many folk there, in fact, as there often were for Sunday worship. Hector Stubbins was well known in the church family; but most of them were there, if they were honest, for the sake of the lovely young bride whom they had taken so readily to their hearts since she came into their fold. Maggie spoke to several people who said, most sincerely, how they wished the young couple well and what a beautiful bride Molly was; but, Maggie sensed, not without just a hint of doubt that all would go smoothly, and the feeling that Hector and the new Mrs Stubbins would need the prayers of all who knew them to help the marriage on its way.

These Methodists were great on praying, Maggie gathered, and she uttered her own little prayer quietly to herself that all would be well with Molly and this man she had chosen for her husband. It could do no harm. No; she corrected herself in her thoughts. It was Hector who had done the choosing, and Molly ... what had she done? Acquiesced, Maggie supposed; just gone alone with it. It could well be that the lass was not nearly so happy as she was pretending to be. Oh dear God, please help them to be happy together, she prayed, almost frantically.

The wedding breakfast – or luncheon, really, as it was almost midday – was very much like the chapel teas which took place there periodically. It was a cold meal which would be much easier to prepare, of course, in the small kitchen, but Maggie had to admit that the chapel ladies, the stalwart band who customarily presided at these gatherings, had done them proud. There was a plentiful helping on each plate of boiled ham and salad, with beetroot and pickled onions in glass dishes. The plates in the centre of the long tables were piled high with bread and butter, and the ubiquitous tea ladies did the rounds with lashings of strong tea poured from large enamel pots. There was trifle to follow, a goodly helping for each person, topped with fresh cream sprinkled with hundreds and thousands. Quite tasty, was Maggie's verdict, as she savoured the jelly and custard and tinned fruit, and the sponge cake moistened with fruit juice at the base of the trifle. One vital ingredient was missing, though: the sherry which always gave that necessary tang to any trifle. But she reminded herself that she was among Methodists and that such a thing would be strictly taboo.

The wedding cake was magnificent, one which could quite easily have graced the most elegant society wedding; three tiers coated in glistening royal icing and topped with a silver vase containing orange blossom. It had been made by Mrs Makepeace, the confectioner from Jubilee Terrace and Molly's former employer. She and her husband were guests at the wedding and the cake was their gift. It was ceremoniously cut by the bridal couple and Hector made a fitting little speech – those who knew him well were amazed at the brevity of it – thanking the guests for being there and for their most acceptable gifts, and paying the homage due to his new wife. What a fortunate fellow he was, he told the assembled gathering, promising he would always cherish this lovely young woman – his wife, he said with pride – who had been committed to his care.

How could she doubt his word or his sincerity? thought Maggie, perceiving the ardour in his eyes as he looked at his bride. But, as she remarked to Bill later that same evening, how could you expect the marriage to be happy when the toast to the couple had been drunk in lemonade?

Chapter 15

The wedding portrait of Mr and Mrs Hector Stubbins and their closest relatives and friends was to be the main attraction in the window of the photographic studio in Jubilee Terrace for many months. It stood on an easel in the very centre of the window, a large sepia study of Hector and Molly; their bridesmaids, Emily and Flo; the best man, Martin Stubbins; Mr and Mrs Stubbins, Hector's parents; and, in the absence of any relatives of her own, Maggie and Bill Winthrop with two-year-old William seated on Maggie's knee. They posed in front of a velvet curtain with a large potted palm to the side of them.

They all looked a little wide-eyed with surprise, this being the result of the sudden flash from the lamp held by the photographer, Mr George Musgrove, who owned the studio. They did not look at all happy, not one of them, Molly thought whenever she glanced at the photograph on her way to the chemist's shop. But this was by no means unusual. People rarely smiled on these stiffly posed studio portraits. Queen Victoria was an obvious example; no one had ever seen her looking pleased with life.

It had been quite an ordeal that photographic session, and had taken a good half-hour, with Hector on pins all the while that they would miss their train. They had all trooped round to Mr Musgrove's studio when the wedding breakfast was over. William by this time had been growing tired and was more than a little irritable. He had wriggled and whimpered and refused to keep still, earning him several looks of annoyance from Hector, although the bridegroom had stopped short of actually scolding him. It was a miracle that the photograph had been taken at all, but Mr Musgrove was a patient soul, used to dealing with children. It was his popping in and out of the black tent around the camera and tripod that had finally captured the attention of the little boy, and in a rare moment of stillness the photographer had seized his moment.

And so, there they were, captured for all time on that photographic plate, that afternoon in late May 1899. Only as Christmas approached did Mr Musgrove change the window display, much to Molly's relief. The portrait was a constant reminder to her of the dreadful mistake she had made, for by this time Molly was having cause to regret her marriage to Hector Stubbins. What was more, she felt that all who looked at the expression on her face in that photograph – apprehensive and far from joyful – would guess that her marriage was not at all the serene and contented one that it might appear to be on the surface. For, so far, she had told no one, neither did she think that anyone, even her closest friends, had guessed at her unhappiness. There were certain matters within marriage that you had to keep to yourself; they were not to be discussed with anyone, not even a best friend.

Hector had instilled in her, right from the start, that her allegiance, her loyalty – her very life, in fact – were now subject to him, and that her former friends and acquaintances, even her small family, were of minor importance. She accompanied him to chapel, Sunday by Sunday, sitting at his side in the congregation, or just with William by her side, if Hector were preaching. She smiled and exchanged pleasantries with everyone, just as she had before her marriage, determined to put on a brave face and not to let anyone see the hurt and disillusionment that was hidden deep at the heart of her.

Maybe, though, her marriage was no different from the dozens she saw around her, she sometimes pondered. After all, she had nothing with which to compare it and there was no one whom she could ask. Yes, there was – there was Maggie, but Molly always pushed away the thought of her friend, knowing that Maggie had believed all along that she was making a mistake in marrying Hector. She did not want to admit that the older woman had been right. Perhaps this nightly attack upon her body, for this was how she viewed it, was quite normal within marriage, the price she had to pay, so to speak, for a roof above her head and her food and clothing. And maybe it was not so unusual for a husband to chastise his wife in the way Hector did Molly whenever he considered she had stepped out of line. She knew, though, deep down, that Bill Winthrop would never lay so much as a finger upon Maggie. Neither, she guessed, would that true gentleman Ralph Prosser ever subject his wife,

Violet, to such indignities and abuse as she, Molly, was made to suffer. And as for her own mother and father – it hurt dreadfully when she remembered them and the tender love they had shown to one another.

But she knew there was nothing she could do about it. She had married Hector for better or for worse; what was more, she had promised to obey him. She tried to console herself that it did not happen all the time. The nightly onslaught on her person – that, of course, was a continuing ordeal except for the times when she was, mercifully, indisposed. But the other only happened occasionally, whenever Hector considered she was in need of a reprimand. So she tried never, never to displease him.

After the photographic session the newly wed couple had gone to Hector's rooms above the chemist shop, a few doors away, to change into their going-away clothes. The rooms were by this time empty of furniture as this had all been transported to their new home on Warbreck Road, where Hector had been living for the past few days. But there was a full-length mirror and a peg on which Molly had previously hung her outfit, in the still carpeted room, which had formerly been Hector's bedroom, and a small washroom and lavatory along the corridor.

Hector, much to her relief, had left her alone to change out of her bridal clothes. She wished that Flo had come along to help her to dress, as she had done earlier in the day in readiness for the wedding service, but she had not offered to do so. Probably her friend believed that Molly would wish to be alone with her new husband. And so she should have done; Molly knew that this was, in truth, how she should have been feeling, but now they were, at last, alone together as man and wife Molly realised, at the heart of her, that she was afraid. But at least he had given her these few moments of privacy in which to prepare herself for the journey. As for their honeymoon on the shores of Lake Windermere – well, she would think about that when the time came. They would not arrive there until very late evening and Molly, in spite of her nervousness about certain matters, was looking forward to the change of surroundings. She had never been out of Blackpool in her life, not even to Preston, only eighteen miles away, and she had heard that the scenery in the Lake District was very beautiful. And she could not help but be excited at the thought of dressing up in her going-away outfit, the most stylish dress and jacket she had ever worn.

She made use of the facilities in the washroom, then, dressed only in her camisole and drawers, scurried back along the corridor to the bedroom. She gave a gasp of surprise when she saw Hector standing there in the middle of the room and, instinctively, her hands flew to her bare neck and shoulders.

'Come here, Molly. And take your hands away. I want to look at you.' His voice was not stern or unkind, but it was authoritative and Molly found herself automatically obeying him. She put her hands to her side, but still she fingered nervously at the white cambric of her knee-length drawers.

They were new too, trimmed with lace and blue ribbon; the 'something blue' which Flo had insisted a bride must wear. She tried to smile at Hector, but her face felt frozen. He was staring at her with the ardent, almost lustful look she had seen in his eyes several times before, but always, in the past, his actions had not matched up to the impassioned glances he gave her. It would be different, though, now they were married.

'Hector...' she began falteringly. 'I must ... get changed. Please ... let me get dressed. We have a train to catch. You said yourself we would be late.'

'There is time enough,' said Hector briefly. 'I told you to come here, Molly.' She made no move so he strode towards her, taking hold of her by her shoulders, not roughly, but very firmly.

'You are my wife now, Molly. You belong to me. Do you understand?'

She looked into his pale grey eyes, nodding numbly. She could not, in honesty, say he was being unkind or unreasonable. His voice might even be called tender, but it held a decisive tone that she knew at once would brook no resistance.

She stood impassively as his mouth came down upon hers, much more demandingly than ever before, and she felt his moustache scratching her upper lip and cheeks as he pulled her close to him. She felt herself, involuntarily, straining away from him as his tongue pushed against her lips and teeth, forcing its way into her mouth. This was something she had not experienced before, nor had she been aware, indeed, that this might happen. This, then, must all be part of marriage, she told herself, as Hector's hands caressed her shoulders, then fondled her breasts beneath her camisole. He was kissing her neck now, then her shoulders, grasping her buttocks tightly and pressing himself towards her. With a sense of shock that almost made her cry out she felt the hardness of him pushing against her. Then, just as suddenly, he released her.

'You are right, Molly. There is no time. We must hurry if we are to catch our train. Come along now.' He frowned slightly as she did not move. 'Come along. Get into your dress, quickly now. I will go and call a cab.'

Her hands were shaking as she drew the green dress from its hanger and put it over her head. Don't be such a silly little fool, she told herself. You are a married woman now. This is all part of it. Hector is your husband and you should have known what to expect. But she had not known, not entirely. She and Flo had only guessed ... at some of it. She recalled the sounds she had heard coming through the wall from her parents' room, giving her some intimation of what was happening there, but she had not told Flo about this, of course. To do so would have been to sully the memory of her mother and father. There were parts of marriage which still remained a mystery, to be revealed to her before long.

She could not help but be pleased at the sight of herself in the mirror. The floor-length dress which flared out behind her was trimmed at the hem with a band of darker green velvet. The matching short jacket with a velvet collar moulded itself closely to her waist and hips, and her wide brimmed hat was trimmed with toning green ostrich feathers. Molly, in spite of her agitation and the trauma of the last few minutes, smiled at her reflection. It was the first time she had ever shopped in Donnelly's dress department. She was proud of the way she had saved, little by little each week, from the proceeds of the dinner shop, to buy this going-away outfit. It was the height of elegance – Flo's expression – and she knew it suited her colouring to perfection. It would have to last for many, many years, of course. And it would, most likely, be the last outfit she would ever buy from her own money.

Hector had made it clear that her working for a living was now a thing of the past. As his wife the only work she would be required to do was supervising the household affairs – the cooking, cleaning, washing and all that sort of thing, he had said airily – but most of the hard work, he had told her, would be done by Rosie, the maid of all work. And, of course, she, Molly, would be required to keep the children in order; that was her responsibility.

When Molly looked back on their honeymoon on the shores of Lake Windermere it was the balmy and sunlit, long spring days that she endeavoured to recapture in her mind. Not the nights. The couple were there for a week and on each of the six full days they spent there Molly tried to push to the back of her mind the thought of the coming night with all its fears and indignity and pain.

It was as though Hector were two different people. Molly could almost be said to enjoy the days she spent in his company, had it not been for the dread of what she knew lay ahead. During the day he was pleasant and amiable, very protective of her on the walks they took near the lake and up into the lower slopes of the hills around, making sure she did not stumble on a steep path or lose her footing on the slippery shale.

They stayed at Waterhead at the north end of the lake, near to the small town of Ambleside. The hotel was comfortable and homely, and Molly enjoyed, probably most of all, the well-cooked food. They were provided with three ample meals a day, or a sandwich lunch on the occasions when Hector told the proprietress that they intended to stay out for the whole day. It was such a pleasure not to have to cook for herself and for dozens of clamouring customers, although she knew, if she were honest, that that was something she was going to miss.

There were even times when Molly felt she could grow quite fond of her new husband, although she knew that her contentment in his – daytime – company stemmed rather from the loveliness of the scenery around than from Hector's personality. This was, indeed, a most beautiful part of the country, more so to Molly after being used to the flat treeless landscape in and around Blackpool. Not that the resort was without a certain appeal, with its sea and sand and the vastness of the ever-changing sky, but never before had Molly seen such greenness as in the lush fertile valleys of the Lake District and grandeur like that of the soaring mountain peaks.

From Ambleside they walked to Stockghyll

Force, about a mile away; an impressive waterfall set in woods. Again, it was the first time Molly had ever set eyes on such a breathtaking phenomenon of natural beauty. They took the steamboat to Bowness and Windermere, to Lake Side at the southern tip of the lake, and across to Sawrey. They hired a pony and trap to take them to Hawkshead near the head of Eskthwaite Water, and to Grasmere, the village where the poet William Wordsworth had lived. They looked at his home, Dove Cottage, and found his grave, marked by a simple stone, in St Oswald's churchyard. Molly knew his poem about the daffodils, but little else about him. She had learned 'I wandered lonely...' at school and could recite all of it, but Hector, it appeared, knew several other of his works. He could quote from 'On Westminster Bridge' and 'To a Highland Girl', which he did ... at length. Molly could not help but be impressed, if a little amused. This was an example of the pomposity that made some of the chapel folk snigger behind his back. It was only later that she realised that these poems were some of Wordsworth's more simple works that Hector had, undoubtedly, remembered from his schooldays, and that he was, in reality, no more cognisant with the Lakeland poet than she was. On the whole, though, he was a pleasant enough companion during the day.

It had been late when they arrived at their destination that first night, after changing trains twice, at Preston and at Lancaster, then taking a pony and trap from the station at Windermere, some five miles away from their hotel. The proprietress, having been informed of their late arrival, had kept a simple meal of shepherd's pie and apple crumble warm for them, then they had retired, almost immediately, to their bedroom. Molly, remembering the incident above the chemist shop earlier in the day, was bracing herself for the inevitable, but Hector, to her surprise, announced that he would get undressed in the bathroom. 'Just for tonight, my dear,' he said. 'We are both tired and I know you will be glad of a little privacy. I will not trouble you tonight.'

She wondered at his choice of words – surely what was about to take place should not be regarded as trouble? – but was, nevertheless, relieved. When he returned from the bathroom in his voluminous nightshirt Molly was already attired in her simple cambric nightdress. She made use of the bathroom along the corridor and went back to find Hector on his knees at the side of the double bed, in an attitude of prayer. Molly was startled. Since her newly found faith she had tried to say her prayers, but it was usually in chapel, or in the comfort of her bed before she went to sleep. She got into bed and after a few moments Hector rose from his knees, extinguished the gas lamp, and got in beside her.

'Good night, my dear.' His kiss on her cheek was a perfunctory peck and in a very short while she could tell by his rhythmic breathing that he was asleep. It took Molly considerably longer to drop off, tired though she was. It had been a traumatic day, though not an entirely unpleasant one. And now, for better or for worse, she was

Mrs Hector Stubbins. Dear God, please take care of William and Em, she prayed, as she did every night now ... and please help me to be a good wife to Hector.

'I could not help but notice, Molly, my dear, that you did not spend any time on your knees before getting into bed,' said Hector the following night. 'I was prepared to let it go last night, but as my wife, I will expect you to join me, from now on, in the act of prayer.' They were both clad in their night attire, Hector this time having stayed in the room, watching Molly quite openly as she undressed. She was more than a little unnerved by his fervent glances, but was determined to face up to whatever must be faced, and to stand up to him now, as best she could.

'I do say my prayers, Hector,' she said quietly. 'I say them in bed, just before I go to sleep.'

'I am afraid that will not do, my dear, not now,' he replied. 'You must learn to humble yourself before the Lord, as I do. Come along now, Molly; kneel down and join with me in prayer.'

'Very well, Hector,' said Molly, falling to her knees at one side of the bed while he knelt at the other. She knew she had no choice. To give Hector his due he did now give thanks to the Almighty for the precious gift of his new wife, but then he went on to ask the Lord to help Molly to be a good and obedient wife, 'and to learn, day by day, more of your holy will and commandments.' But not a word did he utter about helping him, Hector, to be a good husband.

'Amen,' intoned Hector sonorously.

'Amen,' repeated Molly in a whisper, rising, with relief, from her knees.

'Perhaps, another time, you could offer your own prayers to the Lord,' suggested Hector as he put out the light.

'Perhaps...' mumbled Molly, already in bed with the bedclothes pulled around her. But she felt she would never be able to do so, not in front of Hector. Prayer, to her, was something personal, just between herself and her newly found Friend.

Hector did not lie down next to her. He threw back the cumbersome eiderdown, blankets and sheet, staring down at her. 'Take this off, please, Molly,' he said, pulling at the ribbon fastening at the neck of her nightdress. It was Hector, though, not Molly, who pulled the garment over her head and flung it to the floor. He gazed for a few moments at her nakedness, with Molly all the while wanting to fold her arms across her breasts or cover up that other, much more intimate, part of her. Then, in one quick movement, he ripped off his nightshirt and threw himself on top of her, covering her face, her neck, then her breasts with impatient, almost savage kisses.

She felt his hardness growing against her, and she had already guessed, mainly by instinct, at what would happen. But she was unprepared for the sharp stab of pain that seemed to tear right through her as he pulled her legs apart and thrust himself inside her. Nor for the weight of his body upon hers as he pounded away, breathing heavily all the while, as she lay rigid, unable to move a muscle, just longing, longing for it to come to an end. It did, at last. Hector rolled away from her, then turned back, briefly, to kiss her cheek.

'I'm sorry if I hurt you, my dear,' he said in a dismissive tone. 'It won't hurt the next time, but you must try to relax. It is something you will have to get used to. You are my wife now.' His pale grey eyes bored into hers with an intensity she found alarming. She was afraid he would start all over again, but he did not. He leaned over and kissed her wetly on the mouth, then said, surprisingly, 'I love you, Molly. Now, go to sleep. Good night, my dear.' He picked up her nightdress from the floor and thrust it at her, then pulled his own nightshirt over his head.

'Good night, Hector...' she breathed, easing her sore limbs down beneath the cool comfort of the sheets. She could feel hot tears of disillusionment and disappointment oozing from her eyes and running down her cheeks, dampening the pillow, but she knew she must try not to cry out loud. She had guessed, correctly, at what the act of love entailed, but she had not expected it to be so dreadful, so painful and humiliating as that. Surely it should not be so? Not between two people who loved one another? She knew, though, that she did not love Hector and wondered if she ever could. The strange thing was that he said he loved her, and, stranger still, she believed him. Despite his treatment of her she truly believed that he loved her, in his own way. And he had said it would not hurt the next time. Maybe it wouldn't. Maybe it would not be so awful again.

After a while she found herself relaxing, on the

347

verge of sleep. Hector was already snoring, though not too loudly, at her side. One thought came to her with outstanding clarity as she found herself slipping into unconsciousness. This had not been the first time for Hector, as it was for her. She was not sure how she knew, but she was sure that her new husband was not without experience in these matters. He had not been married before, he was a pillar of the church, upright and sanctimonious – but the act of love, if it could be so called, was not something new to him. Molly was convinced of it.

It did get better, slightly so, and Molly learned, on their honeymoon and, later, in their new home, to relax more, as Hector had instructed her to do and to make a pretence at acquiescence, if not enjoyment. There were times when she felt revulsion at some of Hector's more excessive demands, but when she resisted it was then that his treatment of her became more fierce and relentless. When she submitted herself to him he was calmer and behaved in what she considered a more normal manner, although she still experienced no fulfilment or joy in the act of love, as she had hoped she might, in time, come to do. Instead she looked forward to those times in the month when Hector left her alone. As he did at such times. She learned he was fastidious in the extreme, shying away from any mention of normal bodily functions and abhorring dirt or disorder and slovenliness.

It had been very soon after they arrived home from their honeymoon that Hector had started to complain about William's eating habits. 'For goodness' sake, Molly, can't you stop that child from dribbling his food all over the place? Ugh! What a disgusting mess. I really cannot put up with this at mealtimes.'

The child sometimes tried to feed himself now, with a spoon, and Molly believed in letting him do so. His wilful streak was showing no sign of abating. He often pushed Molly's hand away when she tried to feed him, which was why she had decided to let him have a go himself. What did it matter if the mashed potato and gravy dribbled down his chin? He was wearing a protective bib and he could soon be wiped clean afterwards. But to Hector the sight of a grubby child was obnoxious. 'I have finished my meal, anyway. I will partake of a cup of tea in the sitting room. Please see to it that Rosie brings me one.' He had flung down his serviette and departed hurriedly that first time.

Thereafter Molly had made sure that little William had his meals in the kitchen, whenever possible, with Rosie, the maid. Emily, too, had asked if she could do the same so that she could help William with his eating. Molly had agreed, knowing full well that her sister preferred the company of her little brother and Rosie to that of her new brother-in-law. Em was very wary of him. Molly could tell by her sidelong glances and her diffidence when in his company, although she had done nothing, as yet, to provoke his displeasure or censure.

It was not so with William. The child was beginning to talk and, therefore, learning to enjoy the sound of his own voice. He sometimes shouted out loud for no reason at all and still had the occasional tantrum although these, mercifully, were becoming less frequent as he found more and more to engage his active little mind.

'Stop that din!' Hector frequently shouted at him. 'For goodness' sake, child, can't you keep quiet for two minutes? Molly, you really must learn to control him better than that.' Hector hated to have his peace disturbed when he was reading or, worse, when he was preparing a sermon. 'You must keep him quiet when I am studying. How many times do I have to tell you?'

Although Hector retreated to the privacy of the sitting room or even upstairs to their bedroom when he was working, he still complained that William's voice could be heard all over the house. 'When I was growing up I was told that little boys should be seen and not heard. You have been too lenient with him, Molly. Have you never heard that to spare the rod is to spoil the child? What he is short of is a good beating.'

'You leave him alone, Hector, do you hear?' Molly had replied quietly, but in an ominous tone. She did not know how she had found the courage to stand up to Hector, but she knew that where the children were concerned she would fight tooth and nail. 'I have never laid a finger on William and I never will. But I will try to keep him quiet. I will try to make sure that he doesn't disturb you again.'

At that time, a month or so after their marriage, Molly had been unaware of any violent streak in her husband. He used her roughly, and selfishly, too, she guessed – surely he ought to consider that sometimes she might be tired or simply disinclined towards lovemaking? – but he had not, as yet, struck her. She had a feeling, though, that it might be as well to distance the children from him as much as possible. This had been what she had argued against when Hector had suggested they should hire a nanny but now it seemed that young Rosie Hewitt was taking on the task of nursemaid more and more, and she, Molly, was seeing less and less of the children. But if this meant that it kept her husband in an agreeable mood, then Molly decided it might be worth the sacrifice. It was not as if she did not see them at all. Whilst Hector was busy in the shop she tried to spend most of her time with William, and she made sure, too, that she and Em always had an hour or so together at bedtime, chatting or reading well-loved stories.

But Molly was growing increasingly bored. She had been used to filling every moment of her day, from when she rose at the first light of dawn to when she retired to bed, frequently in the early hours of the next morning. It had seemed a luxury at first not to have to cook and bake and clean and wash and iron, in addition to running a shop. Now she was finding she missed the shop and the company of the neighbours and, oddly, the hard work; the satisfaction she had always felt after the completion of a hard task well done.

Which was why, in September, she decided to join the cleaning rota at the chapel. This was at the suggestion of Violet Prosser, and Hector, although he did not like the idea of her working her fingers to the bone in their own home – that was Rosie's job – raised no objection to her cleaning and polishing in the chapel. This was working for the Lord.

She was there on her own a few days before the Harvest Festival, Violet just having gone home to prepare the midday meal, when Philip Mercer, one of Hector's fellow stewards at the chapel, entered the building.

Chapter 16

Philip Mercer was the youngest of the chapel stewards. He was only twenty-two years of age, very young to be the holder of such a responsible position; but it was well known that the minister of Ebenezer, the Reverend Richard Allbright, regarded him as a rising star in the life of the chapel, a potential lay preacher and class leader, even a possible candidate for the ministry. Molly, from what she had seen of him, liked this young man very much. He was earnest and diligent, but without the piety – the 'holier than thou' attitude – that Hector was guilty of, and she was sure Philip Mercer would go a long way in the church. With his fresh-complexioned boyish face and his short fair hair he reminded her a lot of Sam, Flo's young man.

'Hello there, Mrs Stubbins,' he greeted her as he strode down the centre aisle towards her. 'You're very busy, I can see. Don't let me disturb you.'

Molly was on her knees, polishing the oak communion rail, but she got up when she saw him. 'No, that's all right. I've nearly finished, Mr Mercer.' She emphasised his name. 'I'll just stand up and ease my back for a moment.'

He smiled. 'Why the "Mr Mercer" all of a sudden? Everybody calls me Philip, don't they?'

'Just like everyone calls me Molly,' she replied.

'At least I would like them to.' She smiled back at him. 'Tit for tat, I suppose ... Philip. If you will remember to call me Molly, then I will call you Philip.'

'Fair enough, Molly,' he replied. 'I suppose it has always seemed the right thing to do, to call you Mrs Stubbins, because of you being married to Mr Stubbins. I would never dream of calling him Hector, you see. Nor has he ever invited me to do so,' he added musingly.

'No, he wouldn't,' replied Molly. 'He is rather inclined to stand on his dignity, is Hector.' Then, fearing she might have sounded a mite disloyal, she continued, 'What I mean to say is, well, he is the senior steward this year, isn't he? And very proud of his position.'

'Yes, and don't we know it!' replied Philip meaningfully. 'Sorry, Mrs Stubbins ... Molly, I mean. That wasn't very tactful of me, was it? I must admit he's doing a grand job. We all think so. It's just that – how can I put it? – he tends to make me feel ... not exactly inadequate; more ... immature. I feel so young and inexperienced compared with Mr Stubbins. I'm always afraid of putting my foot in it – you know, scared of saying anything he might not agree with.'

I know the feeling, thought Molly. She nodded, but she did not speak.

'I suppose I had always thought of you as some-one more mature as well, Molly,' Philip went on, 'being married to him. But you're not, are you?' He looked at her as though he were seeing her for the first time.

Molly gave a little laugh. 'No, I'm not, Philip.

There are times when I feel very immature, just like you say you do. As a matter of fact, I am younger than you, a couple of years or so, I would say.'

'Yes, I suppose you must be.' Philip was looking at her thoughtfully and she felt a little embarrassed though she was not sure why she should.

She kneeled down again, rubbing her cloth into the tin of polish. 'If you will excuse me, Philip, I must get on with this. My husband will be coming at one o'clock to lock the chapel and I want to be finished by then.'

'Of course, of course,' said Philip. 'I've just popped in to sort out one or two small matters for the Sunday services. I'm on duty, you see, and as we have a visiting preacher I want everything to run smoothly. I mustn't be long myself. I'm on my dinner hour, due back at half-past one.' He hurried away into the vestry at the side of the building and Molly continued with her polishing.

A pleasant young man, she mused, and very efficient and businesslike too, she guessed. She knew he was employed in an insurance office, not very far away, but that, like Hector, he spent much of his spare time on church matters. She had heard Hector refer to him, however, as being 'only just out of the nursery' and not ready for responsibility. It was possible, though, that Hector might be a little envious of the young man's standing with Mr Allbright. She knew there were times when her husband and the minister did not see eye to eye.

She gave the communion rail a final rub, then stood back to admire the gleam of the highly polished oak just as Philip emerged from the vestry. 'All done and dusted, Molly?' he asked. 'Yes, that looks grand, doesn't it? You'll be in on Saturday morning as well, I dare say, to help with the decorations?'

'Yes, I expect so,' replied Molly. The Harvest Festival was one of the big events in the chapel year, when the building was lavishly decorated with all kinds of produce: fruit and vegetables and flowers; sheaves of corn, too, if these could be procured from one of the farms in the Fylde, and loaves of bread baked in fancy shapes by local confectioners. 'I really enjoy the Harvest Festival,' Molly went on. 'I remember going to one at my friend Flo's chapel, that was before I started coming here. I enjoyed it, but I think it was mainly because the chapel was so beautifully decorated and they sang such rousing hymns. But that's not really the right reason for being there, is it? I mean, there should be more to it than that.' She felt she could talk so easily to Philip Mercer and he was listening to her very intently. 'It meant so much more to me last year, when I came to the one here, giving thanks to God for all his gifts and everything. I expect the place will be packed on Sunday morning, won't it?'

'Yes, I should imagine it will,' replied Philip. 'And who are we, after all, to question the reasons why people come? It's something if we can get them here at all, once or twice a year, even though some of them are only cabbage worshippers.'

He chuckled, leaning towards her as he spoke,

and Molly laughed out loud at his words. 'Cabbage worshippers! Oh, that's very funny. I've never heard that before.' Her laughter, in truth, was disproportionate to what he was saying. It was not all that amusing really, but it was a long time since Molly had laughed at all and Philip, at that moment, seemed such a pleasant companion, such a well-needed tonic. 'Cabbage worshippers...' she repeated, putting her hand on his arm in an impulsive but perfectly natural gesture as her peals of laughter rang out across the empty chapel, echoing back from the walls.

Neither of them had noticed the door at the back of the church opening, but suddenly they both became aware of Hector striding down the aisle towards them. His face was like a thunder cloud, his dark brows drawn closely together over eyes that were as cold as steel.

'Whatever is the meaning of this?' He grabbed hold of Molly's arm, pulling her towards him and away from Philip. 'Restrain yourself, woman. I have never heard such disgraceful behaviour. Laughing out loud, in the house of God! It is a wonder He doesn't strike you dead on the spot. And you too, Mr Mercer. You have not heard the last of this. What will Mr Allbright think of you now, I wonder, when he hears you've been fooling about with someone else's wife?'

'But ... I wasn't,' gasped Philip. 'It's not like that at all. Molly and I, we were just talking and ... and I made her laugh at something I said. That's all.'

'Molly indeed! How dare you refer to my wife as Molly?' Hector's eyes blazed into those of the

357

younger man. 'This is Mrs Stubbins – my wife – and I know what I saw. I saw you philandering with her. Now, get out of here before I kick you out. Go along, get moving. I am waiting to lock up.' Hector's voice, though angry, was not loud. He appeared to be in full control of himself.

'I'm sorry ... Mrs Stubbins.' Philip turned to Molly, his eyes full of concern. 'And I can assure you, Mr Stubbins, there was nothing wrong in what we were doing. We were having a little joke, that's all. I am sorry if we displeased you, and I want you to know it was my fault, my fault entirely.' Philip, though clearly disturbed, was showing that he did not mean to be intimidated.

'Get out!' said Hector again, and Philip, with a last sorrowful look at Molly, made his escape. She was glad to see he did not scurry away as though frightened, nor did he have a hang-dog expression on his face. Why should he? As he maintained, he had done nothing wrong. Neither had she, but that did not stop her from being terrified.

'You too. Go along. Get out,' said Hector, still in a quiet, though ominous, voice when Philip had departed. Firmly he took hold of Molly's elbow and propelled her out of the chapel, locking the door behind them. Out on the pavement he again seized her arm in a vicelike grip and they walked along the streets to their home in complete silence. Molly knew she should try to explain, but she was too frightened at that moment to speak; also, she guessed that whatever she said it would make no difference.

Hector flung open the door of the house and

pushed her inside. 'Upstairs,' he ordered. 'I will deal with you in a moment.' She heard him open the door that led into the kitchen and speak to Rosie. 'Have our meal ready in ten minutes' time, and keep the child out of the way, if you please. Mrs Stubbins and I have something to discuss.'

She was standing in the centre of the room, taking the pins out of her hat, when Hector entered. He seized hold of the hat and flung it to the floor before striking her across the head with such force that she fell on to the bed. 'Hector ... please!' she cried, stunned out of her silence by the totally unexpected blow. She had expected angry words, but not this. He had never struck her before, nor shown any signs that he might do so. 'I can explain. I know it was wrong ... to laugh like that, in church. But it was nothing. We were only–'

'I know what I saw,' said Hector, still not raising his voice. 'I saw you flirting with that ... that Philip Mercer. Goodness knows what would have happened if I hadn't come in when I did.'

'Hector, how can you think such a thing? As if I would...' Molly raised herself up from the bed where she had fallen, but he pushed her down again.

'You will have to be punished, Molly. Stay there!' he ordered as she made to get to her feet. He strode to the chest of drawers and pulled open the bottom drawer. She watched in horror as he drew out a long thin cane, testing its weight in his hands.

'Hector, no!' she cried as he pushed her face downwards on to the bed. She felt him lift up her cumbersome skirt, then he held her down, his hand in the middle of her back, before the blows began to fall on her buttocks, her lower back, the tops of her legs. Her teeth bit into the pillow while tears of humiliation and pain streamed from her eyes. She must not cry out loud. The children, Rosie, they must not hear. She had forgotten, momentarily, that Em would have gone back to school.

At last he stopped, then flung the cane away. It clattered across the floor as he pulled her skirts down and laid a hand, almost gently, across her shoulders.

'You had to be punished, Molly,' he said in a voice that was almost a whisper. 'Remember – whom the Lord loveth he chasteneth. Now, wash your face, then come down and have your meal. I have told Rosie to have it ready.'

'I don't want any lunch,' murmured Molly. 'I'm ... I'm not coming.' She was too shocked, too hurt, both physically and mentally, to face anyone. How would she ever be able to face the children, or Rosie, or Hector, again? The shame was too great. She buried her face in the pillow, feeling at that moment that she would be glad to die.

'Very well, my dear. I will tell Rosie that you are feeling a little unwell.' She was astounded that he could sound so calm, so casual, as though nothing had happened. 'I hope you will have recovered by the time I come home this evening.'

And so she had. She lay still for half an hour or more, shocked and shamed, in the depths of despair. It was the first time in her life that anyone had struck her. Her parents had never believed in chastising their children in that way; and at school too, though a cane was often used as an instrument of correction, Molly, an obedient and reasonably clever little girl, had managed to escape it. At last, though, her innate common sense prevailed. Hurt and humiliated though she was she knew that she would survive. She had to. The children were depending on her and she couldn't let them down. After all, she had survived worse things than being beaten.

She raised her aching body from the bed, then washed her face and combed her hair. Little William would be wondering where she was. She would try to face Rosie as though there was nothing amiss, and in the same way she would face up to her husband that evening. She knew in her heart that she had done nothing wrong and she was determined not to go around with a cowed expression as though she were, indeed, guilty. Surely Hector could not really have believed she was guilty of even so much as thinking about another man, when she had made her marriage vows before him and in the presence of God? Hector was her husband, for better or for worse, as she had already reminded herself many times. But she knew that from now on she must try never, never to displease him, in any way at all.

'Hello there, Mrs Stubbins. Feeling better, are you?' asked Rosie when Molly, taking her courage firmly in both hands, appeared in the kitchen. She felt as though her experience, her mortification, was writ large on her face for all to see, but it seemed that it was not so. Rosie did not appear to realise there was anything amiss.

'Moll, Moll!' cried William, who had been hanging on to Rosie's skirt. He lifted up his arms and ran towards her. 'Up, up...' Molly actually managed to smile as she picked him up and lifted him towards the ceiling, his sturdy little legs kicking furiously as he laughed with delight. She swung him round, then put him down on the floor again.

'Yes, thank you, Rosie,' she said. 'I am feeling much better now. A severe headache, that was all.'

'What about one of them headache powders then?' said Rosie. 'There's some in the cupboard, and I'll make you a nice cup of tea to have with it. And perhaps a buttered scone, eh? You haven't had any dinner, you know.' Rosie always referred to the midday meal as dinner, as did most of the people Molly had known until she married Hector. Now she was trying to get used to saying lunch, but she feared she would never get Rosie to do so.

'Yes, that would be very nice,' she said, feeling, for once, in need of a little spoiling; she would, normally, have insisted on making the tea herself. She had realised that her head was indeed thumping. The powder would relieve it and, she hoped, have a calming effect as well. By the time she came to face Em then, later, Hector, she was in full control of herself, though disinclined, still, to talk very much or to eat a hearty meal.

'Is there something the matter, my dear?' asked Hector, tucking into his lamb chops, mashed

362

potato and green beans as though he had not a care in the world. 'You seem to have lost your appetite. You are very quiet too. Come along, Molly; this is not like you. You are feeling a little under the weather, perhaps?'

'No, thank you, Hector. I am feeling perfectly well,' she replied, politely but a shade coolly. 'I am not very hungry, that's all and ... and maybe I have nothing much to say.'

She had hoped he might have left her alone that night. After all, she had displeased him and given him cause, or so he believed, to be angry with her. But he made claim to her body as usual, as he did every night, at least three weeks out of four. Not one word of regret did he utter for the way he had used her earlier in the day. His kisses and embraces were as passionate as ever. She supposed they might even be called loving, at least to Hector's way of thinking, but Molly could find no response within herself that night, although this was something that, at times, she feigned. She was astounded that he could carry on as though the morning's incident had never occurred. She began to wonder if correction of his wife for misbehaviour was, in Hector's view, a part of marriage; if, in fact, he had only been waiting for her to step out of line so that he could chastise her. She came to the sickening realisation that the cane had been there all the time, though unknown to her, at the bottom of Hector's chest of drawers. Never, never, she resolved, must she give him cause to use it again.

Molly did not find out whether or not Hector had made good his threat to tell the minister, Mr

Allbright, about what he had witnessed between his wife and Philip Mercer. She made a guess that, even if he had done so, Richard Allbright would have formed his own conclusions in his usual common-sensical and fair-minded way. She kept her distance from Philip – not that she had ever, until that fateful day, spoken more than a few words to the young man. His understanding glance, however, whenever they happened to meet, was tacit avowal that he knew she had borne the brunt of her husband's anger over the incident. Philip could not guess, though, at what had been the result of that anger. He must not know. No one must ever know and, please God, Molly often prayed, may it never happen again.

But she knew that Hector was watching her with an eagle eye and she also knew, in spite of her prayers, in spite of her resolve never to step out of line again, that it was only a matter of time. Hector was waiting. It was inevitable. And when Hector struck her for the second time it was, as before, because he had seen her talking and laughing with a man.

It was Ralph Prosser this time, her friend Violet's husband, with whom she had been sharing a little joke. She had not even thought to glance over her shoulder to see if she was incurring Hector's displeasure because it was just Ralph, the happy-go-lucky fellow who always had a cheerful word for everyone, men and women alike. The incident happened at the annual Faith Tea, exactly two years, Molly recalled later with a feeling of doom and inescapability, since her first outing with Hector Stubbins. If only she had decided not to accompany him to that first fateful meeting, how different things might have been. But if she had not done so then she would never have met all the lovely friends who had made her so welcome, nor would she have found the faith which was helping her now in her time of trouble.

She was sitting between Hector and Ralph at teatime. 'How do you like our minister's new appearance?' asked Ralph, leaning towards her in the friendly, almost intimate, way he had. The Reverend Richard Allbright, who had formerly sported a large bristling moustache, had suddenly appeared in their midst clean-shaven. It had proved quite a talking point in the congregation.

'It's different,' replied Molly, 'but I think I preferred the way he looked before.'

'I always thought he looked like a walrus,' said Ralph, chuckling.

'No more so than all the rest of you,' countered Molly. 'You've all got moustaches, haven't you?'

'Oh, I don't know. Depends on the size of the moustache, doesn't it?' said Ralph, stroking his own. 'Richard looked just like a walrus to me.'

'Why?' Molly giggled. 'Have you ever seen one?'

'Not a real one, no. But there's a picture of one in our Daisy's *Alice in Wonderland* book. You know, the walrus and the carpenter. That drawing's the spitting image of our Richard. I'll bring it to show you sometime.'

It was then that Molly burst out laughing, at the same time suddenly becoming aware of

Hector's stony-faced silence on the other side of her. She turned to glance, even to half-smile at him, but her smile froze on her lips as he narrowed his eyes, staring coldly at her. Then she saw, to her horror, the corners of his mouth lifting slightly in a grim, very meaningful smile.

'Hector,' she began, 'Ralph was just saying how ... how different Mr Allbright looks...'

Her voice petered off as Hector rose to his feet, pushing away his chair and placing his paper napkin tidily at the side of his plate. 'If you will excuse me, I have finished my tea. I have some matters to attend to in the chapel.' His eyes bored into Molly's, then into those of the flabbergasted Ralph as he strode away.

'Oo ... er, what have we done?' said Ralph, putting his hand to his mouth in mock fear. 'We've been and gone and done it now, eh, Molly? We really should try to control ourselves. Such hilarity is most unseemly.'

Molly tried to smile back at him. 'It's all right, Ralph. He'll ... he'll get over it. He doesn't have much of a sense of humour, that's all.'

She hid her fear from her friends, from Hector, too, all evening. It almost seemed as though he might have forgotten the incident. He made no reference to her behaviour until after they arrived home and were in their bedroom. Not until Molly was in her nightgown and they had gone through the nightly ritual of prayer time did he attempt to chastise her.

Then: 'I will not have you behaving in such a disgraceful manner with other men,' he said quietly. 'I will have to punish you, Molly.'

366

She had known what to expect. The shock was not so great this time, but the humiliation and the pain were just as severe.

That was in November, and by the time Christmas was approaching Molly was becoming, not immune, not even resigned, but frighteningly aware that this was a part of her life with Hector and that there was nothing she could do about it. She felt too ashamed to talk to anyone. Besides, who could she possibly tell? Maggie, or Flo, or Violet Prosser...? She had deliberated from time to time about confiding in one of these very good friends, but for various reasons she had kept her silence. Maggie would sympathise. Molly knew that her older friend, moreover, would be horrified at Hector's treatment of her, but she might be inclined to say, 'I told you so; I knew all along you shouldn't have married him,' or words to that effect, and Molly could not bear that, although she knew herself by now what a disastrous mistake she had made. As for Flo and Violet, they were chapel folk, holding Hector in high esteem, even though they might not feel any particular fondness for him. It would be like telling tales out of school to divulge that a highly respected church official was guilty of ill-treating his wife. Her sense of honour would not let her betray her husband. Besides, she had been married to him for less than a year. It was far too soon to admit to failure, and she felt, in some way, that she must have failed or he would not abuse her so.

Christmas was a rather lacklustre affair in the Stubbins household – no Christmas tree or crackers or fancy trimmings – although it passed by peacefully enough. Hector was in an amiable mood. He even unbent sufficiently to joke a little with the children. Molly had been able to indulge her sister and brother a little more this year with a few toys from Mr Merryweather's toyshop on the terrace. Hector was not mean with the allowance he gave her and she still had a little money of her own saved from the dinner shop days, hidden at the back of her wardrobe in the old family tin box. Em was eleven years old now, just growing out of the playing-with-dolls stage, but she was delighted with the set of grown-up cardboard dolls and the book of fashionable clothes to cut out and dress them in. She also had a jigsaw puzzle, a hoop and stick to play with out of doors when the weather was warmer, and a copy of *Through the Looking-Glass*. William's presents were building bricks, an alphabet book and a nursery rhyme book, and a wooden Noah's ark with lots of tiny animals; a plaything which Molly had often admired in the toyshop window and which was deemed a very suitable gift by Hector, because of the biblical association.

Molly and Rosie, between them, cooked the Christmas goose with all the trimmings, and the pudding which the two of them had made a couple of months previously. For once they all dined together; Hector, Molly and the two children. Molly was on tenterhooks all the while lest William should spill his dinner or Em should put her elbows on the table, but they were both on their best behaviour. She had hoped that Rosie might be allowed to dine with them, but

Hector did not suggest it and Molly did not dare to do so. The girl seemed satisfied to eat her portion in the kitchen and then to be allowed the rest of the day to go home to her family.

Molly had hoped, also, that Hector might have invited his mother and father to dine with them on Christmas Day, but he had not done so. From the little she had seen of Hector's parents Molly liked them, but she sensed a certain restraint between them and their only son, but in this, as in other matters, she had learned to keep silent.

The year 1900 dawned uneventfully, and as the months went by – January, February, then into March – Molly was relieved that Hector found no reason to beat her with the cane, although he would sometimes lash out and knock her to the floor, kicking her or punching her with his fists, when she was late home, maybe, after a visit to her friend Flo, or if she kept him waiting when they were going to a chapel meeting. She had learned to keep her distance from the men in the congregation, even the Reverend Allbright, knowing, above all else, that her husband was insanely jealous.

She asked herself, from time to time, why she did not stand up to him. If she had heard such a tale as this from someone else she would have said, 'Why on earth don't you stick up for yourself?' But the truth was that she might only make things worse if she challenged him. Hector was a man who hated to be opposed or questioned in the slightest degree about his actions.

She had thought seriously of running away from it all. Maggie, she knew, would take her in

as a temporary measure until she found somewhere else to go. But running away seemed such
a feeble thing to do and Molly was not a coward.
Besides, Hector would force her to return to him
and he would be well within his rights to do so.
By marrying him she had become his by law, his
property. Unless she ran away further, to
somewhere where he would not think to look for
her...?

However, so long as the children were safe and
Hector left them alone – which he had done, so
far – Molly decided she must accept her lot and
just go on hoping and praying that things would
improve.

It was one afternoon in the middle of March
that Molly came home from taking William for a
walk, to find Em sobbing in the kitchen with
Rosie's arms around her. She appeared to be in
such distress that she had not even noticed her
sister and little brother come in. Hector was
nowhere to be seen, although this was not
unusual. It was Wednesday, his half-day, when he
usually worked on a sermon or a talk for his class
meeting.

'I hate him! I hate him!' Em was sobbing
uncontrollably. 'Rosie, oh Rosie.' Her words were
muffled against Rosie's clothing. 'Help me,
please help me. It hurts. An' I want Molly.
Where's Molly?'

'Emily, whatever's the matter, love?' Molly
dashed over to her sister and Em, hearing her
voice, lifted her head for a moment, then moved
away from Rosie to cling to Molly now in the
same way.

'Molly, Molly, he hit me. I hate him! I really, really hate him. I want to kill him...' Molly had never heard her so distraught. She kneeled down, taking her little sister into her arms, stroking her hair and her damp forehead.

'Hush, darling, hush. It'll be all right. There now...' Gently she kissed Em's brow, although she could feel a tremendous rage boiling up inside her. Hector had dared to lay a finger on her sister? Had he hit Emily in the way that he had chastised, her, Molly? Oh dear God, no! That didn't bear thinking about.

'I hate him! Oh, Molly ... take me away, please.' Em was still sobbing, her words almost inaudible as she clung to Molly, burying her head in the folds of her skirt.

'All right, love. Don't worry. We'll do something.' Molly looked anxiously towards Rosie. 'Whatever had happened?' she asked. 'Is this true what she's saying. My husband – he has ... hit her?'

'Yes, I'm afraid so, Mrs Stubbins. I was busy cleaning t'silver in the sitting room and I couldn't help hearing all the commotion going on. Emily, she came home from school, and she went into t'kitchen, didn't you, love?' Rosie smiled fondly in the direction of the little girl who was still hiding her face, as if too stunned and shamed to look anyone in the eyes; Molly knew the feeling. 'I think she was happen a bit hungry,' Rosie continued, 'and she thought she'd help herself to a biscuit. I often let her do that, Mrs Stubbins. No harm in it as I can see, and I know you don't mind. Anyroad, she must've dropped the tin.

371

There was such an almighty crash, and then I heard him – Mr Stubbins – going into t'kitchen. Shouting, he was, fit to raise the dead. Saying she was a thief and a wicked girl and she had to be punished. I daren't interfere though, Mrs Stubbins. None of my business, is it?' She stopped for a moment, looking imploringly at Molly.

'But when I heard the little lass screaming, then I had to do summat. I had to go and see what were going on.' She lowered her voice almost to a whisper. 'He'd got her on t'bed, your bed, Mrs Stubbins, and he were laying into her with a ... with a cane. I could scarcely believe my eyes. He stopped when he saw me, thank the Lord. I thought as how he might tell me to get out and mind me own business, but he didn't. He just pushed past me and left me to see to her, poor little mite.'

'Thank you, Rosie,' said Molly calmly, although the fury inside her was almost uncontrollable. She realised she must be in command of this awful situation. It was even worse now that Emily also, was involved and Molly knew they must prevent gossip and rumours. It might be common knowledge soon enough. 'Thank you for telling me, and for looking after Emily. I'm trusting you, though, not to breathe a word about all this to anyone else. Your family, I mean, or the people at chapel. What happens in this house is our affair, mine and ... er, my husband's, and it must not be talked about outside these four walls. You do understand, don't you, Rosie?' She looked pointedly at the girl and Rosie nodded.

'You may have heard ... things before, things

that may have surprised you a little?'

'Happen I have, happen I haven't.' Rosie shrugged, but her eyes were full of concern as she looked back at Molly. 'Like I say, it's nowt to do wi' me, is it, but...' She faltered; then, her words tumbling over one another, she blurted out, 'But I'm surprised at Mr Stubbins; I am that. I would never have believed it if I hadn't seen it with me own eyes. An' other things I've heard an' all. But I won't say owt. You can trust me, Mrs Stubbins.'

'Thank you, Rosie.' Molly tried to smile at her. 'I know I can trust you. Where is my husband now?'

'Upstairs, I reckon. He dashed out o' t'room, but I dare say he's back there now. He were working on his sermon when Em came home. He'd told me earlier, like, as he didn't want disturbing.'

'I'll give him sermon!' breathed Molly. Then, more loudly, 'Just look after Em for a few minutes, please, Rosie,' she said, 'and William, of course.' The little girl had stopped crying now although there was still an occasional sob shaking her body. Molly put her arms round her again. 'Listen, Em, I'm going to pack a few of your things, then I'm taking you to stay with Auntie Maggie for a while. You'll like that, won't you?'

The child nodded. 'And William as well?' she asked. 'Can he come with me? And you, Molly. Don't leave me, Moll. Come with me, please.' She started to cry again, clinging desperately to her sister. 'I don't want to be on my own. Let's all go away. I hate it here.'

'William can stay with you,' replied Molly. 'I'm

sure Auntie Maggie won't mind looking after you both for a while until ... until I decide what to do. You know you'll be all right with Maggie, don't you? And Sarah – she'll be thrilled to bits, won't she?' Molly, in truth, had no idea what she was going to do, but her first thought had been an instinctive one. Maggie would help, of course. 'But ... but I can't stay there with you, Em. I have to stay here, you see. This is my home now and ... and Hector is my husband.'

'But he's horrible!' cried the little girl.

Molly did not respond to the remark. 'Just stay here for a little while with Rosie and William, there's a good girl,' she said impassively. 'Stop crying. It'll be all right, you'll see. I'll make sure that nobody hurts you, ever again. Come along now, love. Rosie can get you a biscuit and a nice cup of tea, and then ... then we'll go and see Auntie Maggie.'

Hector was in the bedroom working on his sermon, as Rosie had said. He was seated at his desk which he had placed in the prime position in the large bay window. He looked up, frowning slightly, when Molly entered, and looked at her enquiringly. Surely he must have been expecting a visit from her, a reaction to the dreadful thing he had just done?

'I am taking the children away, Hector,' said Molly without preamble. 'What you have done to Emily is unforgivable. There is no way I can let her stay here, or William either. They are not your children, and for you to chastise Emily in that way is ... is outrageous.'

'I shall do as I wish in my own house.' Hector

flung down his pen, seemingly unaware of the splatter of ink drops on his pristine sermon. 'This is my house and I am the head of this household. You knew that when you married me. I was good enough to take your brother and sister as well, so how I choose to discipline them is up to me. You have been too lenient with them, Molly. That girl is underhand and sneaky. I actually caught her thieving.'

'A biscuit, Hector, that's all,' replied Molly. 'What she usually has when she comes home from school. And I certainly have never found her to be dishonest. I know she has never liked you,' she went on, not sure how she was finding the courage to stand up to him, 'but you have never given her any reason to like you, have you, Hector?'

'And William is completely out of control,' Hector continued, as though she had not spoken. 'There will be trouble with that lad if he is not disciplined, and pretty quickly too.' Molly had had doubts about taking William, as well as Emily, away from the house, but Hector's words strengthened her resolve. 'However, what you are suggesting is ridiculous.' He gave a smug smile. 'Of course you are not taking the children away. I forbid it. They will stay here with you ... and with me. Emily will get over it, although it would be as well if she learned to do as she is told. There is no reason why we should not be a happy family when the three of you have learned the lessons of obedience.'

'They are my children, my brother and sister,' replied Molly quietly, 'not yours. They do not even have your name. My parents, God rest their souls, have given them into my care. I know they would both be trusting me to see that their children are loved and well cared for, and that is what I intend to do. I am taking them to stay with ... a friend – for the moment. And if you try to stop me, Hector, then I will tell Mr Allbright and the rest of your church stewards about your behaviour, about how you have treated Emily ... and me.'

Hector's eyes narrowed, and his silence told Molly she had won. She had thought, for one wild moment, of threatening him with the police, but she knew they would not be willing to interfere in what they would see as merely a family matter. She had guessed rightly, however, that Hector would not want to lose his good name at the chapel.

'You will be staying here,' he said, more a statement than a question. 'Maybe the children are not entirely my concern. I only took them in out of the kindness of my heart, and look at the thanks I have got. But you will not even think of going with them. Your place is here, and this is where you will stay. Do you hear me, Molly?'

'Yes, I hear you, Hector,' she replied, meeting his possessive glance with a cool stare. 'I will be back, never fear.'

Chapter 17

'Well, well, this is a nice surprise,' said Maggie Winthrop, opening her front door to see Molly and the two children standing on the doorstep. 'I haven't seen you for ages. We were beginning to wonder what had happened to you. Sarah sees Em at school, of course, doesn't she, dear...?' Her voice faltered as she caught sight of the large bag at Molly's side, her friend's anxious face, and the hansom cab disappearing into the distance, quite an uncommon occurrence in Larkhill Street. 'What's up, Molly? Summat the matter, is there?'

'I'm afraid so.' Molly nodded. 'I'm ever so sorry, Maggie, to descend on you like this, but I just had to come. You were the first person I thought of when...' She glanced at the tight-lipped little girl at her side. Em had not spoken a word since they'd left the house.

Maggie intercepted her glance and gave an understanding nod. 'Well, come along in then, and your luggage, an' all, then you can tell me all about it. Go on, Em, love. Sarah's in the back room.' She gave the child a gentle push. 'She'll be ever so pleased to see you and little William. Go on, Will – William, I mean. Go with your sister and say hello to our Sarah, and Billy and Betty.' She took hold of Molly's arm, holding her back for a moment while the children went on ahead. 'What's up then, lass? You've left him, have you?'

Molly shook her head. 'No, I can't do that. Just the children. I'm really sorry to impose on you, Maggie, but...' She had been strong till now, but at the sight of her good friend she could feel tears welling up in her eyes. Hastily she dashed them away. She mustn't cry, not now. She had to keep calm for the children's, especially Emily's, sake. 'If you could look after them for me, just for a little while... Oh dear. I didn't know which way to turn.'

'Well, thank God you turned to me then,' said Maggie, in her usual brusque way that Molly found, somehow, so comforting. 'Come on, lass. Bear up if you can. We'll get the youngsters settled with a slice of bread and jam or summat, then you can tell me all about it. I take it they've not had their tea?'

'Er ... no, they haven't,' said Molly, reflecting that they usually had something a little more substantial than bread and jam these days. If they were to stay with Maggie, though, they would no doubt soon get used to her haphazard domestic arrangements. Moreover, certainly as far as Em was concerned, it would seem like heaven here compared with the Stubbins' household.

Maggie's children had finished their tea – it was turned five o'clock by now – but were pleased to munch a biscuit whilst their two friends tucked into thick slices of bread spread lavishly with strawberry jam. 'Off you go and eat it in t'backyard,' said Maggie, 'then Molly and I can have a chat.' Molly knew that she could not object to these less than satisfactory eating habits. Besides, she was only too relieved to see that Em had perked up at the sight of Sarah, and was actually smiling again.

'Now, tell me all about it,' said Maggie, when she had made a cup of tea for her friend and seated her in the best, though shabby, armchair. 'What's been going on?'

'It's Hector. He's ... not very nice to me,' Molly began, unwilling, even now, to divulge details of Hector's treatment of her. 'I know what you'll say, Maggie. You'll say I should've thought about it more, that I should never have agreed to marry him. Well, I know all that, and I can put up with it all – at least, I think I can – if it's only me. But now ... well, he started on Emily and that's something I can't allow. I came home this afternoon and she was sobbing her heart out. He'd ... He had...'

'Come on, lass, tell me,' said Maggie, coaxingly, as Molly hesitated.

Molly took a deep breath, which she let out in a long sigh, before she went on. 'He was ... he was beating her. Like he beats me,' she added in a whisper.

'What! He actually strikes you? You're telling me that he beats you?' Maggie looked and sounded horrified. 'Goodness me, lass, that's dreadful! I thought that things might be none too good. I guessed he might be a bit stern, like; harsh with the children, happen. But this! And you say it's happened with young Em, an' all? That's why you've brought her here?'

'Yes. I didn't actually see it happen,' said Molly. 'It was while I was out, you see, with William, and when I came back Em was crying and Rosie was trying to comfort her. And all she'd done was take a biscuit and drop the tin.' Molly went on to tell her friend what had happened, and she found that once she started it was much easier to talk and talk. It all poured out of her; all the misery and hurt and humiliation of the last few months.

'I can put up with it for myself,' she said again, 'but I won't have him chastising the children. He's started on Em, and I know from what he says that it wouldn't be long before William gets the same treatment. He doesn't like them, Maggie. I should have realised. He has no time for them at all. He hasn't tried to get to know them or ... or tried to show them any affection. Oh, why didn't I listen? But I thought it would be all right, really I did.'

'Never mind all that now,' said Maggie, gently. 'What you are asking me is – will I look after them for you? Can they stay here for a while? Well, the answer is yes, as you knew it would be. Of course they can stay here. We haven't much room, mind...'

'I know, that's what I'm worried about. And I will pay you, of course. I don't expect you to do it for nothing, and I can well afford it ... now.'

'Oh, never mind all that.' Maggie flapped her hand impatiently. 'We can budge up. Your Em'll share a bed with Sarah, won't she? And I've got a folding bed as little William can have in t'lads room. We're already using t'front room – what your mam used to call the parlour – for Sarah and Betty, now as Sarah's growing up, y'see. Aye, they'll all be as happy as Larry, don't you worry.'

'It's ever so good of you, Maggie. And after all

I've said, too. I can't forget the way you offered to help when my parents died. You wanted to look after William for me and ... and I refused. Real stubborn, I was, insisting on doing everything myself...' And looking down my nose at Maggie and her slovenly ways, Molly thought. Well, they always say pride comes before a fall. It would serve me right if Maggie were to tell me so.

But her friend did not do so. 'You wanted to be independent, lass,' said Maggie, 'and I can't say as how I blame you for that. I like a girl with spirit, and you've always had that by the bucketful. But I'm glad you've had the good sense to ask for help now. And you can pay me an' all, if it'll make you feel better. Not much, though. I'm glad to help. You can't leave the bairns with a monster like that, 'cause that's what he sounds like to me; a monster. What are you going to do, though, Molly? Are you going back?'

'What else can I do, Maggie? He's my husband, isn't he? I married him; I promised to obey him. That's what I keep trying to tell myself. And maybe, once the children have gone, it won't be too bad. I'm no worse off than lots of women, am I? Some of 'em round here, for instance. We've always known, haven't we, about the husbands who come home from the pub and beat their wives black and blue? But we don't say anything. None of our business, is it, what goes on in some-one else's marriage?'

'When it happens to be your marriage then it most certainly is my business,' replied Maggie. 'I can't stand by and see you suffer like this. You can't compare Hector with the fellows round

381

here, the ones as knock their wives senseless when they've had a skinful on a Saturday night. It's the drink that's got into 'em and in a way they can't help it. Oh aye, I know they shouldn't get drunk, but they do and that's that. But as for Hector Stubbins, what he's doing is far worse in my book. Never touches a drop, does he? Calls it the "demon drink"! Huh! Well, he's a demon all right without the drink. Proper evil, he is. He knows what he's doing – takes a delight in it from the sound of it. All this preaching and praying is sheer hypocrisy as far as I'm concerned if he can't treat his wife properly. What would they think about him at chapel, eh, if they knew what he was up to? Why don't you tell 'em? Tell that minister that you seem to like so much. That'd take Hector Stubbins down a peg or two. He should be drummed out of the place and serve him right, an' all.'

'I can't, Maggie. I just ... can't do it,' said Molly. 'In a lot of ways he is good to me.' She ignored Maggie's snort of derision. 'I'm not short of money and he ... well, he wants to – you know – make love to me all the time.' She lowered her voice although there was no one else in the room. 'And he tells me that he loves me. Quite often he says that, although ... I can't say the same thing to him. In fact, I never do say it.'

'Because you don't love him?'

Molly shook her head. 'No, I'm afraid not. But I can't tell tales about him. Not to anyone else. I've had to tell you, but I can't tell the chapel folk.'

'What about Flo? Doesn't she know?'

'No, I don't see Flo as much as I used to. Well, I haven't seen you either, just lately, have I, Maggie? Hector is very possessive, you see. Everything I do, everywhere I go, he likes it to be with him. But that's marriage, isn't it? Cleaving to one another, like it says in the marriage service.'

'Huh! Not much sense in cleaving to a fellow that ill-treats you like he does.'

'But married couples should stay together, shouldn't they? For better or worse, like you promise. You can't just walk away. I belong to Hector now. That's how he sees it, and it's how the law sees it as well.'

'Then it's time the law was changed,' said Maggie. 'Oh, don't get me wrong, lass. I believe in my marriage vows as much as anyone else, but I've got a good 'un, haven't I? Never laid a finger on me, my Bill. I'm not saying as we don't have our ups and downs. We can shout fit to raise the roof when we get going, but we know as we belong together and we always will. But it's 1900 now. Start of a new century – well, almost. Time to look at things a bit differently, happen. I reckon that after a few years have gone by women won't be putting up with anything like as much as they do now. And I don't see why you should put up with beatings like that, lass. It isn't as if you'd done owt wrong.'

'I suppose you could say I've made my bed and now I've got to lie on it,' said Molly. 'I married him, didn't I? I could have said no, but I chose to go ahead with it. Nobody made me.'

'You married into the Methodist church, you

mean,' replied Maggie. 'I reckon that's the real reason you married Hector Stubbins, isn't it? You weren't just marrying him; you were marrying all t'rest o' t'folks who'd shown you a bit of friendship.'

'I ... yes ... I felt I needed them, Maggie. They'd been so good to me at a time when everything seemed hopeless. They made me feel welcome. It was like going into – what can I say? – a nice warm comfortable home, all safe and secure, full of friends. That's what it felt like going into that Methodist hall. I'd never had many friends before, except for you and Flo.'

'And you thought you couldn't have 'em without taking Hector, an' all?'

'I suppose so. Something like that. It all sounds very silly when you put it like that. But that wasn't the only reason. He really was kind to me at the beginning. And then I ... well, I started to look at things differently. You remember how my parents used to say they didn't believe in God? Never sent me and our Em to Sunday school like other parents did – like you did, Maggie? Well, now I think they were wrong. It's given me something to believe in, something to hang on to when things are bad. I know I can go on trusting – and believing – that things'll get better.'

'It certainly sounds as though you're going to need to, lass. Supposing he turns nasty – even nastier, I mean – when he discovers you've taken the children away? Have you thought about that?'

'I don't think he will, Maggie. I know he said at first he would forbid me to take them, but he soon realised he couldn't do that. I'm hoping

384

things might be better. He never cared for our Em and William. Maybe he was even a bit jealous of them. I've told you how possessive he is. So perhaps when he's got me to himself, without the children, he might be better...' Her voice petered out. She knew it was a forlorn hope, but at least the children would be out of harm's way.

'Anyway, I'd best say my goodbyes to 'em and get back home.' Molly bit her lip, trying to stem the threatening tears. 'And your Bill'll be home from work soon, won't he, and Tom? You'll have a meal to get ready for them. I'm sorry, Maggie – I'm hindering you.' She thought again about how many there were in Maggie's family: Tom, who worked as a butcher's assistant in town; Arthur, the next eldest lad, about to leave school quite soon; Sarah and Billy and Betty, now playing in the backyard with Em and William; not to mention Maggie and Bill. A houseful already without the two extra children.

'Oh, ne'er mind them,' said Maggie, flapping her hand again in a casual gesture. 'If they have to wait a few minutes it'll do 'em no harm. And don't you start worrying, neither, about what Bill'll say. He'll be only too pleased to help, like I am. He told you so when your dad died, remember? What are friends for if they can't help out when you're in a spot of bother?'

Molly stood up, ready to depart. 'I know. I'm grateful. You'll never know how much. I'm just wondering... It might be better if I slipped away without telling them. They seem happy enough and I don't want to cause ructions.' A glance through the window showed Betty and Emily

385

turning a long skipping rope while the irrepressible Sarah jumped up and down in the middle, and Billy and William building a tower with a pile of stones and pieces of coal. All of them looked thoroughly absorbed in what they were doing, oblivious to what was going on in the house. 'Our Em, she was so distressed. It's like a miracle, almost, to see her playing with your two as though she hasn't a care in the world. And William is inclined to cling to me, as you know. Yes, it might be best if I just went. I've already told them, of course, that they'd be stopping here for a little while. What do you think, Maggie?'

'I think you're right.' Maggie nodded. 'Off you go, before they notice. It seems hard, I know, but we don't want them upsetting any more than they need be. And you can come and see them anytime you like. Well, you don't need me to tell you that, do you, Molly love?' Impulsively she flung her arms round the young woman and kissed her cheek. 'Look after yourself, lass. Try not to let things get you down. Happen, as you say, it'll be better without the bairns. But if there's any more trouble, well, you know we'll do owt we can, Bill and me ... An' I'll say a little prayer, an' all,' she added quietly. 'It'll not do any harm.'

Molly was touched by Maggie's spontaneous hug and kiss. She was not normally given to such unreserved behaviour. 'Thank you,' was all she could utter. She was anxious to leave before she gave way to a flood of tears that she feared, once started, she would be unable to stop.

'How will you get home, lass? Are you going to

look for a cab? You'll have to go to the end o' t'road, though.' Maggie gave a little chuckle. 'They don't often get 'emselves down here.'

'No, I'll walk,' replied Molly. 'It'll help to clear my head and ... and there's plenty of time.' The truth was that she needed to be able to compose herself fully before facing Hector, and she was in no hurry to get home – even though it would, by now, be time for their evening meal; even though she knew she would be keeping him waiting.

'Goodbye, Maggie, and thanks again, for everything.' She squeezed the older woman's hand as she stood on the doorstep, then walked quickly away.

Maggie gave a tremendous sigh as she watched the girl walk briskly away. She'll be back, she thought to herself, and not just to see the children. Before long she'll be needing a refuge for herself too. And then what the heck were they going to do? Maggie knew that Molly had not thought beyond the next week, the next month, maybe. She had assumed, correctly, that her friend would take the children in. But for how long? And after that? One step at a time, Maggie told herself. Sufficient for the moment that she, Maggie, should provide a loving haven for those two children. But one thing she felt sure of, as sure as her name was Maggie Winthrop: Molly Rimmer – she still could not think of her as Molly Stubbins – would be back before many weeks had passed.

'You are late, Molly. You have kept me waiting.

Rosie has had our meal prepared this last half-hour and more.'

Hector always insisted that their evening meal should be on the table promptly at six o'clock, and woe betide Molly if she should be even so little as five minutes late for this arrangement. She had told Rosie, before she left with the children, to carry on as usual. She'd hoped she would be back in time for the meal, and to postpone it would only provoke Hector's wrath even further. But she had stayed to talk with Maggie rather longer than she had intended, and then even the knowledge that she was late did not force her to quicken her footsteps. Maybe she had hoped, just this once, that her husband might be more lenient; maybe it was that she did not care. She had been successful in getting the children away from him; her suffering, for the moment, would have to take second place.

'Come along, now. The meal will most likely be ruined, and it will be your fault entirely, not the fault of Rosie. You should know by now that one thing I cannot abide is overcooked meat.' Hector glanced critically at the well-browned steaks on the serving dish as Rosie carried it into the dining room. They were just the way Molly preferred them, but Hector liked to see the blood running out of the meat when he stuck his fork in it. The sight of it always turned Molly's stomach, but underdone or overdone, she doubted she would have much appetite tonight.

'As I feared – burned to a cinder. Thank you, Rosie, that will be all. You have done your best, I know. Go and get your own meal now. For these and all Thy mercies, we give Thee thanks, O Lord.' Hector spread his crisp white napkin over his knees, then motioned to Molly to serve out the meal.

It was a silent mealtime. During the first course Hector did not speak at all. Pointedly he left half of his meat, although it was very palatable and Molly, in spite of thinking at first that food would choke her, actually found herself enjoying it. The apple charlotte, it seemed, was much more to Hector's liking. His dish was emptied in no time at all and there was that rapacious glint in his eyes that Molly had noticed whenever something was particularly pleasing to him. She gave an inward shudder. It was a look she had learned to fear, meaning, as it so often did, that his attentions towards her would be more demanding than usual.

'Delicious! I think that is one of the puddings that Rosie makes exceedingly well.' He licked his lips, then dabbed them precisely with his napkin. 'I would like you to accompany me to the class meeting tonight, Molly. It is rather important to me that you should be there.'

'I ... had not intended going, Hector,' said Molly, bravely. 'I have a slight headache.' She did not always go with Hector on a Wednesday evening and he did not always insist that she should.

'A headache which will soon disappear when you get out into the fresh air.' His tone was dismissive. 'It is my wish that you should be there. Now – please tell Rosie that we are ready for our coffee.'

She knew it was pointless to argue further. He

had not mentioned the children since her return, had not even enquired where it was she had taken them, although he would most likely have guessed. She knew that he had been made to lose face. She had stood up to him and, in his own eyes at least, he had been seen to lose a little of his dominance. The children were no longer there under his control, but she, Molly, was.

'He that spareth his rod hateth his son; but he that loveth him chasteneth him betimes.' She might have guessed what his text would be at the class meeting that evening. That one from the book of Proverbs which he quoted so meaningfully, or something similar. But then all Hector's texts referred to judgment, obedience, chastisement, repentance...

Why had she imagined for one moment that it might be easier once the children had gone? As the tears of anguish and humiliation dampened her pillow later that night she knew, from now on, that it would only get worse.

She visited Em and William at Maggie's home a couple of times a week, timing her visits to coincide with Em's arrival home from school. She stayed with them for an hour or so, but always made sure she arrived home in good time for the evening meal. It would be foolish to give Hector any more reason than he already had to be displeased with her. She knew that never since that time she had departed so hurriedly with the children had she stepped out of line. She was obedient – submissive, even – believing that this would be in her best interests, but that one supreme act of disobedience was, it seemed, sufficient for Hector. His chastisement of her was a nightly occurrence now.

She was pleased to see that the children were happy with Maggie and the rest of her family. Em appeared to understand the situation and, in her usual taciturn way, said very little about it. Molly guessed she was trying to blot out of her mind the awful experience she had gone through with Hector. Would that she, Molly, could do the same! Em did not ask when they would be going home, and Molly knew she would meet with total resistance should she ever try to take her back to the house on Warbreck Road. William sometimes said, 'Go home ... go home with Molly', or some such thing, but once again Molly would explain to him that he must stay with Auntie Maggie, 'just for a little while'.

A little while... It lengthened into a fortnight, a month. Molly made sure that Maggie did not lose financially from her kindness; shortage of money was not, now, one of Molly's problems, but she had learned there were far, far worse things than poverty. To Maggie's enquiries as to how things were going with Hector, Molly answered evasively, 'not too badly', or, 'I think it's a little better' – although she was sure Maggie knew it was a lie – or 'Please don't ask me, Maggie'.

Maggie did not know how long Molly intended leaving the children in her care, and at first Molly was not sure herself. She had seen Maggie as an anchor to cling to when she was drowning in despair, but she knew she could not presume on her friend's good nature for ever. However, a plan was slowly forming in her mind.

By the beginning of May, when the children had been with Maggie some six weeks, Molly knew that her plight was such that she could put up with it no longer. She waited until Hector had gone to the shop, then packed the largest bag she could find with her most essential belongings. She knew she could not go without telling Rosie, and though she hated asking the girl to lie on her behalf, she knew that some deception might be necessary.

'I'm sorry, Rosie,' she said. 'I can't tell you where I am going, but I will not be coming back. Tell my husband ... tell him that you don't know where I am. Tell him that I went without speaking to you, if you wish. But you realise, don't you, that I can't stay here any longer?'

Rosie nodded. 'I know things are bad, Mrs Stubbins. But what'll I do? I can't stay here on my own ... with him.'

Molly had thought of that too. 'I'm so sorry, Rosie,' she said again. 'I know it's causing problems for you as well. I can see that you can't stay here. It would not be considered ... quite right, nor would you want to carry on living here when I have gone. Maybe you could go back and live at home? And come in each day to do the cleaning and such cooking as my husband requires? It will have to be his decision, of course, but I am sure he will still need you – that is if you wish to continue working for him?'

'Don't know as I do, really. Not if you're not here, Mrs Stubbins. But I can't see as I've any choice. Me mam needs the money, don't she? And I still won't say owt, you know, to the folk at chapel, about all the, er, goings-on.' Molly was touched to see tears come into the girl's eyes. 'Oh, Mrs Stubbins ... Molly ... do take care of yerself. I shouldn't be thinking of meself, not when you're in such trouble. I know you've been miserable. I know you've got to get away from 'im. You're going to get the little 'uns, are you? You're all going away together somewhere?'

'I think the less said about my plans, the better,' replied Molly, realising she could talk quite calmly now her mind was made up. 'Thank you, Rosie, for everything you've done for me. You've been a good friend. Now, you stay inside while I see if I can find a cab. It's best if you don't see me go, then you don't have to tell too many fibs, eh?' She smiled at the girl, then put her arms round her and gave her a hug; she had never been able to think of her as a servant. 'Goodbye, Rosie. God bless you.'

'Goodbye, Molly. An' God bless you, an' all. I'll think about yer. I'll say me prayers for you every night.'

There was no disguising Maggie's open-mouthed astonishment on seeing Molly on her doorstep, complete with luggage, for a second time. This time it was an even larger bag.

'Oh, so you've finally done it, have you? You've gone and left him? Well, I can't say I blame yer.' Nor could she hide her slight sigh of exasperation as she turned and led the way into the house. 'Well, you'd best come in, hadn't you – and your luggage, an' all – and we'll see if we can sort summat out for you.'

Chapter 18

'Maggie, I don't intend stopping here.' Molly knew she had better put the matter straight at once as she could see her friend was jumping to the wrong conclusion. 'I know you haven't room and I wouldn't dream of putting you to any more trouble. You've been far too good to me already. But I couldn't go without explaining to you. You see, I'm on my way to Preston.'

'Preston?' She may well have said Timbuktu or darkest Africa, not the nearby town, only eighteen miles away, from the incredulous way in which Maggie repeated the word. 'Why on earth d'you want to go to Preston?' She did not wait for an immediate answer. 'Well, like I said, you'd best come in and tell me all about it.'

William was playing with a pile of building bricks on the hearthrug when Molly entered the living room. He jumped up at the sight of his sister, scattering the bricks in all directions, and ran to her. 'Molly, Molly, you've come to see Willum.' He flung his arms around her, just below her waist level, then tugged at her skirt. 'Look, Moll, look. I'm building a house.'

'It's falling down, I'm afraid, darling,' she laughed, stooping down and kissing his cheek. 'Go and build it up again, there's a good boy, while I have a chat with Auntie Maggie.'

He grinned at her, then went obediently back

to his play. She could see how happy and contented he was with Maggie. She knew she would be able to talk quite freely, even with William in the room. He was always totally engrossed in whatever he was doing, to the exclusion of all else. Besides, much of what she was saying would go over his head. It would not have been so with Emily. She would have been all ears, but Em was safely out of the way at school.

'I have decided I can't stay with Hector any longer,' Molly began, amazed at how composedly she was able to speak now that she had made the ultimate decision and got away from Hector, with luck, for good. She was relieved, however, to sit down in Maggie's most comfortable chair before continuing with her tale. 'Life is just intolerable. I thought I might be able to stand it. I even thought it might be better, that he might not treat me quite so badly once the children had gone. But I was wrong. It made him even more determined to ... teach me a lesson, I suppose.'

Maggie turned away from the kitchen range after placing the blackened kettle, once more, on the slow-burning fire. There were not many times during the day in Maggie's home when the kettle was not boiling ready for the next cup of tea. She sat down opposite Molly. 'It got worse then, lass?'

Molly nodded. 'I couldn't tell you. I haven't told anybody. I can't find the words, I suppose, to explain what he is like.'

'Try, love,' said Maggie gently. 'There's only you and me here, and there's not much as I don't know or haven't heard about. In my line of business you see and hear all sorts. I'm not being nosy, like, but I think somebody ought to know what that husband of yours has been getting up to.'

'He beats me,' said Molly, quite unemotionally, but almost in a whisper, so that William should not hear. 'With ... a cane. I told you that before, didn't I? What I find hard to explain – to understand – is that he seems to ... to enjoy it. And now he can't...' She paused for several seconds before going on. 'He can't – you know – make love to me until ... until he has ... punished me.'

Maggie let out a long low sigh. 'Aye, I've heard tell of fellows like that. Sadists, or summat, they call 'em. They like making people suffer pain. Never could understand it meself an' I never will. But he's evil. I've said so before an' I'll say it again. He's downright wicked. A monster, that's what Hector Stubbins is.'

'And yet he tells me he loves me,' said Molly. 'He sounds quite sincere about it too. At times he can't do enough for me: making sure I'm warmly wrapped up when we go out, making a fuss of me at chapel, always calling me "dear" and "love"...'

'In front of other folks, aye.' Maggie gave a sniff. 'He wouldn't want all that lot at chapel to know what he was like, that's for sure. But they'll soon know, won't they? They'll find out, now as you've gone and left him.'

'Not from my telling, they won't,' said Molly. 'Nobody knows but you, and that's the way I want it. Oh, and Rosie – you know, Rosie Hewitt, our maid. She's heard things, sure to have done, but she says she'll keep quiet about it. It always amazed me that Hector behaved in the way he did, with Rosie around. It was as though he thought she was invisible, because she was a servant, or that nobody could hear ... on the other side of the bedroom door.'

Maggie stared at her, slowly shaking her head, her eyes full of sadness and concern and a deep affection. 'To think it should come to this. And after such a short time. Less than a year, isn't it? I never liked him, I'll admit it, but I never thought you'd have to suffer owt like this, lass.'

'Yes, it'll be a year at the end of the month since Hector and I were married. And ... I know I'm doing wrong. I know it's a woman's duty to stay with her husband. I've tried, Maggie. I really have tried to honour and obey him, like I promised. I know now that I should never have promised to love him, to cherish him, like it says in the service, because ... I can't. It was wrong of me to marry him, knowing that I didn't really love him. But now – well – I think it's best if I go, quietly, without any fuss.'

'I think you've done right to leave him,' said Maggie. 'It's a big step you're taking, lass, and I know you won't have done it without thinking long and hard about it. But, Preston, you said? You're thinking of going to Preston? Wouldn't you be better off here, in Blackpool, where all your friends are? And the children...?'

'I'm taking Em and William with me,' said Molly, glancing affectionately at her little brother, who was still playing happily on his own. 'Oh goodness me, how stupid of me! I should have said. Surely you didn't think I would go away and leave them? I said it would only be for a little while, didn't I, that I would leave them with you, until I decided what to do? Well, now I've made up my mind. I can't take them today, of course. I thought I'd go and find somewhere for us all to live, and then I'll come back for them.'

'I'll just mash the tea,' said Maggie, shaking her head bemusedly, 'then you'd best tell me what the big attraction is in Preston.'

'It's where my mother and father came from,' said Molly, when she had taken the welcome mug of tea from Maggie's hands. It was also the place where a young man called Joss lived, but Molly had not allowed this fleeting thought to stay in her mind, nor did she mention it now. Maggie had never heard of him anyway, and Molly tried not to think of him. 'It's the only place I know of where I have any relatives at all ... and only one at that. I can't stay in Blackpool, Maggie. You must realise I can't. Hector would find me and make me go back, and he would be within his rights to do so, I'm sure. Wives don't leave their husbands. It's unheard of. I know I'm doing wrong,' she said again.

'Seems to me as though you've no choice,' said Maggie. 'You've suffered a good deal more than any lass of your age should have to suffer; or any age, come to that. You're not twenty-one yet, are you?'

'No, not till September. But I feel that I grew up years ago, Maggie. As soon as me mam and dad died, that was the start of it. Looking back on it, I feel I was just a child ... till then.'

'Aye, mebbe you're right,' said Maggie. 'That

was when things started going wrong for you, but you always had lots of pluck, even as a little girl, and that'll stand you in good stead. What about that friend of yours, Flo Palmer? Doesn't she know owt about this?'

'No, I decided not to tell anyone I was leaving, only you. I feel awful about it, in a way. Flo's always been my best friend – of my own age, I mean, Maggie. You've been just as much of a friend to me.'

'But a bit longer in the tooth, eh?' Maggie grinned.

Molly shook her head. 'Age doesn't matter. But Flo and I both worked on the terrace for a few years. We had some good times together. I haven't seen as much of her since I got married; I told you, Hector didn't like me going round seeing people unless he was there as well. Anyway, Flo and Sam have been courting for ages – three years it must be by now.' A transient thought flickered through her mind as she recalled the night that Sam and Flo had met. 'I think she knows I'm not too happy with Hector, but she doesn't know why. And I could never bring myself to tell her. I feel years older than Flo now. How can you tell a young woman about to be married about ... that?'

'Aye, that's true enough. True of all of us, I suppose, that you don't know a fellow until you've married him. And none of us knows what goes on behind other folk's closed doors, do we?'

'I'll get in touch with Flo later,' said Molly, 'when I know where I'm going to be living. I'm sure she'll understand. Word'll get around like wildfire once I've gone – unless Hector tries to hide it. He might pretend I'm ill or ... or gone to visit relatives. I can't really imagine what he will do, or say, to people. I feel dreadful about not telling Violet Prosser as well, and one or two of the others. They've been kind to me, especially Violet. But I think she may have realised that things are not too good. There was that time when Hector was annoyed with me for having a laugh with Ralph.' She shuddered at the thought of what Hector's rage might be when he discovered she had gone, but even this did not deter her.

'He'll not be able to hide it for ever that you've gone and left him,' said Maggie. 'And then folks'll start asking themselves why. Don't you worry, the truth will out, and it'll serve him damn well right. Can't for the life of me see why you want to protect him.'

'It's the chapel, I suppose,' said Molly. 'I don't want the place to get a bad name. I don't want anyone to point their finger and say, "He's supposed to be a man of God and look how he carries on", or something like that. Because most of the folk there are really good people, so sincere and kind. They don't deserve this – the shame of it.'

'They don't deserve a hypocrite like Hector Stubbins in their midst, that's for sure,' said Maggie. 'Look, lass, I may not be much of a churchgoer myself, but I know better than to judge the whole lot of 'em by just one bad 'un. There's a rotten apple in every barrel, so they say, and Hector Stubbins is rotten to the core. You'll shed no more tears over him if you've any sense. Now, what about this relation of yours in Preston? Who is she? Or he ... or whatever? I know yer mam and dad came from there, but I never heard tell of any relations that they kept in touch with.'

'Uncle Silas,' replied Molly. 'My dad's uncle; my great-uncle he would be, if he's still alive. Like you say, my parents never spoke much about the past, but I heard my father say that Uncle Silas was his only living relative. I don't know anything about my mother's side of the family, whether any of them are still living or not.'

'And do you know where he lives, this long-lost uncle?' asked Maggie. 'What do you intend to do? Go and knock on the door and ask him to take you in?'

'No, of course not,' said Molly. 'He's just somebody to contact, that's all. Somebody from my own family. I haven't anyone, you know, apart from Em and William. It came home to me when my mother died, then my father, that I had nobody of my own there, at the graveside with me. I should have got in touch with this Uncle Silas then, I suppose, but ... I didn't. It all happened so quickly and I just felt stunned, as though I didn't know what I was doing most of the time.'

'Do you know where he lives then, apart from somewhere in Preston?' asked Maggie again. 'His proper address, I mean?'

'Yes, there was a little address book in the tin box in the cupboard,' replied Molly, 'where we kept all the important bits and pieces – the rent book and policies and all that. I took it with me when I got married and it's at the bottom of my bag now. Most of the other addresses in the book were Blackpool ones – you know, the doctor and the undertaker and some of Dad's workmates; they hadn't many friends, you remember. I don't think they kept in touch with Uncle Silas – well, I'm sure they didn't – but his address is there. He lives in somewhere called Winckley Square.'

'So you're going to Preston to seek out some old uncle that you know nothing about, just because you think he's the only relation you've got? How d'you know you'll be made welcome? Have you ever met him before?'

'Not that I know of,' said Molly. 'Perhaps when I was a baby... No, I don't suppose I have. There was some sort of quarrel, I believe, when my parents got married. Uncle Silas wasn't too pleased about it and he said he wanted nothing more to do with my father.'

'It gets worse,' said Maggie, scratching her head. 'So how d'you know as he'll want owt to do with you?'

'I don't,' said Molly. 'But that was my father's quarrel, wasn't it, not mine? He can't have anything against me, surely, because he's never met me. And they always say that blood's thicker than water, don't they? Can't you see, Maggie, it's a link with the past, with my parents, the only one I know of? I can't stay here in Blackpool, it's too risky, and Preston isn't a million miles away. I thought it would be far enough away, but not too far.'

'And what do you want from him, this Uncle Silas? You want to be careful, Molly, or else he might think you're going there cap in hand.'

'As if I would!' Molly was indignant. 'You surely can't think that, Maggie. No, I've looked after myself before and I'll do it again. I know you were always there, and I'm grateful,' she added, aware that she may have sounded a little unappreciative of her friend's continual help. 'But I was never afraid of hard work and that's what I intend to do again once I've found somewhere for us all to live: work for my living. I just want to feel I've got someone near that I can turn to, for friendship, and guidance, maybe. I'm hoping that this uncle may be able to help me to find somewhere to live. I don't know Preston or anything about the place. And I'm hoping he may be able to tell me something about my parents' past life. It's always been a mystery to me. There may even be other distant relatives that I know nothing about.'

'Hmmm ... I see.' Maggie gave a grunt, not entirely of displeasure. 'Well, as I said before, you've got guts, lass. And I suppose it makes sense to get right away from here, somewhere he can't find you. Just for the time being, eh? P'raps you could come back later, once the dust has settled? But I should be careful, if I were you, about delving too much into the past. Happen it's better left as it is. Happen there were things yer mam and dad felt it was best you should know nowt about.'

'What things?' asked Molly, aware from Maggie's tone that she might know more about

William and Lily Rimmer than she was letting on. 'You know something don't you, Maggie?'

'Not really,' said Maggie. 'I don't know all that much. They were always very secretive. But I do know that yer mam never got over losing her own mam when she was only about eight years old.'

'So I believe,' said Molly. 'My father did tell me about that. I know it's a very tragic thing to happen. But surely that sort of thing must have happened to lots of children? I can't see why it should make her sad for the rest of her life. Especially after she married my father; he was so good to her.'

'Aye, well, you don't know the true story, not the whole of it,' said Maggie. 'I'll be straight with you, lass. It's only fair you should know. William told me, in confidence, that Lily's mother committed suicide. And to make matters worse it was Lily – your mother – as found her. She'd hanged herself, y'see, and I suppose ... well, yer mam never got over it.'

'Oh! That's dreadful!' exclaimed Molly. 'I had no idea there was anything like that. My poor mam, how awful for her. Even so, it was a long time ago.'

'Only thirty years or so before your mam died herself,' said Maggie. 'Not a very long time really, not in the whole scheme of things.'

'And why did she kill herself, my ... grandmother? Strange that, my grandmother, and yet I've never heard anything about her.'

'That I don't know,' said Maggie. 'Yer dad hinted – only hinted, mind – that it was because she'd found summat out about her own mother,

404

some scandal or tragedy, and she couldn't stand it. Yer dad didn't tell me any more than that, so I didn't ask. Some skeleton in the cupboard that's happen best left where it is. It sounds to me as though she was a very highly strung, nervy sort of person, your grandmother.'

'Some scandal ... or tragedy ... about my ... great-grandmother?' said Molly wonderingly.

'Aye, that's who she would be,' said Maggie. 'But I don't see as it'll do any good to go bothering yer head about it. You've enough problems of yer own, haven't you?'

'Seems to me that the past casts a long shadow, though,' said Molly. 'My great-grandmother – we don't know what happened to her, but my grandmother found it so dreadful that she took her own life. And that affected my mother, didn't it? I suppose I can understand now why my parents turned against God; well, my mother at any rate. Maybe she felt that God was against her, that it was all His fault for letting it happen. Or that he wasn't there at all, just didn't exist.'

'Yer mam was a sad sort of person,' said Maggie. 'Could be downright miserable at times, then your dad would try to jolly her along a bit. I don't think she could help it really; it was just part of her make-up, the way she was. But Lily had got it into her head that the women in the family were doomed to disaster, that there was some sort of misfortune continually stalking them. Will tried to tell her it was all nonsense; that was why he never told you the truth about your grandmother's death, in case you started thinking the same way. Happen when Lily died

405

he'd start thinking differently, though.'

'It seems as though there may be some truth in it,' said Molly, thoughtfully. 'Bad luck, misfortune, disaster – whatever you want to call it. As Mam said, it does seem to happen to the women, doesn't it? My mother lost her life, didn't she? And my marriage – well, it's nothing short of a disaster, is it?'

'Don't you start thinking like that, Molly Rimmer, or I shall be sorry that I told you. I'll tell you one thing: you're nothing like yer mam, except in looks, and I have to admit you're the image of her in that respect. No, you've got your father's spirit in you, and a lot more besides. Don't start thinking you're beaten, lass, because you're not. Eh dear, we've wandered a long way from your plans about going to Preston, haven't we? If you're really intent on going then you'd best get off as soon as you can. Happen you're right. It'll do no harm to have a fresh start. But I'll miss you, Molly. I will that; more than I can say. What about the bairns then? What shall I say to them? Or are you going to tell William yourself, now?'

'I don't suppose he will understand,' said Molly. 'He's quite used to me coming and going anyway. In fact, he seems to have settled down much better than I thought he would, thanks to you, Maggie. I'll have to leave it to you to explain to Emily. Tell her the truth, or as near to the truth as you can. Say ... that I've had to go away for a little while, that I'm looking for somewhere for us all to live, and that I'll come back and see them when I've found a nice place. Then we can all be together again.' Molly opened the clasp of her large holdall and took out two books, one a picture book of animals and the other a story book *The Water-Babies*. 'Here, give them these, would you, Maggie? A little present, to show them that I'm still thinking about them.'

For the first time since entering Maggie's house Molly could feel the pricking of tears against her eyelids. She looked at William again. She had missed him more than she had thought possible, and whatever she did now, whatever decisions she made, she knew that her brother and sister must always be of primary importance. And what was most important now was that she should find somewhere suitable where they could all live together happily again.

'I'll write to you as soon as I can,' she told Maggie. 'When I've found somewhere to stay I'll write and let you know. It shouldn't be more than a week – probably less –before I come back for Em and William.'

She spoke confidently, knowing she must summon up all the courage she could find within herself before taking the next step of her journey. All the same, she did not refuse when Maggie offered to accompany her to the station to help with her luggage. As well as her large holdall she had a smaller bag and a handbag. She had hired a cab to bring her from Warbreck Road, but it would not be worth doing so again, always supposing she could find one on Larkhill Street, as Talbot Road station was only five minutes' walk away.

'What about William?' she said at first. 'Won't

he be upset if he sees me going away on a train?'

'Not him!' said Maggie confidently. 'If I know William he'll be more interested in the engine than in you. It'll be the first time he's seen a train close to – quite an adventure for him, especially if you tell him he'll be going on one, an' all, next week. Come on now, William, there's a good lad. Leave yer bricks and off you go down the yard to the lav. We're going to help Molly to carry these heavy bags to the station – you know, that place where they have all them big trains...'

William did not need much persuading, and trotted along happily at Molly's side, holding tightly to her hand. Like all young children he was interested only in the here and now, and did not question why Molly had all those bags or where she was going. As Maggie had predicted he stared spellbound at the huge giant of an engine, laughing excitedly when it gave a great snort then let out a hiss of steam.

'I'n't it big, Molly,' he said, gazing at it in wonderment. 'Look, Auntie Maggie, look! Big engine, just like "E for engine" in my book.' An engine was pictured on the 'E' page in his alphabet book, along with an egg, an elephant and an Eskimo. He could recognise all the pictures, but the engine, with a funny face painted on its front, was his favourite. 'It's got no face,' he said now, sounding a little puzzled. 'No face, not like Willum's.' But the engine, as the women had hoped, was proving to be a distraction.

The trains to Preston left fairly frequently and the women were pleased to find there was one leaving in less than ten minutes. 'Don't wait with me,' said Molly, when they had hauled her bag up on to the luggage rack and she had chosen her seat in the corner of the compartment. All had gone well so far with William. She didn't want tears at the last minute, although the tears that might be shed would be hers, she feared, not those of her little brother.

He seemed to realise, suddenly, that Molly was going somewhere and that he was to be left with Maggie. 'Willum go too,' he said, pulling at Molly's skirt in the way he so often did when he wanted to attract attention. 'Willum go on train.'

'No, not just now, William,' said Molly, swallowing hard to get rid of the lump in her throat. 'Next week – soon – I'll come back, then we'll all go on a train, you and me and Em. Won't that be nice?'

'And Auntie Maggie?' asked the child.

'Perhaps...' said Molly, evasively. Oh dear, this was all getting very complicated. She would have to leave it to her good friend, as usual, to come to the rescue. Which Maggie did, seizing her moment straightaway.

'Come on, young man. Let's be off, shall we? We've got to make dinner for your Em and Sarah, and it'll never be ready at this rate.'

'An' Billy and Betty,' added the child.

'Aye, and them an' all,' grinned Maggie. 'Come on; give Molly a kiss and then we'll get going. Ta-ra lass. Take care of yourself.'

Molly was glad that her friend's farewell was perfunctory. Better for William, better for every-one concerned than a prolonged goodbye with a waving of hands until the train had vanished out of sight. She blinked rapidly, watching the corpulent figure of her friend, with William skipping along quite contentedly at her side, as they made their way out of the station.

'Your little boy, is he, luv?' asked the middle-aged woman in the opposite seat. 'Bonny little lad, but not much like you, is he? More like his dad, I expect. And that'll be yer mam, eh?'

'No, no, he's not my child,' said Molly, trying to answer politely, although she did not feel like entering into a conversation. 'He's my little brother, and the lady is my friend who's looking after him.' She smiled at the nosy woman in a dismissive manner, then took her *People's Friend* magazine out of the small bag at her side and pointedly opened it. She stared hard at the words, not wanting to read – not even able to read, her mind was in such a turmoil – but hoping it would do the trick and procure her some peace and quiet. The woman gave an audible sniff, of pique, Molly supposed, but she did not have to stay silent for long. Just before the train pulled out another middle-aged woman entered the compartment and the two of them chatted contentedly throughout the journey to Preston, leaving Molly alone with her thoughts.

She was almost as much of a stranger to trains as was her little brother. It was only the second time that Molly had been away from her native Blackpool, the first time being a year ago on her honeymoon to the Lake District, an experience she did not want to relive in her mind at all. She had never before visited Preston, but she had seen it from the train window a year ago and it had been there that they had changed trains. She was impressed again by the tall, tall spire of St Walburge's church as the train trundled by. It had been Hector, of course, who had told her the name of the church. On the outskirts of Preston, surrounded by numerous mills and rows and rows of small red-brick terraced houses, it was a landmark that could be seen from miles away. To Molly it signalled the end of her journey – only a short journey, little more than half an hour, but it could well have been a whole day's journey and a destination hundreds of miles away, so strange did it all seem to Molly.

A gentleman who had boarded the train at Kirkham assisted her with her luggage, pulling her holdall off the rack, then holding the door open for her to alight. 'Thank you, thank you so much,' she said, returning his cheerful smile. She was, indeed, grateful to him, and she felt her spirits lift a little at his helpfulness. She began to feel more optimistic as she stared at the hustle and bustle of the busy station going on all around her.

There were porters pushing huge trucks laden with luggage; railway officials in peaked caps and jackets with gold buttons, standing around looking important; hundreds of people dashing hither and thither, some emerging from the waiting rooms and the station buffet room, others standing at the edge of the platform await-ing their trains. And what a multitude of platforms there seemed to be, several on either side of Molly; and all those miles of gleaming railway lines, converging or branching away at some distant point, all in the charge of the skilful men, in their signal boxes, whose job it was to ensure that the trains ended up on the right track and got to their correct destination; London or Manchester or Birmingham...

Molly shook herself. It was no use standing there wool-gathering about distant places she would probably never see. She was here in Preston and she had to find her Great-uncle Silas.

She picked up her bags and approached one of the important-looking men. 'Excuse me, sir, I wonder if you could tell me the way to Winckley Square? Is it very far?'

'Certainly I can, my dear young lady,' replied the man, a mite pompously but smiling at her in a most friendly way. 'No, it's not far. Nobbut a hop, skip and a jump away. Turn right once you've got out o' t'station, on to Fishergate, then it's ... let's see...' He pondered a moment. 'Aye, it's t'fourth turning on yer right. That's Winckley Street, see. Go down there an' you'll be in Winckley Square. Where all the nobs live,' he added. He glanced down at her luggage. 'But happen you'd best get a cab, eh? That bag looks rather heavy for a young lass like you.'

Molly suddenly realised that it might not be a good idea to arrive on her uncle's doorstep with a large bag, as though she were looking for lodgings. 'Yes, it is heavy,' she said, 'and I won't be needing it just yet. I wonder, is there somewhere I could leave it for a while?'

'Aye, t'office over there,' said the man, pointing. 'They'll give you a ticket an' look after it for you for as long as you like.'

'Thank you, thank you very much,' said Molly, touched by his willingness to help and by the homely sound of his northern accent; very similar to the ones she was used to hearing in Blackpool, but possibly a shade broader. It made her feel that she was not so far away from home.

When he had left her holdall at the office she made her way out of the station and up the cobbled incline, then turned right into Fisher-gate. This, she guessed, was the main street of Preston, a busy street thronged with horse-drawn carriages, ponies and traps, bicyclists and hun-dreds of people who all seemed to be in a hurry, but who all knew exactly where they were going, just as Molly did when she was on her home ground. She stared around for a moment at the impressive-looking buildings on either side of the road, strange to her eyes as yet, but soon, she hoped, to be more familiar to her; then she set off walking again.

Winckley Street was a quiet, rather broad thoroughfare with elegant houses leading into a square where there were more stately buildings, all looking on to a tree-lined garden in the centre. Molly gulped in astonishment. It seemed as though her informant at the station had been right in saying that this was where the nobs lived. She hadn't realised her great-uncle lived in such grandiose surroundings as this. However, she had not come so far just to turn round and walk away again. And her life with Hector, awful as it had been, had given her the courage to face up to anything. Nothing venture, nothing win, she told herself as she strode bravely up the path to the door whose number was written in her little black book. She took hold of the lion-headed knocker and tapped three times. Then she stood and waited.

Chapter 19

After a few moments the door was opened by a maid in a black dress and a long white apron and cap. Molly was surprised, although she had not known what it was she had expected. That her great-uncle lived alone, maybe, without any servants? But one look at the imposing residence in front of her should have told her that this was not likely. The truth was that she knew nothing whatsoever about Silas Rimmer except that he was her father's uncle.

'Good afternoon, miss. How can I help you?' The maid, a young woman of roughly Molly's age, was polite, though a mite self-possessed for a servant, thought Molly.

'Er, good afternoon,' she answered. She had assumed that it was still morning – she was on the wrong side of her dinner – but from the maid's words she guessed it must be turned twelve o'clock. 'I wonder if I could see Mr Rimmer? Mr Silas Rimmer? He does live here, doesn't he?'

'Yes, that's correct, miss. Step inside, won't you? Whom shall I say wants to speak to him?'

'Miss ... Rimmer,' said Molly, seeing the maid start a little – but only a little – at her words. 'Miss Molly Rimmer. I am ... well, he's my uncle, sort of. My great-uncle, actually.' She did not hesitate to use her maiden name, white lie though it might be. Molly was not usually one to resort to untruths, but to admit at the start that she was married, that she had, in fact, just walked out on her husband, would be to complicate matters unnecessarily.

'Very well, Miss Rimmer. Would you wait here a moment, please?' Again she was aware of the slightly raised eyebrows of the maid.

The young woman ushered her into the passage beyond the vestibule, a gloomy hallway with dark brown paintwork and wallpaper of a similar dingy hue. The only light was that which filtered through the stained-glass panels on the door, a pleasing pattern of leaves and flowers which provided a splash of colour in otherwise dismal surroundings. A massive hallstand towered at the side of Molly, on which hung a couple of sombre overcoats and two bowler hats, with a selection of walking sticks, some with bone or silver handles, at the side. It was obvious that this was solely a gentleman's residence; it was also most obvious that it had seen better days.

'Excuse me, Mr Rimmer, sir, there's a young lady to see you.' The maid had opened the further of the two dark brown doors and stood on the threshold. 'Miss Molly Rimmer. Your ... niece, Sir?' Molly could hear the questioning note in the young woman's voice. She did not think, however, that it was because the maid did not believe her, but because she had not been aware of any such person. The answer that came from within the room confirmed this.

'Niece? What niece?' The voice was gruff and not at all welcoming. 'I haven't got any niece, not so far as I know, anyroad.'

'Your ... great-niece, actually, sir. That's who she says she is.'

'Great-niece? There's no great-niece neither, not that I'm aware of. There's nobody left but me, like I told you. What did you say her name was?'

'Miss Molly Rimmer, sir.'

There was a few seconds' pause. Then, 'Well, you'd best show her in, I suppose,' said the voice.

Molly noticed a touch of sympathy and understanding in the glance and half-smile that the maid exchanged with her. She showed her into the room. 'Miss Molly Rimmer, sir,' she said again, quietly closing the door behind her.

It was Molly's turn to start as she set eyes on the figure seated in the high-winged armchair to one side of the very small fire. It could almost be her father come back to life, though this man was much older, of course. The same shock of unruly hair – not dark brown, though, as William's had been, but grizzled, completely white at the temples and balding slightly on top; the same rugged face and ruddy cheeks, with a network of broken capillary veins; the same piercing blue eyes but, alas, without her father's glint of humour, which had never been far from the surface. This man's glance was hostile, his wide mouth – again, an exact likeness of William's – unsmiling and unwelcoming in the extreme.

'Good afternoon,' said Molly, trying to smile in spite of the stony visage that confronted her. 'I am sorry to disturb you – I can see you are resting – but I have come to introduce myself.'

She took a deep breath. 'I believe you are my uncle ... my great-uncle, I should say. I am the daughter of your nephew, William.'

'Never knew as he had a daughter. Never heard owt about him since he ran off wi' that Grimshaw lass, and neither have I wanted to. Ran off to Blackpool, so I heard tell.' His eyes narrowed as he peered closely at Molly. 'Your mother, I reckon?'

'Yes, that was my mother's name, I believe,' replied Molly, determined not to be intimidated. 'Lily Grimshaw.'

'Aye, Lily Grimshaw.' The old man – Molly guessed him to be in his late sixties or thereabouts – nodded slowly. 'It was bad enough that he broke my daughter's heart. They should've been wed, him and my lass, my Bella...' His eyes softened momentarily. 'But then what did he do but go and run off wi' one o' that lot. Bad blood there was in that family. Bad blood in the whole lot of 'em. That was what I couldn't forgive. My Bella never forgave him neither; never forgot him and what he'd done. That's why she ended up the way she did.'

'What happened to your daughter?' asked Molly quietly. Her hackles had started to rise at the mention of her mother, especially at the remark about bad blood in the family. Bad blood indeed! This was her gentle and unassuming mother he was talking about, not some harlot! But there was a mystery here, another one, something she did not understand, and the old man, tyrant though he appeared to be, was visibly disturbed. Without being invited to do so she sat

418

down in the chair opposite him and leaned forward. 'I did not realise you had a daughter,' she said, when he did not answer. 'What happened to her?' she asked again.

'Dead,' said Silas Rimmer, his eyes glazing over as he stared into the pitiful apology for a fire. 'Dead these twenty years and more. Knocked down by a dray horse, she was, right there in Fishergate. Wasn't looking where she was going. I tell you, she never got over it; never got over him, your father. So was it any wonder I never wanted any more to do wi' William an' his lot? There's only me left now an' I reckon I'll not be here much longer. What's there to live for, eh?'

He raised his eyes then, staring at Molly quite impassively. He nodded gravely. 'Aye, I can tell you are who you say you are. Molly you say your name is? Aye, you're the spitting image of that other one, that Lily. But there were bad blood there in that Vidler family, going back generations. An' it comes out, you can be sure o' that. It's true what they say. What's bred in the bone comes out in the blood. I allus said no good would come of it, him marrying one o' that lot.' He paused for a moment and Molly had to bite her tongue to prevent herself from retaliating, as she knew she would have to do before long. She certainly would not be able to take much more of this abuse of her family.

'What happened to him then, our William?' he asked, a little less abruptly. She could not help but notice his use of the possessive pronoun, and it was probably this which softened her attitude a little.

'He's dead,' she replied quietly. 'My father died – in an accident in Blackpool – three years ago. Just after my mother died. She died in childbirth, giving birth to my little brother. He is called William as well,' she added.

'I see.' Silas Rimmer stared at her, his eyes still unfriendly, not a trace of the sympathy in them now which she thought she had seen there a few moments ago. 'So ... what do you want? What are you doing here, in Preston? William and that Lily, they settled in Blackpool, didn't they?'

'I have come to Preston to try and make a fresh start,' said Molly, endeavouring to curb her emotions. 'We have had some family problems, myself and my little sister and brother. Things have not been easy ... since my parents died. I decided to come to Preston because it is where my parents came from. The only place where I have any relations. You ... Uncle Silas,' she added, a little more diffidently.

'Oh, I see.' He glanced at the bag at her side. 'So you've come looking for lodgings, have you? You've come cap in hand? You thought I'd be a soft touch, did you?'

Molly sprang to her feet. Cap in hand, indeed! That was the very expression that Maggie had used, the one that Molly had so vehemently denied. And she would deny it now. 'Indeed I have not!' She raised her voice for the first time. 'And if that is what you think then I will go this minute. I came because ... I have told you ... because you are my only living relative that I know of. And because I believed you might be pleased to see me. I can see now that I was wrong.' She picked up her bag, making for the door. 'I will trouble you no longer, Uncle Silas.'

'Here, here, hang on a minute.' He almost, but not quite, rose from his chair. 'There's no need to carry on like that. Sit down again, lass. Go on – sit thee down,' as Molly still hesitated. 'Happen I shouldn't've said that, but what was I to think, eh? You turn up out of the blue. Not a word to say you were coming. Why didn't you write, eh? Let me know what was in yer mind?'

'I'm not sure,' said Molly, sitting down again, her anger slightly appeased. To write would have been to waste precious time. She had needed to get away from Hector, and quickly, but she could not tell her great-uncle this. 'Look, I don't want anything from you. I only wanted to make myself known to you, because of who you are ... my father's uncle. I am sorry about your daughter, really I am, but you must believe me that I knew nothing about her, nothing whatsoever. My parents never spoke about the past.'

'No, they wouldn't, would they? Wanted to forget, didn't they? But my Bella, she didn't forget.'

Molly carried on as though he had not spoken. 'There is so much that I don't know, so much that is a mystery to me. It has been very strange growing up without any relatives. I never knew my grandparents, not any of them. I thought I might have found someone,' she looked her great-uncle straight in the eyes, 'someone who might ... be a friend to me?'

As he stared back at her, his glance softening just a little, she suddenly found herself unable to contain her anger, the emotion that had been slowly building up inside her since she had set foot in the room. 'But all you have done since I came here is pull my parents to pieces. To spoil the memory I have of them. I don't care what they did; they were my mam and dad, and I loved them!'

For the first time she could see a hint of a smile playing round his lips. 'Aye, happen you did, and happen I shouldn't go on about 'em. It's not your fault, not any of it. I'm sure you loved 'em and I'm sorry you've lost 'em both so soon. You're nobbut a young lass, I can see that. Aye, I loved my Bella an' all, but life can be very cruel.'

'You said your daughter and my father were going to be married?' asked Molly, feeling slightly calmer now at her uncle's change of attitude. She was aware that his stony antagonism towards her was beginning to thaw a little. 'But ... they were cousins, surely?'

'Aye, they were cousins, right enough, but what does that matter? The old queen married her cousin, didn't she? Childhood sweethearts, they were, William and my Bella. She worshipped him, right from being a bairn; used to follow him around, she did, everywhere he went. He could do no wrong in our Bella's eyes. Mind you, the missus, my Flossie, she weren't so keen on t'match as I were. Thought as how he weren't quite good enough. She had big ideas, my Flossie.' Molly did not enquire what had happened to Flossie. Silas's wife had died, she guessed, as well as his daughter. He had said there was only him left. As for herself, she was feeling more and more bemused by the minute at all these revelations. She was forming an opinion, however, that this childhood love affair might have been somewhat one-sided; that it had been the unknown Bella who was doing the running and that her father, possibly, had just been caught up in it all.

'But they'd've been happy. Nothing more sure than that. They were happy ... till Lily Grimshaw came along.' He gave a deep sigh. 'He was like a son to me, young William – your Dad – the son I never had. Then he went and spoiled it all.'

'What about his own parents? My grandparents?' asked Molly. 'I've never heard anything about them.'

'They died,' said Silas, quite unemotionally. 'Both of 'em, Jacob and Esther; they both died o' t'fever when William was only a little lad. That was why he came to live with us, wi' me and Flossie and our Bella.'

'I didn't know,' said Molly slowly. 'He never said.'

'Aye, well, happen he had his reasons. Wanted to forget the past, I dare say. But when he got mixed up wi' that Vidler lot – well, I just washed me hands of him. Bad blood,' he muttered again. 'It were all wrong...'

Molly thought it best to ignore his last remark, lest she should lose her temper again. Instead she picked up on the name her uncle had used. Vidler; it was the second time he had mentioned that name. 'Vidler?' she asked. 'Who were the Vidlers? My mother was called Grimshaw, wasn't she?'

'So she was, but her mother – your grand-mother – she was a Vidler till she got wed.'

'My grandmother,' said Molly thoughtfully. 'She was the one who ... she killed herself, didn't she?'

'So I believe. The shame of it, that's what it was. Finding out about her mother. So you know about that, do you?'

'I know about my grandmother,' said Molly carefully. 'But I only found out the true facts fairly recently, from an old family friend. My parents had kept it from me. All I knew, before that, was that my mother never got over her own mother's death. It's only lately I've begun to understand why. My grandmother hanged her-self and it was my mother that found her. It must've been a terrible shock for such a young girl. And my mother was always...' she paused a second before deciding on the right word, '...sensitive.'

'Aye, mebbe she was. Unstable, I'd say, like the whole lot of 'em. Like I've said before, it taints each generation. You can't get away from it. Still, I dunno...' He looked keenly at Molly. 'You seem like a sensible enough lass. Happen it's worked itself out.'

Once again she tried to disregard his derog-atory remarks about her mother. 'Uncle Silas,' she began, detecting just a slight tinge of warmth in the old man's eyes at the use of his name, 'there seems to be some mystery, something I don't understand. You keep hinting about bad blood.' All of a sudden she raised her voice. 'And I must say I don't like that; I don't like it at all.

There was not one drop of bad blood in my mother, I can tell you that for certain. She was the most gentle person you could ever meet.' Having got that off her chest she continued more restrainedly. 'But there's something, isn't there, much further back? My great-grandmother? What happened to her?'

Her great-uncle frowned, looking at her in some surprise. 'D'you mean to say you don't know about Phoebe Vidler?'

'No.' Molly shook her head. 'I wouldn't be asking if I knew, would I? All I know is that there is something ... something that no one wants to talk about.'

Her uncle sighed. 'Then if you don't know, lass, it's not for me to tell you. Best forget it, that's my advice. Forget the whole lot of 'em. No, I don't suppose you can do that. You'll not forget yer own mam and dad, but you can forget about t'rest of 'em. They're not worth it. It does no good to keep looking back to the past.'

That was rich, she thought, coming from him. All he had done since she came was harp on about past wrongs. Her father, William, who had been a son to him rather than a nephew – she had not known that; his daughter, Bella, and her fascination for her cousin, who had probably thought of himself as more of a brother; then the advent of the tragic Lily ... Molly thought she could make some sense of all that. But this other thing, this mystery concerning the Vidlers, a name she had never heard of until today...

'How do you know about it, Uncle Silas?' she asked, 'seeing that it's so long ago. How do you know – whatever it is – about this Phoebe Vidler?'

'Everybody in Preston knows about Phoebe Vidler,' said her uncle. 'At least they did sixty year ago. I reckon it'll be about sixty year since it happened. I know I were only a young lad – ten or so, I'd be – at the time. Happen folk'll've forgotten now. An' it's best forgotten. An' that's what I'm telling you to do. Forget it, lass. Get on with yer own life, whatever it is you want to do. Got any plans, have you?'

'I have some plans, yes,' replied Molly. She did not yet feel very kindly disposed towards him, although he had mellowed somewhat from the disagreeable old man she had first set eyes on. But he was still unsure of her, she could sense that, as she was of him. 'I want to find some lodgings, where there will be room for my sister and brother as well. And I intend to get a job.'

'A job, eh? What sort of job?'

'I have worked in a shop,' replied Molly in a controlled voice. 'As a matter of fact, I used to have a small shop of my own.' She hoped he would not ask why she no longer had one, but he did not do so. He continued to look fixedly at her. His penetrating glance was disturbing and she found herself faltering a little. 'I ... I expect I will be able to find something in that line. A confectioner's or a grocer's shop, perhaps. And somewhere to live.'

'Aye, you'll need a roof over yer head, that's for sure.' He paused significantly, taking his eyes from her and letting them wander around the room.

It was a dark, gloomy room with heavy plush

curtains of a deep maroon shade, pulled back only a little as though he had no wish to see the daylight. A cumbersome mahogany sideboard filled one wall, and a huge matching table and four chairs completed the furniture in what was obviously the dining room, although there was no other sign that meals were taken there. The gilt-framed pictures on the walls were of mountain scenes, highland cattle, and one of horses, but apart from these there was nothing of interest or any touch of lightness in the room; no ornaments or vases or photographs. It was as though Silas Rimmer had tried to banish all reminders of his wife and daughter, even though he talked quite a lot about them. Molly wondered, fleetingly, if he was thinking of offering her lodgings here. That thought certainly seemed to be crossing his mind as he contemplated his surroundings; it was as though he was seeing them for the first time or with different eyes. But if he were to offer, then she would refuse. She could not easily forget his insulting words about her mother or his insinuation, earlier, that she had come on a begging errand.

Whatever might have been in his mind he soon dismissed it, as his next remark revealed. 'Well, I hope you soon find somewhere. There are shops in plenty along Fishergate and Friargate. Not that I see 'em myself – I hardly ever goes out – but I dare say some of 'em'd be glad of a pretty young assistant.' Molly was surprised to see a touch of warmth in his eyes and, for only the second time, a semblance of a smile curving his lips. 'I'm sure you'll soon find yerself some lodgings. There's lots of women wi' rooms to let, wanting to make a few extra bob.' He rose to his feet and she knew it was a signal for her to go. She, also, stood up. He seemed to be hinting he had given her enough of his time, and she had no wish to overstay her – lukewarm – welcome. 'Well, you'd best be on yer way, hadn't you? Don't let me hinder you.'

She had thought from the way he huddled in his armchair that he might be bent and unsteady on his legs, but it was a straight-backed, tall man who faced her now. He could almost have been called dignified were it not for the shabbiness of his clothing – his jacket and shirt were clean but decidedly well worn – and his slight air of dejection. And the forlorn look in his eyes. She had noticed the world-weariness that had come over him as they were talking. It was there again now.

Molly held out her hand. 'Goodbye ... Uncle Silas.' She could not say, in honesty, that it had been nice to meet him, but she hoped she knew her manners. 'I am glad to have met you.' She did not say she would see him again. In all probability he would forget about her – or try to – when she walked out of the door, and would resume what she assumed to be his lonely reclusive life. The fleeting glimpses of friendliness she had seen on his face had been of short duration. She guessed he would prefer to be left alone.

'Goodbye ... Molly,' he said, taking hold of the hand she offered. His own hand felt cold and lifeless. 'I'm sorry to hear that William has gone.

Look after yerself, and...' He hesitated. 'Well, look after yerself.' Whatever else he had been going to say, he had changed his mind.

The maid appeared, right on cue, as soon as the door was opened. Uncle Silas hovered in the doorway of the dining room as the maid led the way to the vestibule, then the front door, opening them for Molly to go through.

'His bark's worse than his bite,' she whispered as Molly took her leave. 'He doesn't have many visitors. He's so ... well, he can be so rude to 'em if he's that way out; then they don't come back.'

'So I've gathered,' said Molly, with a wry smile. She guessed that this young woman had got her uncle's measure and that she was possibly the only one who knew how to handle him. 'But you get on all right with him, do you?' she asked.

'We jog along,' said the girl cheerfully. 'He needs somebody–'

'Lizzie...?' Molly could hear the voice of her uncle from within the house. 'Tell her ... tell her to come and see me again.'

'He says, will you come and see him again, miss?' Molly did not answer. 'Well, goodbye then, miss. I'd best go and see to him now. He'll be wanting his lunch, I dare say.'

Molly realised that she too was hungry. She had not been offered so much as a cup of tea in that parsimonious household. It would not have occurred to her uncharitable old uncle to offer her one, and it was not up to the maid to do so of her own accord. Lizzie, her uncle had called her. She seemed a pleasant and friendly girl, not one to get upset easily. She would need to be easy-going, looking after a curmudgeonly old man like that. Molly wondered if she lived in, or went back to a home of her own at night. She assumed that Lizzie would be the only servant her uncle employed. There was a great deal that was perplexing to Molly, although she had already learned a lot that she had not been aware of before. She had discovered that her father, in marrying her mother, had been guilty of breaking a young woman's heart; or so her uncle would have her believe. And the mystery concerning her maternal great-grandmother was growing ever deeper.

But there were other matters too that puzzled her. Why, for instance, did her Uncle Silas live in such a huge house, in a lifestyle that was quite clearly middle-class? Miserly he undoubtedly was, but all the signs seemed to indicate that he was, in reality, not without a good bit of brass. From the little she knew of her father and his forebears Molly had gathered that they had been ordinary working-class folk, mill workers, as so many were in Preston. And so, she deduced, had her mother's ancestors been as well; mill hands for the most part. Had her Great-uncle Silas married into money? If so, then none of it had come her father's way. No, of course it would not have done so; Silas had told her, hadn't he, that he had wanted nothing more to do with William Rimmer after his unsuitable marriage?

But Molly's immediate concern was with finding something to eat, then lodgings, then a job. She found a little café in a side street just off

Fishergate and after a satisfying meal of steak and kidney pie, green beans and a strong cup of tea she felt refreshed and heartened to continue her search. She came upon a small grocer's shop, the sort that sold anything and everything, at the point where Fishergate merged with Church Street, and in the window were several cards advertising rooms to let. She had noticed she was approaching the slightly less affluent part of the town and she knew it was here she must try to find lodgings. She could not afford to be too fussy, so long as the place was reasonably clean and there was room for Em and William as well as herself.

After one or two disappointments – sorry, luv, no children ... sorry, no cooking allowed in the rooms, miss; guests eat in the dining room – Molly found a place she thought would be ideal. The house on Stoneygate, just behind the impressive Parish Church of St John the Divine, had seen better days, but the two rooms on the top floor which the landlady, Mrs Marsden, offered to Molly, would, she was sure, do splendidly. They were sparsely funished, but all the essentials were there. Two single beds, a wardrobe and dressing table in the one; a table, four bentwood chairs, a shabby armchair, a small gas stove, a sink, and a cupboard in which to keep crockery and provisions in the other. Mrs Marsden, a thin-featured woman who did not look as though she would give much away, did not object to children, in spite of her rather forbidding air, and she took the fortnight's rent which Molly paid in advance with a grunt and

431

curt nod. Molly had a little ready money to meet her immediate needs – her own money, saved from the dinner shop days, not Hector's – but it was imperative, now, that she should find a way of earning her living to support, not only herself, but the two children.

One problem she had unwittingly overlooked was that of young William. He was still only three years old; it would be more than a year before he was old enough to start school. What had she thought she was going to do with him? she chided herself as she was turned away several times. There were jobs available, not an overabundance, but enough of them, and the shopkeepers along Church Street and its environs – the grocer, the confectioner, the draper – would all have been willing to employ Molly, but not with the encumbrance of a child. Why, oh why had she ever thought she might be able to take him with her? She realised she had closed her mind to this most obvious problem, so keen had she been to make a fresh start in life.

She knew, by half-past five on that first day, when all the shops were closing, that she would have to admit defeat, for the moment at least. She dashed into the nearest grocer's shop and bought a small loaf, two rashers of bacon, two eggs and a quarter-pound of tea. At least she would not starve, and tomorrow was another day.

Back in her new home on Stoneygate the rooms did not appear nearly so satisfactory or pleasant. The carpet squares were threadbare, the springs were showing through the split fabric on the armchair, hidden beneath the grimy cushion, and the gas stove was covered in a film of grease. The living room, if it deserved such a grand title, felt chilly in spite of the mild May evening, as though there had been no fire lit in there for ages. There was a fireplace, just a small one as this would, originally, have been a bedroom, with a coal scuttle at the side containing a few small lumps of coal. And, wonder of wonders, there was a crumple of paper and a couple of sticks already laid in the hearth. Molly placed the coal on top, only to realise she had no matches. She searched around and discovered a few, however, in the cupboard near the gas stove. Mrs Marsden, it appeared, had grudgingly provided the barest necessities and no more.

Molly lit the fire, then with a grubby cloth which she found on the bathroom floor, and lukewarm water, she proceeded to clean the worst of the grease from the gas stove. She had already been informed she could use the bathroom, but would be allowed only one bath a week, and that applied to the children, too, when they arrived. That was no hardship. All they had had when they lived in Larkhill Street was a zinc bath. A bathroom was a luxury to which she had only recently become accustomed, since marrying Hector. An indoor lavatory, too, but Molly would gladly have gone down the yard to the closet for now and evermore, and washed at the kitchen slopstone, if needs be, rather than stay another day with Hector.

The cooking utensils were very few and very basic. She cooked the rashers of bacon in the wobbly frying pan, blackened round the rim, then dished them out on to the cracked plate with the egg she had just about managed to baste with the bacon fat. She had forgotten to buy any lard, or any butter, but it would not be the first time she had eaten dry bread, she thought philosophically, as she cut herself two thick slices. Nor the first time she had drunk tea without milk or sugar; she had, of course, forgotten those as well. Tomorrow she would do a little more shopping, she decided, for essentials, and there were a few items of cutlery in her holdall at the station; knives, forks and spoons of her own, from Larkhill. Not one item that could be said to belong to Hector had she taken away from their home. That was another job that must be done tomorrow; she must collect her luggage from the station.

The flock mattress was lumpy and the blankets well worn, but Molly slept reasonably well, tired out by the events of the day. So much had happened. It seemed ages – more like days than hours – since she had called that morning to see Maggie...

Maggie opened the door at around seven o'clock that same evening to find Hector Stubbins on the doorstep. She was not overly surprised: the knock had been loud and decisive and she had been half expecting him anyway.

'I've come to collect my wife,' he said. 'She is here, isn't she? There is no use in denying it, Mrs Winthrop, because I know there is nowhere else she is likely to be. So if you could just tell her I am waiting...'

Maggie narrowed her eyes as she met his icy glance. Goodness, how she hated him. She had disliked him before, but now she hated him for what he had done to Molly. 'She's not here.' She started to shut the door, but he stuck out his foot, preventing her.

'Don't play games with me, Mrs Winthrop. I know she is there.'

'Don't you dare call me a liar, Mr Stubbins! If I say your wife is not here, then she is not here. I'll swear on the Bible if you like, that damned Bible that you're always ramming down people's throats. You're nowt but a hypocrite, Hector Stubbins, treating your lovely young wife the way you've done. Yes, I know all about you and your brutal carryings-on.' She could detect a flicker of something in his pale grey eyes, nothing as strong as fear, but a certain unease, maybe. 'You're nowt but a pervert, an' if I have my way there'll not only be me as knows about it. You try and come in here an' I'll make sure as everybody knows.'

'You can't frighten me, Mrs Winthrop, with your foolish talk. What you are saying is nonsense, sheer nonsense.' Nevertheless, he withdrew his foot from the door. 'The children are here, though, aren't they? Don't try to tell me otherwise, because I know they are.'

'Yes, they are here, and this is where they are going to stay until Molly tells me any different. You just try to get yer hands on them an' it'll be worse for you, Hector Stubbins. You'd best clear off – we don't want your sort round here. Molly's not here; you have my word as a Christian woman. I may not go to church, but I'm a better

435

Christian than the likes of you. She's not here, and you're not having the bairns.'

'I do not want them,' he replied. The curving of his thin lips showed his contempt for them. 'For what it is worth, I believe you that my wife is not here.' He paused before asking, 'Where is she then? Do you know?'

Maggie found it surprising that he had asked, even more surprising that he seemed to expect an answer.

'Where she is at this exact moment I don't know, and that's the honest truth,' said Maggie. 'And if I did know, d'you think I'd tell you? Huh! You could beat me black and blue, like you've done to that poor lass, an' I still wouldn't tell you. She's not in Blackpool, I'll tell you that much, so you can save yer shoe leather looking for her. And that's all as I'm telling you. Now clear off, or I'll get my husband to make sure you do.' She had been speaking quietly so that the children inside the house would not hear, but now she raised her voice. 'Bill, come here a minute, will you?'

'Good evening to you, Mrs Winthrop.' In spite of the cold disdain emanating from his every pore, Hector politely touched his bowler hat before striding away down the street. But Maggie had the satisfaction of seeing that the anxiety in his eyes had increased.

'That was Hector Stubbins,' she said to Bill, who had joined her at the door, 'looking for Molly, but I've sent him off with a flea in his ear. Look at him – he can't get away fast enough. I've put the wind up that one, sure enough. That'll learn him. He'll not come here again in a hurry.

436

Eeh, I can't help thinking about Molly, though. I hope she's all right, poor lass. I wonder what she's doing, eh, right at this minute?'

Chapter 20

Molly was hoping she might have fallen on her feet. Fingers crossed, though: she still had to mention to Mrs Healey about her little brother, William. The Healeys, who ran a grocer's shop on Manchester Road, had a little girl, Amy, who was about the same age as William. Molly had seen her playing quite happily with a pile of empty boxes and a rag doll in the storeroom at the rear of the shop when Mrs Healey had showed her round. They were an amiable couple, in their early thirties, Molly guessed, and after a few pertinent questions about her previous experience they had seemed satisfied; well pleased, in fact, so much so that they had asked her if she could start work the next day.

Molly had jumped at the opportunity; but she had decided, before she first entered the shop on seeing the notice in the window, that this time she would not tell them about William. She would wait and see if she was offered the position, and then, after a few days, perhaps, she would broach the subject. Little Amy seemed to be giving her an excellent starting point, especially when Mrs Healey made the remark that it was difficult keeping the child occupied whilst she was working. 'She's a good little lass, bless her, but I'm sure she must get fed up of amusing herself while I'm busy. I can't very well leave her upstairs on her own. I like to have her near, where I can keep an eye on her.'

The Healeys lived over the shop, and as well as the grocer's they also ran a market stall on Wednesday, Friday and Saturday, where they sold essential groceries and a selection of vegetables and salad stuffs, grown by Mr Healey's brother in his market garden in Woodplumpton. The husband and wife took it in turns to man the market stall, which is why they had decided to employ an assistant. The shop was a busy one, very near to the numerous mills in the Stanley Street area.

'Yes, she is very well-behaved, isn't she?' said Molly. She had just accepted a make-believe cup of tea in a tiny tin cup from the little girl. Molly already seemed to have found favour with the child, but then she had never had any difficulty in getting along with children. It was mid-morning and there was a momentary lull in the small shop. It would get busier when the mill workers had their half-hour break, and when housewives ran short of something for the dinners they were cooking; children too, often popped in for a ha'penny worth of sweets on their way to or from school. Molly decided to take advantage of the quiet interlude.

'I have a little brother about the same age as Amy,' she began. 'She is three, isn't she?'

'Yes, just turned,' said Mrs Healey. 'It was her birthday in March.'

'William will be three in June,' said Molly. She smiled, a little sadly. 'He was born on the night of the Queen's Jubilee, June the twentieth. That was the night my mother died too. She died ... having William.' She spoke quite matter-of-factedly, not wanting to sound as though she was playing on the sympathy of her employer. She had already told her that she lived alone in rented rooms, but until now she had not mentioned her parents or her brother and sister.

'Oh dear, that's sad,' said Mrs Healey. 'Very sad indeed. How does your father manage? I mean, is there someone to look after the little boy?'

'My father died soon after my mother,' replied Molly. Oh goodness! She did not want to make too much of a sob story about all this, but facts were facts. 'The children – I have a sister as well, aged eleven – they have been my responsibility ever since my parents died. They're with a friend of mine at the moment, but I was wondering, Mrs Healey...' Molly took a deep breath. 'I was wondering if it might be possible for me to bring William to work with me? It was seeing Amy playing there on her own that gave me the idea. He might be company for her. He's a good little boy – well, reasonably good,' she added, in an attempt to be more truthful. 'He does have his moments.'

'Don't they all?' Mrs Healey smiled. She hesitated before she went on and Molly feared she might be about to refuse. Then, 'I had no idea,' she said. 'You poor girl. You mean ... you had no relations, no one to help you?'

'No, not really,' said Molly. 'My friend – well, she was my mother's friend in the beginning – she's been very good, but now I'm making arrangements for them to come and live with me.

There's room for them at the place I've got on Stoneygate, but...' Her employer was still regarding her thoughtfully, not even smiling now; in fact a small frown had appeared on her forehead. 'But ... well, it doesn't really matter,' Molly continued, 'if it isn't convenient for me to bring William here. I dare say I could find some-one who would look after him...' Her voice faded away. Oh dear! She was beginning to realise she had not thought around this problem at all. Leaving William with a stranger was the one thing she had been determined she would never do.

'You will do no such thing,' said Mrs Healey. 'Of course you can bring your little brother here. I didn't answer straight away because I was thinking about what you were saying. You say you have a sister as well, aged eleven?'

'Yes, that's right; Emily. But she will be at school, of course, when I've found one for her. I've noticed there's one not far away.'

'There are no shortage of schools,' said Mrs Healey. 'But she won't be there all the time, will she? They finish at four o'clock, then there are the holidays. They have about four weeks off in the summer.' She smiled understandingly at Molly. 'I don't think you've really considered all the problems, have you, my dear?' Her kind expression was Molly's undoing. To her dismay she felt tears of frustration welling up in her eyes. She dashed them away, then gave a loud sniff, reaching into the pocket of her long white apron for a handkerchief.

'Oh, don't cry, my dear. Please don't cry.

There's a way round it all, I'm sure.' Mrs Healey put an arm round her shoulders. 'Go and make yourself a cup of tea – a proper one,' she smiled, nodding at the tiny toy cup Molly had placed on the counter. 'And you can look after Amy for a few minutes while I serve these customers.' The jingle of the doorbell had just heralded the arrival of two women. 'We'll have a chat later,' her employer whispered confidingly. 'Don't worry now; it'll all come out in the wash.'

Molly felt cheered at hearing the expression, which was a favourite one of Maggie's. She blew her nose, then filled the kettle and set it on the gas stove in the storeroom. She had so wanted everything to turn out right; she had almost been willing it to do so, without really considering all the obstacles. Some girls of Emily's age were almost grown-up. Not so long ago girls of eleven and younger would have been working in the cotton mills; but Em was still very much a child. Some children came home to an empty house, cared for their siblings, cooked the tea, ran errands ... but that had never been the way of it in the Rimmer household. Lily had always been there, and Molly, since the children had been left to her charge, had done her utmost to ensure that if she was not always there herself, then there was someone responsible to see to them. Em would not take kindly to being left on her own in the Stoneygate rooms, and Mrs Marsden, the land-lady, did not seem to be the sort one could ask to be a child-minder.

'Molly, Molly.' Little Amy was tugging at her apron, reminding her poignantly of William.

'Kettle's boiling. Look, look...' Already clouds of steam were misting the air and she hadn't even noticed. 'Make cup o' tea, Molly.'

Molly smiled at her. Children always had the power to lift her spirits.

'So you have no need to worry any more, my dear,' said Agnes Healey as she and Molly sat together eating their midday snack of cheese and tomato sandwiches. It was a snatched meal, with one or the other of them, every few minutes, having to leave her half-eaten sandwich to go and serve a customer; but it would be madness to close the door on trade at such a busy time of day. 'Emily can come here when she finishes school, and at dinnertime too, if you wish. She can have a sandwich with us, unless she would rather take her lunch to school with her? Anyway, we can sort that out later. And during the school holidays I will find her some jobs to do. She could do some dusting and polishing, couldn't she? Or run errands, and of course she would be a great help looking after the children. And I'm sure Fred would be pleased to have her on the market stall with him; it would be a nice change for her.'

That was where Fred Healey was at the moment, manning the Friday market stall. Molly was bemused at the way his wife was making all these plans without his say-so. She had noticed, though, how well the couple got on together, so she assumed that whatever Agnes Healey said would be all right with Fred. Agnes had told Molly she had been thinking around her problem concerning the children, and had come to the conclusion that there was, in reality, no problem at all. They could both come here, and that was the end of the matter. Molly was overwhelmed with gratitude. The woman hardly knew her, and yet she was offering so much. She felt, in return, that she ought to be rather more truthful about her own circumstances. Agnes Healey was taking a great deal on trust. Molly, also, must show her employer that she was ready to trust her with, if not all, then at least part of her story.

'I will never be able to thank you enough,' she said. 'You have no idea how much it means to me to know that the children will be all right. They have been my main consideration ever since my parents died ... at least, they should have been. But I feel that sometimes I might have failed them.' She was thinking of her disastrous marriage to Hector. She knew, now that that had not been fair to the children. She had not considered them enough. She supposed it could be said it served her right that it had failed.

'Not on purpose,' replied Agnes, kindly. 'I am sure it would not have been your fault, if you feel you have let them down. I haven't known you very long, Molly, but I already think you are one of the most honest and reliable people I have ever met. That is why I want to do what I can to help you, and I know Fred will feel the same.'

'Thank you,' said Molly again. She told Agnes, now, that her home was in Blackpool. That was where she had been born and where her brother and sister were still living. She spoke again of her mother's death, then of her father's tragic accident at the time of the Tower fire. And of her struggles to keep the family together, about the house shop, and the initial success of the dinner shop. 'And then ... well, it all went wrong, and I had to leave,' she said.

When it came to the climax of the story Molly found that this was the part she could not divulge. Not yet; she did not know Mrs Healey well enough to tell her about her calamitous marriage, the cruelty, the beatings, her fear for the children's safety. The woman might not take kindly to the knowledge that her new assistant was guilty of turning her back on her marriage. For all she knew the Healeys might well be Catholics, brought up to regard marriage as sacrosanct. She did not think they were, but as yet she knew very little about the couple, except that she liked them and trusted them. Not enough, though. It would have to suffice to say that she had decided to make a fresh start, in a different town. She had chosen Preston, she told Agnes, because it was her parents' home town.

'But you have no relations living here now?' asked her employer.

'None that I know of,' replied Molly. 'But there are certain gaps in my family history that I would like to fill in; when I have time. There is Uncle Silas, of course,' she added, 'but I feel he is best left alone.' She explained briefly about her visit to the house in Winckley Square and her less-than-enthusiastic welcome.

'Yes, I can see you are an independent young woman,' said Agnes, 'but at least you were not so independent that you couldn't ask a favour of us.

445

And we are only too pleased to be able to help you.'

'It was for William's sake,' said Molly, 'and Em's, It was them I was thinking about.' And yet, as she considered it now, she realised what a colossal cheek it had been, wanting to bring her little brother to her workplace. It was a wonder she hadn't been sent packing right away.

'And it will all turn out splendidly, I'm sure,' said Agnes Healey, standing up and straightening her apron, 'Now, if you'll wash these pots, Molly, I'll go and prepare for the dinner time rush.'

'I don't mind. No, why should I mind you giving the lass a helping hand?' said Fred Healey to his wife later that same evening. 'I like Molly, from the little I know of her. She's a good worker. She seems honest and straightforward. But you've got to admit, Agnes, that we don't know a great deal about her. There's some sort of mystery surrounding her, something she's not telling us.'

'I don't suppose it's anything sinister, Fred,' replied his wife. 'She's such a nice girl, it couldn't be anything too dreadful, whatever it is. Perhaps the landlord turned 'em out and they'd nowhere to go; something like that. It does happen, you know.'

'Aye, mebbe you're right.' Fred nodded. 'There's a lot to be said for owning yer own place, even if it is only a little 'un, like ours.'

'And don't forget the other shop as you've got round the corner,' said Agnes. She smiled. 'A man of property, that's what you are, Fred. There are not many fellows of your age as can say they own two shops.'

'Don't make me laugh! Man of property, indeed! It's more like a bloomin' millstone round me neck, that tumble-down old place. Anyroad, it's as much yours as mine, Aggie.' Fred grinned at her. 'D'you remember what I promised you when we were wed? *With all my worldly goods I thee endow...* So it's half yours, lass, for what it's worth. And you're welcome to it, an' all. The place is falling down round our ears.'

'And so it'll continue to do, Fred, if we don't do owt about it. So long as it stands there un-occupied it'll only get worse and worse.'

'We haven't got the money to spare.' Fred shook his head. 'Happen next year–'

'Happen nothing!' retorted his wife, but she was smiling at him. 'Honestly, Fred, anybody'd think you'd been born over t'border in Yorkshire – not right here in the middle of good old Lancashire – you're so keen on holding on to your brass. We've got a tidy little sum put away and you know it. And I've got an idea...'

It had been over a year since Fred's Aunt Maud had died, leaving her favourite nephew the little shop in Church Street; it was just round the corner, in fact, from their own shop on Manchester Road. Aunt Maud had been ill for a long time, living and finally dying, at the home of her daughter; and so what had once been a thriving little confectioner's shop had fallen into disuse and, more lately, into a state of dilapidation and disrepair. His Aunt Maud, no doubt, had thought she was doing him a favour with the bequest, and there had been no ill feeling regarding the legacy with her daughter, Dorothy, who had married a wealthy businessman and had no need of any more property. The small shop, indeed, was something of a liability and Dorothy had laughingly told her cousin, Fred, that she wished him joy of it.

Agnes Healey had been concerned for a while now about the run-down state of his inheritance, but she had been unable to persuade her husband to make any moves in that direction. Their grocery business was thriving, as was the market stall, and it was upon these enterprises that Fred was single-mindedly directing his energies. But now Agnes felt it was time for them to branch out, especially since her husband had told her the property was as much hers as his. They had the premises and – in spite of what Fred might say – they had the capital. And now Agnes had found someone she felt would be a hard-working and worthy tenant.

'Good gracious, you don't let the grass grow under your feet, do you?' laughed her husband, when she had outlined her plan. 'The lass has only just come to work for us, and already you're talking about setting her up in her own business. We're not going to get much benefit, are we, if she's working round the corner instead of here, for us?'

'But it will be our business, Fred, don't you see?' said Agnes. 'She'll be running it for us. We'd have to come to some sort of financial agreement, of course. But as far as I can see Molly would be an ideal manageress, or whatever you want to call her. She used to have her own shop, you know.'

'Only a house shop, luv. That's all it was.'

'All the same, I think she's got her head screwed on the right way. She made it into a dinner shop, she told me. Quite a thriving little business, too, from the sound of it.'

'But then she left it ... and we don't know why.'

'That's true, Fred; but I think she'd jump at the chance of starting something like that up again. And the ovens are already there, you know, from the time when your aunt's business was thriving. And there's enough room upstairs for Molly and her brother and sister. She wants to make a stable home for them, at least that's the impression I get. Reading between the lines it seems to me as though they might have been dragged from pillar to post. Of course I don't really know...'

'No, we don't, do we? That's the top and bottom of the matter, isn't it? We know nowt about the girl. All the same, I like her. Aye, I think you might have something there, Aggie.' Fred stroked his chin ruminatively. 'If you're willing to give this idea a go – and Molly, an' all – then so am I. Let's take it nice and steady, though. Best not to rush into things.'

It was six months before the shop and the rooms above were ready for their new tenants. Six very busy and, on the whole, contented, months for Molly as she worked along with Agnes and Fred Healey, getting the run-down premises fit for occupation again. There was certain essential work that could only be undertaken by expert builders, plumbers and gas fitters, but most of the decorating and painting was done by Molly, Agnes and Fred, and the odd bits of joinery by Fred, himself.

Molly had been quite overwhelmed by Mr and Mrs Healey's suggestion that she should run a business – a dinner shop and confectioner's – on their behalf, and when she learned there would be living accommodation as well she could hardly believe her good fortune.

Her rooms in Stoneygate had proved adequate, although they had never felt other than temporary, and the children had adapted to their new routine reasonably well, William more so than Emily. Em seemed happy that the family was reunited, but Molly knew her sister was missing her friends, particularly Sarah Winthrop. Em had never found it easy to make friends, and she gladly agreed to Molly's suggestion that she should eat her midday sandwich at the grocer's shop rather than at school. 'When can I see Sarah again?' she asked from time to time, and Molly was at a loss as to how to answer her.

Molly, too, missed her friends – Maggie and Flo and Violet – but she knew she would not dare pay a visit to Blackpool. Not that there would be much likelihood of her coming face to face with Hector, but even the thought of being in the same town as him filled her with dread. She tried to convince herself that her home now was in Preston. She was making new friends here; she was sure that, given time, Emily, too, would come to regard the place as her home. And this was where they had to stay.

But it was not just her old friends that Molly

missed. There were times when she longed for the sparkling clean air and the salty breezes of the seaside town. Here, by comparison, all seemed dark, dreary and monotonous: the rows and rows of small terraced houses alongside the mills – Molly herself had lived in such a house, in such a street, but there were many, many more of them here – the mills themselves, an abundance of them in the area where she worked, grim, soot-blackened and forbidding, their tall chimneys belching out clouds of thick grey evil-smelling smoke, despoiling the atmosphere and the buildings and, more personally, one's clothing and clean washing on the line. And only a few minutes' walk away, the sombre, fortress-like edifice of the County Prison at the junction of Stanley Street and Ribbleton Lane. Molly had to suppress a shudder each time she set eyes on it.

She tried, however, to be positive in her thinking. Her fortunes had certainly taken a change for the better. Her meeting with her great-uncle had not been propitious – a disappointing start to her stay in Preston – but since that minor setback things seemed to be going well for her. She sometimes thought about her uncle's remark to Lizzie, the maid, as she was leaving: 'Tell her to come and see me again...' but she felt it had been half-hearted, merely an afterthought, and she pushed it to the back of her mind. She had managed, so far, without the help of relations. Her old friends in Blackpool had compensated amply for her lack of relatives, and the new friends she was making here in Preston, in particular Agnes and Fred Healey, were proving to be ones on whom she knew she could rely.

Little by little she had told Agnes and Fred – which was what they now insisted she should call them – more of her story, especially on discovering that the couple were fellow Methodists. She had been welcomed into the fellowship of their chapel, not far from where they lived; and as she sat in the high-backed pew, with William and Em at her side, one morning in October, she felt that the words of the hymn, 'Count your many blessings, Name them one by one...' were very appropriate. So was the preacher's text: 'The lines are fallen for me in pleasant places; yea, I have a goodly heritage.'

Her surroundings were not particularly pleasant, she had to admit, but the way ahead looked promising and, at last, she was beginning to put the past behind her and look to the future. And to count her blessings, which was what the sermon was all about. If all went according to plan the shop and rooms above should be ready for occupancy by November, and she and the Healeys were looking forward to a grand opening before Christmas. Yes, the outlook was brighter, especially after the surprising news she had received last week.

She had heard very little of Hector. She wrote fairly regularly to her good friends, Maggie and Flo and Violet, and she knew she could trust them to keep her whereabouts secret. All the same, she had not been able to rid herself entirely of the fear that there might be a sudden letter or, worse, a sudden appearance of Hector himself on her doorstep. But when she had answered a knock on her door the previous Wednesday it had been to find Flo and Violet standing there.

'Your landlady told us you were up here,' said Flo, laughing at Molly's astonished face. 'Well, come on then, aren't you going to ask us in?'

'Of course ... of course I am. What a lovely surprise.' She flung her arms round each of them in turn. 'Come on in. I'm just getting our tea ready. Em and William will be ever so pleased to see you. Em, William, look who's here. Auntie Vi and Auntie Flo, isn't that lovely?' She could hardly contain her excitement. 'I've got some bubble and squeak cooking on the stove. I was just going to dish it out, but it'll stretch to two more, there's plenty. You'll have some, won't you?'

'No thanks, Molly,' said Violet. 'We had some sandwiches before we set off, but we'd love a cup of tea, if that's all right.'

'Why ever didn't you let me know you were coming? But I didn't realise...' Molly frowned a little, completely overwhelmed at seeing her friends there, 'I didn't know that you two knew one another.'

'Well, we do now,' laughed Violet. 'Don't we. Flo? We made it our business to get acquainted after ... after what happened. We knew one another by sight before, that was all, but we're good pals now, aren't we, Flo?'

'Yes, I'll say we are,' said Flo. 'And Maggie as well. We mustn't forget Maggie. She couldn't come with us, but she sends her love and she says she hopes she'll see you soon. Perhaps you'll

453

come back to Blackpool, and see us all before long, eh? You might even decide to come back for good.'

'No fear!' Molly gave a shudder. 'I can't; you know I can't. I daren't even come back for a visit, not so long as ... you know.' She glanced warningly at the children, then back at her friends. She was always careful not to mention Hector's name in front of them. All that was in the past, and she was trying so hard to make a new life for them here.

'But that's what we've come to tell you,' said Violet. 'He's gone.'

'Who? Who d'you mean? You can't mean ... Hector?' Molly spoke his name almost in a whisper.

'Yes. Hector. He's left Blackpool, at least that's what everyone seems to think. Come on, Molly. Sit down and have your meal, you and the children. I'll make us a cup of tea.' Flo busied herself with the kettle and the teapot and cups and saucers. 'Then we can tell you all the news.'

Word had got around quite quickly when Molly disappeared from her home in Warbreck Road and from the congregation at the Ebenezer chapel. Maggie had made it her business to go to see Flo Palmer at her place of work on Jubilee Terrace, and whilst taking a stroll on the prom during Flo's dinner break, had told her exactly what had been going on in Molly's unfortunate marriage and exactly why her friend had left.

'It's no skin off my nose, telling you about it,' Maggie had said. 'I didn't promise as I'd keep quiet an' I don't see why I should. As far as I'm concerned all t'world can know. He's a monster an' he wants locking up for what he's done to that poor lass. Of course, I know you chapel folk stick together, don't you? So it's up to you whether you keep yer trap shut or whether you drop him right in it. He'd deserve it, there's nowt more sure than that.'

Flo had been horrified. She had received a somewhat guarded note from Molly with the address of Stoneygate, Preston, saying she was sorry she had gone away so quickly without even saying goodbye, but she was sure her friend would understand she was not happy and that she had to get away for a while. It was Maggie who told Flo that it was likely to be for good and not just 'for a while', and that the children, also, were going in a day or two. The arrangement had been that Maggie should take them on the train to Preston and Molly would meet them at the station.

'What on earth shall I do?' Flo had said to her fiancé, Sam Leadbetter, after she had heard Maggie's awful revelations. 'Poor Molly; I sort of guessed that things weren't too good, but I'd no idea it was as bad as that. What a scandal it'd be at their chapel if this was to get out. We don't want folk tittle-tattling, and we certainly don't want the Methodists to get a bad name just because of Hector Stubbins.'

'Neither should he be allowed to get away with it scot-free,' Sam had replied. 'Molly was very friendly with Violet Prosser, wasn't she? You know – a nice sensible woman, she is; looks after the babies' class at their Sunday school. Why don't you go and have a word with her?'

'I hardly know her,' Flo had answered. 'I know who she is, of course…'

'Well, you're not exactly shy, are you?' Sam had laughed. 'And this is important. Why don't you go and meet her out of chapel and have a chat?'

Vi, also, had been aghast at the disclosures. Like Flo, she had guessed that Molly's marriage was far from happy, but had been unsure as to how she could help. 'Mind you, who would be happy with a strange chap like that?' she'd said to Flo. 'Goodness knows why she married him in the first place, a lovely young woman like Molly. You'd've thought she could've had her pick of fellows. I always thought he was strict, a bit severe with her, happen – I know he likes his own way – but I never imagined anything like that. If what you say is true then the fellow's a fiend.'

'It's true enough,' Flo had said. 'Molly doesn't tell lies, neither does Maggie Winthrop. Anyway, why should they?'

'Why indeed?' Vi had answered. 'I wasn't suggesting they were lying. It's just that it's so hard to take in. But what on earth are we going to do? Hector Stubbins has been very quiet about Molly going, you know. All he'll say is that she's gone away for a while. And that girl that was working for them, Rosie Hewitt, she's left as well. She's got a job as a chambermaid in a boarding house.'

All this had happened in the early summer. By mid-August there had been rumours aplenty flying around the Ebenezer chapel, although no one was sure where they had originated. Hector

456

Stubbins had employed a young woman of dubious reputation to act as housekeeper for him; some said she lived in, others that she went home each night, but left very late. He had been seen walking along the clifftop path arm in arm with the same young woman; no, it was not the same woman, said others – she was a dancer from the summer revue at the North Pier Pavilion... He had had a blazing row with his parents. His father was removing him from the chemist's shop and installing Martin Stubbins, his cousin, in his place... He had resigned from his position as the senior steward; he had given up his class leadership and his preaching...

The last were not merely rumours, but fact. And when, in early October, Hector had disappeared from the scene, everyone was relieved, but completely mystified. Again rumours abounded. His housekeeper had disappeared too... No, not his housekeeper, the dancer from North Pier with whom he had been carrying on; he had run off with her when the revue came to an end... He had left Blackpool... His house was empty and up for sale...

It was undoubtedly true that the house was for sale, and that Martin Stubbins was now working at the chemist's shop on Jubilee Terrace. 'But you don't know definitely that he has left Blackpool,' said Molly, who had been listening to her friends' story with a mixture of relief and incredulity.

'It certainly looks like it,' said Violet. 'Nobody's seen neither hide nor hair of him for nearly a month now. We decided to wait a while, didn't we, Flo, before we told you. We feel it'd be safe for you to come back now – if you wanted to.'

Molly glanced at the two children who were playing happily on the floor with a wooden jigsaw puzzle. Em instructing William as to where the more tricky pieces should go. Em's ears had pricked up at first at the mention of Hector's name and a faint tremor of alarm had crossed her face, but then she seemed to have grasped what the women were talking about – that he had gone – and she had grinned at Molly. Now she was engrossed in her little brother's toy, although Molly guessed she would be bending one ear towards the adults' conversation as well.

'It isn't that I don't want to come back,' said Molly. 'I can't ... I daren't. In spite of what you say, I still have this fear. I'm still married to him, even if he has disappeared. Besides, we're making a new life for ourselves here, the children and me.' She told them about the plans, well under way, for the shop with living accommodation. 'I've really fallen on my feet. Sometimes I can't believe it, how well things have turned out.'

'Yes, God's good,' said Violet Prosser, in her usual prosaic way. 'Sometimes we're tempted to think He's not listening, but He is, you see. You'd best tell Molly your own good news, hadn't you, Flo?'

Flo's news was that she and Sam had now fixed a wedding date; it was to be the Saturday before Christmas.

'What, this Christmas?' said Molly. 'Good gracious, that's quick. What's the rush?'

'Nothing like that,' said Flo, rather primly and blushing pink. 'Not so much of a rush either:

we've been courting for more than three years. As a matter of fact, we've got somewhere to live. Do you remember Mr Merryweather, the owner of the toyshop?'

'Of course I remember him,' said Molly indignantly. 'I've only been left five minutes ... well, six months, to be more exact.'

'Anyway, Mr and Mrs Merryweather are moving out. They've bought a little house just off Cocker Street – I've an idea he might be getting ready for retiring – and he says we can have the rooms if we want them. So of course we jumped at it, Sam and me, and we both fancy the idea of a Christmas wedding. You'll be my bridesmaid, won't you, Molly? You'll have to come back for that.'

'I ... don't know. Yes ... perhaps ... I might,' said Molly guardedly. 'But the dinner shop'll be open by then. We might be busy.'

'Oh, you and your blessed shops!' said Flo. 'You're my best friend, aren't you?'

'Of course she is,' broke in Vi, ever the peace-maker. 'You can be sure Molly will be your bridesmaid if she can.'

'Then she'll have to hurry up and decide,' said Flo. 'I've got dresses to make, don't forget. And I was wondering about your Em as well.'

'Ooh yes, please. Can I, Molly?' asked Emily, who was quite openly listening now.

'Well ... yes, all right then,' said Molly. 'If you're sure it will be quite safe for me to come back. I expect Agnes will be able to find somebody to stand in for me that weekend.'

There was other news as well concerning

Jubilee Terrace. Mr Finch from 'High-Class Boots and Shoes' had definitely retired, and Mr and Mrs Makepeace, the confectioners, had decided to buy the next-door shop and extend their premises. 'Upstairs as well,' said Flo. 'There's some talk of them opening a restaurant up there. It's early days yet, though. The workmen haven't even started, but that's what they intend to do.'

'Goodness me! The shop must be doing well.'

'It wasn't just that. From what I've heard, Dolly Makepeace's father died and left her a mint of money. And she'll be taking on extra staff. There'd be a job for you, Molly, anytime you wanted one. I do wish you'd think about coming back; for good, I mean.'

Molly shook her head. 'My life is here now, Flo,' she said, aware that she sounded resigned, if not a mite regretful. 'It wouldn't be fair to Agnes and Fred to leave them in the lurch after all they've done for me. Besides, you know I can't.'

Flo and Vi departed later that evening to catch their train back to Blackpool. They had chosen to come on a Wednesday because it was Flo's half-day. Even so, they hadn't spent very long in Preston, knowing that Molly would be working until at least five thirty. Long enough, though to evoke in Molly feelings of nostalgia, almost of sadness. It had been good to hear news about Jubilee Terrace and her old friends and acquaintances there. But she decided – or it might be truer to say she convinced herself – on reflection, that she must have no regrets. She must never look back.

Chapter 21

Molly did not often wander as far as Fishergate – what she thought of as the posher part of Preston. This was the continuation of Church Street, where the more affluent folk shopped and where the grander establishments – the milliners, tailors, drapers and silk mercers, jewellers and the like – were situated. She had seldom ventured up there since her first day in the town, the main reason being that on a Thursday, her half-day, when Healey's grocer's was closed, all the other shops were closed as well. However, this particular day was a Wednesday, not a Thursday, and Agnes had given her a few hours off to do some shopping. Next Monday – the last Monday in November – the confectionery and dinner shop was due to open, and once that happened Molly knew she would have very little time to spare for shopping, or for anything else. Agnes had willingly agreed, though, to her having a weekend off to be a bridesmaid at her friend's wedding; moreover she had promised to assist at the new shop herself for that weekend. They had already employed some new staff in readiness for the opening: a trained baker who would be responsible for the bread – Molly felt she did not have the experience to deal with that as well as the cakes and the meals – and a girl to serve in the shop.

Molly and the children had now moved into the rooms above the shop, so as to be settled in their new surroundings before the 'grand opening'. That was how Agnes and Fred and Molly thought of it and spoke about it. There had already been an advertisement in the *Evening Post* stating that Healeys, the well-known grocers from Manchester Road, were opening a new shop on Church Street:

All kinds of confectionery will be produced in the bakery at the rear of the premises. Loaves, fancy breads, toothsome cakes of many varieties, meat pies and savoury products. In addition there will be a small café area for the convenience of those customers who wish to partake of their purchases on the premises. Alternatively, meals can be ordered in the morning and collected at dinner time for consumption elsewhere. Meat and potato pie, shepherd's pie, sausages in gravy, and peas (both parched and mushy) will be amongst the delicious meals which are available. Customers are requested to bring their own basins for the savoury dishes.

Molly could not help but feel a stirring of excitement at the thought of the challenge that lay ahead, even though it would involve a great deal of hard work. When they had moved into their new premises the previous week she had felt for the first time since leaving Blackpool that she was really and truly in her own home again. No, not just since leaving Blackpool, she amended her thoughts; since leaving Larkhill. Never since her days in Larkhill Street had she felt that the place she lived in was really her home. Warbreck Road had been Hector's house, not hers. Even now she could not suppress a shudder whenever she thought of it. And the lodgings on Stoneygate had been merely a stopgap. But here, in her rooms on Church Street, though they were almost in the shadow of the prison, Molly felt at long last that she had come home. The feeling was intensified by having some of her mother's possessions there with her: the display cabinet with its delicate flowered china that Lily had prized so much, and the two armchairs, rescued from the little parlour when Molly had opened the house shop. Maggie had been looking after them for her during the year of her marriage to Hector. Molly could never have explained why she had not wanted her mother's treasures to be assimilated into Hector's household. She just knew it would not have felt right to have them there. But now they had been brought over to Preston by carriers, the breakable china stored carefully in packing cases stuffed with straw.

'Isn't that nice?' Em had said, seeing her mother's cherished belongings with them once more. 'All Mam's cups and saucers and her vases and things. Wouldn't she be pleased, Molly?'

'Yes, I rather think she would,' Molly had replied, touched by her sister's words. 'She would be very glad we're happy again. We are happy, aren't we, Em? I mean ... you like your new school now, don't you, and ... everything?'

'It's not so bad,' Em had said, a shade dismissively. 'I'm going to like it here, though. I

463

know I am. It's home, isn't it? Just ours – yours and mine and William's.'

Molly had smiled and nodded. 'It is indeed. Not very posh, but it'll look better when I've got the curtains up, an' I've bought some remnants from the market to make us some nice bright cushion covers. And Agnes has given us a lovely eiderdown for our bed. Look, it's got big pink roses all over it. Isn't that kind of her?'

The furniture and carpets were by no means new, but were all Molly could afford from second-hand shops and salerooms, plus a few items given by kind friends. She did not desire luxury or splendid surroundings; all Molly wanted was a degree of comfort – and safety.

'And Hector won't be able to find us here, will he?' Em had said, almost taking the thought out of her sister's mind. 'We'll be safe, won't we, Molly?'

'Yes, of course we'll be safe, love,' Molly had assured her. It was very rarely that Em mentioned Hector. 'You remember what Vi and Flo said, don't you? That he had disappeared; they don't know where he is.'

'And neither do we,' Em had replied.

Just for a moment Molly had felt a chill in the atmosphere, as though her fiend of a husband might suddenly appear; but the living room, though still untidy with all the upheaval of unpacking, was warm and cheerful, and she'd quickly dismissed her fears. 'Don't you worry your head about him,' she'd said. 'That's all in the past now, Em, and we've a lot to look forward to. Aren't you excited about the new shop? I know I am. And you'll be able to help at weekends, like you used to do at Larkhill.'

'Mmm, yes. So I will...' Em had still appeared preoccupied. 'Molly,' she'd said after a few moments, 'd'you think Hector's mam and dad knew what a bad man he was? They were quite nice, weren't they? I remember seeing them at ... at the wedding.' She'd almost whispered the last few words. 'And another time when they came to see you, just once – they only came once, didn't they – but I thought they were all right ... you know.'

'Yes, I know just what you mean,' Molly had said. Her little sister was, perhaps, not so 'little' now. She was growing up considerably and maybe it was time for Molly to confide in her and not treat her as a child. 'Parents never know how their children are going to turn out, do they, no matter how well they bring them up? And it isn't always the parents' fault when things start to go wrong. Yes, I expect Mr and Mrs Stubbins are displeased with Hector, although I'm not sure how much they know about ... what has happened. They must be disappointed, with him being their only son. I always felt he was ... off-hand with them; you know, he didn't seem to care for them, like a son should. Martin is in charge of the shop now in Jubilee Terrace. You remember – the young man who was our ... best man.' Molly had realised she did not want to think about it at all. 'Forget it, Em,' she'd said. 'Put it all behind you. That's what we've got to do. Here, take these books into the bedroom. Fred's going to put us a shelf up in there. But mind you don't wake our William.'

Molly, also, had wondered about Hector's parents. Had they any idea how he had treated his wife? Was there anything in his past that might explain his brutal behaviour? She had thought they might have tried to contact her, but there had been nothing but silence from Mr and Mrs Herbert Stubbins, as from their son. There were many secrets to be discovered within families; that much she knew. She still had not unravelled the mysteries of her own, but maybe there would be time for that later, when the new business was up and running.

Fishergate was busy on this Wednesday afternoon and Molly was enjoying her few hours of freedom, mingling with the shoppers and gazing into windows of shops she had never before had time to stop to look at. Agnes was looking after William as well as Amy. Em would go to the grocer's shop, as she usually did, on finishing school, so there was no need for Molly to rush back. It was rather early for Christmas shopping, but she hoped to find presents for her brother and sister and also her employers – not forgetting Amy – while she had the chance. She had a little money to spend; not a vast amount as she was merely an employee of the Healeys and would continue to be so, even when the new shop was opened, but the wage they paid her was quite generous.

Now, what would Agnes and Fred like? she pondered. She had thought about a pair of gloves for Agnes and perhaps the same for Fred. Or a nice silk scarf, and a tiepin? But that would mean buying two presents and her funds were rather limited. It might be more sensible to buy them a joint present. She stopped at the window of a shop which sold pictures; a gallery; she thought that was the correct name for such a place. Agnes liked pictures. She had quite a few on the walls of her living room, mostly of animals and children. Molly would not be able to afford an original one, of course; she knew there was a great difference in price between what were called 'originals' and the ones that were copies. There was a lovely one there of a cocker spaniel ... or perhaps the one of that dear little girl; she looked a bit like Amy...

Suddenly Molly stopped her perusal of the reasonably priced pictures to one side of the window. She gave a gasp as her eyes alighted on the portrait in the very centre of the window. There it stood, on an easel; a picture of an auburn-haired girl wearing a hat with green ribbons and a green and white blouse. She was gazing out into the sunset, the sun was shining on the turquoise-blue sea making it glitter with gold. And the girl in the picture was ... herself! She gasped again, relieved there was no one near enough to hear her long sigh of drawn-out breath. Her legs felt unsteady and her hands were beginning to shake, but she took a firm hold of herself. It was a shock, but a very pleasant one; nothing like the dreadful shocks she had received from time to time throughout her life. She looked again, this time at the hand-printed caption below the picture, *Beyond the Sunset*, and underneath that a notice which said 'This picture is not for sale.'

Her eyes moved, looking for the signature. Artists always signed their work. Yes, there it was in the corner. Joss ... Cunliffe. So that was his name. She had not known his surname any more than he had known hers. Would it have done her any good to have known? she wondered. Probably not, but the opportunity was there now for her to find out more about him, if she wished to ... if she dared.

It would not be true to say she had never given a thought, since arriving in Preston, to the mysterious young man she had met on that dim and distant evening, on the cliffs at Uncle Tom's Cabin. Three and a half years; not all that distant, she supposed, but so much had happened to her since then that it seemed like a lifetime ago. Yes, she had thought of him; she had even looked for him at first, wondering if she might pass him in the street and, if so, would she recognise him? Then the thoughts of him had once again receded, until they were just a memory on the fringes of her mind. But this picture proved, surely, that he was here, that he was still living in Preston; and she, Molly Rimmer, was going to find out, at last, exactly who he was.

She hesitated a moment before entering the shop as a thought struck her. She did not want to be recognised. Was it possible she might be identified as the girl in the picture? She thought not. Molly knew she had matured a great deal since Joss had drawn that sketch of her. She felt she had aged; she was no longer the same carefree young lass. However, just in case, she tucked a little more of her auburn hair beneath the large brim of her velour hat and turned up her coat collar.

The door pinged pleasantly as she pushed it open and she saw, to her relief, that the shop – or gallery or whatever it was called – was not busy. There were only two people, a man and a woman, studying the paintings at the far end, and now an assistant – or possibly the owner? – came forward to greet her. He was a middle-aged man wearing a pin-striped suit, with a pair of pince-nez perched on the bridge of his nose.

'Good afternoon, madam. How can I help you?'

Molly enquired, first of all, about the picture she wished to buy. Reproductions, the man called them, seeming to understand exactly how much she would be able to afford. She decided on one similar to the one she had noticed in the window; a little girl resembling Amy, playing with a fluffy grey kitten entangled in a ball of wool. She waited patiently whilst her purchase was wrapped, her change given and the receipt made out; then she plucked up courage, especially as the shop was now empty of customers.

'Excuse me, Mr Middlehurst,' she began. She had read the name on the billhead and had guessed, correctly, that he was the owner of the gallery, 'I wonder if you could tell me something about the picture in the window, the one that is not for sale. Well, not exactly the picture,' she went on. It might be better not to draw too much attention to that, 'but the artist. Joss ... Cunliffe? I've heard the name somewhere, but I can't quite remember where. Could you tell me ... a little about him, please?'

'Ah yes, Joss Cunliffe.' Mr Middlehurst smiled, nodding decisively. 'It would be surprising, my dear young lady, if you had not heard of the Cunliffes. That is if you live in Preston? You do, don't you?'

'Er ... yes,' said Molly. 'But I haven't lived here long.'

'The Cunliffes are one of our mill-owning families. Not in such a big way as the Horrockses, of course, but pretty fair all the same. Yes, pretty fair... That's why you will have heard the name. Henry died a couple of years ago – very sudden it was – a heart attack – and the mill went to his sons. Well, to two of them, I should say; the eldest two, Percy and Edgar. Joss is the youngest son. He didn't come in for a share in the mill, though nobody seems to know why. Still, it's nothing to do with anybody else – family business, I dare say.' Mr Middlehurst nodded again, as though he might know a thing or two, but wasn't letting on. He was something of a gossip, Molly decided. She was agog at his revelations, though trying not to appear overly interested.

'But it is as an artist, of course, that I know Joss Cunliffe; a very talented one as well. I have a few of his paintings for sale. I think you might find they are ... possibly ... within your reach, my dear.' He looked at her assessingly, but she did not find his scrutiny offensive. What she was most concerned about, still, was that she should not be recognised. 'Come along, I will show you.

No obligation, of course.'

She followed him a little further along the gallery to where there were several landscape paintings displayed on the wall, all watercolours, as was the picture in the window. The captions told her the locations, although there were just one or two she could identify. The River Calder near Hebden Bridge (she thought that was in Yorkshire); a Lancashire moorland scene; a deserted Blackpool beach at sunset; fishing boats at Fleetwood. 'And this is our own Avenham Park,' said Mr Middlehurst, pointing to a pleasant scene of trees in their autumn foliage, 'with the River Ribble in the background.'

'Yes, he certainly is very talented,' said Molly, marvelling at the subtle shading of colours and the delicate brush strokes. She was no artist herself, but she could appreciate the skill of others when she saw it. This seemed to her to be not merely talent but brilliance. 'But I don't think... That is...' She knew she could not afford the price that was being asked for the paintings.

'No, I told you there was no obligation.' The man smiled at her. 'It was just that you had shown an interest; I thought you might like to see them. I pleaded with him to let me display the painting in the window, although he has his own reasons for not wanting to sell it. But I felt that everyone should have a chance to see it; everyone in Preston, that is.'

'Yes, of course.' Molly averted her head a little. 'And he is ... still living in Preston?' She tried to make the question casual, though she was aware of the fluttering of hundreds of butterflies inside

471

her. To think that he might walk through that very door, at that moment.

'Yes, he was away for a while, then he came back home when his father died. That was when I got to know Joss Cunliffe, when I started to sell his paintings. Of course he no longer works at Cunliffe Mill...' More people had entered the shop now, and a lady was hovering near the desk as though she wished to make an enquiry. Molly decided it was time she departed, especially as Mr Middlehurst's attention was now shifting to his next customer.

'Thank you very much for all your help,' said Molly. 'And for showing me the paintings.'

Out in the street she stared once again at the picture, *Beyond the Sunset*. Yes the girl's eyes – her eyes – were fixed at a point beyond the red-gold of the sunset, which Joss had painted so exquisitely, as though gazing at something just out of reach. As, indeed, she was. Joss Cunliffe, as she now knew he was called, was out of reach. He always had been.

Molly found her thoughts moving from that faraway June evening, back to the present time; to the facts that were staring her in the face. It was all becoming clear to her now. Joss was the son of a mill owner, one of the wealthiest families in Preston. It was little wonder that he had not wanted her to know his name. And if she had turned up to meet him on that Sunday afternoon it was more than likely that he would not have been there. Or, even if he had, their friendship could have come to nothing. Sons of mill owners did not marry penniless nobodies like Molly

Rimmer. Their families would never allow it. She had told that man, Mr Middlehurst, that the name Cunliffe was familiar to her. That had not been strictly true, but now she realised she had, in fact, heard the name before. Cunliffe House – that was the name of the large house on the cliffs, near to Uncle Tom's Cabin. It was along that stretch of the cliffs that several wealthy industrialists had their homes; second homes, no doubt. That would be where Joss had been staying that night, the reason he had been so cagey about where he lived and why he quite often came to Blackpool.

Cunliffe Mill... That was one, she thought, that was not in the Stanley Street area, near to where Molly lived and worked, but at the other end of the town, near to the North Road. But what did it matter? Mr Middlehurst had said that Joss no longer worked there, so it was of no consequence where the mill was situated. And there was no point in building up false hopes about a young man who was, and always had been, way, way beyond her reach.

Molly turned homewards, heading towards the market where she might find some reasonably priced toys and knick-knacks to enliven the children's Christmas. The flame of longing which had suddenly blazed inside her at the first sight of the picture in the window was dying down as common sense took the place of fancy. But there remained, deep at the heart of her, a tiny spark, a glimmer of hope. Joss Cunliffe, for some reason, had not wanted to sell the picture; and with what loving care it had been executed.

Molly would have been astounded had she known that Joss passed the end of Manchester Road, and her new home on Church Street, almost every day on his way to work. He was now employed as a textile designer at Bleasdale Mill, one of the smaller, but none the less thriving, mills in the Stanley Street area. His home, where only he and his mother now lived, was a good mile and a half away, near to Cunliffe Mill. Joss had been making tentative suggestions for the last few months that it might be sensible for them to move to a smaller residence, one which was in a more pleasant area; near to the Miller and Avenham parks, maybe, which would also have the advantage of being nearer to his place of work. But Charlotte seemed reluctant to move and he did not want to pressurise her. It was, after all, her house in which they were living – it had been left to her unconditionally – and it was scarcely a year since his father had died so suddenly. As for the distance he had to walk to work each day, Joss hardly noticed it, whatever the weather. He was young, fit and strong, and his long strides covered the miles quickly and easily.

After his year's course at the Manchester College had finished in the summer of 1898 he had found employment as a designer at a weaving mill in Blackburn. He had had no wish to return to Cunliffe Mill. In any case, he had been replaced in the textile and design shed by another young man who, his father had made quite clear, was more satisfactory for their needs.

'We don't reckon much to that there fancy stuff at Cunliffe's,' Henry had told him, 'so it might be as well if you took yerself elsewhere, you and your big ideas. It's bread-and-butter stuff we're interested in, not pretty patterns to please t'womenfolk.' Household cottons for domestic use were what Cunliffe's had always specialised in and, seemingly, what they would continue to do, despite the qualifications of the youngest son.

Charlotte had been hurt by her husband's intransigent attitude towards Joss, but, as usual, she did not argue. Joss understood how she felt. His mother would have liked him back home again, but he had enjoyed such warmth and friendliness – and peace, too – at the home of his Uncle Walter and Aunt Miriam in Oldham that he did not feel he could live under his father's roof again. Blackburn was not far away, however, and he did not object to spending many of his weekends in Preston, although he endeavoured to keep out of his father's way as much as possible. He was thankful that Henry had now stopped pushing him in the direction of Priscilla Cartwright. Priscilla, to Joss's satisfaction, was now engaged to a young man who was a solicitor, the son of a well-known Preston practice. Joss was pleased for her. He had always been fond of her, though in a brotherly sort of way, and he wanted her to be happy.

His father threw out hints quite regularly that it was high time Joss was 'wed and settled down, like thi' brothers. Tha's getting left behind, lad'. It was useless for Joss to protest that he was, in fact, still only twenty-five. Whatever he did it seemed to be wrong. If he had declared his intention of getting married, that announcement, no doubt, would have been greeted with scorn. He had come to the conclusion that, with his father, he just could not win, though he was at a loss to know why. He had always tried to be dutiful and respectful and had shown none of the wildness and the wilful streak that was apparent in Percy and, to a lesser degree, in Edgar. Maybe, though, that was what his father liked: sons who were self-willed and inclined to be wayward, more like Henry himself, in fact. It was certainly true that he, Joss, and his father were like chalk and cheese.

Edgar had married Betsy Pringle, the girl from the weaving shed, in the autumn of 1898, soon after Joss had started work at the mill in Blackburn. Henry's objections, which Joss had seen as only bluff and bluster, were quickly dispelled, most likely because Henry could see he had no choice but to agree to the marriage. Betsy was pregnant, and the child, a boy – Henry Joseph, after both grandfathers – arrived a mere five months after the wedding. Eddie and Betsy had a nice comfortable home in Deepdale, not far from the home of Percy and Hannah. Both wives had one child and another on the way; both husbands were settled into contented domesticity.

It had been in early December 1899 that Joss had received a telegram at the mill in Blackburn. His father was seriously ill; he was wanted at home immediately. Joss caught the next train – Preston was only a half-hour's journey away – but by the time he arrived at the house Henry had died. He had lived only a couple of hours after the massive and unexpected heart attack.

His mother, understandably, was in a state of shock, not weeping unconsolably, however, but withdrawn inside herself as though she could not believe what had happened. Her tears flowed, though, when she saw Joss, and it was on him that she relied, rather than Percy or Edgar, to see her through the next few days. His brothers made the funeral arrangements and kept up a token attendance at the mill – it was agreed that Henry on no account would have wanted the mill to close, except for a few hours on the day of the funeral – whilst Joss stayed at home with his mother, helping her to cope with the visits of friends, neighbours and acquaintances coming to express their condolences and to take a customary look at the body of Henry Cunliffe.

'It was so sudden,' Charlotte was to say, time and time again. 'If only we'd had some warning. One minute he was as right as rain, they tell me, the next minute he was lying there on the floor of the weaving shed.'

'He died in harness, lass, so to speak,' said one of Henry's mill-owning associates, 'an' that's the way he would've wanted it, old Henry. Now, you just make sure as you look after yerself. He'll've left you well provided for, there's no doubt about that.'

These words were echoed by Seth Cartwright when he came to visit Charlotte, accompanied by his wife and daughter, Priscilla. 'Now, I know there's no need for you to worry. Henry'll've made sure you're all right, and the business is doing well, I know that for a fact. But if you're ever worried about anything ... well, you know where I am, don't you, lass? And you must never be afraid to ask. We were always good pals, Henry and me, more so when we were younger, of course.' Seth paused, staring down at the floor. 'Aye ... well, as I say, lass, you know where we are; doesn't she, Gertrude?'

His wife gave a tight-lipped little smile, nodding half-heartedly. Joss fancied there was not much love lost between his mother and Gertrude Cartwright. But as Seth said, it was the husbands who had been friendly. 'And you'll take care of your mother, won't you, lad?' Seth said as he took their leave. 'You're working in Blackburn now, aren't you, but I dare say you quite often get home?'

'Yes, I'll look after Mother, don't worry,' said Joss. 'I might even move back here.' That was what he and Charlotte had already been discussing.

'Well, if you're wanting a job, come and look me up an' I'll see if I can do summat for you.' Seth grasped Joss's arm in a comradely manner. 'It might not be at my place, but I've got a few contacts.'

'Thank you, Mr Cartwright; I'll bear that in mind,' said Joss. Seth was a pleasant chap, friendly and mild-mannered, nothing like the brusque and abrasive character Henry Cunliffe had been. Joss was sure it would be a darned sight easier working for such as he.

The will was read by Mr Sowerbutts, the family solicitor, after the funeral guests had departed.

Joss heard it with a sense of shock, though not altogether with dismay; after all, it was only what he might have expected. His two brothers, in his father's eyes, had always been the most worthy of sons, capable and industrious and ready to fall in with all of Henry's plans. And so it was to them, Percy and Edgar, that he had left the mill, to be managed by them jointly, plus a goodly share of the capital. His widow, Charlotte, was to receive the house in Preston, hers to do with as she wished, a not ungenerous sum of money, plus the interest from certain stocks and shares, the bulk of which were to be held, again, by Percy and Edgar.

Joss was to have no share in the mill. The money he had been left was by no means as large as the amounts left to Percy and Edgar, but Joss knew it would be more than sufficient for his needs. It was, indeed, quite a substantial amount, but when compared with the share his brothers were to receive, plus their interest in the mill, he realised he had been treated unfairly. He had always known, of course, that he was the least favoured of Henry's three sons, but he had not expected his father to show his partiality quite so blatantly.

'My youngest son, Josiah, has never shown the same aptitude for the mill as his elder brothers, and as he is no longer in my employment I leave him no share in Cunliffe Mill,' the will stated. 'I leave him the aforesaid sum of money which will enable him to pursue the career of his choice; designing, painting, or whatsoever he wishes.' Joss detected a note of irony in the last few words. His father had always dismissed his artistic bent as a trifling thing, certainly not the sort of career a real man would choose.

'The sea property at Blackpool, known as Cunliffe House, I leave to my wife, Charlotte, and thereafter to our youngest son, Josiah.' This last bequest was certainly a bonus, compensating for the feeling of inadequacy Joss had experienced – which he was sure was what his father had intended – on hearing the first part of the will. One fact stood out clearly, however. Henry Cunliffe had been an extremely wealthy man, far wealthier than any of them, even his wife, had realised.

'I've had little to do with money matters,' said Charlotte that evening, after Percy and Eddie and their wives had left. They had found it difficult to hide their satisfaction – more like glee, in Percy's case – although they tried to be circumspect and solemn-faced, having only a few hours ago buried their father. 'Not that I couldn't manage my money well enough if I had to, but your father never let me have any dealings with it. So I'd no idea he was so well off. Like folks keep telling me, I'll be all right. He's made sure I'm well provided for. Very generous of him, considering...' she added in a quieter voice. She glanced sideways at Joss, then stared down at the floor. It was almost as though she were inviting him to question her remark; which he did.

'Considering what, Mother?'

She looked at him candidly. 'I'll tell you in a moment, Joss. But tell me first. Were you surprised at your father's will? A little ... piqued, maybe? Hurt that you haven't been left the same share as your brothers?'

Joss gave a slight shrug. 'I felt slighted, I suppose. Especially when I saw the look of triumph in their eyes, Percy and Eddie's. They couldn't disguise it, Mother. I felt belittled, but then I always was 'little' in Father's eyes, wasn't I, compared with the other two?'

'And you have no idea why?'

'No, not really. Percy and Eddie are more like Father, aren't they? Much more shrewd – more businesslike, I have to admit – than I am. So he could relate to them far better than he could to me. He thought I was namby-pamby, I know he did. I was his least favourite son. I suppose it's as simple as that.'

Charlotte nodded, smiling at him a little sadly. 'I was never sure whether or not he knew. Now, I believe he did. You see, Joss, Henry was not your father.'

Joss looked at her blankly for a moment. 'What ... what did you say? He was not my father? Then ... who?' But before his mother spoke he knew what her answer would be.

'Seth Cartwright; he is your father, Joss. But I have never admitted it to either of them. I don't think Seth has any idea, even now and Henry would never admit that he knew. If he had done so it would have been like admitting he was second best, and Henry always had to be top dog. Oh dear...' She gave a long shuddering sigh. 'I know I did wrong. Seth and I, we both did wrong, but I have had to bear the guilt of it on my own all these years. I had to tell you now, though. It's only fair you should know. It explains so much – your father's will, his attitude towards you. I always thought he might have an idea, and this seems to prove it. It's his way of showing, perhaps, that he knew. But I really believe he tried to be fair, Joss. Henry was a good man underneath all his roughness and short temper. I suppose he couldn't help it if he felt closer to the other two.'

Joss found he was momentarily speechless. All he could do was stare at his mother. 'But ... I don't understand,' he said after a few silent seconds. 'You and ... Seth Cartwright? I had an idea you were friendly at one time. But that was ages ago, surely, before you met ... Father.' That was how Joss thought of Henry Cunliffe and always would. And as his mother said, if he had known her secret and kept quiet about it, then that said quite a lot for him, considering what a cocksure character Henry had been. He could have made her suffer, but he had not done so.

'I'm not proud of what I've done,' said Charlotte. 'I've been deceitful – wicked, some might call me. But I am proud of you, Joss, and the way you have turned out, so I can really have no regrets.'

She went on to explain that she and Seth had become friendly when she was a girl working at Cartwright Mill, but he had already been engaged to Gertrude. It had been one of those family commitments and there was no way out of it. Then Charlotte had caught the eye of Henry Cunliffe, Seth's friend, and the two had married. But the affection that had been there between

482

Seth and Charlotte had never entirely died, and whilst Henry was away on business for a week in Manchester they had arranged a rendezvous; just the once. Charlotte insisted they had only met the once, but that had been enough. She had guessed a little while afterwards that she was pregnant.

'But surely ... the child – I mean, I – could have been Henry's?' said Joss. It was difficult to speak to his mother about such intimate matters. 'How could you be so sure?'

'Because you were born almost nine months to the day after what happened,' said Charlotte. 'And Henry and I ... well, we weren't ... together for another month. He was ill when he came back from Manchester. He had caught a severe chill.' She went on to explain how, when Joss was born, she persuaded the doctor, a family friend she had known since her girlhood, to say that the child was four weeks' premature. As Joss was a small baby, rather delicate during his first year, no one was any the wiser. Or so she had tried to believe.

'But I don't understand,' said Joss again. There was so much he found perplexing. 'You can't have forgotten how Father tried to push me into marrying Priscilla. Surely he wouldn't have done that if he had known?'

'Who knows what his reasons were?' said Charlotte. 'He was probably just being perverse – he was good at that – knowing all along it would come to nothing. Because it was obvious, wasn't it, that you and Priscilla were not keen on the idea. He may have wanted to see how I would react. And I did, didn't I? I suppose I played right into his hands by reacting the way I did. Priscilla is a lovely girl, but I knew it would not do ... and Seth seemed to realise it too. But even then, he didn't say anything. Joss, I know you are going to find it hard to forgive me for what I've done. But I hope you will try to understand. I had to keep quiet about it all, for everyone's sake. And Henry has been good to me ... considering that he must have known.'

'Yes, perhaps he did know,' said Joss, still stunned at the revelations. 'But you don't need to ask my forgiveness. It isn't me you have wronged, is it? And it's too late now to ask ... Father to forgive you. Forget it, Mother. Try to forget you ever told me. You can be sure I will never breathe a word, certainly not to Percy nor Edgar, nor to anyone for that matter. This is our secret.'

He tried to smile convincingly at her, but Joss was aware that something inside him had died. He still loved her as much as ever, but despite what he said to her he felt he had been betrayed. His mother, whom he had idealised as the perfect woman, was found to have feet of clay.

Chapter 22

Joss knew, however, that Charlotte was now his responsibility. His brothers had families and concerns of their own whereas he was free of any encumbrances. He worked a month's notice at the mill in Blackburn, in the meantime finding employment as a textile designer at Bleasdale Mill in Preston. He found the work satisfying, giving him plenty of scope for his feeling for colour and design, but he also found he had ample leisure time in which to pursue his all-consuming hobby of painting.

This was, in fact, becoming more than a mere hobby. He had found an outlet for his work at Mr Middlehurst's newly opened gallery in Fisher-gate. Mr Middlehurst had suggested the prices he should ask for the paintings as Joss had, until recently, regarded himself as an amateur, albeit a talented one. But the gallery owner had seemed very impressed and had assured him that his work would sell. They could not demand an exorbitant price – after all, he was still unknown – but the scenes he painted were, on the whole, familiar ones to the Preston clientele, and they were original paintings, not reproductions. Joss was very satisfied with the sums he received after Mr Middlehurst had taken his commission. He knew he could not yet make a living solely from the sale of his work, but maybe one day, sometime in the future, he hoped he might be able to do so.

The future was not something that Joss dwelled upon overmuch, nor the past. He had realised it was best to take each day as it came, and he had settled into a comfortable routine – his new position at Bleasdale Mill, his painting, his home life with his mother – without thinking too much about whether he was happy or fulfilled in what he was doing. He knew that his mother and his brothers, particularly his brothers, thought it odd that he was still unattached and, what was more, seemingly uninterested in members of the opposite sex. The same comments he had endured from his father were levelled at him by Percy and Edgar, plus other more pertinent insinuations from Percy that it might not be the opposite sex that Joss was interested in. He laughed them off good-humouredly; he had learned that the best way to treat Percy was not to rise to the bait. Joss had, in fact, taken young ladies out from time to time, to make up a foursome, maybe, or to partner a lone female to a charity concert or dinner, but there had been no one at all, who had caused his pulses to race or make him feel, in any measure, that this was someone with whom he would like to spend more time, let alone the rest of his life. The only time he had ever felt like that was when he had met the enchanting Molly, the girl to whom he had given his heart at their one and only meeting, and then, just as suddenly, had lost again.

The painting of her, which he knew to be his best work, had taken ages to complete because he kept adding more and more finishing touches, to make it as perfect as he felt it deserved to be. He knew that he would never sell it, but he had been unable to resist showing it, firstly to his mother, who had been captivated by it, then to Mr Middlehurst who had persuaded him that such a work of art must be seen and appreciated by the people of Preston. He had described the subject of the painting to the gallery owner as 'a girl I once knew'. He felt guilty to be speaking of Molly in such dismissive tones, but he was unwilling to confide further in the man. After all, looking at it matter-of-factedly, that was what she was. Mr Middlehurst's enigmatic smile, however, had suggested that the man guessed there was more to it than that.

During the time Joss had been studying in Manchester, then working in Blackburn, he had hardly visited the Blackpool house at all. The rest of the family, though, had continued to spend the odd weekend, or even a full week there, Percy and Eddie now being family men. Since his return to Preston after his father's death, Joss, accompanied by his mother and a maid to do the necessary work, had visited the house occasionally. They remained at the north end of the town, not venturing into the centre of Blackpool to sample the more boisterous and brazen delights the resort had to offer. Charlotte enjoyed the solitude of the cliffs at Little Bispham, delighting in the clear sky and the bracing sea breezes after the grime and greyness of Preston. Joss was contented with his paints and easel, working on yet another view of the sea in one of its many moods; calm and still and bluey-green, or rough and angry with dark foam-capped waves dashing against the sea wall, or sparkling with diamonds as the sun set on the far horizon. He had never visited Uncle Tom's Cabin since that Jubilee night; the memories were too poignant. And he remained disinclined to begin his search again for Molly, knowing in his heart that he would be doomed to disappointment.

When they returned to Preston after one of these weekends Joss would be even more aware of the drabness of their environment. The house near to Cunliffe Mill was a well-built and substantial one. It had been the family home for four generations, modernised according to each owner's needs, and would be considered by many to be a desirable residence were it not for the location. Although it stood in its own grounds it was merely a stone's throw from the mill, and the same acrid smoke that affected the mill workers in their small terraced homes affected the owners too, in their more palatial dwelling, soiling their clean washing and stunting the growth of the plants and flowers in the garden. But Henry Cunliffe, like his predecessors, had never seemed to notice the surroundings. They were living on top of their work, able at all times to keep their finger on the pulse, and that was all that mattered.

At least we do have a garden to enjoy, was Charlotte's view, which was more than could be said for the mill hands in their two-up, two-down houses. She had been brought up in such a home and had never ceased to count her blessings since marrying Henry. She was deeply sorry for her one lapse, and she knew the guilt would never entirely leave her because Henry had been a good husband to her. She hoped that Joss, in time, would forgive her too. In spite of his saying there was nothing to forgive she knew she had hurt him by her confession. He had not said so, but she could see it in his eyes; that look, though it was only slight, of disappointment and disillusion on discovering that his mother was not quite the saint he had thought her to be. She had been loath to move from the family home because it had been Henry's home before it was hers, and memories of him were strong. She had loved him, in her own way, though it might seem to Joss that she had betrayed him. Young people sometimes tended to see things as either black or white. Only as you grew older did you appreciate the many, many shades of grey that there were in between. Charlotte made up her mind that if Joss mentioned it again she might well be persuaded to move from here. Maybe they were both ready for a change of scene.

Joss had noticed the work going on at the shop in Church Street which had been derelict for more than a year. He could not say he was particularly interested, as he rarely went into any of these small shops near to his place of work, but he could not help but see there were quite drastic changes being made. Plate-glass windows had replaced the small panes, then a mahogany counter had been installed, running the full length of the shop, with glass shelving beneath and wooden shelving at the rear. He began to take more interest as he saw small tables and chairs stacked at the side of the shop. It looked as though it might be going to open as a café. It should do well, he thought to himself, so near to the many mills in the area, although most of the mill workers, himself included, took sandwiches to eat at midday.

The next day a notice appeared in the window stating that the shop would be opening the following week. It was to be a dinner shop and confectionery business, owned by the people who ran the grocer's shop round the corner in Manchester Road. And, sure enough, the next Monday the shop was open for business.

It was a dull November morning, cold and misty, as Joss hurried along Church Street, and the smell of freshly baked bread at the new shop made him feel hungry again although he had, less than an hour ago, eaten a hearty breakfast. He glanced at the window where crusty brown-topped loaves were displayed, together with a variety of cakes – gingerbread, almond and jam tarts, swiss rolls – nothing too fancy, but all looking very delectable, as well as sausage rolls and meat pies. A peek inside showed him there was more of the same produce beneath the counter, and there were four or five people waiting to be served. Joss hurried on; he was a minute or two late. But perhaps, one day, he would treat himself to one of those delicious-looking meat pies, he decided.

When he passed by after he had finished work the shop was closed, but he could see that the signwriter had been busy. There was a newly painted sign over the window and another smaller one above the door. Joss's heart skipped a beat when he saw what was written there: 'Molly's Meals'. Don't be such a fool, he told himself. How many hundreds of young women there must be called Molly? But his Molly had worked for a confectioner, hadn't she...? Admonishing himself again not to be so ridiculous, he went on his way.

All the same he made sure he was in good time the next morning, and once more he took a surreptitious glance into the shop. There was a young girl serving; she looked about fifteen or sixteen, with dark hair tucked away beneath her white cap. It was not Molly, not his Molly at any rate. It was just possible, of course, that there might be another person out of sight, helping in the bakehouse maybe. This young girl did not look old enough to be the Molly whose name was on the sign and on the new notice that had appeared in the window. This stated that the new shop was under the managership of Miss Molly Rimmer. Wishful thinking, Joss told himself as he hovered for a moment or two, but without any luck. No one else appeared.

He could see the shop was still open as he approached it after his day's work was over. He had made sure he finished a little earlier tonight, although he was cursing himself for being no end of a fool. The stock in the window was depleted; just a couple of loaves remained, a solitary meat pie and a few remnants of cakes. There was one customer in the shop, a lady was being served

491

by... Joss gave a gasp, blinked rapidly, then momentarily looked away. Surely his imagination must be running away with him, making his eyes see things that could not be there. Cautiously he looked again. The young woman was slim and of medium height, her trim figure almost enveloped by her long white apron, and her glorious rich auburn hair, that which was not tucked away beneath her cap, curled alluringly around her forehead and ears. As he watched, totally mesmerised, she smiled at the customer, that enchanting smile that he remembered so well, lighting up her lovely face, making her eyes sparkle with warmth and friendliness.

He opened the door, hearing a welcoming jingle from the shop bell as he stood aside to let the customer pass him.

'Yes, sir,' said Molly, glancing up from the counter. 'How can I help...?' Her voice died away as she stared at him.

Joss stepped forward. 'Hello ... Molly,' he said.

Molly could not believe her eyes. She certainly could not speak. She just stared at the young man who had miraculously appeared out of the blue, her lips parted, trying to form the words her mind could not quite accept. Eventually, 'Joss...' she gasped. 'Is it ... really you?'

'I'm real enough, Molly,' he smiled. 'And so are you, I hope, although I thought at first I was seeing things.'

'So did I...' All she could do was gaze at him. Although she had known he was living in Preston, and she now knew his full name, she still had not quite believed that she would ever see him again. Her attention was diverted for a moment as her young assistant, Susan, came out of the bakehouse. 'Thank you, Susan; you can go now,' she said. 'I'll clear up here. It's turned half-past five.'

'Thank you, Miss Rimmer, if you're sure.' The girl glanced questioningly at the young man.

'Yes, it's all right, Susan,' said Molly. 'Mr Cunliffe is a ... a friend of mine.'

'So you know my name?' said Joss quietly, as Susan departed. 'How did you know?'

'I saw the painting in the window in Fisher-gate,' replied Molly. 'I went in and asked about you. Mr Middlehurst told me ... that you lived in Preston. He didn't tell me much else, though,' she went on, not wanting Joss to think she had been gossiping about him. 'I didn't say that I knew you. And I don't think he recognised me – you know – from the painting.'

He smiled at her then, and she remembered the smile that had captivated her so long ago. His blue, so very blue, eyes were shining again with the same light she recalled seeing there when she had parted from him in Talbot Square, a glow of warmth and tenderness and affection that she had hoped, then, might grow into love. Could she, possibly, hope for the same again?

'It's all I have to remember you by, Molly,' he said gently. 'What happened to you? I waited and waited that Sunday, but you didn't come. Then I looked for you all over Blackpool.' He shook his head disbelievingly as he continued to gaze at her. 'It's like a miracle. I feel I must be dreaming.

But what are you doing here, in Preston? And if you knew my name, then why didn't you come and find me?'

'How could I, Joss?' Molly spoke his name more confidently now. He was not a vision. He was real enough, though she could not quite grasp the fact that he was there, talking with her again after all this time. 'It was all so long ago. How could I assume that you would still want to see me? I'm in Preston because I work here now, and this is where I live, above the shop ... with my sister and brother... It's a long story, Joss,' she added. 'A very long story.'

'Your sister and brother?' he repeated. 'They are upstairs, now?'

'Yes.' Molly nodded. 'Emily's twelve now. She's quite capable of looking after William when she comes out of school. During the day my friend looks after him, with her own little girl. That's Mrs Healey, the owner of the grocery shop, and of this shop, of course.'

'But ... what about your parents?' asked Joss. 'I seem to recall that your mother was expecting a baby, wasn't she?'

'Yes, William.' Molly smiled sadly. 'My mother died when William was born, Joss. Both my parents are dead. That's the reason we came to Preston – well, one of the reasons, anyway. As I've said, it's a very long story.'

'And one I want to hear,' said Joss. 'Listen, Molly, when can I see you? I must meet you again. This is just too incredible for words.' He stopped, as something had obviously occurred to him. 'That Sunday when you didn't meet me –

was it because ... your mother...?'

'Yes, Mam had died,' said Molly simply. 'She died the very night I met you, Joss. And William was my responsibility. He still is.' She wanted that to be clear from the start; but there were other complications, far more serious ones than a younger brother. It was wonderful that she had found Joss again; but how would he feel when he knew her full story, as she was determined he must do?

'What a dreadful time you must have had,' he said, still staring at her in wonder as though he could not quite believe the evidence of his eyes. 'And I had no idea. To think that I even imagined you might have changed your mind about meeting me.'

Molly smiled at him. 'That is just what I tried to tell myself, when I knew I couldn't see you. That you would have changed your mind anyway, that you wouldn't have turned up.'

'Never,' said Joss. He took a step towards her, just as Emily appeared through the doorway that led to the upstairs rooms.

'Oh, I thought the shop was closed.' The girl gave a start at seeing a strange young man there with her sister. It was unusual to have customers of his ilk – well-dressed men of business – in the shop at any time of day, certainly not at closing time. 'I was just wondering, shall I start peeling the potatoes, Molly?'

'Yes, thank you, Em. I'll be with you in a few minutes, dear. You're quite right; the shop is shut. At least it should be.' Molly quickly turned the sign on the door round to read 'Closed'. 'Emily, this is Mr Cunliffe. I used to know him when we lived in Blackpool, quite a long time ago. He lives in Preston and so ... he's called to see me.' She could not help thinking of the time she had introduced her sister to Hector Stubbins, and how the child had taken an instant dislike to him.

'Hello there, Emily.' Joss grinned at her in a friendly way, not bothering to hold out his hand and say 'How do you do?' which children often found intimidating; and Em, after a first dubious glance, responded with a shy smile.

'Hello,' she said; then, to her sister's surprise, 'Are you going to come and see Molly again?'

'I certainly hope so. And you and your little brother as well. You're looking after him, are you?' Joss sounded genuinely interested.

'Yes, he's quite a good boy, isn't he, Molly? I'd better get back to him, hadn't I, although I shut the living-room door like you said, so that he can't fall down the stairs. Goodbye, Mr Cunliffe.'

'My name's Joss,' he said. 'Quite easy to remember, isn't it?'

'Yes.' The little girl nodded. 'Goodbye then ... Joss.'

'She's a charming little girl,' Joss said as she departed. 'She's a real credit to you, Molly.'

'Thank you, I hope so,' said Molly. 'I've done my best. She used to be dreadfully shy and insecure. But helping in the shop brought her out of her shell quite a lot. I used to have a little shop – just a house shop – before we left Blackpool. So much has happened, Joss. It would take me ages–' She looked at him apologetically.

'And you can't tell me now; I realise that. You

must get back to your family and I mustn't hinder you.' He took hold of her arms, looking deep into her eyes. 'Molly, this really is a miracle, finding you. And I shall never let you disappear again, I promise.' He leaned forward, then very gently and tenderly kissed her on the forehead. 'Now ... when can we meet?'

They agreed that their first meeting should be just for the two of them. There was so much to talk about. They decided to meet outside St John's Parish Church on Sunday afternoon at two o'clock. That was five whole days away. So it had been that first time when they had arranged to meet at the North Pier entrance; but this time nothing and nobody would stop Molly from being there. She wished it could have been sooner, but it was winter time, dark at four o'clock, not the kind of weather or the time of year for a leisurely evening stroll. The children would be all right on their own for an hour or two; and Molly, encouraged by Em's empathy towards the newcomer, suggested that Joss should come back to their rooms afterwards to have tea with the three of them.

She told no one of the surprise meeting, not even Agnes. She felt a little scared that her bubble of happiness might burst, as it so quickly had done before, but she knew at the heart of her that this time it was different. Joss was not an impossible dream, a poignant memory, which was how she had been forcing herself to think of him, but a living reality, soon to become part of her life – if all the obstacles could be overcome.

His delight at seeing her again on Sunday

afternoon was apparent in the glow in his eyes and the warmth of his greeting, and the way he tucked her hand comfortably into the crook of his arm as they started to walk away from the town. He led her along little side streets she had not encountered before, towards Avenham Park.

'We're very proud of our parks,' he told her. 'So near to the town centre, and yet they're oases of green away from the grime and the smoky chimneys. This one leads into Miller Park; they're almost one and the same, really. They get quite busy in the summer, but it's peaceful here at this time of year, I'm pleased to say.' He smiled down at her. 'I want you all to myself for a while, Molly,' he said quietly.

She had visited the park only once before. There had been so little time since she'd come to live in Preston for anything but work and preparing her new home. She was impressed now by the beauty of the parkland area; the formal laid-out gardens, now bare of flowers, the flights of stone steps and terraces flanked by impressive urn-topped balustrades; and the landscaped vistas, stretches of grass and tree-lined paths leading down to the river.

'I'd no idea it was so beautiful,' she said as they strolled along the riverside path. 'It's just like being in the country. I've never seen anything like this, not even when I lived in Blackpool. There must be nice countryside round and about, but we didn't get out very much.'

'You hadn't been away from Blackpool a great deal, I gather, till you came here?' asked Joss. 'You don't know many other places?'

'I went to the Lake District once,' said Molly quickly, dismissively. 'Joss ... there's something I've got to tell you.' She cast him an apprehensive glance, but the look he gave her in return was encouraging and very comforting.

'Whatever you have to tell me, I will understand. Please trust me, Molly.' He reached out his hand and very lovingly traced his finger along the curve of her cheek, her chin, the tip of her nose. 'You must not be afraid to tell me ... everything.'

It was almost as if he knew, she mused, as they found a sheltered seat beneath a cluster of trees, and she began to tell him her story. It was as though nothing she said had the power to shock him or make him feel any differently about her. She knew, even before he told her, that he had fallen in love with her, as she had with him. She told him first about her father's death on the night of the Tower fire, and at that Joss did show more than a little surprise.

'Rimmer?' he said. 'That's your name, isn't it? I thought it rang a bell when I read your name on the notice. Yes, of course – William Rimmer. Oh, Molly, you've no idea how near I came to finding you.' He explained how a man he had met on the promenade had told him about the accident, had even told him about the family the poor unfortunate man had left behind. And how he, Joss, had expressed sympathy and regret ... and then had moved on. 'But I didn't know your name was Rimmer. Oh, Molly – what a waste of all these years.'

'A waste indeed, Joss,' said Molly, a trifle grimly. She smiled at him, a wry smile. 'When we stood outside the Tower on Jubilee night watching the illuminations – you remember? – I nearly told you then that my father worked at the Tower, but I didn't. If only I had, it would have been something, wouldn't it, a way of finding me? Instead I lost you, and things started to go wrong. Then I went and made the biggest mistake of my life.' She looked at him candidly, not smiling now. 'Joss ... I have to tell you, my name is not Molly Rimmer, not any more. I got married. I'm ... Molly Stubbins.'

There was just a momentary flicker in Joss's blue eyes, but not of shock or even disquiet, more of deep concern. 'Just tell me about it, my love,' he said. 'I take it you are not a widow?'

'No, I'm afraid not.' She shook her head. 'That sounds dreadful, doesn't it? But it's true. I sometimes think I must be a very wicked person, because I have wished that he were dead. No, perhaps not dead, but I have wished that he would just disappear, that I would never need to see him again. Well, now he has disappeared, but it's no better because I know I'm still married to him.'

'Tell me about your marriage, Molly,' he said.

She began to tell him, hesitantly at first, the story of how she had met Hector Stubbins. Of how she had believed he was a good worthy man who would take care of her, and of her bitter disillusionment and unhappiness on discovering that, although he professed to be a man of God, a pillar of the church, there was a dark and cruel side to him. It was not easy to speak of Hector's cruelty, but with Joss's arm around her shoulders and his hand holding tightly to hers she was able to find the courage to do so. She held nothing back: her fear that he would start on the children as well; that he had, indeed, begun to chastise Emily in the same way; culminating in her decision to move to Preston and start a new life.

'And the awful part is that I knew – I knew almost as soon as we were man and wife – that I had made a dreadful mistake. How could I have been such a stupid fool? And I'm still married to him. I don't know where he is, but there's no way I can get out of it. I'm still Mrs Hector Stubbins.'

Joss drew her closely into his arms, then, for the very first time, his mouth came down upon hers in a kiss of more sweetness and tenderness than Molly, in her wildest dreams, had never imagined. There was underlying passion there too, but she felt safe and secure in the warmth of his embrace and she knew that with Joss she need have no fears; his love for her would be pure and wholesome, and this was where she truly belonged.

'Molly, you know how much I love you, don't you?' he said, holding her away from him a little, looking into her eyes. 'I think I must have fallen in love with you that first night. I know now that I have never stopped loving you. Some might say that I hardly know you, but I feel as though I have known you forever, and that is how long I will go on loving you – forever.'

He kissed her again and she found herself responding, her mouth opening beneath his, her arms folding around him, drawing him even closer to her in an intimacy she had never experienced before. 'I love you too, Joss,' she whispered when they drew apart for a moment. 'It's impossible I know, but I do.'

'Nothing is impossible, my love,' he said, releasing her from his arms, but clasping both her hands tightly in his. 'You may be married to this ... Hector Stubbins, but it is only in name. You are mine now, Molly, and I am yours – forever. I realise I can't ask you to marry me, but I want you to belong to me, just as I want to belong to you, in every way. Do you understand what I am saying, Molly? We must be together.'

Molly nodded. 'Yes, I think so,' she said. What was he suggesting? That he should come and live with her in the rooms above the shop? That would not be possible. There were the children to consider. She shared a bedroom with Em and William... Or did he mean that she should go and live with him and his mother? He had already told her he and his mother lived in a house that was far too big for them, in the vicinity of St Walburge's church. But it all came back to the problem of her marriage, to the indisputable fact that she was the wife of another man and, therefore, she could not belong to Joss, as he was proposing. Marriage was out of the question, but for them to be together – really together – in a close relationship outside of marriage, surely that was impossible as well?

'You have gone very quiet, my dear,' Joss said. 'And I can guess what you are thinking. You are a very moral person, aren't you? And so am I. I have always believed myself to be an honourable man, and I will not make you do anything that you are not completely happy about. I will not rush you, Molly. I am content, for the moment, that I have found you again; that we can meet and talk and find out more about each other. Oh, Molly, you have no idea how happy you have made me.'

'Yes, I have, Joss,' she replied, 'because I am just as happy myself. But happy is not a strong enough word to explain how I feel. Blissful, joyful – that's how I feel.'

'Jubilant, radiant, over the moon,' he added. 'The nearest thing to heaven on earth. That is what I feel, being with you again, Molly.'

The early dusk was falling as they left the park, although they had scarcely noticed the chill and the slight mistiness in the air. Their way home took them through Winckley Square and Molly pointed out to Joss the home of her Great-uncle Silas. She had already told him about her unsuccessful visit to that house.

'Are you sure you don't want to call and say hello?' Joss said now, though a trifle jokingly.

Molly shook her head.

'I can't help thinking you are being a wee bit too critical of the old man, my dear,' he went on. 'He's probably very lonely, but finds it hard to say so. It sounds to me as though he has a tremendous chip on his shoulder about all that's happened in the past. He finds it hard to forgive and forget. Perhaps if you were to meet him halfway...? You know, make the first move then leave it to him. He did ask you to call again, didn't he?'

'As an afterthought,' said Molly. 'He told

Lizzie, the maid, not me. So you really think I should see him again?'

'Sometime soon, maybe,' said Joss. 'But not today; it's too late now.' They were already back on Fishergate. 'We all have skeletons in the cupboard, Molly. I'm sure all families do; I know there are one or two in mine. Your uncle is living in the past instead of looking to the future. And perhaps he thinks there is not much future ahead of him.'

'Perhaps so,' said Molly pensively. 'He's quite an old man. And it must be awful to be alone and friendless. Oh, Joss, I've been very thoughtless, haven't I?'

'Not so, my dear. You could never be thoughtless. Anyway, you've been too busy to think of anything just lately except your work and your family, haven't you? But I hope I may be able to make things a little easier for you before long.'

She looked at him questioningly. 'What do you mean? I can't give up the shop. It's only just opened and Agnes and Fred are depending on me. I can't let them down.'

'Nor would I want you to. But you must find it hard, doing all your own housework as well: looking after the children, washing, cooking meals...'

'Thousands of women do it, Joss.' Molly smiled at him a little teasingly. That was the great difference between the two of them, of course. Joss and his mother would have servants to wait on them hand and foot, to cook their meals and clean their floors and do their bidding, although he had told her – no doubt to set some of her

504

fears at rest – about his mother's humble beginnings.

'Yes, I'm sorry,' said Joss. 'That was insensitive of me. I realise, of course, that thousands of women don't know any other sort of life. And you would be quite right if you were to say that I know next to nothing about what they have to put up with. I've had an easy life – I admit it. But I'm determined I'm going to make things easier for you too, Molly. Just trust me, my love. I promise I'm going to look after you – and Emily and William – forever. And very soon you must come and meet my mother. I've told her about you. She's seen your portrait and she knows I've found you again. She'll love you, Molly, just as much as I do. No, not just as much – that isn't possible – but she'll like you, Molly, and I know you'll like her too. And now I'm looking forward to meeting Emily again, and little William...'

Chapter 23

Silas Rimmer blinked – surely he must be seeing things! – then he looked again at the portrait in the window. Yes, it was her, Molly, his great-niece. If not, then it was someone uncannily like her. He had been trying to find her for the past few months, but without any success. And now, here she was – a picture of her, at any rate – right in front of his eyes. Not that he had been putting himself out a great deal in his search for her; that would not have been his way. He had cast a cursory glance through the windows of shops on his occasional trips along Fishergate, remembering how she had said she might get a job as a shop assistant; and he had asked Lizzie to keep an eye open for her, all to no avail. She seemed to have vanished off the scene. It served him right really, he supposed. He should have made her more welcome that day in the early summer when she had called on him. It was not her fault, all that had happened in the past. Now Christmas was approaching once again, and Silas was admitting to himself, for the first time for years, that he was lonely.

He knew Albert Middlehurst. They had been boys together at school, although Albert had been a few years below him, and at one time they had attended the same chapel. Perhaps Albert would be able to tell him about the young woman in the picture; he might even know her whereabouts. He pushed open the door and went in.

'Good afternoon, Silas. It's been a long time.' Albert Middlehurst looked at him in some surprise. 'We don't often see you these days. Janie was only saying the other day she hadn't seen you for ages.'

'Aye, well, I don't get around much.'

'So, what can I do for you? Is there a picture you would like to look at more closely? A Christmas gift, perhaps?'

'That one in the window,' said Silas abruptly. 'That girl with the ginger hair. Who is she?'

'I'm sorry; that particular painting is not for sale.'

'I know that. I can read, can't I? I don't want to buy it. All I'm asking you is – who is she?'

Albert Middlehurst smiled. 'It's strange you should ask that. If you had asked me a fortnight ago I would have had to say I didn't know. But now I do know a little more about the young lady. Tell me though, Silas, why do you want to know?'

'Because I think she's my niece, that's why. My great-niece, to be more precise; our William's lass. She called to see me a while ago, then she vanished into thin air. I've been trying to find her. I'm sure it's her. Molly, she's called. Molly Rimmer, same name as me, of course.'

'Then I have good news for you. The young woman is, indeed, called Molly, although I have not been told her second name. It's Rimmer, you say, and she's your great-niece? Well, that is very interesting.'

'And where is she? Do you know?'

'No, I'm afraid I don't know her exact whereabouts,' said Albert Middlehurst carefully. 'But I know someone who does; Mr Joss Cunliffe, the young man who painted the portrait. He would be able to tell you where to find her. It's a very romantic story, Silas, one with a very happy ending, I'm pleased to say...'

Mr Middlehurst recounted the tale of how a young woman had come into the gallery a few weeks ago enquiring about the painting. He had not recognised her at the time, not fully, although he had thought there was something a little mysterious about her. It was only later, when he was thinking about her, that he had wondered if she might be 'a girl I once knew' whom Joss had referred to; she had certainly seemed very interested in the artist. He had even wondered if there might be a romance there; if he, Albert Middlehurst, might be the means of reuniting them. Then, the very next week, there was Joss Cunliffe in the gallery, like a dog with two tails he had been, telling Albert how he had found her again, his Molly, the girl in the painting whom he thought he had lost. And the information that the picture had been painted from a lightning sketch done on the cliffs at Blackpool was enough to convince Silas Rimmer now that the young woman was, indeed, Molly, his great-niece.

'Mr Cunliffe is coming in again at the end of the week,' said Albert Middlehurst. 'He has a few more paintings to show me. If you wish, Silas, you could arrange to come here at the same time and meet him. I am sure he will be able to tell you what you want to know: where to find your niece. Another happy ending, eh?' Albert's eyes, behind his pince-nez, were shining with delight. It had warmed his heart to hear Joss's romantic story. And here, perhaps was another fairy-tale ending. He had thought he was too old to be stirred by such sentimental stuff.

Silas, however, was looking a mite sceptical, glad though he was that he might soon locate Molly again. 'Cunliffe?' he said. 'Did you say the young fellow was called Cunliffe? Would he belong to the same family that own the mill then?'

'Yes, that's right,' said Albert. 'Joss is the youngest son, although he doesn't actually have anything to do with the family business now. He works at Bleasdale Mill now, apparently. His father, Henry, died about a year ago.'

'Yes, so I heard,' Silas rubbed his chin thoughtfully. 'And you say this young fellow, Joss, is, er, friendly with Molly?'

Albert smiled. 'It was my impression that the two of them are friendly, yes. And it would be my guess that if that young man has anything to do with it, they may very soon be more than just friends. Anyway, you are most welcome to call in again and meet him. He will be here on Saturday afternoon, around two-thirty.'

Silas walked home in a brown study. It was possible that Molly would not want anything more to do with him after the way he had treated her on her one and only visit. He knew he had been less than welcoming to the poor lass; it was hardly surprising that she had not come to see him again. But to find out she was friendly with the young Cunliffe chap, that was staggering news indeed. Why, it had been her great-grandmother who had... Goodness, it didn't bear thinking of. Silas shook his head ruefully, tutting to himself as he walked along. Did Joss Cunliffe know, he wondered, that this young lady friend belonged to that infamous family? It was quite possible he did not; the name was different, after all. The women of the family had changed their names when they'd married.

Or had Molly delved into the history of her family as she had seemed so keen to do? Silas had warned her to let sleeping dogs lie. Now, even more, it would be wise for her to do so. He would have to tell her again to leave well alone – that was if she agreed to meet him.

Joss was a regular visitor to the rooms above the shop now. The children had taken to him immediately and without restraint. Sometimes he shared an evening meal with them, staying until William and then, much later, Em, had gone to bed so that he and Molly could spend some time alone together.

'Molly, you know you agreed to spend Christmas with my mother and me?' he said, one evening in the middle of December.

'Yes,' Molly replied. 'We are all looking forward to it. Em has never stopped talking about your house. It's the grandest one she's ever seen. That isn't why she wants to go again, though. She took an instant liking to your mother, and so did William. She's lovely, isn't she, Joss? She was so kind and friendly to us all. Why, is there some problem about Christmas?'

'No, there's no problem, darling. At least, I hope not. I just wanted to warn you ... there will be an extra guest.'

'That's all right, Joss. It's your house, isn't it, and your party? You can invite whoever you like, can't you? You mean, it's someone who might not understand ... about me?'

'I hope he'll understand. I know he's anxious to see you again. He seemed rather cagey about something, though. As you say, he's an odd sort of chap.'

'Joss, you're talking in riddles. Who is he?' Molly looked at him curiously. 'You don't know anyone that I know, do you?' Suddenly light began to dawn. 'You can't mean...? Is it my...?'

Joss grinned at her. 'Yes, it's your Great-uncle Silas. He's coming to spend Christmas with us.'

Molly listened in astonishment as Joss told her of his meeting with Silas Rimmer in Mr Middlehurst's gallery; how he had been anxious to know the whereabouts of his great-niece, and Joss had suddenly thought what a good idea it would be for them all to spend Christmas together. The old man had seemed reluctant at first to accept an invitation to the Cunliffe's home, but the thought of seeing Molly again had swayed him.

'He does seem to want to make amends,' said Joss. 'He admits he's wasted precious years in bitterness about what he considered to be the wrong your father did him – yes, he told me a little about that. But he realises none of it is your

511

fault. He kept insisting, in fact, that you and I have to look to the future, never mind what has happened in the past. I wasn't sure what he was going on about, to be quite honest. He was rambling a bit, I think. That's what comes of living alone and having no one to talk to; he's sure to be confused.'

'He doesn't know about me – about my marriage, I mean,' said Molly. 'There didn't seem to be any point in telling him, so he can't be referring to that. Anyway, we got off on the wrong foot, him and me.'

'Something I hope will soon be put to rights, my love,' said Joss.

'And your mother – she doesn't mind? She's never met my Uncle Silas, has she?'

'No, but she's a very hospitable person and I'm sure she'll charm him. She has that way with her. She didn't mind at all. My mother has grown very fond of you, Molly, in the short time she has known you, and she will be more than willing to welcome your uncle.' He clasped hold of her hands as they sat together on the sofa. 'Oh, Molly, it will be such a happy Christmas for us all. We'll make sure the children forget all about the unhappiness of the past.'

'I think they've forgotten already, Joss,' said Molly quietly. 'They never mention Hector. They hardly ever talk about Blackpool now, although I know Em is looking forward to seeing Sarah again when we go to Flo's wedding.'

'Flo ... what a friendly and likeable girl she is,' smiled Joss. 'I do hope that she and her Sam will be happy together, just like we will be, Molly.'

Except that Flo and Sam are able to be married, thought Molly, but as for herself and Joss ... there was little likelihood of it. Flo had informed her, on her recent visit to Preston to do the final fitting for the bridesmaids' dresses, that there was still no sign, no word of Hector Stubbins. No one had any idea where he had gone.

'I remember Flo from that first night at Uncle Tom's Cabin,' Joss continued. 'I think she was a little wary of me. She thought I was bent on leading you astray.'

'She thought I was getting ideas above my station,' laughed Molly, 'but she's changed her mind about you now. She was really delighted we have found one another again.'

'I have been giving some thought to Flo and Sam's wedding,' said Joss. 'I realise that I cannot be an invited guest. You and I – we must not be seen together, not in Blackpool where people know your circumstances. It's a great pity, my love, but that's the way of it, I'm afraid.' Molly nodded in agreement, smiling a little sadly at him. 'But there is no reason why I should not attend the marriage service. I would like to do that, to wish them both well. My mother and I will stay at Cunliffe House that weekend. We'll sit at the back of the church – sorry, chapel, you call it, don't you?' Joss, when he worshipped any-where, went to the Church of England. 'We can all travel there and back together on the train. Now, what do you think about that?'

'I think it's a lovely idea, Joss,' said Molly. 'It would make me happy to know that you are there, even though we can't be together, though we can't be a ... a proper couple.' She bowed her head as the hopelessness of it all struck her once again. She loved him so much; already their relationship had begun to blossom, to strengthen, as they discovered more and more about each other. It would seem, at times, as though the past was forgotten, thoughts of her ill-fated marriage banished to the far corners of her mind; then she would remember with a sickening jolt the great obstacle that prevented them from belonging to one another.

Joss put an arm around her shoulders. 'You mustn't be sad, my darling. We already have so much. And one day, I promise, we will have everything.'

Flo and Sam's wedding was quite a grand affair for a chapel do. Flo was a truly beautiful bride in her gown of ivory satin, and her four bridesmaids, in their dresses of deep gold-coloured velvet, made a cheerful splash of colour, the sunshine that was missing, in the gloom of the mid-winter day.

Molly found it strange to be back in Blackpool. It was her first visit there since her hurried departure at the end of May. She and the children stayed at Maggie's home. It was a tight squeeze, needing a shoe horn to get them all in, Maggie joked, but Molly was happy to see her old friend again. Em and Sarah were delighted to be together again, especially as Flo had asked Sarah to be a bridesmaid along with Em, Molly, and Minnie, the other assistant from 'Marianne

Modes'. Maggie, Flo and Vi Prosser had become great friends, drawn together by Molly's misfortunes.

And those three women were the only ones in the chapel who knew the reason for the sparkle in Molly's eyes, the glow in her face, as she received the wedding bouquet from Flo's hands, then listened to the voice of the minister as he read the marriage service. It was not the Ebenezer chapel, but the one at the other end of town, which Sam and Flo attended, but many of the congregation gathered there were the same. Tales had been flying around, losing nothing in the telling, about Hector's disappearance, and the reason for it. It was now well-known that Molly had had a dreadful life with him. Her friends and acquaintances were pleased to see her again, though somewhat surprised at how well she looked. One might have thought that this wedding would bring back a host of unhappy memories, but the young woman looked positively radiant.

Beneath the glow of happiness, however, there was a niggling fear at the back of Molly's mind that remained with her throughout the weekend; the fear that Hector Stubbins might suddenly reappear. Foolish though she knew it was, she could not help looking over her shoulder, scanning the faces of the congregation milling outside the chapel, even looking warily at strangers waiting on the platform at the railway station. But her husband was not among them. She had known, deep down, that she was not likely to see him; it was possible that she might never set eyes on him again, but the fearful memories of the way he had ill-treated her could not be erased completely.

Christmas Day was a happy one, starting with the customary opening of stockings in the bedroom before Molly and the children were even dressed or had eaten breakfast. Em was still young enough to enjoy the fun of surprises, and her delight matched that of William as they pulled out the sugar mice and gold-foiled chocolate coins, the tangerines wrapped in silver paper and the little toys that did not cost a great deal, but provided hours of enjoyment. Em's main present this year was a furry hat and a muff to match, and William's a clockwork engine. And Em had saved her pocket money to buy Molly a miniature woven silk picture of summer flowers which Molly declared with sincerity was the nicest present she had ever received.

Joss called for them mid-morning to escort them to his home where they were to spend the rest of the day. He insisted they should take a cab as it was a long way for William's little legs to walk. When they alighted outside the house there was Silas Rimmer, also getting out of a cab. Any embarrassment or shyness on the part of the children was soon dispelled by Joss's good humour and Charlotte Cunliffe's warm welcome to everyone.

Molly saw another side to her great-uncle that day. There was, beneath the acerbic exterior, a more benign aspect to his personality and she found herself warming to him. She learned that Silas, as she had guessed, had 'married into money'. His wife, Flossie, had been the only child of a solicitor, the head of an old-established family firm, hence the imposing house in Winckley Square which Flossie had inherited on the death of her parents. Charlotte and Silas reminisced about old times, although he was many years her senior, discovering they had several mutual acquaintances. He had never worked in the mill, however – he had met his wife through his position as a solicitor's clerk – and seemed disinclined to bring Preston's cotton mills into the conversation. Molly noticed, on one occasion, how he steered the talk around to Albert Middlehurst, and the subject of Joss's paintings when it seemed as though Cunliffe Mill was about to be discussed.

It was quite a small gathering, just the six of them sharing the elaborate Christmas luncheon, then the equally sumptuous spread that Charlotte's cook had prepared for a late tea. Joss explained to Molly that his two brothers and their families were spending Christmas in their own homes, but would all be coming to spend Boxing Day with their mother and younger brother.

Silas left soon after tea, expressing the wish that Molly and Joss, and Charlotte too, might come to visit him before very long. Joss escorted him into the hallway then tactfully left Molly and her uncle alone together.

'I'm a crochety old man sometimes,' he confided in Molly. 'I've lived too long in the past, and it doesn't do any good. When you came along out of the blue – well – I was dumbstruck; I didn't know what to make of you or what to say.

I hope you'll ... er ... forgive me if I was rude.' He mumbled the words and Molly knew what an effort it was for him to say them. Impulsively she leaned forward and kissed his cheek.

'I know it was a shock, Uncle Silas, and I do understand. I will come and see you again, I promise. Joss and I, we will both come.'

He looked at her intently. 'You've got a fine young man there. You and him, you're going to make a go of it then? You'll be getting wed?'

He still did not know about Molly's marriage. The time was not yet ripe for such a disclosure. 'I hope so, Uncle,' she replied casually. 'Eventually. It's early days yet. We've only just met again and ... well, there are one or two problems.'

'Family problems, you mean?'

'Er ... sort of,' said Molly.

His eyes looked searchingly into hers. 'Ne'er mind about your families, Molly, neither of 'em, yours nor his. I thought at first it wouldn't do, you and him, not after everything that's gone on.' He stopped, shaking his head confusedly. 'But now I've seen you together I can tell that you're right for one another. You mustn't let anything spoil it, though. Don't let her come between you.'

'Who, Uncle Silas? What are you talking about?'

'That Vidler woman. Her I was telling you about before.'

'My ... great-grandmother? Is that who you mean?' Joss had said that Silas was rambling when he met him at the gallery. He had seemed quite coherent all day, but now she feared he might be getting confused again. Poor old fellow; as he said, he had lived too long in the past.

'Aye, her, Phoebe Vidler. I told you to forget about her, didn't I, not to go stirring up the past? You haven't, have you? No, I reckon you can't have done, or else...'

'No, I haven't found out anything else about my family,' said Molly. 'There hasn't been time.' But what on earth had her ancestors – her great-grandmother – to do with her and Joss?

Silas looked relieved. 'Then take my advice and leave well alone.' He lowered his voice to a whisper although he was already talking quietly. 'And whatever you do, don't mention that name to young Joss. D'you understand?'

'What name, Uncle?'

'Phoebe Vidler. Promise me – you mustn't say anything.'

'Very well then. I promise.' She was even more convinced now that he was rambling, but just as quickly he recovered and held out his hand. 'It's been grand seeing you again, Molly. Now don't forget to come and see me again, any time.'

The maidservant had been given the rest of the day off so Molly opened the door for her uncle, watching him stride away into the night; he had said he would walk home as it was a calm, though cold evening.

What a strange old man he is, she mused, wondering what on earth he was going on about. Probably he didn't know himself; but whatever it was she was sure it could make no difference to her and Joss. It had only made her more determined than ever to get to the bottom of her family mystery – when she had time – whatever her Uncle Silas might say. She wouldn't tell Joss though. Silas had been adamant about that, and she had given her promise.

Molly and the children were to stay the night at Joss's home, leaving before the rest of his family arrived on Boxing Day. Although she had been invited to join the extended family party she did not feel yet that she was ready to do so. Perhaps by this time next year she and Joss might be able to plan their future with a little more certainty. She knew very little about the grounds for divorce; neither did Joss. The word was still anathema to respectable folk, spoken of in hushed voices, but Joss had a solicitor friend who would be able to give them some advice.

It was when Em and William had both gone to bed – in one of the guest rooms that Em declared was the poshest room she had ever seen – that Charlotte and Joss told Molly of their plans for their future, and her future, too.

'Joss has been trying to persuade me for ages to move from here,' said Charlotte, 'but I was reluctant to do so. There are a lot of memories here, Molly, most of them happy ones.' She smiled reminiscently. 'This house is convenient for the mill. That is why it was built here, of course, and the reason Henry stayed. But now I have come to realise there are nicer places to live. Where your uncle lives it is very pleasant and peaceful, with that lovely view of the gardens in the centre. Or one of the terraces overlooking Avenham Park, maybe...'

'What Mother is saying, Molly, is that we have

decided to move from here,' said Joss. 'It was her idea in the end that we should do so; she didn't need any persuading. So we are selling this place just as soon as we can, and we shall look for somewhere near to the park. It will be nearer to my place of work, and it will be nearer to yours as well, Molly. Because that is one of our main reasons for moving; we want you to come and share our home with us. And you and I – we will be able to be together, my love.'

'But ... what do you mean?' Molly was open-mouthed, wide-eyed with surprise. 'There are the children to consider as well. And you and I, Joss...You don't mean that we should...?' She was embarrassed at speaking openly in front of Joss's mother, although she knew what was in his mind. He wanted them to have a place where they could be truly alone together, in a way they had not been able to be so far.

'You would have your own rooms, Molly.' Joss smiled at her understandingly. 'A bedroom for you, and one for Em and William – one each if you prefer. And your own sitting room too. When we first thought of moving my idea was to get something smaller – this place is too big for Mother and me – but now, since I met you again, the situation has changed.'

'Molly, my dear, I have only known you a short while,' said Charlotte, 'but already I have grown very fond of you, and of the children. I'm sure you realise that. And I also know how much you and Joss care for one another. I know your circumstances, my dear, Joss has told me, and I understand ... believe me, I do understand.' Her

521

blue eyes, so like her son's, were warm with sympathy. 'You need to have a place where you can be together. Goodness knows how long it may be before the pair of you can marry. It might be ages before things can be sorted out.'

'Yes, it's quite a predicament,' agreed Molly. 'In fact it may never be sorted out at all. Hector – my ... husband – has disappeared. It's possible he may never be found. I want to be with Joss, of course I do, but I can't let you rearrange your lives – where you live and everything – for the sake of me and the children. It's too much and ... and it's all happening so quickly. I can't take it all in.'

'Molly, my love,' Joss moved across to the sofa where she was sitting and put his arms around her, 'this is what we want, both Mother and I. You are part of our lives now, forever. And not just you – Em and William as well. That's true, isn't it Mother?' he asked, turning to Charlotte.

'Most certainly it is.' Charlotte's smile was sincere. 'That is – if you don't mind sharing your home with a middle-aged woman like me?' Her eyes twinkled. 'I won't call myself old, Molly. I don't consider that I am, not yet. I plan to be around for a long time, God willing, but I don't think I could live on my own, nor with Percy or Edgar.'

'But this is your home, Mrs Cunliffe,' cried Molly. 'And the new house, that will be yours as well. It is me – I – who am the intruder. How could you think–'

'Not so, my dear. You must never think of yourself as an intruder. And please, call me

Charlotte. I have already told you – you are part of our lives now.'

Molly nodded. 'It is kind of you, so very kind. I'm just ... overwhelmed. But you did say, didn't you Joss, that I could have my own room? I don't think I could–'

'Molly,' Joss stroked her hand, then held it tightly in his own, 'I told you when we first spoke about it, that day in the park, that I would never expect you to do anything you are not completely happy with. Mother and I think this is the ideal solution – for the time being. You and I can be together whenever we wish, but to the outside world – and I know we must observe the proprieties – you and the children are just sharing our home, as family friends. Mother understands everything, don't you, Mother?'

Molly noticed the look of empathy, of complete understanding, that passed between Charlotte and her son. 'Oh, most certainly, I do,' said Charlotte fervently. 'Believe me, Molly, my dear, I do. And now I'm going to leave you two on your own for a while.'

It was then that Joss gave Molly her Christmas present, as he had promised her he would do when they were alone. It was a small heart-shaped brooch, exquisitely formed from tiny diamonds, seed pearls and rubies, to be worn as a token of their love until such time as he felt he could buy her a ring. And he knew that her present to him, a gold tiepin with a garnet in the centre, though it was nowhere near as costly a gift, was given with all her love; a promise that one day – quite soon, they both hoped – they

523

might be able to tell the world of their regard for one another.

Molly had felt a little apprehensive – guilty, even – at telling Agnes and Fred Healey that she was vacating the premises over the Church Street shop. They had both been so good to her. Not only had they given her the managership of the shop – when, in fact they had hardly known her – but they had provided her with living accommodation as well. But, as things turned out, Molly need not have worried. Agnes and Fred were very understanding and rejoiced with her over her good fortune. They knew her story now almost in its entirety; Agnes in particular kept saying how much like a fairy-tale it was that Molly had met Joss again. They were delighted to hear that Molly would continue to manage the shop for them, in spite of the change in her circumstances. The living accommodation was taken over with alacrity by the bakehouse man, Joe, who was pleased to move in with his wife and little son almost at once. He had been living more than a mile from his place of work and he was glad not to have to walk there any more at five o'clock in the morning.

At the end of April Joss and his mother, Molly and the children, moved into their new home on Ribblesdale Place. It overlooked Avenham Park, one of the houses Charlotte had fancied from the start which, luckily, had come vacant, and was only a stone's throw from Winckley Square where Molly's great-uncle lived. The old mill house had been sold quite quickly, to their surprise, to a couple of unmarried ladies who intended to start a private school for young children.

Britain was entering a new age. Queen Victoria had died peacefully at Osborne House on the Isle of Wight at the end of January, and with the succession of her son, Edward VII, it seemed that many of the restraints that the old queen had symbolised were being thrown off with the advent of a more tolerant, fun-loving way of life. No one epitomised the new age better than the new king. With his obvious enjoyment of the good things in life – enormous cigars, racehorses and pretty women – he set the pattern of social life for rich and poor alike.

It was a new beginning too for Molly and Joss. He had said he was determined to make life easier for her, and at first she found it difficult to get used to the idea of servants waiting on her; cooking her meals, doing her washing, cleaning her rooms. The Cunliffes did not employ an army of servants; just a cook and kitchen maid and a housemaid, but to Molly it was all undreamed of grandeur. She marvelled at the high-ceilinged rooms, the deep pile carpets and velvet curtains, the oak banisters, the Adam-style fireplaces and the elegant furniture in the living rooms and bedrooms, the glossy patina preserved by years of loving care. Her own rooms had been furnished specifically to her requirements; Charlotte had insisted she must have a say as to what she would like. Her sitting room was carpeted in cherry red with matching curtains, and with her mother's display cabinet and two easy chairs from the Larkhill Street days – which by no means looked out of place in their new luxurious surroundings – it felt cosy and friendly.

It was a warm and peaceful haven where Molly and the children could relax and spend some time together after the pressures of the day; for she was still working just as hard at the shop. She opened up early in the morning before the first customers arrived, having left William in the capable hands of Charlotte, his new 'granny', whom he had taken to as readily as he had once taken to Maggie. They all dined together, however, in the handsome dining room, waited on by Mabel, the maid. And at night Molly slept in her bedroom overlooking the park, with its mid-blue carpet and matching daisy-sprigged curtains, in the double bed with the pale blue satin eiderdown.

It was there that Joss joined her on the second night in their new home. He had knocked and waited for her to invite him in, although they had both known that their coming together was inevitable; they had waited so long for this moment. Molly knew that she loved Joss totally and unreservedly, and that was how she wanted to belong to him, but even this knowledge could not stop her feeling more than a little afraid. She had known nothing but roughness and insensitivity, even violence, in the act of love, and it was hard to imagine that it could be a thing of beauty, an expression of complete oneness and perfect accord between two people who were truly in love.

And that was just what she discovered it to be. Joss set her fears at rest immediately. 'Molly, you know how much I love you, don't you?' He sat on the edge of the bed, first holding her hands, then stroking her auburn hair as it tumbled around her shoulders and the nape of her neck. She had been sitting up in bed awaiting him, and now she felt herself responding eagerly to the gentleness of his touch and the fervour of his kisses. She was no stranger to his embraces, but they had both known during the winter and early spring that the time was not yet ripe to consummate their love.

'I love you too, Joss,' she whispered, 'so very much.' She opened up now as his loving hands caressed her neck, her shoulders, her breasts, every intimate curve and line of her body... Then she experienced the most bitter-sweet sensation, a mixture of both pleasure and pain, as she gave herself fully to the man she loved.

'You are mine now, Molly, my dearest love,' Joss whispered. 'You are truly my wife. That is what you must believe. You are mine in everything but name. And that doesn't matter, does it?'

'What's in a name?' She smiled up at him. 'Isn't that what Shakespeare said? And it's true, isn't it? It doesn't matter what I am called. I love you, Joss. I will always love you.'

'Just as I will love you, my darling.'

She called herself Miss Molly Rimmer; in her heart and mind she belonged to Joss; but Molly knew, in reality and in the eyes of the law, she was Mrs Hector Stubbins. There was no getting round it.

Chapter 24

The trees in the park were bright with springtime green, the daffodils and crocuses already dying back and being replaced by tulips and early sweet-smelling wallflowers as Molly made her way towards Fishergate one Thursday afternoon towards the end of April. It was the same in Winckley Square. The trees that edged the path were putting out more and more green shoots, some were already in full leaf and the flowerbeds were gay with primulas. Children played on the grass whilst their mothers or nannies sat on nearby seats, keeping a watchful eye on their charges. On such a day, her half-day away from the shop, Molly usually spent her time with William, but William, now almost four, had recently started at a nursery school, a friendly little place, not far from home, which he attended three afternoons a week. And so Molly had decided to go to the churchyard to see what she could discover about her ancestors; a mission she had long been putting off, but now knew she must fulfil.

She had told Charlotte very little about her quest, merely that she would like to try to find the graves of her grandparents and great-grandparents, those unknown relatives who had lived in Preston many years ago; perhaps put a few flowers on the graves to show they were not forgotten. Charlotte had agreed that it was a nice idea although she knew nothing of the curiosity that was niggling away at Molly. The only person Molly had confided in about the family history was Agnes Healey. Agnes had suggested that the best place to look for ancestors – the only place, in fact – was in the churchyard, and in all probability Molly's relations would be buried in the graveyard of St John the Divine, the parish church on Church Street, only a few minutes' walk from the shop. Then the parish records might be of some help to her. Molly, in truth, had little idea how to go about her search. She realised, as well, that it might only lead to frustration and in the end it was possible she would discover nothing at all. Besides, hadn't Uncle Silas warned her about leaving well alone? But she knew she was unable to do that; her curiosity was too great. She bought a couple of bunches of tulips and freesias at a little shop on Fishergate, then she went into the churchyard.

She began to fear, after she had been searching for about ten minutes, that it was like looking for the proverbial needle in a haystack. There were so many graves. Simple stone headpieces were in the majority, but there were more elaborate gravestones as well, crafted from black or white, or curiously red-mottled marble which reminded Molly of the potted brawn in the butcher's window; some of the stones in the shape of crosses and some topped with statues of angels or, poignantly, cherubs on the graves of children who had died in infancy. With the death of Queen Victoria's beloved Albert, mourning had become something of a cult and not just amongst the upper classes. Poorer folk, too, spent more than they could really afford on a fitting memorial for their loved ones.

Molly had no way of knowing how her ancestors would have behaved, what sort of tombstones they would have chosen, but she decided to concentrate on the simpler ones. She knew she came from a family of mill-workers in the main, although Uncle Silas had done well for himself. Her grandfather's name was Grimshaw. She remembered her father saying that Albert Grimshaw had been old to be Lily's father, more like her grandfather, in fact. And Molly's grandmother, the unfortunate young woman who had committed suicide, had been called Alice. She scanned the headstones for the name of Grimshaw, and as she did so a thought suddenly struck her. Hadn't she heard that suicide victims were not allowed to be buried in consecrated ground?

She was just pondering on this problem when she found the first grave with a simple headstone of black marble. 'Alice, beloved wife of Albert Grimshaw. Died 29 January 1866, aged 32 years. Rest in Peace.' Yes, that would be right. She did a quick calculation. Her own mother, Lily, was eight, so Molly had been told, when she made the grim discovery of her mother's dead body, hanging. Molly shuddered at the thought. But it was not necessarily true then, what folk said about suicides? Or maybe there had been a very understanding vicar, for this was assuredly the same Alice Grimshaw. The gravestone also told her that Albert, her grandfather, had died in 1879 at the age of seventy. And it was soon afterwards, Molly realised, that her parents had moved to Blackpool; she had been born later that same year.

There was a small urn on the grave and Molly saw, to her surprise, that it was filled with fresh flowers: pink and white tulips and some green leaves, all nicely arranged. She had intended leaving some flowers here herself, but they would be superfluous. Thoughtfully she recommenced her search. Her great-grandparents, concentrating on the female branch of the family, the distaff line, had been called Vidler. Alice had been Alice Vidler until she married Albert Grimshaw. It was an unusual name. The grave, therefore, might not be too difficult to find. Vidler... That was the name that had caused such strong feelings of hostility in Uncle Silas. Phoebe Vidler ... Molly felt herself shuddering again, although she could not have explained why.

To her surprise she found the grave quite quickly. It was not too far from the Grimshaw plot and was marked by a stone cross. The first names on the headstone were those of two children, Rebecca and Edwin, who had died in infancy in 1851 and 1852. The next name was that of 'Caroline, beloved wife of Joseph Vidler, died 7 April 1880, aged 50 years.' Caroline? But she had been told, so many times, that her great-grandmother's name was Phoebe. Who, then, was Caroline? Had the woman had two names? No, another quick calculation told her that this person could not possibly have been Alice's

531

mother. The dates did not fit. This woman was not much different in age to Alice. Caroline must have been Joseph's second wife, and the mother of the ill-fated Rebecca and Edwin, but not of Alice; Alice was Phoebe's child. Joseph Vidler, whose name was the last one on the stone, had died in 1882, aged seventy-two years.

Where, then, was Phoebe's grave? Molly made another search through the headstones round and about, but to no avail. She frowned to herself, thinking hard. Yes, more than likely that would be the answer. Perhaps Phoebe, also, had committed suicide. And the clergyman in those days, some – what? – twenty or thirty years earlier, might not have been so accommodating. Poor Phoebe, alas, must have been buried in unconsecrated ground.

Molly looked down at the flowers in her hand. She must get them in water soon or they would wilt. She might as well leave them all on this Vidler grave which was bare of flowers; after all, the unknown Joseph had been her great-grandfather. There was a water tap by the church wall and she went there to fill the glass jar she had brought with her, although there were several jars on the ground for the use of visitors. She returned and placed the jar of tulips and freesias on the Vidler grave, pushing it well into the soil so it would not topple over. Then she made her way again to the grave of Alice and Albert, pondering as she stood there who it might have been that had placed the flowers there.

Could it be Uncle Silas? No, of course not;

whatever was she thinking about? These ancestors of hers had not been related in any way to Silas Rimmer; this was her mother's family, not her father's. All this delving into the past was making her confused. She was not sure how long she stood there, deep in thought, but her attention was diverted by the appearance of a figure at her side. A grey-haired man in a long black robe, but his absence of any dog collar told her that this might be the verger, not the vicar.

'Good afternoon, miss,' he greeted her politely. 'I have been watching you for a little while; I'm not prying, you understand, but I noticed you seemed to be searching for something and I wondered if I might be of some assistance. I am the verger, you see,' so she had guessed correctly, 'and I do know a little about some of the folk who are buried here. Many of their descendants still worship with us at St John's.' He looked at her enquiringly. 'I don't think we've had the pleasure of seeing you here, though?'

'No, I'm a Methodist,' replied Molly. 'I haven't ... er ... actually been inside the church.'

'You would be very welcome, my dear. After all, we're all bound for the same place in the end, aren't we, though we may think we have different ways of getting there. Now, can I be of any help?'

'I have found a couple of graves,' replied Molly, 'those of my grandparents and ... great-grandparents.' Obliging though the man was, she found herself loath to divulge the name of her great-grandparents or to tell him she had been searching for the missing grave of the mysterious Phoebe Vidler. What was she afraid of hearing?

Molly did not know, but something deep inside her told her to keep quiet about this. Instead she concentrated on the grave in front of her. If she could find out who had placed the flowers there – it might even be a relative she had not known about – then maybe she would be a little closer to solving the riddle that was nagging at her.

She pointed towards the headstone. 'Albert and Alice Grimshaw – they were my grandfather and grandmother. They died before I was born. I was wondering who had put the flowers there. Do you know who it might be? I wasn't aware that I had any more living relatives.'

'Indeed, I do know,' replied the verger, beaming at her. 'It's old Kitty – Kitty Proctor. That's who puts the flowers on the grave. Winter or summer, whatever the weather, old Kitty manages to bring a few flowers to put on her friend's grave. She was very fond of Alice ... your grandmother, you say? I never knew her myself, of course. It was long before I came to St John's, but Kitty has told me about her. It's quite a tragic story, I believe.'

'Yes, so I have heard,' said Molly, beginning to feel a stirring of excitement. 'Tell me, this Kitty – do you know where she lives?'

'I do indeed,' said the verger again. 'Kitty lives in Alsop Street, up near Moor Lane. The same house as she's lived in since she was a girl, as she's fond of telling us. Of course we don't see her in church as much as we used to. She's well into her eighties now, is Kitty; eighty-five, possibly more.'

'But she still comes with the flowers?' said Molly.

'Yes, whenever she can. If she doesn't come herself she gets her daughter to come. Why don't you call and see her? Kitty would be pleased to see you, I know, and to have a chat about your grandmother. Do you know the area? I dare say you do. It's near to the mills; Green Bank Mills and Moorbrook, and Cunliffe Mill's up there, an' all. Kitty was a mill hand, of course, for many a long year. She'll tell you...'

'Yes, I do know where it is,' said Molly. She had already made up her mind to go and see this Kitty Proctor. She did not know the exact location of the street, but it could not be far from the house where Joss had lived when she first met up with him again. 'You wouldn't happen to know the number of the house?'

He was unable to help her with that, but he assured her that anyone living in the area would be able to tell her the whereabouts of Kitty Proctor. Molly thanked him warmly and made her way home, determined to go and see the old lady as soon as she could.

She hated to be secretive, especially with Joss, but she was still remembering what her Uncle Silas had said about leaving well alone. What he'd said was nonsense, of course; the maundering of an old man; nothing could possibly come between her and Joss. Molly decided she would go on her mission on the following Thursday afternoon. It was her half-day from the shop and she knew Joss had a meeting in town to discuss the forthcoming Preston Guild. She had heard him say he would not come home that day, but would go straight to the meeting when he

535

finished work. The menfolk were to partake of a meal, she gathered, at a local hostelry, before getting down to their discussion. Preston Guild was to be held in the September of the following year, 1902, but plans were made well ahead and Joss had been invited to be on one of the committees. And Charlotte, on the same day, was to visit a friend on the outskirts of Preston, so there would be no one to ask awkward questions when Molly returned from her visit. She hated being deceitful, but this was one matter best kept to herself.

She found the little street of terraced houses – very similar to Larkhill Street in Blackpool – without any difficulty and the woman at the first house she knocked at was able to tell her where to find Kitty Proctor.

The door opened a few moments after Molly's knock to reveal a very small woman whose face was criss-crossed with a network of deep lines; her hair was snowy white and abundant, springing around her head like a bush, and her deep brown eyes were bright and needle-sharp. But Molly was unprepared for the reaction of the old woman when those penetrating eyes first looked upon her visitor.

'Oh ... my goodness!' The woman put her hands to her breast, gasping to catch her breath as she stared in amazement at Molly. 'Oh, God help me! It can't be ... I must be seeing things.'

'Mrs Proctor?' Molly spoke to her gently, taking hold of her arm. She realised what had happened. The old lady had mistaken her for her mother, Lily, maybe – it was possible she had known Lily – or for her long-dead friend, Alice. 'I am sorry if I startled you. I didn't mean to, but I think you knew my grandmother, Alice Grimshaw. She was a friend of yours, I believe? I'm Molly Rimmer, Lily's daughter. You might have known my mother as well?'

'Oh, so that's who you are.' Kitty's breath escaped in a long sigh. 'So silly of me. I should have known it was summat o' t'sort. But it was just seeing you standing there ... like a ghost from t'past. You're the image of her, and I were thinking of her only t'other day, looking at some photies. That's what did it, I dare say. I thought as how I were seeing things. I thought she'd come back from t'dead.' She shook her head vigorously. 'Silly of me. But then I'm getting old, y'see, lass. Eighty-eight next birthday. I reckon it can't be long before I'll be joining 'em all. Anyroad, you'd best come in.'

She led the way into a room at the back of the house, which was almost a duplicate of the one Molly had lived in as a child. There was a similar black range with a small fire burning and a rag rug in the front, two shabby armchairs, a huge towering sideboard crammed with vases, knick-knacks and photos, a table with a chenille cloth spread over it and a threadbare carpet on the floor. Another similarity with Molly's old home was that everything was scrupulously clean; the range was ebony bright and the fire irons and brass candlesticks on the mantelshelf gleamed with recent polishing.

'I'm here on me own.' Kitty Proctor smiled at her a little more confidently now she had got over her first shock. 'So we can have a nice chat and you can tell me why you've come to see me; why I've heard nowt about you afore. Turning up out o' t'blue, nearly giving folks a heart attack.' She tutted disapprovingly, but Molly could see the glint of humour in her eyes. She guessed that even at her advanced age Kitty still saw everything clearly without the aid of spectacles.

'Yes, I'm sorry,' said Molly again. 'It must have been a shock, me turning up like this. I should have let you know I was coming, but I didn't know the number of the house. Do you live on your own, Mrs Proctor?'

'Call me Kitty,' said the old lady. 'Everybody does... No, me daughter, Elsie, lives here an' all, and her husband, Fred. But they're both at work. At t'mill, you know. I don't mind being on me own. I've a big family, nearly all of 'em still round and about. I'm never lonely. Sit yerself down, lass. Molly, did you say you were called?'

'Yes, that's right.' Molly sat in the sagging armchair opposite Kitty. 'I'm Lily's daughter. Do you remember my mother?'

'Aye, I remember her.' Kitty nodded. 'I never knew her all that well, mind. She got wed and went off to Blackpool, didn't she? So what are you doing here then? Have they moved back?'

'No; I'm sorry to say my mother died.' Molly explained how she had lost both her parents and was now making a new life for herself in Preston, with her sister and small brother.

'I'm sorry to hear about yer mam,' said Kitty. 'She died young then, didn't she? Like they all do, all t'women in that line... Seems as though there might be summat in it after all, the gypsy's curse.'

Molly felt a tremor of fear which she tried to suppress. It was not the first time she had heard of the ill luck that hounded the women of her family, but she had not heard anything about a gypsy's curse. She did not enquire, however, as Kitty had seemed to be talking half to herself. 'It was Alice I knew best, of course,' the old lady went on. 'She was always special to me, that little lass, especially after her mam ... died. Like another daughter, you might say. That's how I allus thought of her, and my lot never minded how much fuss I made of her. They could hardly complain, not after what had happened to her mother. You're the spitting image of her, you know. That's what gave me such a turn, seeing you standing there.'

'I know I'm like my mother,' said Molly. 'I have always been told so and I can see it for myself. So you say I'm like my grandmother, Alice, as well?'

'Aye, you've a look of her,' said Kitty. 'But it wasn't her I was thinking of. It was Phoebe – Phoebe Vidler, God rest her soul. You're the living image of her; I can't get over it. And she'd be about your age an' all ... when it happened. How old are you, lass?'

'I'm twenty-one,' replied Molly. She leaned forward in her chair. 'Tell me, Kitty, what happened to my great-grandmother – to ... Phoebe Vidler?'

'You mean to say as you don't know? You've never heard?'

'No,' said Molly. 'If I knew I wouldn't be asking, would I?' She remembered saying the self-same words to her Uncle Silas, but he had refused to tell her.

Kitty did not answer straight away. She got up and went to the sideboard, rummaging in a drawer for a minute or two. She thrust a photograph into Molly's hands. 'That's Phoebe and me when we worked at t'mill. You can see for yerself what I mean.'

The somewhat faded sepia snapshot showed two girls smiling into the camera. Both were dressed in long working overalls and had shawls around their shoulders. One girl was recognisable as Kitty, except for the halo of hair, dark then, and the bright eyes, but the other one could well have been Molly. She did not need colour to tell her that Phoebe would have had the same auburn hair as herself.

Kitty sat down again. 'Are you sure you want to hear? It's a sad tale.'

'Yes, I'm sure,' said Molly in a quiet voice. 'Tell me what happened to Phoebe?'

It was in 1830 that Kitty and Phoebe first met. They were both sixteen years of age and were working at the same cotton mill. Molly had guessed the name of the mill even before Kitty told her; it was Cunliffe Mill. The two girls became close friends and in a couple of years, both of them were married to weavers from the same mill. Kitty married Albert Proctor, and Phoebe, Joseph Vidler. And it was not long before each of the girls gave birth to her first child. For Phoebe it was to be her only child, a dear little girl called Alice with the same mass of auburn curls and deep brown eyes as her mother.

Phoebe, and Kitty too, carried on working at the mill, leaving their children in the care of willing neighbours. Money was scarce – then as now – and it was necessary for both husband and wife to work to make ends meet. Phoebe did not mind working long hours if it meant she could buy a few bits and bobs to make her little home more comfortable. What was more, she was determined her husband should do the same. It was not long before Joe became an overseer, commonly known as a 'tackler'. This was a responsible job, putting him in charge of many looms. It was his task to put the warps on the looms and to keep them in running order and he was paid according to production.

'Aye, he were a good worker,' said Kitty. 'A nice steady lad, Joe Vidler. I don't think Phoebe realised how lucky she was, having a fellow like Joe. My Albert, he were a good sort, an' all; not so ambitious, though, as Joe. Mind you, it were Phoebe as did the pushing; I thought so all along. She was always a cut above the rest o' t'lasses. Some of 'em thought she were stuck up, full of fancy ideas, but I would never say a word against her. She just wanted a nice little home wi' a few extra comforts, and who could blame her for that? And she allus made sure as Alice had the best of everything, as much as they could afford, o' course.'

A trait that the women of the family seemed to have inherited, Molly thought to herself, remembering Lily and her parlour and the sometimes derogatory comments of the neighbours. And she, Molly, had always tried to keep her home nice. She could almost imagine herself to be there as Kitty described vividly the life of the mill workers in the 1830s.

Waking as the knocker-up tapped at the window with his pole capped with umbrella wires, to a twilight world of hissing gaslamps and yowling cats; then washing in icy cold water before joining the hordes of workers bound for the mill, the clatter of their iron-shod clogs on the pavement sounding like an army on the march. Then the lightening sky would be filled with grey billowing smoke, blotting out the rising sun, as the boiler fires were lit. It was not so much different today, thought Molly, but Kitty told her that inside the mills conditions had now improved.

'Aye, some folk look back and call 'em the good old days,' she said, 'but it weren't all good, not for us workers. Sometimes, in t'winter, we could hardly feel us hands for the cold; like blocks of ice they were; we could scarcely tie the knots in t'thread. And then there were t'cotton fluff and dust what got on our chests, to say nothing o' t'steam. Some o' t'bosses filled the place wi' steam, y'see. It were good for the cotton – high humidity or summat – but bad for t'weavers. Anyroad, Parlyment put an end to that twenty year ago.'

Molly wished Kitty would get on with the important part of the story; all the same she was finding it fascinating. 'We kept cheerful, though, most o' t'time, and old Jacob Cunliffe weren't a

bad sort of a boss, not compared with some o'
t'others we heard about. Mind you, we all had to
watch our Ps and Qs when he did the rounds.
Nine o'clock every morning, regular as clockwork, old Jacob'd come walking down t'broad
alley. We'd all wave and mee-maw to one another
as he were coming, then we knew as we hadn't to
gawp, we'd just to get on wi' our work, or else...
It were Isaac really, though, that we had to watch.
He were ten times worse than his dad. A real
stickler, Isaac were, for keeping us noses to
t'grindstone. They put on a bit of a do for us,
though, for t'Queen's coronation. Trimmed
t'weaving sheds up wi' streamers and flags, then
we had a party in t'yard. That were when Phoebe
first caught young Isaac's eye, I reckon.'

At last, thought Molly. She heard how, in 1838,
at the time of the Coronation party, Phoebe
became friendly with Isaac Cunliffe, the mill
owner's eldest son – a ruthless, self-seeking man,
from all accounts, though not without a certain
charm and a most winning way with the ladies,
those who took his fancy.

'I can't understand to this day why she went
along wi' it,' said Kitty. 'Her wi' a good husband
and a nice home and a bonny little lass. But she
were flattered, I reckon. He made a fuss of her,
and she liked to be noticed, did Phoebe. I warned
her to be careful, like, but even I had no idea how
far it had gone. I didn't know they were meeting
at night in one o' t'offices that weren't used any
more. Proper little love nest, so we found out
afterwards, wi' a bed and fancy sheets an' a
sheepskin run on t'floor. It seems as though he'd

543

made her go along with him, at least that's the tale Phoebe told. Joe had a good job – highly thought of he were; one o' t'best tacklers in t'mill – but Isaac were threatening that Joe'd lose his job if Phoebe didn't keep on meeting him, keep on giving into his wicked ways.'

'So what happened?' prompted Molly as Kitty paused, staring for a moment into the embers of the fire.

She listened, mesmerised, as Kitty recounted the tale. Joe Vidler, a good-hearted, amiable sort of chap, had remained in ignorance of what was going on, but the affair was not the secret that Isaac and Phoebe imagined it to be. And one person who had heard rumours was Harriet Cunliffe, Isaac's wife. She was a proud and haughty woman, of gypsy stock, who had given up many of her old ways when she married Isaac; but she still hung on to some of the superstitions and had the fearsome temper and the desire for revenge for which many of her race were renowned.

She surprised Isaac and Phoebe at their trysting place one night in the winter of 1838. Phoebe, by that time, was fully dressed again, but the crumpled bed linen was evidence enough of what had been taking place. Harriet loved her husband, and she was not going to stand by and see him make a fool of himself with some low-bred mill girl. She had always had a reputation for being a hellcat, and she flung herself at Phoebe, shaking the girl almost senseless, pulling her hair, slapping her face, kicking and thumping her, all the while shouting out, 'I curse you ... you and your children and your grandchildren. I curse the whole lot of you. You'll rue the day you stole my husband, you no-good trollop. You are cursed, to every generation...'

Harriet knocked the younger woman on to the bed. She was a tall, statuesque woman, powerfully built, and the delicately boned Phoebe was no match for her. She was defenceless against the blows that rained down on her face and body. Isaac tried, vainly, to pull his wife away, but she was a good match for him as well. Phoebe was fully clothed, even to her 'brat', the working apron which covered her clothes and in the pocket of which a mill girl always carried the tools of her trade: a hook, a comb and a pair of scissors. It was the scissors that Phoebe reached for, struggling beneath the weight of Harriet's flailing arms to extract them from her pocket. She stabbed wildly, scarcely aware of what she was doing, feeling the blades sink into the soft flesh of Harriet's abdomen. The woman gave a cry and rolled off her, landing on the floor with a sickening thud. The thrust of the scissor blades must have pierced her heart, because in a few moments Harriet's lifeless form and staring eyes told Phoebe that the woman was dead. She had killed her; some might say it was murder...

That was what they did say when the police came to move the body and to take Phoebe away to the prison on Stanley Street. She protested that she hadn't meant to do it; it had been an accident; she told them so at her trial. Isaac too, to give him his due, spoke up in her defence, but all to no avail.

'What ... what happened to her?' asked Molly, in a voice that was almost inaudible, although she thought she could guess. No wonder she had been unable to find poor Phoebe's grave. No wonder the prison, so near to the Church Street shop, had filled her with dread every time she set eyes on it, though she had not known why.

'Can't you guess?' said Kitty, so very sadly. 'She was hanged for murder, poor lass. In the spring of 1839, it were.' She had been moved, though, from the Preston prison and hanged at Lancaster Castle, as all murderers were.

'It were self-defence, of course,' said Kitty. 'But they wouldn't listen. In their eyes she was a wicked woman who had pinched somebody else's husband and she deserved to die.'

'And everybody knew about it?'

'Oh aye. It were quite a scandal for many a long day. T'newspapers were full of it. Then folks stopped talking. They do in the end when summat else takes their fancy.'

'And the present Cunliffe family?'

'What about 'em?'

'Well, do you suppose they know about it?'

'Sure to, though I don't suppose they talk about it any more. Isaac took over t'mill when old Jacob died, then it went to George. He were the only son, Harriet's son, although Isaac wed again. Then it passed to Henry. He died a couple o' year back and his sons have got it now; two of 'em, I believe, although t'other one's working somewhere else.'

'Yes,' said Molly faintly. 'Joss. I have met Joss Cunliffe.' The names were going round and round in her head: Henry, George, Isaac ... Isaac and Harriet. They had been Joss's great-grandparents, just as Phoebe and Joseph Vidler had been her, Molly's, great-grandparents. Joss's great-grandmother had died at the hands of her own great-grandmother, and she, Molly Rimmer, was the descendant of a murderess.

Joss would certainly not want to marry her now, even if such a thing were possible. No wonder her Uncle Silas had warned her about delving into the past. Why could she not have heeded his words and left well alone? But it was something she had had to discover. The not-knowing would have niggled away at her if she had tried to remain in ignorance. And it explained such a lot: her mother's all-pervading sadness and the feeling that ill luck was hounding her. Had Lily known about Harriet's curse? It was the first that she, Molly, had heard about it and at one time she would have dismissed such a thing as nonsense, just so much mumbo-jumbo. But who was she to say it was nonsense? Had she not already suffered more than her share of bad luck; the death of both her parents, then a disastrous marriage? She had thought that her meeting with Joss had broken the chain of tragic events, but it seemed that it was not so. He would not want to go on seeing her now.

Molly's mind was in a turmoil, nevertheless she listened to the rest of Kitty's story of what had happened, subsequently, to poor Phoebe's offspring. Little Alice had been five years old and had never been told, of course, of her mother's fate, except that she had died. Joe Vidler left

Cunliffe Mill, finding employment as a tackler in a mill on the other side of the town, and within a few years he remarried.

It was some years later, when Alice was about seventeen or so, that the girl had come to tell her mother's old friend Kitty that she was to be married.

'I was real pleased to hear that,' said Kitty. 'Quite a surprise, it were. I don't think she'd had many young men, although she were a pretty lass. Like her mam to look at, of course, but she were nervy and highly strung, frightened of her own shadow, she seemed at times. Not surprising, really, although she knew nowt about what had happened. But there must've been summat troubling her. Anyroad, this weren't exactly a young chap as she were going to marry. No, Albert Grimshaw were at least ten or twelve years older. She brought him to see me. He weren't a mill hand; he were a sales assistant in one o' t'posh shops in Fishergate and I could see as how he'd be good to her. More like a father, I couldn't help thinking. Maybe that was what she wanted. I don't think she'd been all that happy wi' Joe, her own dad. He'd changed, gone all broody, like, after what had happened, but who could blame him? And I think she was glad to get away from her stepmother. They'd never really seen eye to eye.

'They seemed happy enough, Alice and Albert, although the poor lass lost a couple o' bairns – stillborn, they were – before she had Lily. That was your mother, of course, but I never knew Lily as well as I knew Alice and Phoebe. Anyroad, everything seemed to be all right, and then Alice found out...'

'About her mother?' asked Molly.

'Aye, some folks can't keep their traps shut, can they? Some nosy parker of a neighbour it were: goodness knows why she told her, but she did. And the poor lass never got over it. Albert was nearly out of his mind wi' worry. She were that bad, screaming and shouting and carrying on, then other times she'd lock herself in her room for hours on end. He even thought of having her put in one o' them asylums. And then ... well, I dare say you've heard what she did?'

'I know she hanged herself,' said Molly, 'and it was my mother who found her.'

'Aye, that's right. What a tragedy, to be sure. I could scarcely believe it. Phoebe, then Alice...'

The gypsy's curse, thought Molly, experiencing a stab of fear. She found herself unable to shake off the feeling as Kitty went on with the rest of the tale.

She had lost touch, though never completely, with the family then. Kitty saw Albert and Lily only occasionally, but she knew that Albert had never remarried, caring devotedly for his little daughter. And when he considered she was old enough he told her the tragic history of her family. Molly knew the rest of the story, but now she could understand it more fully. Lily had been so affected by what she had seen as a child, then what she had heard later about her grandmother, that it had evoked a melancholy which she had never been able to shake off entirely. Even though she had married William and, after the death of her beloved father, had moved to Blackpool in the hope that a fresh start would dispel the unhappy memories, Lily still had not managed to cast off her sadness.

Molly fell silent as Kitty finished her tale. She could think of nothing else to say. A feeling of dread had enveloped her, a premonition that something terrible was about to happen.

'Aye, it's a sad story,' said Kitty. 'But you wanted to hear it, didn't you? I suppose that's why you came, to find out about yer great-grandmother, God rest her soul. Here, lovey, you mustn't take on so. You've gone as white as a sheet. I know it's been a shock to yer, but it's all in t'past now. We've got to get on with us lives, haven't we, all of us? It weren't easy for me as first.'

Molly found, to her dismay, that her hands were shaking and she felt cold, sick to her stomach. She grasped hold of the sides of the chair in an attempt to stop the trembling. Kitty was looking at her in alarm. 'I'll mek us a cup o' tea,' she said, jumping to her feet with the agility of a much younger woman, 'an' I'll put a drop o' brandy in it. That's allus good for a shock. You'll be all right, lass, won't you? You're not going to faint or owt?'

'No ... I don't think so,' said Molly leaning back against the cushions. She did feel faint and light-headed, but she had never fainted in her life and she had had enough shocks, goodness knows, to make her do so. 'It was just the shock of it all. It was far worse than I thought. I don't really know what I had thought, but nothing ... like that. I'll be all right again in a minute.'

'Here – this is hot and strong, an' I've put a big spoonful o' sugar in and some brandy, an' all.' Kitty pushed a mug of tea into her hands. 'Sup it up, lass, an' you'll soon feel better. Aye, yer colour's coming back a bit now. You had me worried for the minute. I could kick meself, though, for telling you all that rubbish about the gypsy's curse. Tek no notice o' that, Molly lass. It's all a load o' nonsense. I shouldn't o' said owt. Was that what made you go all queer?'

'No...' Molly tried to smile. 'I don't think so. As you say, it's all nonsense. Everything that happened – to Alice, then to Lily ... my mother – it's all coincidence. It must be.'

All the same, Molly knew that hearing about Harriet's curse had alarmed her, nor did she think that Kitty was as dismissive of it as she was making out. Had she not said, on hearing of Lily's death, that there might be something in the gypsy's curse after all? An involuntary remark that she may not have realised Molly had heard. But Molly had, and she was scared.

Chapter 25

She would have to tell Joss. Molly made her way back along the unfamiliar streets, feeling as though she were walking in a dream, or, more truly, a nightmare. She knew, deep down, that there was really no need to tell him anything. He had never enquired about her ancestry, beyond the knowledge that both her parents had been Preston people, and he was not likely to do so now. Joss, indeed, always seemed more concerned with putting the past behind him and looking to the future. She did not need to tell him ... but she knew that she must. She had always been truthful, and she knew, also, that it was not right for couples who intended to marry to keep secrets from one another. The slate must be wiped clean before they became husband and wife.

She brought her wandering thoughts quickly to a halt. What on earth was she thinking about? She and Joss could not be married. She was married already. And when she told him what she had discovered he would not wish to marry her at all. She was sure he would try to be kind about it. Joss was always kind, but she would have to leave her nice new home on Ribblesdale Place and find lodgings again, for herself and the children. If it were not for the fear of meeting Hector she might even return home to Blackpool. She still thought of the town as home, though she had been happy in Preston, especially of late. Very happy, ecstatically so, since she met Joss. But she could not keep the knowledge of her frightful discovery from him. That would be very wrong.

Her mind was in a complete turmoil and by the time she arrived back at the house on Ribblesdale Place she had convinced herself that the best thing she could do – the only thing – was to disappear, to get away from there as quickly as possible, herself and the two children. No longer did she feel she must tell Joss. She knew she was too ashamed to tell him anything. She hated herself, her ancestry, her background, everything about herself. She was not a fit person to associate with Joss, and when he knew the truth about her he most certainly would not want anything to do with her.

How opportune it was that both Joss and Charlotte were not at home today. Hastily, and scarcely giving a thought to what she was doing, Molly grabbed her largest holdall and began to cram into it her clothing and underclothing, as much as she could carry, then, into a slightly smaller bag she shoved some of William and Emily's clothes. She glanced at her small bedroom clock. It was time to collect William from nursery school, then Em should be home a few minutes later. She ran all the way to the next street where William's nursery school was situated. On seeing him emerge from the house, his face, as always, wreathed in smiles at the sight of her, she grabbed hold of his hand and began to run, dragging him behind her.

'Moll, Moll, stop!' he cried, his little legs scarcely able to keep up with her. 'Stop it, Molly. I'm tired.' She stopped then, picking him up and carrying him the last fifty yards or so.

'I'm sorry, William, but we've got to be quick. We've got to get away. We're going on a train, you see. Won't that be nice?'

William did not look too sure. He scowled at his sister and pouted, something he had not done for ages.

Em was even more perplexed.

'But why, Molly, why?' she kept asking, watching in dismay as her sister frenziedly flung their belongings together then went out and called a passing cab. In no time at all they were bowling along Fishergate towards the station, and about fifteen minutes later, during which time Molly, appearing almost demented, paced the platform, they were on a train bound for Blackpool.

'Why, Molly?' Em persisted. 'Why are we going back to Blackpool? You know what you said. You couldn't go back, because of ... him. So why have you changed your mind?'

'Hector's not there,' Molly snapped. 'It doesn't matter anyway, not now. I've got to get away. Don't ask so many questions, Em. I won't ... I can't answer them. Just leave me alone.'

'Have you had a row with Joss?'

'No, of course I haven't. Just leave it, Emily.' Molly looked at her sister's stricken face and felt a pang of guilt. None of this was Em's fault, nor was it fair to the girl to be dragging her away in this manner, but she knew she could not tell her the true facts. 'I just felt that I ... that we needed a change. So we're going to Blackpool for ... for a few days.' Molly had not thought beyond that day; in fact she had not thought at all about how long they would be away; a week, a month, forever? 'You know you've kept asking me about going back. Well, now we're going.'

'To Auntie Maggie's?'

'Mmm...' Molly nodded, a little unsurely. What on earth would Maggie say when the three of them arrived on her doorstep?

'What about the shop? Have you told Mrs Healey you're going? And what about my school?'

'Oh, for heaven's sake, Em, can't you be quiet? I've told you not to keep pestering me. We're going because ... because it's for the best. At the moment it's the only thing to do.' Molly closed her eyes, leaning back against the seat. Her head was thumping and she couldn't take any more questioning. She listened to the rattling of the train wheels, taking her away from the tragic and awful story she had just heard, away from the scene of that dreadful happening which she could not get out of her mind ... and away from the man she loved. She felt tears pricking at her eyelids at the thought of Joss, but she knew she had to put him right out of her mind. Joss Cunliffe was not for her. It might have been as well, she told herself, if he had stayed where he was, out of reach ... beyond the sunset. Then she would not have known either the rapture of meeting him or the agony of losing him again. This was the second time she had lost him.

Em gave her a hurt, exasperated look, then

settled to the task of looking after her little brother, who was clambering on the seat next to the window; fortunately they had the compartment to themselves. It seemed as though Molly had given up on everything. Em knew this wasn't like her sister at all. Em was sure she had had a row with Joss, whatever she might say. Why else would they be running away like this? Oh well, Auntie Maggie would be able to sort it out. She was very good at sorting out problems ... and it would be grand to see Sarah again.

'That lass is cracking up,' said Maggie Winthrop to her husband, Bill, later that night. 'She's going to have a breakdown, sure as eggs are eggs; that's why we've got to do all we can to help her. And is it any wonder after all that's happened to her, poor lass? Losing her mam and dad like that, then looking after little William and the shop, then being married to that ... monster. Then, when she thinks she's found happiness she finds out her great-grandmother's a murderess! Murdered her young man's great-grandmother; isn't that what she said? It were such a garbled tale she were telling us.'

'Aye, that were the gist of it,' said Bill. 'As if it mattered. If the fellow loves her, and it sounds as though he does, he won't give a toss about it.'

'That's what I've told her. We've both told her, haven't we? But it seems as though there's no getting through to her. She's nearly demented with the shock of it, coming on top of all the other shocks she's had, of course. It's no wonder she's at the end of her tether. Anyroad, we'll do what we can to straighten things out for her. She's in such a state she's run off without leaving a message for her employer, that Mrs Healey. I reckon I'll have to get on t'telephone tomorrow and see if I can contact her, though I'm blessed if I can cope with all that new-fangled how-d-you-do; I might send a telegram instead.'

'And what about her young man?' asked Bill. 'Are you going to get in touch with him an' all?'

'I don't rightly know. No, I think I'll leave well alone there. If he's the fellow I think he is he'll come and find her.'

'He might not know where to look.'

'He'll know where to look all right. Where else would she run, eh, except to us? Of course we can't put her up for more than a day or two. If she's set on staying, and if he doesn't come looking for her, then she'd have to find somewhere else to live. She knows that. There's a house vacant at the end o' t'street. I dare say she could move in there, unless t'landlord's already let it.'

'Then she'd be back where she started.'

'Don't let's look on t'black side, Bill. It'll happen work out all right. She's sleeping peacefully enough just now, bless her. She must be worn out, what wi' one thing and another. That poor, poor lass. If anybody's had more than their fair share of problems it's Molly Rimmer. Eh, dearie me, I don't know. When is summat going to go right for her for a change, that's what I'd like to know...'

Joss stared at his mother in disbelief. 'What do you mean, she's ... gone? How can she have gone?

And where has she gone, for heaven's sake? If you ask me, that woman next door must have got it all wrong. She is quite old, you know. Perhaps she was mistaken. Perhaps it wasn't Molly that she saw at all.'

Charlotte looked back at him in dismay. 'I know that is what you would like to think, dear, and so would I, but Mrs Reade seemed certain enough of her facts. I told you, I went out into the garden at about seven o'clock – soon after I got back from Clara's – because I felt worried about Molly being out so long. I don't know why I should, but I had this strange feeling. You must have noticed she's been a little odd just lately; you know, sort of preoccupied.'

'Maybe...' Joss nodded uncertainly. 'But she worries quite a lot about that husband of hers, though I've told her not to, about whether he'll turn up or stay missing; so I put it down to that.'

'Anyway, I went down to the gate and looked out into the road. The house seemed so dead without Molly and the children. I knew she wouldn't want little William to be out late, wherever they were; she always insists on him being in bed by seven o'clock. And that was when Mrs Reade came out of the house and told me what she had seen. She didn't shout to me, of course; she's such a well-bred dignified sort of lady. She beckoned to me, then she told me quietly, over the privet hedge, that she had seen Molly – "that nice young lady who stays with you", was what she said – and the two children go off in a cab. About half-past four, it was, and they had some luggage with them. Yes, I know Mrs Reade is an old lady, but she's got all her chairs at home, Joss, and she told me because she could see I was worried.'

'Worried? I'm nearly out of my mind!' cried Joss, running his fingers through his hair. 'What on earth is she playing at? And you're sure she's left no note?'

'Quite sure,' said Charlotte. 'I've looked everywhere. I was going to phone Mrs Healey to see if she knows anything, but I thought it best to wait until you got home, just in case you knew—'

'Of course I don't know!' Joss almost shouted. 'I know nothing, except that I've got to find her. I'll ring Agnes Healey now. It's only ten o'clock. They won't have gone to bed yet.'

But Agnes was just as mystified as Joss and Charlotte at Molly's disappearance. She was distressed too, and not because she realised she would be without an assistant the following day, but because they were all beginning to recognise that Molly must have had some sort of a brainstorm. Or maybe she had heard some disturbing news; or both.

'She went to the churchyard last week, to put some flowers on her ancestors' graves,' said Charlotte thoughtfully. 'And she seemed as though she didn't want to talk about it afterwards. I thought that was odd because she's usually such a candid sort of girl, but I didn't press her.'

'Very odd, I would say,' said Joss. 'It's something she has never mentioned to me at all.' Agnes Healey also had just mentioned Molly's visit to the graveyard and the fact that she had seemed somewhat withdrawn since that day. Joss frowned and closed his eyes, then, after a few moments, slapped his hands on the arms of his chair and jumped to his feet. 'Silas Rimmer,' he cried. 'Yes, Silas Rimmer; he might have the answer.'

'What about him?' asked Charlotte. 'You mean Molly might have gone there?'

'No, probably not,' said Joss. 'But I'm sure Silas knows something, and I'm pretty sure he'll know what's the matter with Molly. Because something's the matter, Mother. It must be for her to run off like this.' He was pacing up and down the room as he spoke. 'Silas was damned funny at first, you know, when he knew that Molly and I were friendly. He kept harping on about the past, about how it didn't matter what had gone on before, how we had to look to the future. Molly and I both thought he was rambling, but maybe there's something that he knows and we don't. Yes, I'll go and see him first thing in the morning. It's too late now, though I can hardly contain myself. Oh, Molly, Molly ... where on earth are you...?'

His mother rose, putting her hands on his arms to stop his restless pacing. 'Don't worry, my dear. Wherever she is we will find her and bring her back.'

'I warned her to leave well alone,' said Silas Rimmer. 'I told her as how it would do no good to go digging up the past, but she's paid no heed. Aye, you're quite right, lad. I do know something, and now it seems as though Molly knows it, an' all. And that's why she's gone, you can be sure.'

'But what is it? Aren't you going to tell me? You must tell me.' Joss stood on the threshold of the gloomy room into which the maid had ushered him, staring across at Silas Rimmer, seated in the large winged armchair.

'Seems as though I've no choice, have I?' said the old man, beckoning towards the other arm-chair. 'Sit down. I feared this would happen. You say she disappeared last night? And she's been rooting about in the churchyard? Aye, she's gone and found out about it, that's what she's done. And it's frightened her out of her wits, more than likely.'

'What has?' asked Joss. 'Come along, Silas. I love Molly – you know I do – and I want to know everything.'

Silas nodded soberly. 'Aye, you say you do, but it would have been as well if it had never come to light. Anyroad, like I say, I've no choice now but to tell you about it.' He paused, then: 'Tell me,' he said, 'does the name Phoebe Vidler mean anything to you?'

Joss frowned, slowly shaking his head. 'I don't think so... Wait a minute... Yes... It's coming back to me. Wasn't she the young woman who was hanged for murder? Didn't she kill my ... my great-grandmother? I remember hearing the tale from my father, but it was ages ago and... Why?' He looked sharply at Silas. 'What has she to do with Molly?'

'I'll tell you, lad.' Silas's voice was sorrowful. 'She was Molly's great-grandmother, Phoebe

Vidler was. And you're quite right, she was hanged for murder ... for murdering your great-grandmother Harriet. So you can imagine what a shock it's been for Molly to find out. Goodness knows who's told her, but somebody has, you can be sure, and that's why she's done a disappearing act. Because she doesn't want to face you. She's too ashamed, I dare say.'

'But this is ridiculous.' Joss almost laughed in spite of the seriousness of the situation. He was suitably shocked, and amazed too, at hearing the story, but what difference could it possibly make to him and Molly? 'It all happened ages ago. It must be – what? – sixty, seventy years ago? And how can Molly be held responsible for what her great-grandmother did? It's all ancient history.'

'Not so ancient, Joss, lad,' said Silas. 'I remember it well, though I was just a boy at the time. It was talked about for many a long day and most people considered it to be a shocking thing. That young woman, she was a murderess when all was said and done, and no better than she should be neither, from all accounts.'

'She killed in self-defence though, didn't she?' said Joss. 'I remember hearing about it. Wasn't my great-grandmother something of a tartar? Descended from gypsy stock, wasn't she; had a fearsome temper?'

'That's as maybe,' replied Silas, 'but murder is murder. That was what the jury decided.'

'But ... it's not Molly's fault.'

'No, I agree – it's not. But maybe she feels – what? – tainted by it? After all, she is descended from a murderess.'

'That's nonsense.'

'Happen it is, lad, but you can be sure that that's what Molly is feeling. She's a sensitive lass. And she's a good lass too; one of the best. That's why I'm sorry it's all had to come out. You need never have known if she hadn't gone ferreting around. I'll admit that it used to affect my way of thinking, this murder. When my nephew – Molly's father – married into that family I wanted nothing more to do with him. Of course there were other reasons as well that I won't go into... But I feared that the bad blood would come out, you see. What does it say in the Bible? That the sins of the fathers – mothers in this case – are visited upon the children unto the third generation? Summat like that. I didn't want to know Molly at first; then I realised – almost as soon as I met her – that she is a lovely young woman; genuine and honest. I never got to know Lily, her mother, more's the pity, and I'm sorry now.' Silas paused, staring morosely down at his feet. Several seconds passed before he lifted his head again.

'But I've tried to make amends since then, and you've got to get her back. Where do you suppose she's gone?'

'Where else could she have gone but back to Blackpool?' Joss replied. 'At least that's what I'm hoping and praying she's done. More than likely she'll have gone to her good friend, Maggie ... or to Flo. I would have gone after her straight away last night, but I thought it best to see you first. I guessed you would be able to shed some light on it all. Now, all I have to do is convince her that

563

none of this matters one jot.'

'And do you know where this Maggie lives?'

'In Larkhill Street, near the station. I don't know the number, but I'll knock on every door if necessary. Don't worry; I'll find her.'

Molly had been away from Preston less than a day when Joss arrived to take her home. Maggie had kept assuring her that he would come, but Molly did not know what to think or believe. It was as though part of her brain had stopped functioning. She could not say why she had run away, nor did she know what her future plans might be. She just knew she was confused and ashamed, and at the heart of her there was a deep-seated fear that would not be stilled, a feeling that the whole of her life would be touched by ill luck. She had been struck by tragedy many times already and she could see no sign of it abating.

'A visitor for you, Molly.' She had heard the knock on the door and now Maggie ushered Joss into the living room. Molly looked at him blankly, not rising from her seat on the sagging sofa. It was the two children who greeted him with joyful cries of, 'Joss, Joss...'

'We knew you'd come,' said Em. She sounded pleased, but her face was serious. 'Molly won't talk to us,' she added pensively.

'Come along, you two,' said Maggie, in her usual brisk manner. 'Get yer coats on. I was just going to wash the dinner pots, but I think a walk on t'prom'd do us more good. We'll let Molly and Joss have a little chat, shall we?' She bustled them out of the room while Joss sat on the sofa and took Molly's hands in his own.

She hardly responded even when the sound of the door closing told her the others had gone. Joss put his arms right round her, enclosing her in the circle of his love as he had done so many times before. Her only reaction was to lay her head upon his shoulder as he kissed her gently on the forehead.

'Molly, Molly ... don't you realise how much I love you?' he whispered. 'I know why you have run away. I know all about it and it doesn't matter. None of it matters, only you and me. How could you think...? What did you think? That I would stop loving you?'

She lifted her head then, looking at him intently. 'You know? What do you know?' She frowned. 'How can you know? Who told you?'

'Your Uncle Silas, my darling.' He took both her hands again, enfolding them within his own. 'I went to see him – I always felt he was keeping something from us – and he told me the whole story.'

'About...?' She could scarcely believe he knew it all and that it did not matter to him.

'Yes, about your great-grandmother, and mine.' He explained briefly what he had discovered, assuring her again that it made no difference. 'Silas guessed you had found out and that was why you'd gone. There is no need, Molly. I love you. It doesn't matter–'

'How can you say that, Joss?' she interrupted him. 'I am descended from a woman who committed murder and I feel ... I feel so unclean, so ... soiled. And I thought, I really thought, you would want nothing more to do with me. I still can't believe that you do.' But as she continued to look at him she could see his eyes were glowing with the love she had always known he felt for her. Then why did she still feel so sick and empty inside, so full of trepidation and with a sense of impending doom?

'It's all a long time ago, Molly,' Joss sighed. 'It's a coincidence, a very strange one, but we are not responsible for the way our great-grandparents behaved, are we? Come along, love. Surely I have convinced you that it's...' he shrugged, 'it's of no consequence.'

Molly looked steadily at him. 'Of no consequence,' she repeated. 'I wish ... oh, how I wish I could believe that. You see, Joss, it's the consequence of it all that is troubling me. Your great-grandmother Harriet, she cursed Phoebe before she died, before Phoebe ... stabbed her. And not just Phoebe – her children and grand-children and ... great-grandchildren. That means me.' Her eyes grew wide with fear.

'Molly, my love, you must not think like that. I've heard the story – I heard it from my father years ago – and that is one part I don't take much notice of. Harriet was a gypsy – well, of gypsy descent, at any rate. Apparently she came from a very distinguished family of Romanies, not just any rag, tag and bobtail, so the Cunliffe family did not frown upon it when Isaac married her, as they might well have done. I've told you before what they were like, haven't I? But she was a firebrand, from all accounts, and quite liberal with her curses. She'd curse everything and everybody who got in her way, so the story goes. They say it was a very stormy marriage, what with her furious temper and Isaac's philandering. And your poor Phoebe, well, she just got caught up in it all, didn't she? She wasn't the first ... er ... mistress he'd had. Try to put it behind you, darling. It's ancient history.'

'But the curse – it came true,' Molly persisted. 'My grandmother hanged herself, my mother died in childbirth, and as for me ... well, you know what has happened to me.'

'All coincidence,' said Joss briskly. 'I know, my love. I'm not decrying what has happened to you, but lots of people have tragedies in their lives. You've had more than your fair share, but things are looking up now, aren't they? I know you and I can't get married – yet – but it will all work out, I'm convinced it will. Now, what I've come for – as I'm sure you know – is to take you home with me. You will come home, won't you?'

Molly nodded. Yes, she would go home with Joss. She knew the children would be pleased. And how did she, Molly, feel? Relieved, she supposed, that Joss still loved her, still wanted her. Then why did she feel so lost and empty inside, as though her little world, in which she had believed she was so happy, was crumbling to pieces all around her?

'That poor, poor girl,' said Charlotte later that evening. Molly, wearied by the events of the last two days, was in bed. 'Is it any wonder she feels as she does after everything that has happened to her? I tried to make light of that old tale of the gypsy's curse, and I don't really believe in it. But her family does seem to have been plagued with disaster all along the line, the women at any rate. It's been one misfortune after another. I'm not surprised she's scared. Who wouldn't be?'

'Yes, it's certainly shaken her,' said Joss. 'But she'll be all right, given time. Molly's a sensible girl; got her head screwed on the right way, as they say, and I'm sure she'll learn to live with it. I shall help her all I can. She's everything to me, Mother. I love her very much. I'm so relieved she came back with me. It doesn't matter at all that her great-grandmother killed mine.'

Charlotte smiled wryly as she looked across at him. 'Do you realise what you keep saying, Joss? Your great-grandmother. You've said it several times ... but she wasn't, was she? Harriet was not related to you, neither was Isaac. Oh yes, I know they were in law, and as far as everybody else knows, because you were brought up as Henry's son. But your great-grandparents – on your father's side – are the ancestors of Seth Cartwright.'

A look of astonishment spread across Joss's face. 'Damn it all, you're right, Mother! Honestly, it hadn't occurred to me. That's because ... well ... we've hardly mentioned it, have we, since you told me about it just after Father died. Would it make any difference, do you suppose, to the way Molly is feeling? It's what she keeps saying, isn't it – that her great-grandmother killed mine? Well, supposing she were to find out Harriet wasn't my great-grandmother?'

Charlotte smiled. 'You may tell her if you wish. You don't need to divulge who your father is – just that you are not descended from Harriet and Isaac. The lass'll probably be relieved to hear that we've more than one skeleton in our cupboard. I know she felt at first that she was marrying into the upper class, out of her station, like. That is ... if you ever will be able to get wed. Do you think you ever will, Joss?'

'I don't know.' Joss shook his head. 'Apparently he would have to be missing for seven years – her husband, this ... Hector – before we could assume he was dead. The best thing would be if he were to put in an appearance, then perhaps Molly could divorce him for cruelty. Or he might well divorce her – for adultery – if he were to find out about me.' He cast a sidelong glance at his mother.

'And how would you feel about that?' asked Charlotte. 'It would cause quite a scandal, Joss.'

'The scandal wouldn't bother me, Mother, so long as I could have Molly. Ironic, isn't it? A man can divorce his wife for adultery, but she can't divorce him for the same offence, no matter how unfaithful he's been, not unless there's cruelty as well. There's certainly that, we know, but we can't do anything, not so long as he's missing. And that's another thing Molly seems scared of: him suddenly reappearing, although it might be an answer to our problems.' He was silent for a moment. Then: 'Mother, how would you feel about going to live in Blackpool?' he asked.

'You mean at Cunliffe House? But we've only just moved here.'

'I don't mean yet, of course. But you mentioned the scandal there might be if Molly and I were involved in a divorce case. It might not matter so much in Blackpool. The people there who know Molly realise how much she suffered at the hands of that fiend. They would understand, and I think she would like to go back. It's the place she ran to, isn't it, when she felt everything was against her? And I guess it's the unhappy memories of this ... Hector Stubbins that are playing on her mind, as well as this latest discovery. I feel, at times, that she's homesick for Blackpool.'

'What about your job, Joss? There are no cotton mills in Blackpool, and it's a long way to travel each day.'

'Oh, I could find something else,' said Joss airily. 'There is my painting, you know. I've always wanted to make more of a career of it, and my pictures are going very well in Mr Middlehurst's gallery. Besides, Mother, I'm quite wealthy. You and I, we are both wealthy compared to a lot of folk.'

'I know, Joss, I know, and don't imagine I can't count my blessings, because I can, and I do. When I think of the sort of life Molly had before she came to live here I realise I'm very lucky. I always have been, ever since I married your father ... er, Henry. But I can't see Molly ever wanting to give up working to lead a life of luxury. She seems to thrive on hard work. That shop she runs, it's a little gold mine, and it's Molly who's made it that way.'

'Yes, I know. I pass there every day and it's

always busy, and Molly in the middle of it all, chatting and laughing with the customers, obviously enjoying every minute of it.' He smiled fondly. 'There's nothing I would like more than to indulge her and let her live a life of ease, but that just wouldn't be Molly. You don't need to feel guilty though, Mother, about your way of life. You worked just as hard as Molly did when you were a girl. And you are working now, aren't you, helping to look after Em and William? I know Molly appreciates it.'

'And I'm happy to do it, Joss. Molly and those two children – they've brought me such joy, haven't they? More than my own grandchildren do, I have to admit,' Charlotte added pensively. 'They're part of our lives now and I want Molly to realise that. I hope she gets over this feeling of depression, of doom and disaster, or whatever it is. She's certainly not herself at the moment. Yes, Joss; I would be happy to live in Blackpool ... whenever you felt the time was right.'

'I used to love going there,' said Joss reminiscently. 'I remember saying to Molly, that night we met, that it seemed like home to me, sometimes more so than Preston. Then, when I lost her, all of a sudden it lost its appeal. One day, perhaps, when everything is sorted out – if it ever is – it would be a delightful place to live.'

'You mean ... Harriet was not your great-grandmother? She was not a relative of yours at all?' said Molly, the next morning, when Joss told her the secret of his ancestry. For a moment, to his relief, it seemed as though the light was coming back into her eyes; they were losing that blankness, that look of despondency that had worried him so much.

'Yes, that's right, but no one knows about it. Henry was my father according to the law. I always thought he was, until he died. Then Mother told me the whole story. She believes that is why I didn't get a share in the mill, like Percy and Edgar, because I was not his true son. That seemed to prove to her that he had guessed, although he never once said that he knew.'

'Then ... who...?'

'Who is my father?' Joss smiled. 'I'm not at liberty to say, darling. The man himself is not aware of the fact. Or, if he is, then – like Henry – he has kept quiet about it. That is the way of things, you see. It's all tied up with respectability and not losing face. But Mother wanted you to know. She thought it might ... help.'

'Help me to come to terms with my own doubtful ancestry?' Molly gave a sad little smile. 'She's very kind. No, more than kind. It's very brave of her to divulge her secret, to admit that she...' She paused. 'I can't imagine your mother flirting or having a casual sort of affair with anyone. It must have been someone she really loved. And you are quite right, Joss, not to tell me who it was. I shouldn't have asked. Were your father – I mean Henry – and your Mother not happy together?'

'I still think of him as my father, Molly. It's hard not to after twenty-six years of believing he was. Yes, they seemed happy enough. He doted on her – in his own brusque way. He could be rather

572

sharp with her and domineering, but I never doubted that he loved her. And she was a devoted wife and mother – she still is – and she ran his home for him just as he wished. Yes, I would say they were happy. I must admit, when I first found out I felt rather disillusioned, as though she'd let me down, you know. I had thought she was perfect, and now she'd fallen off her pedestal. But I soon got over it.'

'She's a remarkable woman, Joss. When I heard about Phoebe, it hurt dreadfully to think that I would lose you and your mother. It's very generous of you both – very forgiving – to say that all this doesn't matter.'

'Forgiving? But there is nothing to forgive, Molly, as far as you are concerned. You have done nothing wrong, darling, except to run away. That was just … foolish. Anyway, I've told you Harriet was not my great-grandmother.'

'But Phoebe was mine,' replied Molly. 'All right; it was not your relative that she killed – and I suppose I'm relieved to hear that – but I am still descended from a murderess.'

'One who killed in self-defence,' said Joss. 'How many times do I have to tell you? In France she would not have been executed for such a crime, or so I believe. They call it a *crime passionnel*; a crime of passion. But here – well – it's an eye for an eye and a tooth for a tooth, isn't it? No excuses allowed, all very moral and upright. I dare say she was condemned just as much for committing adultery as she was for murder. Listen, darling, you must try to put all this behind you. I love you; my mother loves you.

Promise me you will try to forget, or at least to push it to the back of your mind. And Agnes understands why you felt you had to go away. She doesn't know the full story – just that you had some bad news and were very frightened. When you go back to work perhaps you can confide in her? She's a very understanding person.'

'Very well, Joss... I will try to pull myself together,' said Molly.

Chapter 26

Molly did try to forget and, as she had always found, hard work was a means of diverting her mind from her problems. She had told Agnes Healey the full story of her ancestry. How could she do any other when the woman had been so tolerant about her sudden flight to Blackpool? But Agnes, like Joss and his mother, seemed to regard it as nothing more than an amazing coincidence. Molly returned to the shop and, as before, worked cheerfully and competently. No one seeing her during the day would have guessed at the feeling of unease that was constantly with her, the sense of doom and foreboding, as though there was a dark shadow continually at her shoulder. Once or twice she even found herself looking round sharply, but, of course, there was nothing there. Her fears were worse at night, and the one person from whom she was unable to hide them was Joss.

He came to her room most nights, not always to make love to her, but just to be near her, to chat and to enjoy the intimacy, the feeling of togetherness that had grown and grown between the two of them. He knew that Molly was still disturbed, not the same level-headed and usually optimistic girl whom he had found again, so miraculously, some six months ago; though he still loved her just as much as ever. It was now the beginning of June, several weeks after Molly's visit to Kitty Proctor, and her subsequent visit to Blackpool, but still she was subdued, often miles away in some little world of her own. Moreover, she appeared nervy and ill at ease, something she had never been all the time Joss had known her. The fact that he now knew her so well was what gave him the courage to speak openly to her, more sternly than he ever had before.

'Molly, you still go to church – sorry, chapel – each week, don't you?'

'Yes, of course I do, Joss. Why?' He knew perfectly well she attended chapel. Sometimes, indeed, he went along with her – although he had been brought up as respectable C of E – which had pleased her greatly.

'Because, I just wondered... Does it not help at all?'

'How do you mean, help?' She frowned a little.

'Well, forgive me, darling, for being so obtuse, but isn't your faith supposed to help you with your problems? I remember you told me, once, the real reason you got married. It was because you had found something you didn't have before. Those Methodist people had made you so welcome, and you had accepted their faith as your own. You told me it had made a difference to your life. You said it was the only good thing to come out of your marriage. And so I wondered ... why is it not helping you now?'

Molly, to her shame and annoyance, burst into tears. Joss, at once was all contrition, his arms around her, stroking her hair, kissing her wet cheeks. 'I'm so sorry, darling. Please don't cry.

I'm sorry if I was sarcastic; I didn't mean it. But I'm worried about you, very worried.'

She lifted her tear-stained face to his. 'You're right, Joss. That's why I'm upset, because I know you're right. It should help, I know it should, but it doesn't seem to. I go to chapel, I say my prayers, but it doesn't make any difference. I still feel so ... afraid.'

'What exactly are you afraid of?' Joss spoke gently now, stroking her face, taking out his handkerchief and wiping away her tears. 'Try to analyse it, darling. It might help.'

'I don't know ... exactly.' Molly shook her head. 'It's just a feeling that something awful is going to happen. That ... Hector might come back. I'm so frightened of him, Joss.'

'It would be all to the good if he did come back, my love. I've told you so before. We can deal with Hector.'

Molly nodded numbly. 'I know. I'll try to be sensible, Joss. I'll try to look to the future, like you're always telling me to. I really will try.'

But Molly did not admit, even to Joss, what was troubling her most. She could feel herself becoming more and more like her mother, low-spirited and melancholy, unable to shake off the sense of impending disaster. She feared that the nervousness and lack of self-esteem that had characterised both Alice and Lily were taking hold of her as well.

June, July, into August ... Molly's melancholia continued. It was a dull ache in the pit of her stomach, a dead weight at the back of her mind.

During the day she could cope with it reasonably well, and there were even times when she managed to forget the fear that was hounding her. She had told Joss she was frightened of Hector returning, and so she was. The very thought of him now was a torment to her. The remembrance that she had been the wife of such a man – one flesh, as it said in the Bible and prayer book – made that same flesh of hers creep. When she had met Joss again the dreadful memories had receded; now they were back again with a vengeance. And with them an all-pervading anxiety that tragedy would strike again at her, that it was just round the corner. She had felt that way ever since her visit to Kitty, and she knew the reason for her fear. Joss's finding her and taking her home again had made no difference to how she felt.

She had tried hard to dismiss it from her mind. Her common sense, which she had always had in plenty, told her it was ridiculous to believe in a gypsy's curse. She had not mentioned it again to Joss and his mother. They thought she had forgotten it, but there were times, as the long summer daylight faded, when she saw a menace in every deepening shadow and dark corner. Sometimes she was awake till the early hours, a prey to her anxieties and fears.

Joss, aware that she was losing weight and much of the sparkle and cheerfulness that had been so much a part of her, persuaded her to see a doctor. She went along with his suggestion.

'Yes, maybe I am just tired,' she said. She certainly was after a few sleepless nights. 'And we've been very busy at the shop.' She knew, however, that although she worked hard at the shop, her burden of work was not nearly so arduous as it had been in the days of the little house shop in Larkhill Street. But if Joss could see she was prepared to listen to his advice, then maybe he would stop worrying about her.

The doctor, who came to the house, gave her a tonic and advised her to eat liver and more greens. She obeyed his instructions, though she detested liver, and soon, to her surprise, she began to feel a little better in herself. Yes, the tonic was doing her good, she assured Joss and Charlotte; but Molly was still waiting for something. The strong feeling deep inside her, the dread that something momentous was about to happen, would not go away.

'Miss Rimmer, there are two visitors to see you. Shall I bring them upstairs?'

Mabel, the maid, knocked at the door of Molly's sitting room one Thursday afternoon at the beginning of September. It was Molly's half-day away from the shop and she was alone in the house. Joss was at work, Charlotte was visiting a friend, and the children were at school.

'Yes, of course, Mabel.' Molly put down the magazine she was reading. 'Show them up. Who is it?'

'They wouldn't give their names, Miss Rimmer, but the gentleman said it would be all right, that you know him. He's from Blackpool. There's a gentleman and a lady.'

A gentleman who wouldn't give his name?

Molly's hand went to her throat. She could feel the constriction there, her heart starting to miss a beat. Supposing it were...? She sprang to her feet at the knock on her door, then gave a gasp as Mabel opened it to usher in, not Hector, as she had feared for one awful moment, but his father. Hector's father and a lady, many years younger, with a fragile prettiness and auburn hair of roughly the same shade as Molly's own.

'Molly, my dear.' Mr Stubbins hurried across the room, taking hold gently of both her arms. 'I am so sorry to have startled you. That is why I didn't give my name to the maid, because I knew what a shock it would be. Come along, my dear, sit down. I'm sorry, but I ... we ... had to come and see you.'

'Yes, sit down, both of you.' Molly gestured towards the sofa. 'It's a shock ... yes.' She too, feeling her legs go weak at the knees, collapsed gratefully into an easy chair. 'What is it? Is it ... Hector? You have some news?'

'Yes ... yes we have. We certainly have some news,' said Mr Stubbins. Molly noticed he had made no move to introduce the lady. 'Just let me say to you, my dear, before we tell you ... our news, that I am well aware of what you suffered at the hands of my son. I was shocked – horrified – to hear about it, which I have done now, from several sources, although I was not aware of it at first. I just knew that you had left, and then that Hector had ... disappeared. We had hoped, his mother and I, that marriage would have been the making of him, that he would begin to settle down. He always had a wild streak in him. It was sublimated – to a certain extent, or so we thought – by his religion, but we had no idea what he was really like. We quarrelled, ages ago, when he was only a young man. I dare say you realised that, didn't you?'

Molly nodded, still too stunned to say very much. 'Yes, I guessed that things were ... not right between you.'

'He didn't come back home after he had done his pharmacy training. He found employment as a chemist somewhere in east Yorkshire and we heard nothing of him for years. It was always a great sadness to my wife and to me, but we had Martin, our nephew – a lovely young man; you've met him, of course? – and that made up for a lot. Anyway...' Mr Stubbins let out his breath in a long sigh, 'Hector turned up out of the blue a few years ago. Very contrite, wanting to make amends. And so, eventually we set him up in the shop on Jubilee Terrace. After all he was – is – our son. And when he married you we really thought everything would be fine. We left you alone; we felt it best not to interfere, you know. But now ... now we've found out just why he came home.'

'He's there now? He's in Blackpool again?' Molly was unable to keep the fear from her voice.

'No, he's still missing. We have no idea where he is. I was referring to him coming back after his time in Yorkshire.' He turned to the woman at his side. 'Tell Molly who you are, my dear.'

'I'm Gwendoline Stubbins,' said the woman.

Molly stared at her blankly. 'You're a relation of Hector's? I didn't realise...'

'Yes, you could say I am a relation.' Gwendoline

Stubbins did not smile as she said, quite calmly, 'You see, I am Mrs Hector Stubbins.'

Molly gasped. 'You mean he's got married again? But ... but that's bigamy, isn't it? Oh, this is dreadful. I knew he had done some awful things. But this...' Molly felt her own fears and forebodings being eclipsed as she stared in astonishment at her visitors.

'No...' The woman shook her head slowly. 'That is not exactly how it is.' She glanced at Herbert Stubbins at her side, as if for support.

'Yes, go on. Tell her, my dear,' he said.

'Hector married me six years ago,' said Gwendoline. 'In Beverley, east Yorkshire – that's where I'm still living. We've not been divorced and, as far as I know, he is still alive. He disappeared ... back to Blackpool. I know that now although I didn't know at the time. He is still my husband. And so you see, my dear...'

'I ... I was never married to him...' Molly's voice was the faintest whisper. 'Then I'm not ... Mrs Stubbins at all. I never was. But this is ... it's incredible. I just can't believe it.'

'It's true enough, Molly,' said Mr Stubbins, 'and we've brought you the marriage certificate to prove it. Show her, Gwen.'

Gwen opened her handbag and Molly, still dazed, took the document into her slightly trembling hands. Yes, there it was in black and white. Hector Stubbins and Gwendoline Holroyd, married in Beverley, March 1895.

She listened in amazement, which still amounted to disbelief, as Gwen told her story. Hector had had a small chemist's shop in

Beverley and she had met him at the Methodist chapel where he was a lay preacher. Gwen, too, was a devout chapelgoer and they had seemed admirably suited. Then his violent streak had become apparent and it had got worse and worse. Molly listened in horrified astonishment to the self-same story as her own: the beatings, the cruelty, the humiliation, until Gwen could stand it no longer. As Molly had done, she left him, to go back and live with her parents. But they did not try to avert a scandal at the chapel as Molly had wanted to do. Word of his behaviour soon spread around the congregation and the small town.

'It became too hot for him, and so he scarpered, back to Blackpool,' said Gwen. 'I knew nothing of his parents or any relations; I had no idea where he came from. Lancashire, he had said, vaguely, but that he had wanted to make a fresh start in Yorkshire. I didn't know where to look. He had just ... vanished, overnight. I was relieved, of course, which is why I didn't bother to look for him. But now ... I want to get married again. As, I believe so do you?'

She was a pretty woman, several years older than Molly, but younger than Hector. As Molly looked at her she realised that Gwendoline was very much like herself. Auburn hair which curled attractively round the small hat she was wearing, delicate features and a slim, trim figure. Her eyes, though, were not brown like Molly's, but clear luminous grey. They were full of compassion and concern, but Molly realised suddenly that Gwendoline was the one in need of sympathy.

She was the one who was still married to Hector where as she, Molly, was free.

'Yes,' Molly replied. 'I have a friend, Joss Cunliffe. This is his house, his and his mother's, where I am living with my brother and sister. We would like to be married, but we thought it was impossible. Now, you are saying that ... we can?'

'You can, indeed.' Herbert Stubbins spoke emphatically. 'And you must let nothing stand in your way. I am afraid it is Gwen who has the problems.' He smiled fondly at the woman at his side. What a kind man he is, thought Molly, so very different from his son. She had always thought so and had wished she could know him better. 'But we are trying to find him. We will leave no stone unturned, I can assure you.'

Molly nodded. The truth – the amazing wonderful truth – was just beginning to sink into her muddled mind. 'But how did you and Gwen come to meet, Mr Stubbins?' she asked. 'And how did you know where to find me?'

Gwen told the story. She had not tried at first to search for Hector. She was only too relieved that he had gone. However, only a few weeks ago some friends of hers had been taking a holiday in Blackpool – as a change from the resorts of Scarborough, Bridlington and Filey which Yorkshire folk usually favoured – and they had come across the chemist's shop on Jubilee Terrace, H. Stubbins and Son. As it was rather an unusual name they had made enquiries.

'And Martin sent them along to see me,' said Mr Stubbins. 'The upshot of it was that Gwen made the journey to Blackpool – she is staying with us at the moment – and so we discovered that my son is a bigamist. It has been a shock, Molly, a tremendous shock.'

Herbert Stubbins, at that moment, seemed to age visibly. Molly was aware of the anguish in his eyes as he lowered his head, sadly shaking it to and fro. He was silent for a moment as she and Gwen exchanged understanding glances. They had both been married to Hector, or thought she had as far as Molly was concerned, but this man was his father. He must have loved him once, and probably he still did. It must be a very bitter truth to acknowledge the crimes of which his son was guilty.

He recovered himself in a few moments. 'But, as I say, we are doing our best to put things right. I feel guilty, Molly, that I did not try to find you much earlier, but I have only recently been made aware of the extent of Hector's wrongdoing. My wife and I, we always thought it best not to interfere, you see. When you left him we guessed there was something badly wrong, but he wouldn't say. Silent as the grave, Hector can be ... as we have learned to our cost. All he would say was that you and he had quarrelled. We were able to find you through your friend, Flo Leadbetter. As you know, we do not worship at the Ebenezer chapel, nor at the one where Flo and her husband go, but we made enquiries and someone put us in touch with Flo. It was she who told us – very reluctantly, I must add – about the dreadful time you had with Hector. And Gwen's story substantiated it, of course. I am ashamed of my son; bitterly ashamed... Oh dear, what an upset it all is.' One again he shook his head sorrowfully. 'Sometimes I feel I'll never come to terms with it, and my wife is in a terrible state, as you can imagine... Anyway, Flo gave me your address – I told her it was most important I should see you – so here we are.'

'I'll ... I'll ring for some tea,' said Molly faintly. 'You'll stay, won't you? Have a meal with us...?' She was unsure, in fact, as to what she should do, but Mr Stubbins solved the problem for her.

'No, we must get back, thank you all the same. Ellen – my wife – is quite upset; we mustn't be away too long. A cup of tea would be very welcome though.'

Molly felt as though a great weight had been lifted from her mind, and not just her mind. Her whole body felt lighter, freer. She was liberated from the shackles of a disastrous marriage, which, in reality, had not been a marriage at all. She knew that all her fears and anxieties, and the feeling of doom that had been stalking her, were now things of the past. She realised it was not a gypsy's curse that had been filling her with dread, but Hector, always Hector, the remembrance of what he had done to her and the fear that she would never, ever be rid of him, that he would always be there, a sinister shadow lurking just out of sight. But now ... now, miraculously, she was free.

'Then we can be married, my darling?' said Joss, later that evening. Molly had broken the news to him and his mother – and to Emily, too, who was old enough to understand – and now Joss and Molly were alone. 'There is nothing to stop us?'

'Nothing and no one,' she said happily. 'Oh, Joss, I do love you.'

'I love you too, my darling Molly. I don't think you will ever realise how much.' They kissed and embraced in the joyful knowledge that there was nothing to keep them apart.

It was several minutes before they spoke again. Then: 'How would you feel about going back to live in Blackpool?' asked Joss.

'Oh, Joss, do you really mean it?'

'Do I ever say anything I don't mean?'

'No, you don't.' She knew he was sincere in all he said and did and she could trust him completely with her heart, her life, with everything. 'Oh ... Joss,' she said again. 'That is the thing I want most in all the world – apart from you, of course – and I've only just realised it. Yes. How soon can we go?'

The publishers hope that this book has given you enjoyable reading. Large Print Books are especially designed to be as easy to see and hold as possible. If you wish a complete list of our books please ask at your local library or write directly to:

Magna Large Print Books
Magna House, Long Preston,
Skipton, North Yorkshire.
BD23 4ND

This Large Print Book for the partially sighted, who cannot read normal print, is published under the auspices of

THE ULVERSCROFT FOUNDATION

	81	101	121	141	161	181
62	82	102	122	142	162	182
63			123	143	163	183
			124	144	164	184
			125	145		